THE TRUTH ABOUT MELODY BROWNE

Also by Lisa Jewell

The Night She Disappeared
Invisible Girl
The Family Upstairs
Watching You
Then She Was Gone
I Found You
The Girls in the Garden
The Third Wife
The House We Grew Up In
Before I Met You
The Making of Us
After the Party
31 Dream Street
A Friend of the Family
Vince & Joy
One-Hit Wonder
Thirtynothing
Ralph's Party

LISA JEWELL

THE TRUTH ABOUT MELODY BROWNE

ATRIA PAPERBACK

New York London Toronto Sydney New Delhi

An Imprint of Simon & Schuster, Inc.
1230 Avenue of the Americas
New York, NY 10020

Originally published in Great Britain in 2009 by Century, an imprint of Penguin Random House UK

This Atria Paperback edition April 2022

ATRIA PAPERBACK and colophon are trademarks of Simon & Schuster, Inc.

For information about special discounts for bulk purchases, please contact Simon & Schuster Special Sales at 1-866-506-1949 or business@simonandschuster.com.

The Simon & Schuster Speakers Bureau can bring authors to your live event. For more information or to book an event, contact the Simon & Schuster Speakers Bureau at 1-866-248-3049 or visit our website at www.simonspeakers.com.

Interior design by Erika R. Genova

Manufactured in the United States of America

3 5 7 9 10 8 6 4 2

Library of Congress Cataloging-in-Publication Data has been applied for.

ISBN 978-1-9821-2938-5
ISBN 978-1-9821-2940-8 (ebook)

Dedicated to Ruby Roxanne Seeley
18.09.07

Prologue

Melody Browne opened her eyes and saw the moon, a perfect white circle, like a bullet hole shot through the sky. It was fully lit and beamed down upon her, as if she were the star of the show.

She closed her eyes again and smiled. Around her she could hear the rapturous applause of creaking timber, blistering paint, popping windows, a fire engine's alarm wailing dramatically somewhere in the distance.

"Melody! Melody!" It was her. That woman. Her mother.

"She opened her eyes! Did you see? Just for a second!" Another voice. The man with the bald head. Her father.

Melody breathed in. Her throat and her nose felt like they had been doused in acid; the smoky air burned like fire as it passed down into her lungs. It stuck for a while, halfway to her gullet, like a lit match. She held it there and waited a heartbeat for her body to expel it. But for that tiny moment, lying on the pavement in front of her house, the moon shining down onto her, her thoughts muffled and her parents at her side, she felt suspended somewhere both dark and light, painful and comfortable, a place where her life finally made some sense. She smiled again and then she coughed.

They were smiling at her, her mother and father, smiling with sooty faces and frazzled hair. Her mother put her hand to her hair and stroked it. "Oh thank God!" she cried breathlessly. "Thank God!"

Melody blinked at her and tried to talk, but she had no voice. The fire had taken it. She turned to look at her father. There were tear tracks running through the dirt on his face. He held her hand inside his.

"Don't try to talk," he said. His voice was raw and gravelly, but full of tenderness. "We're here. We're here."

In her peripheral vision, Melody could see the strobe of blue lights playing out in the splintered windows of the house. She allowed her mother to pull her into a sitting position and she gazed around her at an altogether unexpected vision. A house, her house, roaring and alive with flames. Crowds of people, huddled together in dressing gowns and pajamas, watching the fire as though it were a Guy Fawkes Night offering. Two big red engines drawing up in the middle of the street, men in yellow helmets unfurling thick hosepipes and rushing toward them, and the moon still hanging there, fat and bright and oblivious.

She got to her feet and felt her knees trembling precariously beneath her.

"She was unconscious for a while," she heard her mother saying to somebody. "Out cold for about five minutes."

Somebody took her elbow and moved her gently toward the bright light of an ambulance. She was wrapped in a blanket and fed oxygen through a strange-smelling plastic mask. Her eyes were riveted by the mayhem around her. Slowly reality seeped through the layers of smoke and chaos and something hit her like a thunderbolt.

"My painting!"

"It's OK," said her mother. "It's here. Clive saved it."

"Where? Where is it?"

"There." She pointed at the curb.

The painting was propped up against the pavement. Melody stared at it, at the Spanish girl with the huge blue eyes and the polka-dot dress. It moved her in some strange, unknowable way. It soothed her and reassured her like it had always done, ever since she was a small girl.

"Can you look after it?" she croaked. "Make sure it doesn't get stolen?"

Her parents glanced at each other, clearly reassured by her preoccupation with a shoddy junk-shop painting.

"We'll have to take her into hospital," said a man. "Get her checked over. Just to be on the safe side."

Her mother nodded.

"I'll stay here," said her father. "Keep an eye on things."

All three of them turned then, as one, to acknowledge the shocking sight of their home disintegrating in front of their very eyes, to ash and rubble.

"That's my house," said Melody.

Her parents nodded.

"And you're my mum and dad."

They nodded again and pulled her toward them into an embrace.

Melody felt safe there, inside her parents' arms. She remembered a few moments ago, lying in her bed, a pair of strong arms pulling her, carrying her through the roasting house, toward the fresh air. And that was all she could remember. Her father saving her life. The moon staring down at her. The Spanish girl in the painting telling her that everything was going to be all right.

She lay down on the crisp white sheets of the emergency bed and watched as the doors were pulled shut. The noise, the lights, the crackle of destruction all faded away and the ambulance took her to hospital.

Chapter 1

When she was nine years and three days old, Melody Browne's house burned down, taking every toy, every photograph, every item of clothing and old Christmas card with it. But not only did the fire destroy all her possessions, it took with it her internal memories too. Melody Browne could remember almost nothing before her ninth birthday. Melody's early childhood was a mystery to her. She had only two memories of it, both as vague and as fleeting as a flurry of snow. The first was of standing on the back of a sofa and craning her head to see out of a tall window. The second memory was of a perfumed bed in a dimly lit room, a puff of cream marabou, and a tiny baby in a crib. There was no context to these memories, just two isolated moments of time hanging pendulously and alone, side by side, in an empty, echoing room that should have housed a thousand more moments just like them.

But when she was thirty-three years old, and the past was just a dusty fragment of what her life had turned out to be, something unpredictable and extraordinary happened to her. On a warm July night, one of only a handful of warm nights that summer, Melody Browne's life turned in on itself, stopped being what it was, and became something else entirely.

Melody Browne would have been home that night, the night everything started to change, if she hadn't decided, upon feeling a fat droplet of summer rain against her bare arm, to hop onto a number 14 bus after work one afternoon, instead of walking. She would also, most probably, have been at home that night if she hadn't chosen to put on a sleeveless camisole top that morning, revealing her bare shoulders to the world.

"You have the most amazing shoulders," said a man, slipping onto the seat next to her. "I've been staring at them since you got on."

"Are you taking the piss?" was her poetic response.

"No, seriously. I've got a bit of a thing about shoulders, and yours—they're incredible."

She touched her shoulders, self-consciously, and then threw him a suspicious look. "Are you a fetishist?"

He laughed, full throated, showing the three silver fillings in his back teeth. "Not that I know of," he said. "Unless fancying women because they've got nice shoulders makes me one."

She stared at him, agog. He fancied her. Nobody fancied her. Nobody had fancied her since 1999, and even then she wasn't sure if he had or if he'd just felt sorry for her.

"Do I look like a pervert?" he asked in amusement.

She appraised him, checked him out from his loafers, to his pale blue shirt, to his shampoo-fresh hair and his stone-colored trousers. He couldn't have looked more normal.

"Who says that perverts look like perverts?" she said.

"Well, look, I promise you, I'm not. I'm totally normal. I'll give you my ex-wife's phone number if you like. She found me so incredibly normal that she left me for a bloke with a stud through his eyebrow."

Melody laughed and the man laughed back. "Look," he said, getting to his feet. "I'm getting off here. Here's my card. If you fancy a night out with a fetishistic pervert, give me a ring."

Melody took the card from his tanned fingers and stared at it for a moment.

"I won't hold my breath," he said, smiling. And then he picked up his rucksack and disappeared through the puffing hydraulic doors and out onto the busy pavement.

The woman sitting in front of Melody turned round in her seat. "Bloody hell," she said, "if you don't call him, I will!"

She didn't call him. She waited a full seven days and then she texted him, not because she particularly wanted to—the last thing Melody Browne needed in her life was a man—but because everyone, from her son to her best friend to the women at work, wanted her to.

"Hello," her text read, "I am the woman whose shoulders you were perving over on the no. 14 bus last week. This is my number. Do with it as you will."

Less than five minutes later he replied.

"Thanks for the number. Not sure what to do with it. Any ideas?"

She sighed. He wanted to banter.

Melody didn't want to banter. Melody just wanted to get on with her life.

She texted back, somewhat abruptly. "I don't know—ask me out?"

He did.

And so the journey began.

Chapter 2

Now

Melody Browne lived in a flat in a Victorian block squeezed between Endell Street and Neal Street right in the middle of Covent Garden.

She lived with Edward James Browne, not her husband, but her seventeen-year-old son. Their flat was small and sunny, and had no garden, but a balcony overlooking a central courtyard. Having a flat in Covent Garden was not purely the preserve of the very rich. Camden Council owned large swathes of property in the area and Melody had been fortunate enough to have been offered one of their flats when she'd found herself a single mother at the age of fifteen. She and Ed had lived here alone, together, ever since, and the flat had taken on the look of a home that had evolved through times of change and growth. It was a home with layers and piles. They still had the same sofa that they'd been given by a charity for teenage mums when they moved in seventeen years ago, covered with a throw that she'd found in a charity shop when Ed was about ten and now decorated with smart cushions she'd bought from Monsoon in the sale two years ago when she won seventy-five pounds on the lottery.

Melody had bought potted plants when Ed was tiny. In the nineties everybody had potted plants. Most of them had died but one still remained, strong and determined and really quite ugly, sitting on a chipped saucer ringed with rust marks and ingrained dirt. If Melody were to move to a new flat the plant would go, but it was such a part of the fabric of the home she'd known for seventeen years that she didn't see it anymore.

The same was true of the piles of paperwork underneath her bed; Ed's old trainers in the hallway, which hadn't fit him since he was fifteen; and the ugly framed painting of a Spanish dancer on her bedroom wall that had come with her from her childhood home.

Melody's home would not win any prizes for interiors, but it was warm and comfortable, and filled with the smell and feel of her and her son. It was a treasure box of memories; photographs, souvenirs, postcards pinned to a cork board. Melody and her son had grown up together in this flat and she wanted, consciously or not, to make sure that not one iota of that experience ended up in a landfill. She wanted it all to hand, every friend's visit, every school play, every Christmas morning, every last memory, because memory was something that Melody valued more than life itself.

Melody dressed carefully that night, the night her life both ended and began. Melody rarely dressed carefully, because she had no interest in clothes at all. Half the time she wore her son's clothes. She didn't go anywhere, apart from to work as a dinner lady at the school where Ed had been a pupil up until finishing his A levels last month, and she didn't have enough money to buy anything nice, so she just didn't bother. But today she'd been to Oxford Street, to the big branch of Primark, and spent thirty-five hard-earned pounds, because tonight she was meeting a man, her first proper date in eight years.

Melody pulled a necklace from her jewelry box, a pear-shaped pendant in jet and onyx hanging from a thick silver chain, one of the few things she had left of her mother. She looped it over her head and turned to face Ed, who was watching her from the corner of her bed. He was wearing a white polo shirt, the collar turned up and a silver chain around his neck. His black hair was cropped and glossy with something out of a tube, his eyes were navy blue, and his profile was Roman. He had been the best-looking boy in the sixth form: that wasn't just her opinion, it was the opinion of half the girls at his school, and Melody knew it because she heard them whispering it when they thought no one who cared could possibly be listening.

He smiled and gave her the thumbs-up. "You look hot," he said.

"Thank you for lying," she said.

"I'm not, honest. You look really good."

"Well, lying or not, I love you for it." She squashed his cheeks between her hands and kissed him loudly on the lips.

"Urgh!" he said, wiping his mouth with the back of his hands. "Lip gloss!"

"I bet you wouldn't be complaining if it was Tiffany Baxter's lip gloss."

"Course I wouldn't," he said. "She's seventeen years old, she's fit, and she's not my mother."

She turned back to the mirror and appraised what she saw. Faded chestnut hair that had grown out of a short crop into a shaggy helmet. Teeth stained slightly from twenty years of smoking. Slim but untoned physique. Primark tunic top; red, V-necked, and sequined. Old Gap jeans. Primark diamanté sandals. And a slight look of terror in her hazel eyes.

"You don't think I should put some heels on," she said, standing on her tiptoes and examining herself in the full-length mirror, "to lengthen my legs?"

Ed crossed his arms in front of his body and shook his head. "Now we are entering 'daughter I never had' territory. I'm afraid I'm not actually gay."

Melody smiled and stroked his cheek again.

"Right," she said, picking up her handbag and putting it over her shoulder, "I'll be off then. There's pizza in the freezer. Or yesterday's roast chicken in the fridge. Make sure you heat it through *properly*. And er . . ."

"And er, *goodbye*."

"Yes." She smiled. "Goodbye. I'll text you when I'm on my way back."

Ben was waiting for her outside the Leicester Square tube station, in a pale blue shirt and jeans. She breathed a sigh of relief. He'd come. And then she felt her heart sink with terror. *He'd come.*

She glanced at him from across the road, sizing him up before his darting eyes found her. He looked bigger than she remembered, taller and more masculine. But his face was so soft, like something freshly hatched and untouched by life. Subconsciously she lifted her fingertips to her own face and felt the roughness of her skin, the tiredness of it. She knew she looked older than her age (the same age as Kate Moss, as she frequently reminded herself, cruelly and unnecessarily) and the thought repulsed her, somehow.

"You look lovely," he said, touching her bare forearm as he leaned in to kiss her cheek.

"Thank you," she said. "So do you." The unfamiliar sensation of being touched by a man, even on the chaste planes of her lower arm, left her feeling flushed and slightly breathless.

"Shall we get a drink?" he said. "The show doesn't start for half an hour."

"Yes," she said, "let's."

They went to a small pub on Cranbourn Street and she ordered a large glass of white wine for herself and a gin and tonic for Ben.

"So," he said, "a toast. To brazen strangers, beautiful shoulders, and to warm summer nights."

She knocked her glass gently against his and wondered if that was the kind of thing a normal bloke would say. Every time she looked at him, she found fault. His nose was too smooth, his chin was too square, he was too clean, too fresh, his hair was too fluffy, his shoes were too clean.

He was taking her to see Julius Sardo, the famous mind controller and hypnotist. Ben's brother worked for a ticket agency and had managed to get them seats even though it was sold out. Ed had been teasing her all week—"*look into the eyes, not around the eyes, look into the eyes*"—and she knew what he meant. There was something silly and schoolyardish about the idea of hypnotizing somebody, the sort of thing that someone would only learn to do in order to get better-looking people to pay them attention.

"So, have you ever seen his show before?"

"Not live," he said, "just on the telly. You?"

"Same," she said, "just on the telly."

"Did you see that show where he got that woman to rob a security van? And she was a community police officer?"

"No." Melody shook her head. "I must have missed that one." She noticed a Tubigrip bandage peeping out from beneath his shirt cuff. "What have you done to your arm?" she asked.

He touched the bandage. "Sprained my wrist," he said. "Three hours in casualty."

"Ow," said Melody. "What happened?"

"Squash happened," he said, miming a swing of the racket and wincing slightly. "Got a bit carried away."

Melody narrowed her eyes. In the context of her entire existence, playing squash seemed such an arbitrary and random thing for a person to do. "That'll teach you," she said, half meaning it.

"Yes. It will." He smiled. "There must be a better way for me to release all my pent-up energy than battering a little rubber ball into submission."

There followed a short but intense silence. Melody took a large sip of wine and tried to tamp down her sense of rising panic. She'd known this was a mistake, right from the outset. She clearly had nothing in common with this clean, cotton-faced man. Her shiny new shoes twinkled at her, mocking her for her stupidity.

"So," said Ben, breaking through the silence. "You work in a school? What do you do—teaching?"

Melody grimaced. She could either lie, or she could give him the bottom line and see what he did with it. "No," she said bluntly. "I'm a kitchen assistant. Or, a dinner lady, in other words."

"No!" Ben smiled. "Are you really?"

She nodded. "Yup, nylon overalls, hairnet, that's me."

"Wow," he said, "that's unbelievable! I didn't know dinner ladies could look like you. They certainly didn't in my day."

"Oh, I'm sure they did, but as far as kids are concerned, anyone over twenty is an old git, we all sort of merge together into one mass of *sadness*. Anyway, how about you? You're a . . . sorry," she said. "I can't remember exactly . . ."

"I'm a quantity surveyor. You don't need to remember. It's very dull, I can assure you."

"And do you enjoy it?"

"Yes," he said, "I'm sorry to say that I do. I don't know what that says about me as a person. Maybe I should lie and say it bores me to death and I'd secretly like to give it all up and become a . . . *a rock star*." He laughed. "But, no, I enjoy it. It pays the rent. And half my ex-wife's rent." He laughed again. "So," he said. "Have you always lived in London?"

Melody shook her head. "No," she said. "I was brought up in Kent. Near Canterbury."

"So what brought you to London?"

She paused for a moment, unsure whether now was the time to launch into the Story of Her Misspent Youth. He must have worked out by now that she really wasn't his type. Melody could picture Ben's type: she was blond, she was cute, she was sporty, and she was probably called Isabel. This was just an experiment for Ben, something to make him feel better about the fact that his wife had gone off with a bloke with piercings; a small act of rebellion to balance out the scales ("Well, I went out on a date with a *dinner lady*, so there").

She had nothing to lose, she reasoned, so she may as well set the whole sorry picture out on the table and she may as well lay it on thick.

"I ran away from home," she said, deadpan, "when I was fifteen. I was lured here by drugs, alcohol, and an Irish traveler called Tiff, and then I got pregnant and Tiff buggered off and my parents didn't want to know. Well, they would have if I'd agreed to go back home and have an abortion, but I didn't want to and that was that. I was put on an emergency list, lived in a hostel for a while, then got given a flat when I was nine months pregnant."

Ben stared at her for a second.

"Are you shocked?" she asked.

"No"—he shook his head—"not, not shocked. Just surprised. You seem so—well, conventional. And what about your parents? Do you see them anymore?"

She shrugged. "Not for years, since I left home. I spoke to them on the phone a couple of times after Ed was born, but that was it."

"That's a shame."

"Do you think?" Melody glanced at him, questioningly.

"Yeah. I mean, you've got a son. Such a shame for him not to know his grandparents."

She shrugged again. "I never really thought about it like that. I mean, in a way, they never really felt like my parents, they always felt like kindly strangers who'd taken me in off the streets. I was more than happy to leave them behind. Truly."

Ben stared at her. "Wow" was all he could say.

And Melody knew then that less than an hour into their date, she'd already lost him.

They had good seats in the stalls. Too good, as it happened. It was the third foam ball launched from Julius Sardo's giant air gun that landed in her lap. It was pink and had the number 3 printed on it. The entire population of the theater turned to gaze at her, craning their necks to get a better look. Melody sat and stared at the pink ball, feeling shocked, yet strangely unsurprised.

"What's your name?" Julius called up to her.

"Melody," she called back.

"OK, Melody, down you come."

Melody got to her feet, numbly and in something of a state of shock. She made her way down the aisle and a man wearing an earpiece pulled her onto the stage. Suddenly she was standing next to Julius, dazzled by spotlights, staring into a sea of homogenous faces.

"OK," said Julius, once all six audience members were gathered together on the stage, "now, this trick is called the Five Stages of Man. And what I want you good people to do is play out the life story of a man called—oh, I don't know—*Fred*. Now, Fred is a nice man. Fundamentally. *But*, he has some, shall we say, *quirks*. So, I'm going to let you each choose another ball and inside that ball is a piece of paper and on that piece of paper is an age and a quirk I want you to apply to your performance of Fred."

He passed around a bowl of more tennis balls and Melody took one. She pulled out the paper and unfolded it and read the words "Five years old and gassy."

Melody would never be able to explain properly to anybody quite what happened to her during the next five minutes. But from the moment Julius counted down to the number one, she felt small. Small and gassy. She careered around the stage, farting and wiping her nose on the back of her arm and pretending to chase pigeons. Every time she made a farting noise the audience laughed, but she wasn't really aware of them, other than as a kind of vague background noise, like the sound of traffic through an open window.

"Go to sleep, Fred," said Julius, clicking his fingers in front of Melody's nose, and there followed a lull in Melody's consciousness, a void. Not the sort of muffled, hazy void that a state of sleep or drunkenness might bring about, but something different, as if a black hole had opened up in her head for a split second and let in something dazzling and alien, before slamming shut again. She felt her knees buckle beneath her and then she fell, sideways and really quite elegantly, into a pile on the stage floor.

The next thing Melody was aware of was Ben's face close to hers, the citrus smell of his hair, a door with the word "EXIT" illuminated above it, and the scratchy wool of a blanket across her knees.

A woman in a green tunic hove into her line of vision. She had a very shiny forehead and large open pores on her nose.

"Melody? Melody? Can you hear me?"

Melody nodded and the woman's face disappeared again.

"Are you OK?" It was Ben. He had very neat stubble with tiny flecks of red in it.

Melody nodded again and attempted to get to her feet. Ben pulled her back down gently by the hand.

"Where am I?" she said.

"You're in First Aid," said Ben. "You passed out. Brought the whole show to a grinding halt. Single-handedly. They had to call for an early interval."

Melody winced. She felt woozy and confused, too confused to process properly what Ben was saying to her. She touched her shoulder reflexively.

"Where's my bag?" she said.

"Here." Ben showed it to her. "I've got your jacket as well. I figured you probably didn't want to go back and watch the rest of the show."

"No." She shook her head. "No. I don't. I want to go home. Sorry . . ." She felt strangely devoid of any sense of time or place, cut adrift from herself.

"No, no, no, that's fine. Of course. I totally understand. Maybe you're coming down with something?"

"No," she said in a voice that was two tones sharper than she'd intended. "No, it's not that. It's something else. It's my head. Something's happened to my head."

She saw Ben and the first-aid woman exchange a glance and then she saw the door marked "EXIT" open and there he was. Julius Sardo. Smaller than he'd looked on the stage, and much more orange.

"Hey, Melody, you're back. Thank God. You had me worried out there. Are you OK?"

She nodded distractedly. She didn't want to talk to Julius Sardo. She just wanted to go home and get into bed.

"What do you think it might have been?" he continued. "Low blood sugar?"

"I don't know," she said, "but I'm fine now. I just want to go home. Can I go home?"

The first-aid woman nodded her assent and Ben helped her to her feet.

"I want you to know," Julius continued, "that I've been doing live shows for nine years and that's the first time anyone's passed out on me." His smile was slightly too wide and Melody could tell that he was concerned, but she didn't have the energy to discuss it with him.

"It's fine," she said, taking her jacket from Ben and sliding it on. "Don't worry about it."

"Cool." He beamed again, flashing artificially white teeth at her. "Well, I've got to get back now, but talk to the people in the office next door and they'll arrange tickets for you both for another night, make up for what you missed, yeah?"

She smiled wanly. She had no intention of going within a hundred feet of Julius Sardo ever again. "Yeah," she said.

The air outside the theater was cool and chilled now that the sun had set, and Melody shivered slightly in her open shoes and thin jacket.

"I'm really sorry," she said. "What a disaster!"

"No, I'm sorry. It was my idea to bring you here. Next time we'll just go for a nice meal, eh?"

Melody threw him a curious glance. Next time? It was unthinkable that he would want to see her again. She smiled tightly, assuming that he had just said that to be polite, and headed for the tube.

Ed was stretched out on the sofa watching TV when she got home at nine thirty. He jumped as she walked into the room.

"What are you doing back so early?" he said.

She sighed and perched herself on the arm of the sofa. "Disaster struck," she said.

"What—he stood you up?"

"No, he didn't *stand me up*," she replied indignantly. "I got picked on for a trick. Julius Sardo made me pretend to be a five-year-old boy with gas. So, as if running around a stage in front of hundreds of people pretending to fart wasn't bad enough, I then passed out . . ."

"*What?*"

". . . collapsed. In front of everybody. Had to be carted off backstage and given first aid."

"No way!"

"Yes way, unfortunately." She sighed and ran her hands through her hair. "Jesus. This could only happen to me. To Melody Browne. And this," she continued, "is exactly why I have spent the last eight years at home."

"God, Mum, are you all right?"

Melody shook her head. Then she nodded. She didn't know if she was all right. She just knew that she had to sleep. "Yeah. I'm fine. I think it was just too much adrenaline plus a big glass of wine. I'm off to bed."

"Are you sure you're OK? Maybe you should have something to eat?"

She smiled, touched and surprised by the sound of her baby boy attempting to mother her. "No. I just need to sleep. Don't forget to lock all the windows before you head for bed."

She left Ed there, on the sofa, no longer her baby but a strapping boy of seventeen, and headed to her room.

In the darkness she listened to the sounds of a summer night playing out on the estate, the sounds of hot car engines coming and going, voices carrying through open windows, distant music. It was surprising to her that she had so recently been a part of the fabric of this Saturday night. She had been a person on a pavement in the West End in sparkly shoes and lipstick. She had been a person in a pub with a man and a glass of wine. And she had, more unexpectedly, been a person on a West End stage being watched by hundreds of people, a person who would be talked about long after the moment itself: "There was this woman and she *fainted*!" She had left her mark on the night, but now she was here, as ever, in her double bed, alone and sober, a single mum, as if none of it had ever happened.

The red LED of her radio alarm clicked from 9:50 to 9:51 and Melody fell into a deep and immediate sleep.

Chapter 3

1976

When Melody Browne was three years old, she was called Melody Ribblesdale and she lived in a big red house right in the very middle of London. At least, that is how her three-year-old consciousness saw it. She lived, in fact, in one corner of the second floor of a big red mansion block squatted unprepossessingly on a busy junction in Lambeth, south London.

To get to their corner of the big red building, Melody and her parents had to either walk up two flights of cold, bleach-scented stairs or cram themselves into a tiny lift with a crisscross sliding door that was nearly impossible to push open, even for her father with his big hairy arms.

Their flat was bright and airy, though, with huge sash windows in every room overlooking the chaos below. When Melody climbed onto the back of the sofa in the living room and stood on her tiptoes, she could even see a bit of the river Thames.

She slept in a small yellow bedroom with blue curtains and a mobile with wooden butterflies on it, and every morning her mother strapped her onto the back of her bicycle and took her to a house on Walnut Tree Walk to be looked after by a lady called Pam while she went to work. At five o'clock her mother would return, smelling of coffee and cigarettes, and take her home again, sometimes stopping at the convenience store on the corner of their road for a pint of milk or a packet of ham.

Melody's mum was a marketing manager for a contemporary dance company and her dad was a block setter at a print works. They both worked regular hours. Neither of them traveled. It was a quiet life. It was a predictable life. Melody knew what to expect on a day-to-day basis. She liked it like that, bobbing around in the warm, buoyant waters of routine. Sometimes her parents threw parties in the big flat in Lambeth, parties that started at lunchtime and went on until breakfast. Her dad played the piano and her mum doled out a raspberry-hued punch with a big plastic ladle. People stood on the fire escape outside the kitchen to smoke pipes and cigarettes, and Melody woke up with other people's children asleep on her bedroom floor, but she didn't mind. It was normal. It was her life, her family, her world. But when she was three and a half her life, her family, and her world changed forever.

And all because of the baby who never came home.

Her mother told her about the baby growing in her tummy one soft May morning. Even though Melody's life had been nice before the announcement about the baby, it seemed to get even nicer afterward. They went on holiday together to a cottage in the countryside that summer. There was a very big rabbit in a hutch in the garden outside their cottage. He was called Mr. Flopsicle and he liked eating celery out of Melody's hands. Her mum and dad kept hugging each other and holding hands all the time and when they came back to London, Melody stopped going to Pam's house and started going to a nursery school on Lollard Street, where she got her milk in a carton instead of a bottle.

One day her mother came to collect her from school and told her that she'd just felt the baby moving for the first time. This seemed to make her mother even happier. After that her mum got really big, not just on her belly, but all over. When Melody shared the bath with her she could feel the extra weight of her, the way she squished up against the sides of the bath like a big soft cork. After Christmas Melody's mum had her hair cut into a sort of square shape with a fringe. It had been long and tangly before, almost down to her bottom, and Melody wasn't sure if she liked it or not, particularly now that her mum's face was a different shape. But her mum said that when the baby came the last thing she'd want to be bothered with was all that hair.

And then, one night, when Melody's mum was the biggest thing that she'd ever seen, so big that she couldn't even go to work anymore and could barely get off the sofa, she started to make a lot of noise and locked herself in the bathroom and her dad told her that the baby was coming. A lady called Marceline came a little while later and sat in the bathroom with her mum and for a while everyone was really excited and Melody was allowed to stay up even though it was, as her dad kept telling her, the middle of the night. Eventually Melody fell asleep on the sofa and someone put her blanket over her and when she woke up again it was the morning and her mum was still having the baby. Nobody said anything about going to nursery or eating cereal or getting dressed, so Melody just sat at her little wooden table in the corner of the living room and did coloring-in with her big box of crayons.

A few minutes later, her aunt Maggie arrived with Claire and Nicola, her big cousins. Maggie was her mum's sister and they looked exactly the same usually, but not anymore because of her mum's new haircut and new shape. They stayed until the ambulance came and then they took Melody back to their house in Ealing. Melody waved at her mum as they wheeled her into the ambulance and her mum waved back and looked a bit like she might start crying.

"Be good for your auntie," she said, "and I'll see you later, when you're a sister!"

Melody stayed at Aunt Maggie's for two whole days and two whole nights. Nobody really explained why she wasn't at home, sitting on her mum's bed, staring at the new baby and wondering what she thought about it.

On her third morning she awoke to find Maggie's cat, Boots, rubbing her face with his fishy whiskers. He then lay down on her chest, which she found vaguely alarming.

"Off, Boots," she said in a loud whisper, not wanting to wake her cousin. "Off, Boots."

In the distance, she could hear the phone ringing. She pushed the cat off her chest and sat up. She could hear Maggie's voice, muted, sleepy, through the wall of Nicola's bedroom. There was a painting of a Spanish girl on the wall. She had black hair and dark blue eyes and a rose tucked behind her ear. Her lips were all red, like she'd been eating blackberries straight from a bush, and her dress was covered in white spots, like it had been snowing. Melody stared at the picture as she listened to Maggie through the wall, heard her voice turn from sleepy to confused to urgent, from quiet to loud and then to a slow, heavy incantation of the word "no."

The Spanish girl seemed to peer at Melody curiously, as if she too were wondering what the phone call could be about. Melody smiled at the Spanish girl, a hopeful smile, as if to reassure her that everything would be all right.

A few minutes later Maggie came into Nicola's bedroom. She was wearing a blue dressing gown with birds embroidered on it and her long hair was in a plait. Her eye makeup, which was usually quite neat, was smudged all under her eyes, like she'd been rubbing them, and she didn't look as pretty as she did normally, during the day.

"Oh," she said, smiling, "you're awake."

"Yes," Melody said, "I heard the phone ringing."

Maggie nodded. "That was your dad."

"Is the baby coming home now?"

"No," said Maggie, stroking Melody's cheek with her thumb. "No, the baby's not coming home . . ."

Melody glanced away from Maggie and up at the Spanish girl, hoping that she would do something dramatic to make this horrible feeling go away. But she didn't. She just stood there in her spotty dress, looking curious.

"The baby wasn't very well when it came out. The doctors tried to make the baby better, but nothing they tried to do worked. And the baby tried really hard too. But she was too small and too unwell and she stopped breathing. Do you know what happens when you stop breathing?"

Melody did know what happened when you stopped breathing, so she nodded. "You get dead," she said.

"Yes," said Maggie, "you get dead. And I'm so sorry, my precious girl, but that's what happened to your baby sister. She stopped breathing. And your mummy and daddy are very, very sad. And you know what they said, they said, the only thing that will make them feel better will be to see their big, brave girl. So shall we get ready? Shall we get you dressed and take you home to see your mummy and daddy?"

Melody considered this. If she stayed here she could stare at the Spanish girl a little longer and see if she might somehow show her a way to reverse the last two minutes of her life. Then she could go downstairs and have sugary cereal with her big cousins and walk with them to school and then go for a slice of cake with Maggie and then go home to a nice happy place with a new baby sister in it.

"I'm very hungry," she said eventually. "Can we have breakfast first?"

Maggie gave her Sugar Puffs with a strange-shaped plastic spoon and Melody tried her hardest not to spill them down her T-shirt, but a couple landed in her lap and Maggie cleared them off for her with a damp cloth. Nicola and Claire ate toast in their gray school uniforms and were not as noisy as they usually were.

After she'd dropped the girls off at school, Maggie drove Melody back to Lambeth and stood with her in the little creaky lift as it made its way up to the second floor. Melody reached out and held her hand as they approached the front door of her flat, feeling suddenly shy and nervous. Her dad came to the door. His chin was all furry and his eyes were all red and his T-shirt looked sort of tired and floppy, like an old person's skin. "Hello, sweetpea." He leaned down and scooped her up and squeezed her. He smelled like an old tea towel, but she squeezed him back anyway, because she knew he wanted her to.

"Where's Mummy?" she said.

"She's in bed. Do you want to see her?"

Melody nodded and he put her down and took her by the hand. "Mummy's very tired," he said, "and very sad."

She nodded again.

At her parents' bedroom door she stopped for a moment, because even though she was only four, in some unfathomable way she knew that on this side of the door lay her past and on the other side of that door lay her future and that this was the very last moment she would ever spend in the old order.

As the door opened and she approached her mother in bed, and saw her funny square hair all squashed flat against her head and her T-shirt all creased and grimy, smiling blankly at her like she'd forgotten who she was, Melody knew she was right.

She was in a different place now. A different place altogether.

Chapter 4

Now

The strange feeling was there the moment Melody opened her eyes the next day.

She didn't mention it to Ed as she couldn't think of a good enough way to explain it, and it was so fleeting and peripheral that the moment her thoughts turned to anything even slightly distracting she forgot all about it. It was as though someone had opened her up, made a mess in her head, and then tidied it all away again before sealing her closed. But they hadn't quite put everything back in the right place and Melody felt strangely disordered.

Objects seemed to carry an extra resonance. She stared at her toothbrush for a while before putting it in her mouth that morning, feeling oddly as if it weren't hers, but at the same time feeling almost as if she'd only brushed her teeth a moment earlier. Her coffee tasted strange, as though she were tasting it for the very first time and only just noticing the pungent bitterness. When she looked at her reflection that morning, trying to decide whether or not she needed to wash her hair, there was a split second of objectivity, the oddness that accompanies an unexpected sighting of yourself in a shop window. Melody recognized some of the sensations she was experiencing. Ed had only slept for two hours at a time from his six-month birthday until he was eighteen months old, and for a year Melody had lived her life in a feathery state of sleep deprivation, the edges of her consciousness constantly blurred, the pull of lag and delay on all her actions and reactions. She had similar feelings now. She felt hollowed out and temporary. She felt *wrong*.

The day itself was bright and warm, just like the day before and the day before that, but the breeze outside her bedroom window seemed to have developed an extra auditory dimension, a kind of flat, humming undertone as it whistled through the leaves of the tree outside her windows.

Her mobile phone called to her from the kitchen counter where she'd left it to charge overnight. The caller ID came up as Unknown, but glad of the distraction she pressed answer. It was Ben.

"Am I too early?" he asked.

"No, no, it's fine," she replied. "I've been up for a while."

"I was just worried about you. Couldn't really sleep last night. I was thinking about what happened. You don't think it was anything to do with the trick, do you? Being hypnotized. You don't think . . . ?"

"What?"

"That he *did* something, to your head?"

"What makes you say that?"

"Well, the timing. I mean, you passed out literally as he clicked his fingers. It just seems rather . . ."

"I know. It's weird. I feel a bit . . . *weird*."

"You do?" he asked in a concerned tone. "In what way?"

"Oh, I don't know. A bit *undone*."

"Undone?"

"Yes. Like a jigsaw or a ball of wool, or—" She stopped abruptly. As the words "ball of wool" left her mouth, something flashed through her mind. An image, as bright and focused as real life, a ball of pale blue angora wool in a basket, a small hand, a price sticker that said "20p."

As quickly as the image had arrived in her head, it had left. She breathed out.

"Are you OK?"

"Uh-huh," she replied breathlessly.

"Do you think you should see somebody?"

"Like what? A shrink?"

"No. Just a . . . I don't know, someone who knows about this kind of thing. Just to be on the safe side."

Melody had no intention of seeing anyone about this. She didn't even know what "this" was yet. "No," she said over-brightly. "I don't think it's that bad. It was probably just a combination of things—you know, wine, nerves, adrenaline."

Ben paused. "Yeah," he said, sounding unconvinced. "Probably. But anyway, I just really wanted to make sure you were OK. You went off in such a rush I didn't really have a chance to say goodbye properly."

"Yes, sorry about that."

"And there's still so much I don't know about you."

"Oh, trust me, there really isn't much to know."

"Come on, you're a single mother, you're a dinner lady . . ."

"*Kitchen* assistant."

"Oh, yes, sorry, *kitchen* assistant. You live in Covent Garden."

"On an estate."

"Yes, but it's still in Covent Garden. And besides, there's no such thing as a person without a story. Look, I'd really like to see you again. Without the magic man and the dramatic fainting episodes. Next week, maybe?"

Melody sat down and moved the phone to her other ear. This was a most unexpected turn of events and she didn't know how to react.

Ben took her silence as a rebuff and sighed. "Right," he said, "I see . . ."

"No!" Melody replied. "It's just, I didn't think you'd want to and I'm a bit surprised. That's all."

"Well, I don't know why you'd be surprised," he laughed, "but if you can get over the shock of someone wanting to take you out for dinner, I'm free on Friday."

Ed emerged from his bedroom just then, his thick black hair pressed into furrows and humps, his sinewy teenage chest bare and hairless, thin white legs poking out of a pair of gray jersey boxer shorts. He grunted at her, his normal morning greeting, and she smiled and squeezed the back of his neck.

"Erm, I'm not sure about Friday, actually," she continued. "I think I've got something on. I'll give you a call, shall I, later in the week?"

"Now that," said Ben, with another small laugh, "sounds suspiciously like a brush-off."

"No," said Melody, nervously, "not at all, not at all. I'll speak to you later then, yeah?"

She hung up, hurriedly, her hands trembling slightly.

"Who was that?" asked Ed, shaking Honey Nut Corn Flakes into a bowl.

"Ben," she said, "the guy from last night."

"So you didn't put him off then?"

"Apparently not. He wants to go out again. On Friday."

"Cool," said Ed, splashing milk into his bowl and carrying it through to the table in the living room. "And you, do you want to go?"

Melody considered the question. Ben was a real "what's not to like?" kind of a guy, easygoing, bright, considerate. He was the kind of man that a well-meaning friend would set you up with. He ticked all the "good guy" boxes. And he was reasonably good-looking. But she just couldn't face going through it all over again—the nerves, the apprehension, the awkwardness—and then what? Next time there'd be no convenient fainting episode to offer her a quick exit route. Next time the evening would have to play itself out toward a more conventional ending: a kiss, a coffee, full-blown sex, an awkward extraction. And after that, what? Someone would be bound to get hurt, and it sure as hell wasn't going to be her.

"No." She shook her head. "No. I don't think so. He's not really my type."

Chapter 5

1977

Melody's dad stood in her bedroom, rifling through her wardrobe, a look of slightly bemused deliberation on his face.

"I don't think it's going to be warm enough for your green dress," he was saying. "I think you'll need something with sleeves."

"No!" she said. "I want to wear the green dress!"

"OK, OK," he sighed, "relax. But you'll need to wear something underneath it then. Where are your tops?"

Melody sighed too, and got to her feet. "They're here," she said, "on this shelf."

"Well, can you pick one?"

Her mum would never ask her to pick a top. Her mum was always in a hurry and would just spin around the room pulling clothes out of cupboards and drawers and wedging Melody into them. Melody didn't have to think much about clothes usually. But she was having to think about lots of things these days that she didn't normally have to think about. Like whether it was teatime. And what day of the week it was. And how to make her mum feel happy again.

She looked through her bedroom window for a moment. It wasn't what her mother would call a "gorgeous day."

It was a gray, purply sort of day, like a bruise. Like the bruise, in fact, that she had on her elbow when she'd fallen off her little chair in the kitchen the other day trying to reach out for a packet of Viscount peppermint biscuits because nobody came when she called and she was hungry. That bruise was not just gray and purple but had a bit of green in it too, and a red raw bit in the middle where the skin had scraped away. Her dad had put a plaster on it but it had come off in the bath the night before and she didn't like to ask for another one. She didn't like to ask for much at all really, as asking for things seemed to make everyone sigh a lot.

She chose a top with a pink chest and orange sleeves and a word printed on the front. That way, she thought, her mum would have something to look at that wasn't purple or gray and that might just cheer her up.

"You'll need tights too," said her dad.

She pulled a pair of red tights from her tights drawer and a pair of yellow knickers. "I can wear my blue shoes," she said, "then everything I've got on is a different color."

"Great idea," said her dad, pulling her nightdress over her head. "Fantastic."

Her mum was brushing her hair when they went to show her what she was wearing a moment later. She turned sharply as they walked into the room.

"Look," said Melody, "red, and pink and orange and green—and yellow underwear and blue shoes."

"Fantastic," said her mother in the same unfantastic tone of voice that her dad had just used. "You're a little rainbow."

Melody smiled and hugged her mother's knees, pleased by the mention of little rainbows. Her mother stroked her hair absentmindedly, and then stood up. She was wearing a voluminous gray pinafore dress with big pockets, which she'd worn when she was pregnant, and a black turtleneck. Her hair was tied back, but had lots of grips in it to keep it neat because it wasn't really long enough to be tied back anymore.

"Shall we go then?" she said. Melody nodded and slid her hand inside her mother's. But her mother didn't keep ahold of it and it dropped from her fingers like a slippery bar of soap.

The graveyard was a horrible place. It was really big and straggly and full of weird pointy trees and statues with bits missing. Melody's mood brightened when she saw her cousins Claire and Nicola, and for a moment she felt like she wanted to run off with them and play, like she usually did. But then she looked at Maggie's big black coat and down-turned mouth and remembered that this was the baby's funeral and she probably wasn't allowed to play. She turned down her own mouth and followed her parents to a hole in the ground with creamy-colored silk inside it. On a normal day she'd have wanted to climb into the silky hole and pretend to be a naughty pixie, but she could absolutely imagine what her mum and dad would say if she tried that today. So instead, she made herself feel sad and grown-up, and stood primly by the side of the hole and let all thoughts of play and fun leave her mind.

A black car pulled up on the road by the graveside and two men got out. They were wearing suits like businessmen and one of them had really strange hair, like a doll's hair.

"Dad," she whispered, tugging her father's hem, "why's that man got funny hair?"

"Shhh," said her dad.

"No, but what's it like?"

"What do you mean?"

"I mean, is it like real hair? Or is it like pretend hair?"

"I don't know," he replied impatiently. And then he walked away from her, toward the man with the pretend hair, and they said something to each other in very quiet voices and then they pulled a box out of the back of the car. It was a creamy color with silver handles and flowers on the top. It was her. Her sister. The baby who never came home. And for a moment Melody didn't need to make herself feel sad and grown-up, because she just did.

They carried the box toward the hole in the ground and then the vicar said lots of serious things and all around were snuffling noises of grown-ups crying and sighing, and Melody found it hard to believe that there was a baby inside that box—a real, live, tiny baby, except that she was dead—and that she had never even seen her face.

A wind came from between the trees as the vicar spoke. It was low and strong and flipped the hem of Melody's green dress up and down and threw the golden-brown curls of her hair all over her face so that she couldn't see what was happening. By the time she'd got it out of her eyes, she could see that the cream box was being lowered into the silky cream hole, and that Auntie Maggie was crying proper tears and that even Claire and Nicola were crying and they were only children, and the next thing she knew was that her mother was kneeling at the edge of the hole, getting mud all over her gray pinafore dress and making funny noises. They sounded a lot like the noises she'd made the day the baby came, a lot like a cow or a pony or even like the fox who sometimes screamed outside the windows of the cottage they'd stayed in that summer when the baby was still in her mummy's tummy. The noises made Melody feel weird and uncomfortable, like maybe her mum was doing something wrong. And then she started shouting, "My baby, my baby!" over and over again, which was funny to hear because that was what her mum had used to call her before the other baby hadn't come home.

Auntie Maggie and her dad both went over to her mum and pulled her away from the hole and she hit at them with her hands, pushing them away. Her face was red and her dress was muddy and she looked like the lady who lived on the pavement near the church with the newspaper in her shoes and all her things in a shopping trolley. Melody's dad pulled her to him, really tight, and wrapped his big strong arms around her, and for a minute her mum looked like she was trying to push her way out of a straitjacket, like the man with all the chains she'd seen on the TV. But then she stopped pushing and went soft and floppy and let her dad hold her as if she were a big rag doll.

For a second, there was complete silence. Even the wind stopped blowing and nobody sniffed or snuffled. It felt as if they were all playing a game of musical statues. Melody stared at her mum and dad and thought how strange they looked, holding each other like that. Usually when they hugged they looked at each other, or smiled and made out like they were messing around. But this looked more like Dad was rescuing Mum from an accident, like she'd been floating underwater in a swimming pool and Dad had pulled her out.

It was the last time Melody ever saw her parents embrace.

Chapter 6

Now

By the time Melody left the house at midday it had started to rain, the kind of sad, disappointing rain that takes the edge off a bright summer's day. She walked toward the tube, threading her way through the hordes of shoppers that descended on Covent Garden every Sunday. Her feet caught gray puddles as she walked, flicking pear-shaped drops of London dirt across her calves. She was going to a barbecue at her sister's house in Hackney. Well, not her real sister, but as close as she had to one. She and Stacey had lived in adjoining rooms in the hostel when they were both fifteen and pregnant. Stacey was the same age as Melody, but unlike Melody, she was married with two teenage children and a toddler.

Melody stopped at Marks and Spencer on the way to the tube station to pick up some spare ribs, a packet of salmon kebabs, and a bottle of pink Cava. At the till she was served by a woman with very short cropped hair and a wide smiling face. "Good morning, my dear," said the woman, in a soft South African accent. "And how are you today?"

"I'm fine, thank you," Melody said. "How are you?"

"Oh, I am very well. Very well indeed."

The woman smiled again and waved the Cava over the scanner. "Not a good day for a barbecue." She gestured toward the rain outside.

"Not really," said Melody, "but I'm hoping it will have dried off by the time I get there."

"I will say a prayer for you," said the woman. Melody smiled again and glanced at the name badge pinned to her chest.

Emerald.

She was about to say, "What a beautiful name," when suddenly, there it was again, a vivid, Technicolor snapshot in her head. An open newspaper on a pine table. A blue and white striped mug. A woman's legs in blue denim with a patch on the knee, a pair of women's feet in oatmeal socks, a child's voice saying: "Emerald?"

A woman's voice saying, "Yes, like the green stone."

And then the picture was gone, and Melody was standing at a till in Marks and Spencer with her mouth hanging open and a packet of salmon kebabs in her hand.

She gathered her carrier bags hastily, smiled at the woman called Emerald, and headed for the tube.

"So," said Stacey, "how'd it go with your number fourteen man?"

Melody poured herself another glass of pink Cava and grimaced. "Hmmmm," she said.

"Oh dear."

"No. It was fine. I mean, he was fine. But the night was, well, a bit bizarre."

She told Stacey about being hypnotized and fainting onstage and she thought about telling her about the strange feelings she'd been having but couldn't quite stomach the conversation that would follow. Stacey was scathing about anything that she perceived to be in any way "alternative" or "spiritual." She didn't believe in ghosts or tarot or past lives and she certainly didn't believe in hypnotism. Stacey believed only in the tangible and the visible. Anything else made her scowl disdainfully and say things like, "Bollocks," or "Pile of old crap."

Stacey would have no time for the onset of inexplicable flashbacks. She'd say, "Get over yourself, it's just your mind playing tricks on you."

Stacey glanced at her questioningly. "You all right?"

Melody lit a cigarette and shrugged. "Of course I am."

"Right," said Stacey. "You seem a bit off, that's all. You sure you're not coming down with something?"

Melody nodded and inhaled. It was her first cigarette of the day, the first since yesterday afternoon, and, like her coffee that morning, it tasted strange. She glanced at the packet absentmindedly, checking the brand, checking she hadn't picked up the wrong ones. But they were hers, definitely, her Marlboro

Lights. Her cigarette tasted musty and dusty, though, not like tobacco, but like *dirt*, the way cigarettes had tasted when she was just pregnant with Ed.

She stared at the cigarette distastefully and then stubbed it out.

"What's going on?" said Stacey, eyeing the mashed-up cigarette in the bowl.

"Don't know," said Melody. "It just tasted wrong."

"Ha!" Stacey laughed, and banged her hand down on the tabletop. "That Julius bloke—he's hypnotized you out of liking nicotine!"

"Oh God," said Melody, staring at the ashtray. "Do you think?"

"Well, I've never seen you do that before. Never in my life! Ooh, I wonder if he could hypnotize me out of liking chocolate?"

"Yeah, and maybe into liking sex!"

Stacey laughed and her husband, Pete, grunted from the barbecue, where he was turning burgers. "I'd pay for that," he said.

The air was still damp from the earlier shower, but was drying out quickly in a long stretch of sunshine. Their toddler, Clover, sat at a small plastic table arranging miniature teacups and saucers with fat hands while Mutley, their Norfolk terrier, snuffled at a stuffed toy on the decking by her feet. It was, as ever, a picture of domestic bliss.

Melody and Stacey had started their adult lives at exactly the same point: fifteen, pregnant, homeless, and single, but within a year of their babies' being born exactly a week apart, Stacey's life had headed in a completely different direction, because when she was seventeen, she'd met Pete. Placid, strong, and dependable Pete had stuck around and married her even with another man's baby, and now, as they neared middle age, she had a neat little house in Hackney, two teenagers, an unexpected baby girl, and an eternal air of contentment. Stacey and Melody were similar in so many ways, and for a while it had looked like their lives might pan out the same way. But from the very moment that they both discovered they were pregnant at the age of fifteen, Stacey's life had begun.

And Melody's had hit rock bottom.

Chapter 7

1988

Rock bottom wasn't a day or a week or a month. Rock bottom was a moment. And for Melody it looked like this:

A room, ten by ten, with ripped net curtains and a rusty Baby Belling.

A single, unmade bed and a chair covered in clothes.

Her hands, resting helplessly in her lap, holding a scrunched-up piece of tissue paper.

The sound of the front door slamming downstairs and Tiff's scooter buzzing angrily away into the dark night air.

Sudden silence and a sudden desperate realization.

She was alone, in a damp bedsit; and she was pregnant.

Her boyfriend had just dumped her.

And she wasn't even sure it was his baby.

At her feet was a bottle of gin. On the bed next to her was a packet of paracetamols. She glanced from the gin, to the tablets, and then back to her upturned hands. She tried to imagine a baby in those hands, a baby who might look like Tiff, or might look like a man whose name she didn't know because there hadn't been time to find out. She tried to imagine those hands rubbing cream onto a baby's bottom, putting a safety pin into the corners of a terry nappy, clipping a parasol to the bars of a pram. She tried and she couldn't.

After a while she picked up a teacup and filled it to the brim with gin. Then she poured ten paracetamols into the palm of her hand and tipped them into her mouth. She washed the tablets down with the gin, poured herself another, and swallowed that down in three vile gulps.

Down the hall she could hear the bathwater nearing the top. She tiptoed across the landing, clutching her towel. And it was there, halfway across the landing, her stomach full of gin and pills, the bathroom in front of her spewing steam through the open door, on her way to kill her baby, that she felt it; the cold, grimy, sharp surface of rock bottom.

Afterward she sat on her bed, her knees drawn into her chest, damp tendrils of hair curling around her bare shoulders, and she wept soft, hot tears into the fur of a battered teddy bear.

Chapter 8

Now

The sun was shining and Bloomsbury was full of happy students from University College and office workers sunbathing on the grass. The summer air felt sweet against her clammy skin. Usually after work on these warm summer days Melody craved lager or chilled white wine, but today she had a sudden urge for a glass of fizzy lemonade.

She stopped at a café on Sicilian Avenue, took a table on the pavement, and ordered one. It arrived in a tall condensation-coated glass with a yellow bendy straw and a crescent of lemon floating on the top. She stared at it for a while before bringing it to her lips and as she stared another picture appeared in her head. A Formica-topped table, a salmon-pink banquette, a rain-splattered crash helmet, a glass of lemonade, and a huge glass globe of ice cream; three mounds of vanilla, a squirt of strawberry sauce, sugar sprinkles, a fan-shaped wafer, a long spoon, and a man's voice saying: "*Regrets are worse than any mistake you could ever make. Far, far worse.*" And then a smaller voice, a girl's voice: "*Will I still be here, in Broadstairs?*"

"Oh, I doubt that very much. Nobody should stay in Broadstairs forever."

And then the vignette disappeared and a name flashed through her thoughts.

Ken.

That's who that man was. The man with the crash helmet and the long fingers and the wise words about regret.

Ken.

But before she could grab hold of the memory and make any sense of it, it was gone and she was once more at a pavement table in Bloomsbury staring at a glass of lemonade. She pulled her bag onto her knee and opened it with shaking hands, taking out her cigarettes and lighter, but before she'd even lit it up, she knew she didn't want it. She dropped the box back into her bag and sighed.

What was happening to her? She appeared to be going mad. All the signs suggested an encroaching state of insanity. Inexplicable flashbacks. Voices in her head. Paranoia. And a sudden dramatic aversion to coffee and cigarettes.

But no, there was something more to it than simple madness. *Broadstairs.* It meant something to her. It had always meant something to her. All her adult life, whenever she heard the name "Broadstairs" she had a reaction, a sense of nostalgic yearning, as if she'd like to go there. And then *Ken*. She knew someone called Ken. Ken was someone *important*. She just couldn't bring his face to mind. Neither his face nor, indeed, any other detail about him. Except now she had something—a crash helmet. She focused her thoughts on the crash helmet and suddenly she felt a tightness around her skull, a deafening blast of wind in her ears, a rush of adrenaline, a thrill of excitement. And then it was gone.

She dropped two pound coins on the table and headed home, her lemonade untouched on the table, her head in turmoil.

Chapter 9

1977

Nobody smiled in Melody's house anymore. Not properly. Sometimes, if Melody tried really hard to be funny, her mum might squeeze her lips together and stroke her hair, and her dad smiled quite a lot when they went out together, when it was just the two of them, but at home, under normal circumstances, life was very staid.

They didn't have parties anymore and friends didn't come over, not even for tea. But the strange thing was that nobody went around saying things that might make sense of the gloomy atmosphere, like, "oh, I miss my dead baby," or, "I wish Romany were here and not in that cold hole in the ground." Nobody talked about Romany, so Melody was left to conclude that they weren't sad about Romany, but that they were sad about her. She tried as hard as she could to make up for whatever it was she'd done to make her parents so sad. She always put her plate in the sink after breakfast and tea, she never splashed in puddles in her school shoes and didn't make a fuss when her mum brushed the knots out of her hair. But there were some things she couldn't help, like falling over and laddering her tights, like spilling her milk, like sometimes getting cross when she had to go to bed.

One day, about three months after baby Romany's funeral, Melody got *very* cross about having to go to bed. It was a Friday night, there was no school the next day, and earlier in the afternoon her mum had said specifically, "You can stay up late tonight if you like, for being such a good girl."

But it seemed that Melody's idea of late and her mother's idea of late were incompatible, and even though she had only two more cats to color in and said so really politely, her mum started shouting at her.

"Why," she said, her eyes filled with tears, "can't you just do what I ask you to do? Why?"

"I am," began Melody. "I just—"

"No 'just,' Melody. No buts. Nothing. Please. I do not want to hear another word come out of your mouth. Not one!"

"But—"

"*No!* Enough! Get to bed now!"

Sparkles appeared inside Melody's eyes then, and a big feeling of red and black flooded her head and she screamed at the top of her voice, "I JUST WANT TO FINISH MY CATS!!!"

But instead of screaming back, like she might have done in the past, her mother made a strange choking sound, ran from the room, and slammed her bedroom door behind her.

Melody and her father looked at each other. Then her father put down his newspaper, cleared his throat, and knocked gently on the bedroom door. "Janie, it's me."

When he had gone in, Melody rested her crayon on her play table and tiptoed toward her parents' bedroom. She could hear them muttering urgently to each other.

"She's trying so hard not to annoy you, can't you see that?"

"I know she is, I know. She's such a good girl. But I just can't . . ."

"What? What can't you do?"

"I can't do it anymore."

"Do what?"

"This! Just—this! This life. This family."

"Janie, we need you. Melody needs you."

"Exactly. And I can't take it anymore. All the . . . all the *caring*. I don't care anymore, John, do you see? I just don't care! I've lost the only thing that matters to me. I've lost my innocence."

"Jane, you've lost a baby. But you've still got another one. One who needs you. One who loves you."

"Yes, but she's not a baby, is she? She's four years old. I know her. I know her hair. I know her voice. I know that she likes Viscount biscuits and coloring-in and that she prefers your mother to my mother. I know she's got hazel eyes and legs like yours. I know her. That's what I've lost. Not a baby. Not a child. *Potential.* I've lost potential. All the things I will *never, ever know*. And it kills me, John, kills me every time I close my eyes."

There was a long pause then, and Melody held her breath.

"Melody may not be your only baby, Jane, but you're her only mother. You need to find a way out of this, because you owe it to her. You owe her a mother."

"But that's exactly it. That's exactly, precisely it! If I can't be Romany's mother, then I don't want to be anybody's mother at all, do you understand? Nobody's mother at all."

Melody exhaled silently, and very slowly, very quietly, tidied away her crayons and went to bed.

Chapter 10

Now

The summer term finished on Thursday and Melody felt a sense of enormous relief as she left through the school gates that afternoon. Her head was overflowing with memories and ideas. The memories didn't come in a neat, chronological stream, however. They came in fits and bursts, unconnected to each other, as if someone had taken a pair of scissors to her life, thrown the pieces in the air, and let them float slowly back down to earth, scrap by scrap.

The following day, hoping to put some order to the fragments, Melody packed herself a small bag, dressed herself in jeans and trainers, and got on a train to Broadstairs. She stood on the platform at Victoria Station and glanced up and down nervously, almost as if she were expecting someone to appear. A public-address message announced the imminent arrival of her train and with the announcement came another memory. Cold, bare hands in her lap. Bobbly navy tights and a denim skirt. A woman's voice saying, "*You'll just have to freeze then.*" A wave of sadness.

Melody shivered, suddenly cold in spite of the diesel-tinged summer heat.

She took a window seat on the near-empty train that arrived a moment later. She was hoping that she might see something from here that would give her some sense of direction, but the view through the window seemed ordinary and insignificant. It wasn't until she found herself in Broadstairs town that her subconsciousness began to stir again.

Broadstairs was a pretty town, full of slender maritime town houses, squat clapboard cottages, and stucco Regency villas. The streets were tiny and cobbled, and lined with touristy gift shops with striped awnings. It was the first day of the summer holidays and the town was packed with fresh-faced families. Melody didn't recognize anything, but she did feel herself being pulled along in a particular direction, as if being led by the hand by an excitable child.

On the High Street she stopped for a moment to peer through the window of a coffee shop. It was old-fashioned, with an ornate Victorian façade and gingham curtains strung across the window. She felt a burst of surprise as she stood there, as though she'd just seen something wonderful and surprising. She stood for a while, mesmerized slightly by the way she was feeling and waiting for something to come to her, something colorful and full of explanations. But it didn't, and she moved along and waited to see where else she would be taken.

She began to feel a sense of disappointment as she wandered around over the next half an hour or so. She was having no flashbacks and no sense of remembering. She was beginning to think that she was wasting her time, until two things happened within a short time of each other. First of all she saw a house, a tall white house with thin windows and a curved balcony like a sad smile. Her memory opened up and gave her this:

Rain, soft against her skin like feathers.

Three seagulls circling overhead, so close she could see the scales on their feet.

Splat. Like a broken egg. Seagull poo, gray and murky, all over the pavement, just inches from her black plimsolls.

A doorbell that sounded like a clock chiming.

And then a man at the door, a man with long hair, shaved bald above the ears, and a kind face.

He smiled, first at Melody's companion, and then at her. His eyes were gray and his teeth were white. He was wearing a blue shirt without a collar and baggy linen trousers.

"*Hello, Jane*," he said to her companion, "*and hello, Melody. Welcome*," he said, "*welcome to your new home*."

She sat down on the curb for a moment, to steady herself. This was the strongest flashback yet, vivid and overwhelming. Here was fact, strong and irrefutable. She had lived here. With someone called Jane. This had been their home.

She gazed at the house for a while, drinking in the details, the windows, the door, the freshly painted ironwork. It was a beautiful house, elegant and well cared for, very different from the one that had just presented itself to her in her head. That house had been shabby and run-down, its stucco work streaked green, its ironwork peeling and pockmarked. And that man with the long hair. She knew him. She really knew him.

A notice in the bottom window caught her eye then and she got to her feet.

"Rooms available."

She rang the doorbell. A woman of around her own age came to the door. She had a yellow duster and a can of Mr. Sheen in her hands and was wearing an apron. She looked distracted and slightly cross.

"Hello," said Melody, "I was just . . ." She paused for a moment, unsure exactly what she was doing.

The woman stared at her impatiently.

"Do you have a room available?" Melody asked eventually.

"Yes," said the woman brusquely, "but only for tonight. We're fully booked from tomorrow for the rest of the season."

"Could I see it?"

"Yes. Of course."

The woman opened the door and allowed her in. The hallway was neat and elegant, with a tessellated tiled floor and beige walls with lots of framed black-and-white photos of Broadstairs. The house was double fronted and doors went off both sides of the entrance hall. Every angle, every corner of the house meant something to Melody, in some unfathomable way.

"It's only small," said the woman, "but if it's just for you, just for one night . . ."

"Oh, I'm sure it'll be fine," Melody said, hoping she sounded like an ordinary woman doing an ordinary thing, rather than someone in the throes of existential mayhem.

"Have you lived here long?" she asked the woman.

"Well, we bought the place six years ago, but it took us two years to put it back together."

"Was it derelict?"

"As good as, yes. It was in a terrible state. We lived in a caravan for over a year."

"Wow." Melody couldn't imagine this prim, pristine woman living in a caravan. "So who was living here before then?"

"No one, as far as we know. It was a squat in the seventies and then the owner reappeared in 1980 to reclaim it, kicked the squatters out, boarded it up, and left it to rot. We bought it at auction. An act of love. And madness."

She turned and smiled at Melody. "OK, well, this is the room." She pushed open the door to a small box room overlooking the back garden. It was beautifully presented, a cut above the usual guesthouse fare of floral quilts and cheap pine wardrobes. It housed a single bed with a white duvet and pillowcase and two black-and-white cushions, a white French antique bureau and wardrobe, and a framed monochrome photo of Paris at night above the bed. The floorboards were stripped and varnished and full of whorls and knots.

"It's beautiful," Melody said, "really beautiful. But I'm not sure I can really stay tonight. I think I should really get home. I've got a son . . . I've got to . . ." She paused as her eye was caught by a particularly large whorl in the floorboards, and there it came again, memory, clear and fresh: a matted sheepskin rug, a scrunched-up paper tissue, floorboards painted brown, a dark bed with someone in it, her own voice, whispering urgently: "*They're going to call the police! They'll put you in jail! Mum! Don't you understand?*"

Melody gasped. "My mother!" she whispered, louder than she'd expected.

"Oh," said the woman, looking slightly confused. "That's fine."

"Um, I have to go now," said Melody, trying to regain her composure. "But thank you."

"Well, as I say, I am fully booked until the end of summer now . . ."

"Oh, yes, that's right. Never mind. Maybe in the autumn?"

"I'll give you a brochure."

Melody let her eyes take in as much detail as they could hold as she passed back through the house and down to the entrance hall, but the owners had done such a beautiful job of restoring the house that only the layout offered any sense of remembrance.

"So, this place, when it was a squat—any idea who lived here then?"

The woman looked at her sadly, as if the very notion of her house ever having been home to something as unsavory as squatters was too much for her to bear. "No idea whatsoever," she said sniffily. She handed Melody a very tasteful brochure and saw her to the door. "Remember," she said, "book in advance. We're busy all year round."

Melody turned to leave the house, and that was when she saw him. A man—battered looking, time ravaged, bearded and dirty, clutching a can of Diamond White, and careening toward her.

"Are you lost?" he said, breathing putrid cider into her face.

"No, I'm fine," she said, trying to get past him.

"You look lost to me. You sure you're not lost? I can tell you where to go. I've lived here since I was seven. I know this place like the *back of my hand*."

The man was of average height and probably only a bit older than her. If he weren't so unkempt and so drunk she might have liked to ask him about the town and what it was like when he was growing up.

"No, honestly," she said, "I'm fine. I'm just wandering."

"Me too." He smiled. His teeth were discolored but surprisingly straight and intact for a man of the street.

She smiled back at him, willing him to go away, to leave her alone.

"My name's Matthew. What's yours?"

"Mel," she said, not wanting to give her full name in case he found it interesting and prolonged the conversation.

"Nice to meet you, Mel. And what brings you to Broadstairs?"

She shrugged. "Just fancied a day away from London," she said.

He smiled again and passed his can of cider from one hand to the other. "Nice day for it," he said. He looked as though he was planning to join her so she drew herself away from him. He peered at her through slanted eyes, still smiling. "Off you trot, then," he said.

She threw him a nervous smile and headed off.

"Nice talking to you!" he called after her.

"Yes," she said, "you too." She gave him another smile and watched as he turned away from her. And it was then that it hit her:

A grubby tennis ball, a brick wall painted white, a painting of a flying boy, the sound of . . . *a cricket*? No, not a cricket, but a scratchy noise, like wood being whittled. And a child's voice saying, "*Get your mum away from him before she's giving him baths and having babies for him too.*"

She stopped to catch her breath.

By the time she'd recovered herself the man called Matthew was gone, swallowed up by the crowds, taking with him, Melody was sure, some vital clue about her childhood.

Chapter 11

1977

Everything about Melody's old life had been stripped away, not all in one go, but slowly, torturously, layer by layer. First her dad had gone to live in a room in Brixton with mice behind the skirting boards, then her mum had resigned from her job and started getting the dole, which meant that they couldn't afford things like nice cereal and going to the zoo. Then Melody had been taken out of nursery because her mum couldn't afford to pay for it and then they'd packed up all their stuff, left the flat in London, and moved in with Melody's aunt Susie, who didn't have any children and lived in a bungalow on the Kentish coast, just outside Broadstairs.

Susie was Jane's oldest sister and she was known as "the Quiet One." She'd never married and had lived in the same rather damp bungalow for twenty years. She read the Bible for fun and experimented a lot in the kitchen. She was also very, very fat and moved so slowly that she rarely left the house. She was only four years older than Jane, but looked like she might be her mother.

Melody didn't like staying at Aunt Susie's house. There was nothing to do and nothing to play with and nothing to see out of the windows, except another bungalow and some ragged hedges. Plus, there was no normal food anymore, because Jane couldn't afford to go shopping so they just ate what Aunt Susie cooked—things with weird names, like rissoles and soufflés and confits and tagines, things with sauces and herbs and blobs of cream, and even, once, with a whole lemon in it. There didn't seem to be a plan in the offing, or any kind of future goal. Routine, such as it was, revolved around Susie and her churchgoing and TV viewing. Days spilled over into more slippery days without anything solid to hold on to.

Until one day, in early September, when Melody and her mum were walking through Broadstairs with an envelope full of money that had arrived in the post that morning from Melody's dad to buy her school uniform with. A man stopped them in the street, a man with gray eyes and a bunch of peachy roses. He asked Jane how she was and Jane flushed and said, "I'm fine, thank you," in her prim, now-I'll-be-on-my-way voice.

"No, but really," he said, one hand touching the cuff of her cream sweater. "Really, how are you?"

Jane squinted at him. Melody held her breath, wanting her mum to walk away because this was clearly a strange situation, but wanting her to stay too, to see what on earth would happen.

"I told you," said Jane, "I'm fine."

"You look like someone has put their hand inside your gut"—he moved his hand from her sleeve to her belly, where it retracted into a fist—"and *pulled out your soul.*" He turned his fist ninety degrees clockwise and then let it drop.

Melody gulped.

Jane inhaled heavily, audibly, through her nose and her head fell back slightly as if she'd been punched. "I . . . ," she began, but the man quietened her with a finger to her lips.

"I've seen you before," he said. "I've been watching you."

Jane pushed his hand away from her face and grabbed Melody's hand. "Well," she said, "I'd rather you didn't."

"I can help you," he called to her. "Whatever it is that's hurt you, I can make it better."

Jane kept walking, squeezing Melody's hand too hard inside her fist.

"Here," said the man, appearing at their side. "Here. Take a flower. A rose. From my own garden. Take it. It's fine. I've taken off the thorns. You don't need any more hurt in your life."

Jane took the flower without looking at it and led Melody firmly, briskly, away.

Melody turned as they reached the end of the street to see if the man was still there. He was. She smiled at him, just once, and then they turned the corner.

Melody couldn't stop thinking about the man with the rose for days after that. She watched the rose in the vase at Susie's house grow smaller and browner and wither away. And then, on the same day that the very last discolored petal fell from the stem and onto Aunt Susie's Formica-topped sideboard, Jane announced that they needed to go back to Broadstairs to buy Melody some new shoes.

Melody didn't say anything to her mum about the man with the rose, in case she changed her mind about going to the shoe shop. She hadn't said anything about the man, in fact, since they'd seen him.

She saw him the moment they got out of Susie's car on the seafront. He was sitting on a bench, reading a book, the sun shining directly onto him. He looked up when he heard the car door slam, and for a brief moment, he looked exactly like a picture of Jesus that Aunt Susie had on her kitchen wall.

Aunt Susie drove away and they started across the road toward the shops. He got up off the bench and approached them. He was wearing a blue cotton shirt and ripped army trousers and his long hair was tied back from his face. Melody found she couldn't stop looking at him, even when she wanted to.

"Hello again," he said.

Jane jumped at the sound of his voice. "Oh God," she began.

"Listen up, listen up," he said. "First of all, an apology." He put his hand to his heart. "I was way out of line last week. I'm really sorry. That was no way to approach a stranger. But the thing is, I get these . . . *insights*. Instantaneous. *Bam!* Just like that. I see someone, I know them. And I get carried away. Can you forgive me?"

He smiled at Jane and his eyes creased at the corners.

"It's fine," muttered Jane, "honestly. Don't worry about it."

"I wanted to make it up to you. Let me buy you a coffee."

"No, really, it's—"

"You're in a hurry?"

"Yes."

"Where you off to?"

"We've got to get new shoes for my daughter."

"Ah." He smiled. "School shoes?"

Melody flushed and nodded.

"Back to school. I remember that feeling. Which year are you in? One? Two?"

"No." She shook her head. "Reception."

"Reception!" He smiled. "Wow. You look too big to be in reception. I thought you must be at least six."

Melody smiled and pushed herself against her mother's body.

"Well, anyway, I'll let you get on. And if you change your mind about that coffee, I'll be just here." He pointed at the bench, where his paperback still lay. "And again," he said, "a thousand apologies for the other day. I didn't mean to freak you out."

"It's fine," said Jane, a smile just forming at the furthest reaches of her mouth. "Really. Forget about it."

"Then I'm forgiven?"

"Yes," said Jane, "you're forgiven."

The man smiled, wiped imaginary sweat off his forehead, and headed back to the bench.

"By the way," he shouted, as they rounded the corner. "My name's Ken!"

It was raining as they approached the address on the piece of paper Ken had given them last week, with their few meager possessions in battered suitcases and bulging shoulder bags. Neither of them had thought to bring an umbrella and they were damp in their summer clothes. They stopped for a moment on the pavement and appraised the building. It was a battered Regency villa on a square just behind the seafront. Melody looked up at the circling gulls and moved out of the way as one of them released a large monochrome dollop inches from her feet.

Ken appeared at the front door. He skipped down the front steps in bare feet and scooped up their luggage. "Hello, Jane," he said to her mother, "and hello, Melody. Welcome," he said, "welcome to your new home." He showed them to a large room at the top of the house with sloping ceilings and small windows.

It was furnished simply with a single bed dressed in a patchwork quilt, a set of white wrought-iron bunk beds, and a wardrobe made of stripped pine.

"In the eaves," he said, lowering his head to open the window. "Not great for us tall folk, but perfect for you little ones." He turned and winked at Melody and she smiled at him and wondered what eaves were.

After Ken had gone, Melody and her mum sat on the single bed together and stared out of the window. Jane looked tired. Her eyes had changed color over the past year, from an electric aqua blue to a kind of disinterested periwinkle. When Melody looked at pictures of her mum that were taken before the baby had died, it was like looking at a picture of another person entirely. Her hair was dull, her eyes were dull, and there were two big lines on her forehead, deep and painful, like they'd been carved in with a blunt knife.

"I'm hungry," said Melody, who'd eaten only three wine gums since the previous lunchtime because her mother had been in such a hurry to get them out of Susie's house.

Her mother sighed. "Come on then," she said, "let's see if we can find you something to eat."

The kitchen in Ken's house was at the very bottom of the house, a warm subterranean room with a big green oven, an old pine table, and a dozen mismatched chairs. Underneath a window that cowered below street level was an old sofa on which lay a large white dog with droopy jowls. A woman wearing a turban sat at the kitchen table slicing a huge carrot into discs. A black cat sat on a chair next to her, purring very loudly. On the floor by her feet sat a small baby with fat cheeks, chewing on a plastic teaspoon.

Melody and Jane stepped gingerly into the room and the woman looked up.

"Hi!" she said. "Jane? Melody? I'm Grace, Ken's wife. So lovely to meet you."

She raised a ring-laden hand toward them and squeezed their hands with it. "And this"—she pointed at the baby on the floor—"is Seth. Say hello, Seth."

Seth looked up at them curiously and a long string of drool fell from his mouth to his chest.

"Let me make you a cup of tea. Sit down, sit down."

Melody watched Grace making tea. She was very surprised by the presence of Grace, by the existence of a "wife" in the world of Ken. Grace was tall and slender in gray cheesecloth trousers, a tight black T-shirt, and arms laden with clattering bangles. Her hair was pulled back tightly from her face by the red cotton turban. She was very beautiful indeed, with cheekbones that caught the light and dark-framed eyes. The only thing that spoiled her beauty was a big black mole, just by her ear, with a hair growing out of it, which made Melody think that maybe she didn't particularly care about being beautiful.

While she was at the sink, filling the kettle, the kitchen door swung open and another child ran in, a boy wearing camouflage trousers and a brown long-sleeved T-shirt. He stopped when he saw Melody and her mum and stared at them. After a moment, he said, "Hi."

"Oh," said Grace, turning from the sink, "hello there. Melody, Jane, this is my other son, Matty."

Matty had conker-colored hair and bright hazel eyes and looked about ten years old. He smiled at them tightly, and then sighed. "Have you come here to live?" he said.

Jane nodded.

"Great," he said, "just great."

Grace smiled apologetically. "Don't worry about him," she said. "He's just being territorial. Matty, why don't you show Melody the garden?"

He groaned and scuffed the toe of his shoe against the rug.

"Please," said Grace.

"OK."

Melody followed him through a door and into a small paved courtyard. A tall brick wall had been painted white and then decorated with strange paintings of peculiar creatures and flying children. There was a pine bench and an old rocking horse, and a box full of balls and ropes, and a bush of fat peachy roses. "This is the garden," said Matty. "It's not very big. But we like it."

Melody stared at a blob of purple paint, on the wall, which had run and looked like a balloon on a piece of string. She didn't know what to say.

"You can play with anything in that box," Matty said. "That's stuff for the kids. But don't touch my bike." He banged his heel against the wall and put his hands in his pockets. "How old are you?"

"Four," said Melody, "five in November, though."

Matty nodded. "And where's your dad? Is he dead?"

"No. He's in London," said Melody.

"Yeah," he said, "so's mine."

Melody thought of a question then that she'd like to ask, but she felt too shy so she stayed silent.

"So your mum and Ken—are they, you know . . . ?"

Melody didn't know, didn't know at all. Matty's question meant nothing to her, so she just nodded.

"Yeah," said Matty. "I guessed as much. Fuck, this place just gets weirder and weirder." He tutted and shook his head. "Still"—he eyed her up broodily—"you seem like a nice girl. If you were a bit older, we could even be friends. But I'll look out for you. I'll make sure you're OK. Because if I don't, then believe me, nobody bloody will."

He turned then, took his hands from his pockets, and walked back into the kitchen.

Melody stood and stared at the balloon-shaped blob and wondered whether anything in her life would ever feel normal again.

Chapter 12

Now

That night, the night she got back from Broadstairs, the night that Melody could have been having dinner with Ben, she decided to take her son to the pub instead. They went to the Cross Keys, their local, a tiny, fussy pub, spilling over with heavy-handed Victoriana and hanging baskets of petunias. Ed had a pint of Stella and Melody had a pint of shandy. They sat together on a small ledge around a tree on the pavement outside, squeezed between fifty overloud office workers unwinding at the end of the day.

"So," said Ed, resting his pint on the wall next to him, "what's going on with you?"

"What?"

"You? What's up?"

"Nothing's up."

"Oh, come on, Mum. I'm not stupid. Ever since you met that bloke, you've been different. Is everything OK?"

"Yes, of course it is."

"So, what's happening with him? Is he treating you OK?"

Melody laughed. "Ben?" she said, trying to envisage big, soft, soppy Ben doing anything more offensive than failing to hold a door open for her. "Oh God, Ed, if you met him, he's just a . . . he's a sweetheart, he's a gent."

"Then why are you acting so weird?"

"What sort of weird?"

"I dunno. Cagey. And why've you stopped smoking?"

She shrugged. "Just seemed a good time to."

Ed furrowed his brow at her and it was all Melody could do not to fling her arms around his neck and hug him to her, her baby, her only baby, so concerned and so oblivious to everything that was going on in her life.

"You mustn't worry about me," she said. "Maybe I am going through some changes. Maybe it's the idea of you growing up and leaving me that's making me feel a bit . . . out of shape. You know, it's just been you and me for so long, I haven't had to think about anything else, and now I'm having to start thinking about the bigger picture, about what happens next . . ."

"I'm not going anywhere just yet." He smiled and picked up his pint.

"No, I know you're not, not physically, but emotionally, you'll need me less and less every day. And even my job—I only took it so I could be near you, so that I could be around at the holidays, but I don't need to be a dinner lady anymore. I could be anything now. I'm free, you see, I'm free. And I'm really, really scared."

"Oh, Mum, God, you don't need to be scared! What are you scared of? I'll still be around. And you're brilliant—there's loads of things you could do."

"Oh, yes, like what?"

"I dunno, like teaching? You'd be a great teacher. I would never have got my GCSEs without you, and I wouldn't have bothered with A levels. Or you could even get married to someone, have some more kids . . ."

"What!"

"Yeah, seriously. Why not? You're only young. You should have some more kids. You're the best mum out there—wouldn't you want to? You know, like Stacey?"

Melody smiled wryly. "No," she said, placing her hand on Ed's knee. "No. One's enough for me."

"But what about this Ben bloke? He hasn't got any kids, has he? Doesn't he want some?"

"I don't know." She laughed again. "Probably."

"So, then, you know, maybe you and him . . ."

She shook her head slowly. "No, there is no me and him."

"What—it's finished?"

"Well, no, not finished, but not really even started."

"But why not?"

"I don't know," she said. "I just can't quite get my head around him."

"Around him, or around having a man in your life?"

Melody paused and glanced at her son in surprise. What an astute question. Was it possible, she wondered for just a moment, that she'd raised a good man?

"Look, Ed," she said uncertainly. "There is something going on in my life now and it's got nothing to do with Ben. It's got to do with . . ." She paused, feeling that she didn't know enough to start sharing this with Ed, feeling that she wanted to be able to give him more: more absolutes, more facts, more black-and-whites. That was her role, as a mother, to paint the world in the cleanest lines, the brightest colors, to protect him from the vagaries and uncertainties of life. She took a deep breath, chose the right words. "It's to do with my childhood and what happened at the Julius Sardo show."

Ed threw her a confused grimace.

She sighed and continued, "Ever since I fainted that night, I've started remembering things."

"What sort of things?"

"Well, I'm not sure really. They're more like little snatches of time, rather than proper memories, but they're to do with my life, you know, the bit I can't remember, before the fire. I haven't quite made sense of them but I know this much—I used to live in Broadstairs. I went there today. I found the house, and everything."

"What?" said Ed. "You mean, where you lived with your mum and dad?"

"Yes. No. I don't know. I can't remember. I just know that it was a squat and I remember this man called Ken. He had a motorbike. And there was a woman called Jane, and I think . . ." She was about to say, *I think I called her Mum*, but stopped, as she still hadn't properly absorbed the full implication of the memory. "I mean," she moved on, "I even recognized a knot in the floorboards, you know, that kind of detail. I can't be imagining it. It's almost like . . . like I lived a different life."

"You mean like you were adopted or something?"

Melody caught her breath. The possibility had already occurred to her in the deep, muddy darkness of her nighttime ruminations, but she'd discounted it as too far-fetched, even given the unusually pale outline of her childhood recollections.

"No," she said quietly, "nothing like that. But I think I might have been sent away for a while, sent to the seaside, for some reason . . ."

"Oh shit." Ed put down his pint and threw her a nervous look. "You don't think, you know, like those books, that bloke, those, you know, those fucked-up things that can happen to kids?"

"What, you mean *abuse*?"

"Well, yeah." He shrugged unhappily. "What's it called when kids forget bad stuff and then they go to a head doctor and it all comes out and then their dads get sent to jail when they're, like, really old men?"

"*Regression*?"

"Yeah. Because that's like what that Sardo guy did to you, isn't it? He made you think you were five, and maybe when you were five something really bad happened and you shut it all away, and now it's coming back. I mean, seriously, I know it's not very nice, but your dad, do you think . . . ?"

"No!" exclaimed Melody, half amused. "No way!"

"Yeah, well, you say that, but they all look like nice old men, these kiddy-fiddlers. How do you know? If your memory got broken, how do you know?"

"I just do," she replied.

"Well, it might explain some stuff, if it was true."

"Like what?"

"You know, like not wanting a man . . ."

"I *do* want a man!"

"No you don't. And you being so anti your parents . . ."

"You *know* why I'm so anti my parents."

"Well, I know why you *say* you're anti your parents."

"Christ, Ed, stop it, will you! My dad did not abuse me, OK?"

"Then what were you doing living in a squat in Broadstairs with a bloke called Ken?"

Melody sighed and let her head flop into her chest. "I don't know," she said, looking up again. "I don't know, OK?"

"What was it—like a commune, or something?"

She shrugged. "I don't really remember. I remember the man called Ken. He had . . ."—she squeezed her eyes shut—"a tattoo on his hand—it was a symbol—and he smelled . . ."—she sniffed the air—"of rolling tobacco. And his hair, it was long, but shaved off at the sides, like an overgrown Mohican."

"Mmm," said Ed, "sounds really *nice*. You'll have to phone them, then."

"What—Mum and Dad?"

"Yeah. You'll have to phone them and say, 'Mummy, Daddy, what *on earth* was I doing in Broadstairs?'" He said this in the put-on plummy accent he always used when he talked about the grandparents he'd never met, imagining them to be far more genteel than they actually were.

"I can't phone them," Melody sighed.

"Why not?"

"Because," she sighed again, "if they lied to me then, then they'll just lie to me again. I need to know the truth. And I think I need . . ." She paused for a moment to find the right words. "I think I need to let this happen bit by bit, you know, like a jigsaw. I think that if I knew everything, all at once, I might just . . ."

"Explode?"

"Yes. Or implode. Or maybe both. So," she said quietly, "what do you think I should do next?"

"Go back to Broadstairs," said Ed. "Go back and see what else you can get."

Chapter 13

1989

"Pregnant?"

Her mother rolled the word off her tongue like an unexpected piece of gristle.

"Yes," said Melody, pulling at the skin around her fingernails.

"Pregnant?" her mother repeated. "But I—"

"It's OK," said Melody, "I'm dealing with it."

"You're *dealing* with it?" Her father rose from his armchair like a mantis reaching for a fly on a distant branch, his neck wattles quivering, his shiny forehead gleaming in the early evening light.

"Sit down, Clive." Her mother threw him a fearsome look.

He leaned back into the Dralon upholstery and shook his head slowly from side to side. "Whose is it?" he asked. "That boy, is it? The one with the scooter?"

"Yes," Melody said. "Who else would it be?" She hated the inference that she might have slept with someone other than her boyfriend, even though she had.

Her mother turned to gaze through the window. Her blond hair was brittle in the low sun, translucent like the tufts of horsehair and cotton inside an old sofa. Her pretty face looked old, as though someone had unstitched the skin from the bone and let it land where it fell. And her eyes, Melody was pained to see, were glazed over with tears.

"How far gone are you?" she said, turning back abruptly, her tears dried up.

Melody shrugged. "I'm not sure," she said. "I'm five weeks late."

"Five weeks?"

"Nearly six."

"Oh my God."

"What? It's fine."

"Fine! How can you say it's fine? We'll have to take you to the doctor's as soon as possible, get this sorted out. I mean, it could be that you're just late."

"I've been sick every day this week."

"Well, then . . ." Her mother paused and pursed her lips. "We'll just have to ask him about . . . *options*."

"You mean about abortions?"

"Yes, about *abortions*. Oh God, Melody, what were you thinking, what on earth were you *thinking*?"

Melody shrugged again.

"She wasn't thinking, Gloria, that's patently obvious, otherwise she wouldn't be in this hideous mess." Her father rearranged his legs beneath his blanket, slowly and painfully.

"How could you do this to us, Melody? How could you do this to your father after what he's been through these last months? After everything we've done for you?"

"This has got nothing to do with you! This is about *me*!"

"No! It's not! Don't you see? This is about all of us! This affects the whole family!"

"This isn't a family!" Melody yelled. "This is just an old people's home with a teenage girl living in it!"

The words hung there in the still air, cruel and irretrievable. She glanced at her father, at his broken body, his hairless pate, then thought of those strong arms all those years ago, pulling her from her bed, carrying her to safety, saving her life. He didn't deserve her harsh words. But then she didn't deserve these people, this life.

"Fine," said her mother, the hard word sounding incongruous in her small-girl voice, "fine. If that's how you really feel, then go."

Melody gazed at her, half smiling. *As if.* "Go where?" she said with a gruff laugh.

"I don't know. Somewhere else. Somewhere *cool.* Tiff's caravan? The street? You tell me!"

Melody stared at her mother, waiting for her to soften like she always did, but her jaw remained solid, her arms tight across her rib cage. "I mean it, Melody. I'm serious. This is the limit. This is the end of the road. We've had as much as we can take . . ."

Melody turned to her father. He stared resolutely through the window at the cul-de-sac outside. Melody breathed in deeply. This moment had been coming for months, for years. She'd been pushing them away since her fourteenth birthday, and they'd been letting her. It was almost as if they didn't recognize each other anymore, as though, in the way of jaded lovers, they'd become strangers.

That night she packed a bag with a few clothes, her mother's best jewelry, fifty pounds in notes and coins from the "secret" stash at the bottom of their wardrobe, her teddy bear, and the portrait of the Spanish girl and she waited outside on the pavement impatiently for Tiff to appear. Her breath was thick and cloudy in the midnight air, her feet cold in cheap Dolcis pumps. Finally the dense silence was broken by the sound of a scooter approaching the cul-de-sac. Without looking at him, Melody climbed onto the moped, wrapped her arms around his waist, and whispered in his ear the words, "Let's get out of here."

She never saw her parents again.

Chapter 14

Now

The following day, Melody and Stacey went shopping. Cleo, Stacey's eldest, was turning eighteen in a week on Wednesday, and Ed's eighteenth was a week later, so they were meeting up to help each other buy gifts. They'd always used shopping as an excuse to spend time with each other. In the early years of their friendship they'd meet up in Oxford Circus with buggies and spare nappies, babies slumbering in fat snowsuits, while they stormed in and out of Mothercare and the John Lewis toy department. As the kids had got older they'd meet up while they were in nursery or school, and now that their kids were nearly adults, they could meet at their own convenience.

It was a cool day, sunny but fresh, more like April than July. Melody walked the half a mile across town, feeling glad that today she was doing something so mundane and familiar after the weirdness of her trip to Broadstairs the previous day.

She saw Stacey's reassuring birdlike figure scampering up Oxford Street toward her, and smiled. Stacey was a tiny creature, who ballooned to the size of a country cottage every time she got pregnant, then deflated back to a frail size six within a couple of months. She was dressed in her usual uniform of cut-off combats and hooded jacket, her copper hair tied up in a ponytail, sunglasses on her head, and a cigarette burning between her fingers. From behind she looked about fourteen, but from the front her face was prematurely aged by stress, cigarettes, and too many Spanish holidays. If Melody had used a condom on the two occasions she'd had sex in October 1987 she'd never have met Stacey, and chances are she'd have had a best friend she'd met at university who lived in a three-bed terrace in Clapham Junction with mushroom-colored walls and an Audi parked outside. But fate had brought her to this place, and Stacey was not just part of her story, but one of the few things that had kept her sane for the past eighteen years.

"Hello! Hello! Sorry I'm late!" Stacey leaned in for a hug, breathing her last inhalation of tobacco all over Melody and gripping her arms with thin fingers. "The tube stopped in a tunnel at Bethnal Green for eight minutes. Thought I was going to faint, so hot down there."

They marched into Selfridges and toward the luxury goods department on the ground floor.

"So," said Melody, "what are you getting for Cleo?"

"She wants a Mulberry something or other," she said, reaching into her handbag and pulling out a piece of paper. "A Mulberry *Bayswater*," she read. "Over here." They walked toward the Mulberry concession and asked the assistant, who, to her credit, didn't look at all fazed by the two of them in their Primark and New Look and Nice'n Easy home-dyed hair.

"God, is that it?" Stacey looked at the bag disdainfully. It was chestnut brown leather with a flap and two handles. It was beautiful. But Stacey had a penchant for anything with a logo on it. She couldn't see the point in spending hundreds on a bag if it didn't have something written on it to tell the casual observer where it had come from. She turned the bag this way and that, trying to find something redeeming in it, but failed. She pulled her purse out of her bag and began peeling fifty-pound notes out, one by one, into the assistant's upturned hand. "Fuck a duck," she muttered.

Melody didn't want to ask where the money had come from. Stacey always seemed to have just enough money for whatever she needed, and not a penny more, and always in crisp new notes. So if she needed new shoes, she had £50, if she needed fags she had a fiver, and if she wanted two weeks in an all-inclusive resort in the Dominican Republic, then she had £2,500. It was as if she had some magic money pot hidden away somewhere.

"Well, that's me done. What about you? What you getting for Eddie?"

"Oh, guess."

"An iMac?"

"Yes, an iMac."

"You could get it cheaper online, you know?"

"Yeah, I know, but I never go online, do I? And this is more fun, anyway.

Also, I want to get him something special too—you know, something he can keep forever."

Stacey raised her eyebrows at her. She always teased Melody for her sentimentality, her need for every single object to mean something. "Get him a watch."

She wrinkled her nose. "He's got a watch. I was thinking of something more . . . I don't know, something like a pen."

"A pen? What does he want a pen for?"

"I don't know. Just to keep. Just to have. So that he can think of me, you know."

"Why don't you get him a tattoo, instead? 'MUM.' In a heart." Stacey made the shape of a heart with her hands, then nudged Melody and laughed. "Kids today don't want stuff to keep, Melody. They just want stuff to use. Instant gratification. Get him a bottle of Calvin Klein. And a bag of hash." She nudged her again and they made their way to the electronics department.

Melody felt slightly deflated as they sat down half an hour later, surrounded by yellow bags, at the sushi bar in the food hall. She felt hollow and robbed of something but she wasn't sure exactly what it was. This was her only child's eighteenth birthday. She wanted more for him than a box full of gadgets. She wanted *meaning*. It was different for Stacey. Cleo wasn't her only child. She still had Charlie and Clover to live for. She could give her firstborn a leather bag and know that there was more to come, more meaning, more milestones. But for Melody, this was the end of the road.

"So," said Stacey, pulling a plate of noodles off the conveyor belt and breaking open a pair of chopsticks, "have you heard from your man again?"

"Yeah," said Melody, eyeing the plates passing clockwise and anticlockwise before her without enthusiasm. "He's texted me a few times."

"And? You going to see him again? Do you like him?"

"He's all right," she said, reaching absentmindedly for a bowl of chicken teriyaki and taking off the plastic dome. "He's a bit . . ."

"What? Nice? Kind? Good?"

"No, well, yes, he is all that, but he's just a bit . . . *middle-class*."

Stacey snorted with laughter. "But so are you!"

"No I'm not!"

"Course you are. Look at you! And anyway, being 'middle-class' is not a good enough reason not to want to go out with someone."

"He plays squash, Stace. *Squash.* I mean, who the fuck plays squash?"

"OK, I'll grant you that. Squash is a bit, you know. But on the plus side, means he's fit. Anyway," she sighed, "this is just you, Melody Browne, doing what Melody Browne does best. Keeping yourself safe. Keeping those gates locked. Keeping it all out. But I tell you this, Mel, as your best friend, you're not getting any younger. Your boy'll be off soon and then it'll be just you. Just Melody. And unless you think that's enough to keep you going for the next forty or however many years, then that's fine. But if you don't, well"—she paused—"you need to spread your horizons a bit wider. You need to stop making excuses. And I say that"—she laid a gentle hand upon Melody's arm—"as your best friend in all the world because all I want is what's best for you."

"I'm late," said Stacey, over coffee and pancakes later that afternoon.

Melody could tell from the look on her face that she wasn't talking about the time. "What, you mean . . . ?"

"Yeah, only four days, but you know me, regular as clockwork. Only times I've ever been late have been when I was pregnant."

"Oh my God, Stace, are you . . . was it planned?"

Stacey shook her head and pulled her cigarettes out of her handbag. "No, but it wasn't *unplanned.*"

"Are you going to . . . ?"

"Keep it? Yeah, I reckon. Haven't decided yet for sure, but it would be nice, wouldn't it, a little brother or sister for Clove, stop her turning into the spoiled baby? And my contract is up in March anyway. I don't know, what do you think?"

Melody breathed in. "God, yeah, of course! Funny, I always thought of Clover as your happy accident, you know, but of course, you should have another one, definitely. It would be so nice for Clover."

"She wouldn't know what had hit her." Stacey lit a cigarette and Melody glanced at her.

"I'm giving up *after* I've done the test," she said defensively. "But God, the thought of being pregnant again, so scary. And I'm older now . . ."

"You're only thirty-four!"

"Yeah, but still. I could feel the difference with Clove compared to the big ones, and I don't know where we'll put it."

"Put it in a drawer!" Melody smiled at her friend. "By the time it grows out of the drawer Cleo will probably have moved out."

"Yeah, you're right, I suppose. But still, another baby, Mel. Another baby."

Melody took her time walking home that afternoon. It was perfect walking weather, dry, bright, and cool, and London, away from the tourist-laden pavements of Oxford Circus, was still and peaceful. Stacey's words kept echoing through her head as she walked. "*Another baby. Another baby.*" They brought a song to her mind, a song from her youth that played round on a loop with every few paces: "All that she wants is another baby."

Melody loved babies. She loved their formless faces and doughy thighs, their tiny skulls and pathetic sloping shoulders. But babies scared her too. They were so tenuous, diaphanous. One mistake, one missed breath, one blow to the head, and they were gone. And babies, Melody believed, could take with them an entire life's worth of happiness. After Ed was born she'd suffered from what was now known to be postnatal depression. From the moment she realized the depth of her love for her new son and the power he held inside each and every tiny breath to devastate her life, she began obsessing about the myriad ways in which he could die, pictured herself harming him in some way: letting him go under the water in the bath, letting go of his pushchair at the top of a hill, falling down the concrete stairs of her flat with him in her arms. But worse than that was her fear that someone would take him away from her. Every time the phone rang she thought it would be someone from the social services telling her that they were coming for him; when a kindly lady in the supermarket held his tiny hand, she pulled away, fearing that she was about to snatch him from her. She didn't tell anyone how she was feeling, not even Stacey, who had seemed to be having a completely different experience with the infant Cleo.

When Ed was ten months old he'd fallen off the sofa. Melody heard the sickening thud from the kitchen, where she was preparing his tea. She rushed into the living room and found Ed lying on the floor, on his back, beaming at her. His own sense of pride in his part in the accident, his delight at finding himself one moment on the sofa, the next on the floor, had at first disgusted her and then, the moment after, unburdened her. Her baby could fall! He could fall and still exist!

Her depression started to lift from that moment but the memory of it never left her, and she vowed that she would never again bring something as fragile and flimsy as a baby into the world. She had an IUD fitted a year after Ed's birth and lavished her love instead onto Stacey's babies, the second, third, fourth babies of the mothers at Ed's school, the babies of strangers she passed in the street. She felt nothing but happiness at the arrival of every new baby, and nothing but joy for their blessed parents. But for herself, she was done. The very fact that her boy had survived the first eighteen years of his life was a miracle. She didn't want to push her luck.

She'd been wandering aimlessly as she absorbed the possibility of another baby, maybe, probably, taking shape in her friend's body, another baby in her life, another small person to talk about and wonder at, and had found herself, not in Soho, as she'd imagined, but just north of Goodge Street in a tiny cobbled turning called Goodge Place. At the mouth of the turning were two mobile units selling CDs and DVDs in dodgy wrappings and around the bend a terrace of narrow Georgian town houses, some with the external appearance of temporary housing, some smarter with thick curtains at the windows and nickel-plated doorknobs. Melody followed the curve of the street and felt it again, a certainty of place, of time, of having been here before. She stood for a moment, her eyes closed, and let the feeling impress itself upon her.

She saw a bike, and a man, the same man she'd seen with the knickerbocker glory and the crash helmet. He had long hair tied back in a ponytail, and he was waving goodbye. She opened her eyes and looked up at the sky, and then down again at a house in the middle of the terrace. She closed her eyes again and saw this:

A beautiful girl, in a pink tutu, at the top of a flight of stairs.

The sun shining through the window behind her, turning her into a silhouette.

Expensive carpet beneath her bare feet.

A dog, barking somewhere else in the house.

"Melody smells of poo, Melody smells of poo." The girl's face contorted with pleasure, her thin body twisting around itself in a strange dance of loathing. "Melody is a fathead, and she smells of poo."

Then the girl falling, one thin leg turned around the other thin leg, her elbow on one step, her bottom on the next, her head bouncing off the banisters, her tutu tearing with a sound like ripped newspaper.

A woman appearing at the bottom of the stairs, wearing a smocked dress with billowy sleeves and thick coral lipstick.

"Oh my God, Charlotte! Charlotte! What happened?"

Melody's mouth, glued closed, words bubbling in her head but not coming out.

"She pushed me, Mummy. Melody pushed me!"

The woman's face, pursed and furious, her coral lips snarling, her blue eyes sniping, bundling Charlotte into her arms.

Charlotte's screams, shrill and exaggerated, getting further and further away as Jacqui carried her through the house.

A small shred of pink netting, on the floor by Melody's feet.

Then the words finally leaving her mouth, two seconds too late. "It wasn't me. She just tripped."

Chapter 15

1978

Jacqui Sonningfeld lived in a tall, thin house in a quiet turning just off Goodge Street. It was decorated in a very plush way, with whole zebra skins clinging to walls, leopard-print cushions thrown all over velvety sofas, Tiffany lamps with dragonfly wings, piles of heavy books arranged like pyramids on low coffee tables, and every floor thick with the softest, bounciest, most luxuriant cream carpet Melody had ever encountered.

Jacqui was a makeup artist and Charlotte was her seven-year-old daughter. Charlotte went to a private girls' school in Westminster and had friends with names like Amelia and Sophie and Theodora.

Had Melody thought to ask, she would have discovered that her father had met Jacqui on a blind date set up for him by his boss, who was Jacqui's ex-brother-in-law. And if Melody had ever met her father's boss, he might have disclosed to her that he'd set them up, primarily because he'd suspected they might hit it off, but also, and significantly, to get Jacqui off his brother's back, financially, emotionally, and, on occasion, physically.

But Melody was only five and although she thought about things a lot, she rarely asked about things, because sometimes it was just really hard to know what the right question was. So she took on board the fact that her father no longer lived on his own in a rented room in a big house in Brixton, and now lived in a beautiful house in Fitzrovia with Jacqui and her daughter, without demanding to know why. She accepted that she only got to live in the Fitzrovia house with her father for three or four days a month, while Charlotte, who barely knew him, got to see him every single day. And she was resigned to the fact that when she got back to Ken's house by the seaside her mother would ply her with the rare reward of hot chocolate and ask her two hundred questions about Jacqui's house and Jacqui's clothes and Jacqui's makeup and what Jacqui had said and what her father had said and what they'd eaten and where they'd been.

"Why don't you and Daddy live together anymore?" Melody had asked this question once, a few weeks earlier.

Jane had furrowed her brow and grimaced. "Well," she'd said, "we stopped being friends."

"You mean, you had a fight?"

"Not just one fight. Lots of fights. About lots of silly, silly things. And we thought we might just get along a bit better if we lived apart."

"But couldn't you just have lived apart for a little while? Not for so many months and months and months?"

Her mother sighed. "Sometimes," she said, "sometimes, in life, things happen, things that change things forever. And once things have changed forever, it's hard to go backward."

"What things had changed forever?"

"Oh, everything, sweetheart, absolutely everything."

Feeling slightly dissatisfied by this response, Melody had waited a couple of days and then asked the same question again.

"Mummy, why don't you and Daddy live together anymore?"

This time her mother hadn't sighed and paused to think of the right words to answer her question. This time she'd thrown her hands up into the air and stormed out of the room, yelling, "Stop with the questions, will you, for God's sake!"

So Melody had changed tack and asked her father instead.

"Daddy, why do you live here with Jacqui and Mummy lives at the seaside with me?"

There followed a long-drawn-out silence, during which Melody wondered if her father too would leave the room and shout at her. "That's a very good question," he said eventually.

Melody nodded.

"The thing is," he said, drawing her up onto his knees, "when bad things happen, sometimes grown-ups can't find a way to make each other feel better. Sometimes they can actually make each other feel worse. And after baby

Romany died, Mummy and Daddy both felt too sad to be nice to each other. Does that sound strange?"

Melody nodded again.

"Yes, I guess it does. But then grown-ups *can* be very strange. But you do know, don't you, that it had absolutely *nothing to do with you*? That Mummy and Daddy still love you so much, just as much as they did before, and in fact, a load more?"

She nodded again, but inside she was thinking that she wasn't entirely sure that that was true. She felt pretty certain that her mother in particular had loved her much, much more before the baby died. But she didn't say that. Instead she looped her arms around her father's neck and clung on to him for a very long time indeed.

One Saturday afternoon, during the month of March, when her dad was in the kitchen cooking lunch and Charlotte was at her ballet class and Melody was sitting in a window seat on the top landing, watching people passing by on the street below, Jacqui walked up to her and squeezed her shoulder.

"Hello there," she said. "You look very pensive."

Melody had no idea what "pensive" meant but thought it might be something like "sad," or "worried."

"That means 'thoughtful,'" Jacqui said, smoothing down the back of her skirt and sitting next to her. "I'll give you a penny for them."

Melody knew what that meant. Aunt Susie always said it to her. "A penny for your thoughts." She'd never actually given her a penny, so Melody assumed it was just one of those things that grown-ups said because they liked the sound of the words.

She shrugged and turned to look out of the window again. "I'm just looking at all the people. They look really small from up here."

Jacqui glanced down and nodded. "Like little ants," she said. "One day, when you and Charlotte are older, we'll take you both to Paris, to the *tour Eiffel*." She said this in a strange voice. "Have you heard of the Eiffel Tower?"

Melody nodded. "It's in France," she said.

"That's right. And you can climb right to the very, very top of it and see the whole of Paris below. And you look down and see all these tiny, weeny little people, and tiny, weeny little cars, and it looks like Toyland!"

Melody tried to look interested, just to be polite, but the conversation was making her feel a bit strange. Not because of the subject matter, but because it was Jacqui, and Jacqui had never really spoken to her before because she was usually too busy organizing everybody.

"It's very romantic," she continued. "In fact, that was where Charlotte's father proposed to me."

Melody knew that Charlotte had a father. He was called Harry and he was big and garrulous, with very thick hair and hairy hands, and he had a tiny wife from China called Mai. Every so often he'd turn up on a Saturday morning, in a roaring MG Midget, roof down whatever the weather, and announce that he was taking Charlotte shopping. She'd come home a few hours later, laden with big paper bags from posh department stores full of things like cassette players and high-heeled shoes and perfume and teddy bears. It was clear to Melody that he allowed her to choose absolutely anything she wanted without a hint of restraint. It was also clear to Melody that Charlotte didn't appreciate his extravagance in the slightest, as the bags would sit unopened and forgotten about underneath her bed for months afterward.

"Back when I was a young foolish girl of twenty with a head full of marshmallows and fluff, Harry seemed like the most exciting man in the world," Jacqui continued. "I soon learned that exciting men don't make good husbands. But still, if I hadn't married Harry, I wouldn't have had Charlotte, so I'm glad I did. And I'm sure that's exactly how your father feels about your mother, isn't it?"

Melody nodded, not because she knew for sure that that was the case, but because she'd seen no evidence to the contrary.

"You see, children are *the* most precious thing in all the world, more precious and important than anything, and even though your mummy and daddy aren't friends anymore, they'll always be glad they used to be, because it meant that they made you. And I happen to know for a fact that your daddy *adores* you. And, you know, it's really important to your dad that you're happy. And sometimes he worries about how you are when you're not with him. Because he knows you're a brave little girl and you don't always want to worry anyone with your thoughts. So it would be great if I could tell him that I'd had a little chat with you and that you were OK with everything."

"I am," Melody said. "I am OK with everything."

"At home? With your mum? Is everything OK there?"

Melody shrugged and nodded.

"So it's a kind of *commune*, is it?"

Melody smiled nervously. "I don't know," she said.

"A commune," Jacqui said, "is a house where lots of different people who aren't necessarily related to each other live together. Is that what it's like where you live?"

Melody thought about the big, sparsely furnished house by the sea, about Ken and Grace and Seth and Matty, and the fact that Matty wasn't Ken's son and Matty's dad lived in London and so did her dad, and decided that no, although it wasn't a normal house, it certainly wasn't whatever that word was that Jacqui had just used.

She shook her head. "No," she said, "it's just a house. It's Ken's house."

"And this Ken—is he a friend of your mum's?"

Melody nodded. "Yes. He talked to us on the street, when we went to get my shoes, and he said that Mum looked sad, and then Mum had a big row with Aunt Susie and Ken said we could live in his house."

"And Ken, is he married?"

"Yes, he's married to Grace, and she's a lot older than him and she's got a son called Matty, who's ten, and they've got a little baby called Seth, who's eight months old."

"So Ken's not . . . your mum's boyfriend?"

"No!" Melody laughed.

"So they don't . . . hold hands, or anything like that?"

"No!" She laughed again.

"Oh," said Jacqui, "that's interesting to know. And does Ken have a job? Does he go out to work?"

"I think so," Melody replied. "I think he writes books. But not books about stories, but books about . . . *feelings*."

"Goodness," said Jacqui, "that sounds interesting. What sort of feelings?"

"I don't really know," Melody said. "Happy feelings, I think."

"Well, I suppose they must be very good books if he can afford to have a big house by the seaside and pay for lots of people to live there."

"Yes," agreed Melody, "they must be brilliant."

Melody felt like Jacqui was trying to make her say more words than she was able to say. She had a look on her face like someone who wants another slice of cake but is feeling too shy to ask.

There was a short silence until Jacqui sighed, and said, "Anyway—I really hope that as the years go by, you'll feel more and more comfortable with the way things have turned out. And that we can all kind of think of each other as one big, unusual, happy family. Because," she leaned in toward Melody's ear and whispered, "I love your daddy so much I ache and all I want is for us all to be happy. Forever." Then she leaned over and kissed Melody on the cheek, stood up, and walked away, her shoes making no sound at all against the thick, spongy carpet, a smudge of coral lipstick on Melody's cheek and the smell of l'Air du Temps the only evidence that she'd ever been there.

Chapter 16

Now

Melody walked past the house on Goodge Place a total of eight times over the next two days. Each time she remembered something new. A large, bearded man in a tiny sports car; the girl, Charlotte, in oversized sunglasses carrying a dozen carrier bags; herself and Charlotte's mother, silhouetted side by side in the small dormer window in the eaves of the house, the smell of sweet perfume; a Girls' World; patchwork jeans; a lime hairband; and more significantly than any of that, a room with a cot and the brand-new baby. It was up there, one of only two things she remembered about her life before the fire. The room with the baby in it was in there somewhere, still carrying traces within its walls of the sweet honeyed scent of new baby and breast milk.

It wasn't an accident that Melody had found herself outside this house. Her newly aroused subconscious had pulled her here, step by step, while her thoughts were otherwise engaged. And she hadn't lived here, she knew that much, but she had stayed at this neat little house, tucked away in a quiet corner of central London. She had stayed here often. She remembered a man now too. Charlotte's father? He was tall and solid, with a long face, soft eyes, a deep, gentle voice. She felt warm when she thought about this man; she felt loved.

Melody tried to find a way to fit these new memories in with the memories her parents had given her to fill in the gaps in her world, but she couldn't. The world her parents had told her about was a small world, conducted in the hushed environs of a Canterbury cul-de-sac. It was a world peopled by an aloof auntie, a scary uncle, a pair of dumpy cousins, and a friend called Aubrey who turned out to be a sex tourist with a particular liking for green-eyed Moroccan boys. In the verbally reproduced world of her forgotten infancy, there were occasional holidays to a villa in Spain, visits to grandparents in Wales and Torquay, and Easter breaks at a B & B in Ramsgate.

There were no glamorous women with extravagant Fitzrovian town houses, no bearded hippies on motorbikes, no beautiful girls in tutus and yeasty-smelling newborn babies. In the childhood that Melody had previously thought of as her own, London was a place visited infrequently, and under duress. Her parents disliked London, fearing its sophistication, the sheer velocity of its pace of life. It was certainly not somewhere they would have allowed her to stay, unchaperoned. Unless, of course—the thought hit her like a thunderclap—there had been a different time, *before* her parents.

The moment the thought went through her head, she knew it was true. She'd always known it was true and she'd always *wanted* it to be true.

Suddenly all the fragments of her newly remembered life started to swirl around her head, demanding to be put into some kind of order. She turned that very moment to face the front door of the town house, she breathed in, and then she rang the doorbell.

Chapter 17

1978

"I wish your dad had never been born." Charlotte dragged a plastic brush through the tangled nylon hair of her Girls' World. "And you. I wish you'd never been born either."

Charlotte was wearing purple corduroy jeans with a flower appliquéd onto each knee. Her black hair was parted in the middle and tied in bunches with lengths of thick pink wool. She was a beautiful girl. Much more beautiful than Jacqui, who was only just pretty and made the best of herself with lots of makeup and attitude. Charlotte had Harry's dark coloring and aquiline nose, and also looked likely to have inherited his height. Beside her, Melody always felt very small and very ordinary. Melody's hair was lovely, everyone always said so. It hung down her back in thick ropes of chestnut, but she wasn't a particularly nice shape (she had her father's legs, apparently) and her face wasn't all symmetrical like Charlotte's. Charlotte's face looked like someone had sat down with a protractor and a very sharp pencil and spent ages designing it. Melody's face was more slapdash. Unconventional, according to her mother. Melody wasn't sure she liked the idea of unconventional. Anything with an "un" in front of it tended to be a bad thing, as far as she could tell.

"In fact," continued Charlotte, "I wish no one in your whole entire family had ever been born, going all the way back to your great-great-great-great-grandparents."

Melody gulped. She didn't even know she *had* any great-great-great-great-grandparents.

"That way," continued Charlotte, "there wouldn't be even the tiniest chance of any of your relatives getting together and making you, even by accident." She turned the Girls' World around and began to comb the hair at the back. "What shall I do," she said, pulling at the yellow hair with her fingertips, "a plait or a chignon?"

"A plait," said Melody, feeling slightly more confident about the precise definition and pronunciation of the word.

"It's nothing personal, you know," Charlotte said, dividing the hair roughly into three sections. "I'm sure, under different circumstances, that you are completely OK. It's just that this is only a small house and you and your father take up *way too much room*. And also, your dad smells funny."

"No he doesn't!"

"Yes, he does. He smells all vinegary, like a Banda machine."

"Well, that's because he's a printer. He can't help it."

"No, I know he can't. I'm not saying it's his fault. I'm just saying I wish he'd go and take his smell somewhere else. Do you realize," Charlotte said, feeling around in a pot full of elastic bands, "that before my mother met your smelly father, she was about to get back with my dad?"

Melody threw her a skeptical look.

"Yes, she cooked him dinner with champagne and everything. And then your stupid dad turned up on the scene."

"But what about Mai?"

"What about Mai?"

"Well, isn't your dad married to her now?"

"Yeah? So what? Mai's about as important as your stupid dad. If my mum clicked her fingers, my dad would just dump Mai in the middle of the street and come running. Seriously." She wound a lime-green hairband tightly around the end of a plait and smiled. "There," she said, "now that is what I would call a perfect plait."

Melody stared at the plait. It was very neat indeed. And then she stared at Charlotte's fingernails. They were ragged and bitten. They looked incongruous against her flawless skin and perfectly parted hair. Something about them made Melody feel sad inside. She reached out and touched Charlotte's hand, with her fingertips.

Charlotte looked at her aghast. "Jesus Christ, child," she said, "get your grubby hands off me immediately before I scream the whole house down!"

Melody snatched her hand back and let it fall onto her lap.

• • •

Melody hated saying goodbye to her father, knowing that he was going to carry on being there, sleeping in his big soft bed with Jacqui, eating Jacqui's delicious suppers at the lovely shiny table with the big chandelier, watching whatever he liked on the TV that lived in a mahogany cabinet while Charlotte sat on the armchair beside him, wearing her posh pajamas, swinging her long legs over the arm, and eating as much popcorn as she wanted. Ken's house seemed so bare and wooden compared to Jacqui's smothered house. And her mother seemed so lifeless compared to the bustling, colorful Jacqui. And where life in Jacqui's house made perfect sense—Jacqui loved Daddy, Daddy loved Jacqui, Charlotte hated Melody, and Jacqui pretended to like Melody—in Ken's house life was a series of dead ends and cul-de-sacs and strange empty rooms.

Her mother met her at Victoria Station at 2:30 to get the 3:05 train back to Broadstairs. Melody liked it at the station with her mum. She liked the simplicity of it, just the two of them, swallowed up by the cyclone of human activity around them, the strange silence that existed beneath the hubbub of Tannoy announcements and screeching trains.

Her mother frowned at her. "Are you OK?" she said, in a tone of voice that suggested that she didn't think she was.

"I'm fine," Melody replied.

"You look tired."

Melody didn't respond. She was tired because she'd stayed up until midnight last night watching a film with Charlotte. She wanted to be able to tell her mum about it but she knew she couldn't because it was the sort of thing that made her mum go all shaky and emotional.

"Have you had lunch?"

Her mum asked this every time she met her at the station, as if she suspected that one day Jacqui would be so busy being selfish and awful that she might just forget completely to feed her.

"Yes," Melody replied.

"What did you have?"

"Spaghetti Bolognese," she said. "And salad."

"Salad?"

"Yes."

"What sort of salad?"

"Erm, a salad salad. With tomatoes. And cucumber."

"Hmm." Her mother pursed her lips, as if doubting the veracity of her salad story. "Dressing?"

Melody nodded. "Yes, there was a yummy dressing. All pink. I can't remember what it was called, though."

"Thousand Island?"

"Yes!" said Melody. "That's right."

"Hmm," said her mother again.

They sat down on a bench on platform 12 and stared at the announcement board.

"Ten minutes," said her mother. "You warm enough?"

Melody nodded and wished she could think of something to say that would make her mother suddenly forget to be stiff and strange, something that would make her smile and hug her and call her "babyface." "Actually," she said, "I am quite cold."

"Well, then, you should have put your coat on. Where is it?"

"I left it at Jacqui's house."

Her mum raised her eyebrows. "Well, you'll just have to freeze then."

Melody sighed. She'd only said she was cold to see if her mum would wrap her up in her big soft cardigan to keep her warm.

She nestled herself against her mother's body, hoping for an embrace, a heavy arm around her shoulders, a show of affection, but none came.

Chapter 18

Now

A young boy came to the door of the house on Goodge Place. He was about ten years old and dressed in white karate pajamas. He looked at her curiously.

"Hello," said Melody, lightly, her hands shaking gently inside the pockets of her cardigan. "Is your mum here?"

He shook his head slowly, side to side.

A woman appeared behind him, young and blond, wearing the same Primark smock top that Melody had in her wardrobe at home.

"Hi," said Melody.

"Can I help you?" said the woman, in an Australian accent.

"I don't know," said Melody, "maybe. I used to live here, in this house, when I was a child . . ." She smiled, too brightly, trying to compensate for her feelings of vagueness, of silliness, the same way she'd felt at the guesthouse in Broadstairs.

The woman's expression softened. "Did you?" she said. "Wow!"

"Yes, and I don't remember much about it and I was wondering, how long have you lived here?"

"Me?" said the woman. "Well, only about six months, but I'm just the nanny. My boss and her husband have been here, ooh, I don't know . . ."

"Nine and a half years," said the boy, in an accent with a slight American twang.

"Of course, yeah—since Danny was born."

"Are they here, your boss, her husband?"

"No"—the woman looped her arms around Danny's neck and hugged him to her—"no, they're both at work."

"Shame," said Melody. "I'd like to have asked them a few questions, you know, about the house."

"You can ask me," said the boy.

Melody smiled. "Oh, I'm not sure you'll be able to answer the sort of questions I want to ask."

The boy smiled and looked down at his feet.

"But listen, is it OK if I leave my number? Maybe your boss or her husband might give me a ring . . . ?"

The nanny smiled. "That's highly unlikely," she said, her voice laden with skepticism, "but if you come back around six, six thirty, she'll be home then." She winked and Melody smiled gratefully at her.

"OK," she said, "I might well do that."

The nanny's boss was a formidable American woman called Pippa. She was still in her work suit, a conventional navy affair, with a starchy blouse underneath, and her tired blond hair was cut into a practical, side-parted bob. She invited Melody into the hallway and then led her into what she referred to as "the drawing room."

Inside, the house looked nothing like the one Melody remembered. The floors were varnished parquet and the furnishings were elegant and mainly cream in color. There was little evidence of children in this room, though childish noises emanated from elsewhere in the house.

"So," Pippa said, easing herself onto a cream sofa, "you used to live here?"

"Yes," said Melody, feeling that it was unnecessary to go into too much detail. "About thirty years ago."

"Oh, so when you were tiny?"

"Yes. I hardly remember it at all, just that I definitely did and there was a baby up there, in one of the bedrooms, and that this room had lots of stuff on the walls and there was a tiger skin with a head on it on that wall over there, and a glass table there and cream carpets *everywhere*." She stopped and caught her breath. Pippa was looking at her strangely.

"You're not Charlotte, are you?"

Melody gasped. She'd said it! She'd said Charlotte! That meant it was all true! That meant she wasn't mad! And if Charlotte was real, then so was Ken and so was the baby and so was the woman called Jane. Relief flooded through

Melody and the gnawing sense of doubt in herself finally subsided. "Do you . . . ," she began, "do you know her?"

"Well, no, not really, I never met her—but we bought this house from her, back in 1996."

"Oh my God, so she's real!" Melody stopped briefly. "Sorry, it's just they're kind of hazy memories and I've lost touch with everyone who lived here, and it's just great to know that, well, that I hadn't made it all up! So, Charlotte, where does she live now?"

"Well, she was in LA, then. No idea where now. It was her mother's house originally . . ."

"Jacqui?"

"Yes, I think so. She's a very famous makeup artist, in Hollywood, or so I recall. And Jacqui gave it to her daughter as a twenty-first-birthday present, when it was worth, probably, you know, a few pence. I don't know why she sold it, I didn't like to ask . . ."

"And was there anyone else—a brother, or a sister?"

Pippa shrugged and kicked off her court shoes. "I really don't know," she said. "Like I said, I never met Charlotte. This house was empty when we bought it. She'd been renting it out. I never saw anyone or spoke to anyone from her family. I'm not sure I can really help you very much."

Melody sighed.

"Do you . . . would you like to have a look around?" Pippa offered.

Melody could tell she didn't really want a stranger poking around her house, but curiosity overrode politeness and she accepted the offer enthusiastically.

"It's all pretty much as we found it," said Pippa, leading her through the upstairs rooms, "we just changed the décor. These were kids' rooms when we bought it and, as you can see, they still are, and this was the master bedroom. We just put in an en suite . . ."

She switched on the overhead light and Melody gasped again—this was the room, the room with the baby in it! It was so real that she could smell it, the dust burning off a shawl thrown over a lamp, floral perfume, old milk.

"There was a bed there!" she said. "And a table with a lamp on it there, covered with something, like a chiffon scarf, and that's where the cot was, the cot with the baby in it. And I held it—I held *her*. I remember now, I remember properly. I think she was my sister . . ." As the words left her mouth, so did all her breath, knocked from her by an overwhelming punch of sadness, straight to her heart. Tears pricked at her eyes and she stifled a sob.

And then it hit her, another flashback:

A tall glass of lemonade.

A bendy straw.

Her father sitting opposite her, partially obscured by a large pot of paper-wrapped grissini.

The smell of garlic.

A checked tablecloth.

Jacqui, wearing a fur jacket and big sunglasses, smiling at her.

The words: "Jacqui and I are going to have a baby. You're going to have a little brother or sister!"

A moment's silence.

"What do you think?"

Another moment's silence.

"Are you happy?"

And then finally, the words exploding from her lips like bubbles from a shaken bottle of lemonade. "Yes. I think so. But Mummy won't be."

Chapter 19

1978

Emily Elizabeth Ribblesdale was born in October 1978, exactly a month before Melody's sixth birthday. She was born on a Monday, so Melody had to wait five whole days before she could go up to London on the train to meet her.

All that week, Melody's mother was ill. It was a vague, nonspecific sort of illness that seemed to come upon her most profoundly whenever Melody mentioned the coming weekend. Melody thought that maybe she was feeling ill because she was sad that Dad's girlfriend had had a baby who hadn't died, but she decided not to venture this theory. Melody's mum didn't want to talk about the baby at the best of times, and this, Melody could tell, was not the best of times.

On Friday her mother collected her from school, looking dreadful.

"I'm really sorry," she said, "but I don't think you'll be able to go to see your father tomorrow."

Melody felt sick with disappointment.

"Why not?"

"A big bill came in this morning and Ken asked us all to contribute and now I've got no cash left for the train fare."

"But, Mum . . ." Melody felt hot tears coming to her eyes.

"Don't talk to me in that whiny voice! *Don't make me feel worse than I already do!*"

"But, Mum . . ."

"*What do you expect me to do about it?* Sell my miserable body on the streets for a few quid, just so you can go and see your precious father?"

Melody gulped, feeling embarrassed that her mother was shouting at her in front of her schoolmates and also a little shocked to learn that there were people on the streets who would pay her mother for her body. She found it hard to imagine what they would do with it.

"I'll phone him," Melody said, a moment later, having given the matter plenty of thought. "I'll phone him and ask him if he can send me some money."

"And then what? The money won't arrive until next week."

"Well, then, I'll ask him to come and get me."

"Melody, your father has just *had a baby*. Jacqui will not want him disappearing off to the seaside for half the day. Especially not just to come and get you. You can't go tomorrow. You'll just have to wait. Now stop dawdling. We're never going to get home at this rate."

Melody picked up her pace and fell into step with her mother. She couldn't wait another week to see her new sister. There was something small and painful gnawing away at the pit of her stomach, and she knew it wouldn't stop until she'd felt Emily's newborn breath against her cheek.

Ken brought Melody to London in the sidecar of his motorcycle. Melody didn't even realize he had a motorbike until she shared her predicament with him that night. The following morning he took her to a garage at the bottom of the street. As well as the bike, which was cloaked in green tarpaulin, there were several cardboard boxes full of leaflets and lots of big signs on sticks that she didn't get a chance to read.

He lined the seat of the sidecar with a soft blanket, strapped her in, and put a bulbous green helmet on her head.

The journey to London was exhilarating. The wind battered her cheeks and threw the ends of her hair into disarray. Every time they stopped at a traffic light, Ken turned and smiled at her and she smiled back and felt like the most important girl in the world. She scanned the roads as they went for other five-year-old girls in sidecars, but didn't see one. If she'd had any friends at school, she would have been desperate to tell them all about her adventure. As it was, she would tell Charlotte, who would pretend that it was of no interest to her whatsoever.

Ken didn't wait outside for Melody when he dropped her off. He said he had to go and see some people and that he'd be back for her at six o'clock.

"Give your new sister a big kiss from me," he said. And then he wedged his head back into his crash helmet, revved the engine of his bike, and disappeared around the corner, like John Wayne rounding his steed out of the corner of a cinema screen.

Jacqui was lying in bed. The room was curtained and dimly lit, and pungent with a yeasty, milky scent, like Ovaltine. Jacqui was wearing a filmy bed jacket with a bit of cream fluff around the edges and a turquoise nightdress. The baby had been taken out of her with a knife, apparently, and she wasn't allowed out of bed yet. She smiled as Melody walked into the room and Melody smiled back nervously.

"Come," Jacqui said, patting the silky bedspread, "come and meet Emily."

To the side of the bed was a small white crib. Melody held her father's hand and stepped softly around the bed with him. She took a deep breath and peered into the crib. Inside was a tiny creature with a thatch of thick black hair and a full red mouth, set into a pursed-up grimace.

"How do you like your sister?" said her dad.

"Is she really my sister?" said Melody.

"Yes, of course she is," laughed Jacqui.

Melody looked at her again and assessed her. She wasn't very pretty. But she was quite cute. She picked up one of her tiny little hands and stroked it. "She looks like a tiny bear cub."

Jacqui and her dad looked at each other and smiled.

"She looks exactly like you looked when you were a new baby," said her dad.

"What, like a tiny bear cub?"

"Yes, just like a tiny bear cub."

"Did baby Romany look like a tiny bear cub when she was born?"

Her dad smiled sadly. "No," he said, "she had no hair at all, and a tiny rosebud mouth. She looked more like a little leprechaun."

"Did she?" said Melody, forming for the first time in her life the beginnings of a picture of her dead sister. "And did she have brown eyes? Or blue eyes?"

"Well, all babies' eyes are the same color when they're born. The same color as Emily's. Look. A sort of murky blue. And when they're a few months old they become the color they're going to be."

"So did I have murky blue eyes when I was born?"

"Yes, you did."

"And then they turned hazel."

"That's right."

"I wonder what color baby Romany's eyes would have been."

"Well," said her dad, "sadly, that's something that none of us will ever know."

Melody stared at the little baby, stared really hard, trying to bring the picture of her other sister into her head, but already it had started to fade. Already the more tangible, immediate features of this new sister were starting to imprint themselves over the blurred picture of Romany's little leprechaun face that existed only in Melody's imagination. Already her earliest memory was starting to fade.

Chapter 20

1978

Melody kicked a tennis ball across the courtyard and watched it come to a rest between two flowerpots.

"So," said Matty, whittling the tip of a large twig into a sharp point with a Stanley knife, "what's the deal with your dad?"

"What do you mean?"

"I mean, why did he and your mum split up?"

"I think it was because they were cross with each other."

"About what?"

"I think they were cross about me."

Matty stopped whittling and glanced at her thoughtfully. "You sure?"

"Yes. Well, a bit sure. I mean, I had a baby sister called Romany and she died when she was two days old, and I think my mum and dad were sad about that and then they were cross with me. Especially my mum."

Matty nodded sagely.

"I think my mum was annoyed with me because I wasn't properly sad and because I still wanted to keep doing things, like making cakes and going to the playground. And then I think she got cross with my dad because he didn't want to be sad anymore either and wanted to try and have another baby."

"Why would that make her cross?"

Melody shrugged. "I don't know. It just did. Maybe she thought it might die again, or something."

Matty nodded and returned to whittling his stick.

"She got furious with him when he said it."

"God, you'd have thought she'd have been pleased."

"Yes," said Melody, nodding vigorously, "I know."

"But adults are really fucking weird. Like, take my mum."

Melody looked at him expectantly.

"No, really, take her . . ."

Melody furrowed her brow at him, feeling slightly worried that she was being slow.

He sighed. "Sorry. Just a stupid joke. Never mind."

"Tell me, though," said Melody. "Tell me about your mum. Why is she weird?"

He shrugged. "Just is. My dad, right, my dad is this great, great bloke. He's really big and strong and funny and stuff. We lived in this really cool house in London and Dad was really rich and took us to cool places and stuff. And Mum just decided to go."

"Why?"

"I don't know. She said that she didn't like it when he'd been drinking but, you know, he didn't really drink that much. *I* never saw him drunk, not really, just funny. And now my dad's all sad and lonely and my mum's married to some *idiot* who thinks he's Jesus fucking Christ."

Melody wondered who he was talking about for a moment. "What, you mean Ken?"

"Yeah, Ken."

"Why do you think he thinks he's Jesus?"

"Oh, come on, look at him. With his stupid ponytail and his little beard and his big eyes all the time."

"Oh," said Melody, feeling a little deflated. "I really like him."

"Well, then you're an idiot, Melody Ribblesdale."

Melody blanched. Nobody had ever called her an idiot before.

"Ken is just some bloke, that's all, some bloke who's basically *stolen* a house, who's never had to work and gets stupid gullible women to do whatever he wants them to do just by fluttering his big puppy eyes at them."

"Oh," said Melody again.

"Oh God," said Matty, "he's got to you too, hasn't he? Well, listen, Melody Ribblesdale, you're a bright girl and you're young. Take my advice. Get your mum away from him before she's giving him baths and having babies for him too."

He then ran his fingertips around the point of his sharpened stick, held it to the light, examined it from every angle, and turned to leave.

"Where are you going?" called Melody.

"Fishing," Matty said. "See you around."

After he'd gone, Melody stared at the yellow tennis ball really hard, until her eyeballs started to ache. Thoughts and questions flew around her mind like sheets of newspaper in a windy street. What did Matty mean about baths and babies? Why did he need a sharp stick to go fishing? And when was someone going to sit her down and tell her what was happening?

Chapter 21

Now

Melody felt more certain of what needed to be done as she climbed aboard the train to Broadstairs at Victoria Station later that week. She had specific goals and was armed with the reassurance that the strange story that had been stitching bits of itself patchily into her consciousness was real.

She glanced around at the other passengers in the sparsely occupied carriage. She smiled to herself. *Hello*, she wanted to call out, *I'm Melody! I'm on my way home!* Instead she turned her gaze to her phone, to the message she'd received from Ben ten minutes ago, the one that said: "Hello stranger. Not stalking you, just concerned about you. Hope all's OK. Would be great to hear from you (but not holding my breath). Ben x"

Melody paused, halfway between a sigh and a smile. He was persistent, that was for sure, but she had yet to decide whether that was a good thing or a bad thing. Softening to his complete disregard for the Rules of Attraction, she started to type: "Hi. Sorry haven't replied to your other texts, life's been hectic and—"

She stopped, abruptly. What was she doing? She was entering into a dialogue, breathing life into a delicate, fledgling relationship at a point in her own existence when she had barely the slightest idea who the hell she really was. No, she thought, closing down the unfinished message, no, not now, not yet. Maybe later . . .

Broadstairs was even busier than it had been the week before. The gray, lukewarm tones of the day had not dampened the holidaymakers' enthusiasm for wandering in a meaningless way around the few streets that constituted its center. They sported cagoules and brightly colored Crocs, furled umbrellas hanging from crooked arms ready to be employed at the first sad splashes of rain. Melody, with a far greater sense of purpose, headed for the house on the square.

She stood in front of the house, closed her eyes, and tried to think what else may have lain beyond that front door thirty years ago. She saw another baby, this one a boy, fat and solid, chewing on a spoon. She saw a boy, olive skinned and unruly haired. And then she saw a young woman, pale and drawn, with long hair and a yellow dressing gown. She felt the softness of the letter L playing upon her tongue, lelelele . . . *Laura*.

Chapter 22

1978

One day, about a week before Emily was born, a woman called Laura moved into Ken's house. Melody didn't know she'd moved in until she saw her coming out of the bathroom the following morning, in a yellow candlewick dressing gown, clutching a drawstring toiletry bag and looking slightly nervous.

"Hello," she said, passing her on the landing, "who are you?"

"I'm Melody."

"Melody?" she said. "That's a lovely name."

"Thank you," said Melody, who was used to people telling her that she had a lovely name.

"I'm Laura. It's very nice to meet you."

"Nice to meet you too," said Melody.

Laura had long brown hair that was parted in the middle and hung in strands over each shoulder. Her skin was very pale and shiny and she had big splodgy freckles all over her face and neck.

Melody waited for a moment on the landing to see where exactly this new person would head and felt shocked when she saw her casually push open the door to Ken and Grace's bedroom and walk in.

"Mum! Mum!" She leaped up the stairs to the attic floor, two at a time. "There's a woman!"

Her mother emerged from behind her wardrobe door, clutching a green sweater and looking slightly puffy. "What?"

"A woman. In Ken's room! She's called Laura!"

"Oh, yes, Laura. I met her yesterday."

"Who is she? And why is she in Ken and Grace's room?"

"Oh, I'm sure she wasn't."

"Yes, she was. She had on her dressing gown and she just walked straight into their room without knocking or anything."

"Well, maybe she had the wrong room."

"Hmm." Melody sat down on the foot of her bed and stared at her toes. "Mum," she said, "why are we living here?"

"Well," said her mum, in her annoyed voice, "where would you suggest that we live?"

"I don't know," Melody said. "With Auntie Maggie?"

Her mother tutted and sighed distractedly. "Maggie's got her own problems right now. The last thing she needs is her wreck of a sister landing on her doorstep with another mouth to feed."

"Well, what about Auntie Susie?"

"I thought you didn't like it at Auntie Susie's."

Melody shrugged and banged her toes together. "No," she said, "I didn't. But at least . . ."

"At least what?"

"At least she was family."

Jane inhaled noisily. "Melody," she said, "I'm very tired. And you talk too much. Why don't you go and play?"

"I don't want to play."

"Well, then, why don't you go and read a book?"

"I don't want to read a book."

"Well, then, just do anything. Just leave me alone."

Melody sat on the end of her bed for another moment after that, staring disconsolately at her feet. Then she walked to the door and left. She walked slowly enough for her mum to change her mind about being annoyed and call her over for a hug, but she didn't. She just stood there with the green sweater in her hands, looking like she'd forgotten something.

Melody stood outside the bedroom door for a while, and listened to her mother sobbing, quiet and soft as a whispered prayer.

Chapter 23

Now

Melody couldn't find the man called Matthew. She walked around the town three times, peered through the windows of lard-scented cafés, and wandered the aisles of off-licenses. She scanned the beaches and benches and found not a trace of him. In a musty, graffitied man-made cave, dug out beneath the seafront, she came upon two young men with cider cans, stretched out across slatted wooden benches. They didn't look like they were homeless or down-and-out, but they were the only people she'd seen in two hours who looked vaguely like they might know a drunk called Matthew, so she stopped and waited to be addressed.

"You all right?" said the older-looking of the two boys. He seemed nervous, and it occurred to Melody that maybe she resembled a plainclothes police officer.

"Yes," she said, "I'm looking for someone. A man called Matthew."

The youths glanced at each other and frowned. "Matthew? Nah. What's he look like?"

"Forty-ish," said Melody, "dark hair. Drunk."

They glanced at each other again. "Ah," said the spottier of the two, "*that* Matthew. The pisshead?"

"Yeah," said Melody, "I guess so."

"He should be in town. He usually is."

"Is there a special place where he hangs out?" she asked.

"Nah. He just hangs about everywhere, really."

"Yeah," said the other one, "scaring the out-of-towners."

"Where does he live?"

"I dunno," said the older-looking one. "Rough, I reckon. Round here, most probably. This is where the vagrants live, come nighttime, down here in these caves."

"Why d'you want him, anyway?" said the spotty one.

"Oh, I used to live here, when I was a kid. I think he might have known me."

"Yeah. Matthew's been around since we were kids."

"Has he always been a drunk?"

"Yeah, pretty much. But he goes dry sometimes. Every few weeks. He just disappears and comes back with a haircut and some new clothes and then starts drinking again."

"Oh right, so he could be doing that now?"

The spotty one shrugged. "Yeah. I suppose so. If he's not in town."

"And you don't have any idea where it is he goes to?"

They both shrugged. "Maybe to his mum's? Maybe to hospital? Dunno. Never asked."

"Right." Melody bit her lip. "So, you've spoken to him?"

"Nah. Not really. Just in passing. Just like, you all right, that kind of thing. No one really talks to him."

"Why not?"

They both laughed. "Because he's a pisshead, innit!"

Melody smiled, and nodded. She was done here. The man called Matthew was out of town. She would have to come back another time.

Melody stood on the beach with her hands in her pockets, surveying the curve of the town in front of her. It seemed to curl toward her, like arms opened for embrace. A building in the middle of the sweep caught her eye, an ice-cream parlour with a salmon-pink exterior and chrome 1950s signage. She moved immediately, took the stone steps up from the beach two at a time, and was a little breathless when a moment later she pushed open a large pair of heavy glass Art Deco doors into a shiny, brightly lit 1930s-style parlour, all chrome, Formica, and Bakelite fittings in shades of mint and salmon pink. Melody stopped, for just a moment, on the threshold and looked around her, this way and that, across the heads of dozens of waterproofed families. A woman walked past holding a tray. On the tray were four fat goblets, each containing a different medley of colored ice creams, sprinkles, wafers, and sauces. Knickerbocker glories.

This was it. This was the place—she knew it immediately—the place she'd been to with Ken.

Chapter 24

1978

Ken and Melody got back from London at eight o'clock, the day he took Melody to London to meet her new sister. As they approached the coast, the October sun was setting over the sea in streaks of peach, silver, and gold. There was a cruise liner moving slowly away from land, across the horizon, lit up from inside like a lantern. They rode up the seafront, past the flashing neon of the empty arcades, the vinegary fish shops and sickly sweet souvenir shops, and pulled up outside Morelli's Ice Cream Parlour.

"Fancy a sundae?" said Ken, sliding off his helmet.

"What, now?" said Melody.

"Yes, why not?"

"But we told Mum I'd be home by eight."

"Well, we'll just tell her we got stuck in some traffic. Come on, how about a knickerbocker glory?"

Melody gazed through the door at the pastel-hued utopia inside, at the happy families clustered together inside salmon-pink booths, dipping long spoons into oversized goblets of ice cream. She'd seen this place from a distance many times over the past year but her mother always told her that they couldn't afford "unnecessary luxuries" like ice cream.

"My treat," said Ken, as if reading her thoughts.

She felt like someone else as she walked in. Visiting ice-cream parlours after dark with a handsome man and a crash helmet in her hand wasn't the kind of thing she expected to find herself doing. It was the sort of thing that Charlotte did.

She ordered a raspberry ripple sundae and Ken ordered vanilla with chocolate sauce and a cup of coffee. His hair was all messy where his helmet had been and his cheeks were pink from the autumn wind. He looked less like

Jesus and more like a teddy bear, which made her feel less shy about being in a restaurant with him.

"So, you liked the baby, did you?"

"Mm-hm." She nodded. "She was cute."

"I bet. Must be a great feeling to have a new sister."

She nodded again.

"Bet you felt sad having to say goodbye, though, didn't you?"

Melody dipped her head and smiled. She always hated leaving Jacqui's house, even when she'd had a horrible time there, even when Charlotte had been a pig and Jacqui had barely acknowledged her. But this afternoon had been the worst ever. She'd spent the whole day with Emily; she'd helped change her nappy and Jacqui had even let her give her a bottle of milk. Dad and Jacqui's bedroom had become more and more magical as the day went on. By late afternoon the sun had started to sink and Dad switched on the table lamps and they all sat on the big soft bed just staring at the baby.

"You know, in some ways I'm really glad you had to have a Caesarean," her dad had said to Jacqui. "It's forced you to sit still and enjoy this time."

Jacqui had smiled at him and said, "I know, I know, you're right. I'd have been trying to do the hoovering. And I'm glad too, because this is the nicest time. This is the time you look back on when they grow and want to snatch back . . ."

Melody wanted to snatch it back already. She wanted to absorb her sister, drop by drop, into her own skin, and keep her there. She didn't want to leave her in London, to wait a week before she could see her again. She wanted to live with her, sleep with her, watch her wake up in the mornings. She wanted to see her grow, day by day, each sliver of fingernail, each millimeter of hair. She wanted Emily to know her, the same way she would know Charlotte.

She glanced up into Ken's soft gray eyes and felt her jaw go soft and wobbly. Then she started crying, silently and heavily.

"Oh, now, now, now." Ken passed her a paper napkin. "Oh, Melody, you poor, sweet thing."

"I love her so, so much," she sobbed. "I love her and she lives in London and I live here and she'll forget all about me."

"Oh, she won't."

"But she will. All she'll see is Charlotte and she'll think Charlotte's her only sister and when I come she'll cry because she won't know who I am!"

"No, honestly, I promise you. Babies are very clever. She'll remember your smell, and then, when she gets older, she'll remember your face and, you know, she'll save all her best smiles for you, because when she sees you it'll be like a special treat. Not like Charlotte."

"Do you think?"

"Yes, I think. And because you won't see her that often, you'll be much nicer to her than Charlotte. In fact, I'll bet you anything that you and Emily end up being best friends."

Melody sniffed and stirred her spoon in circles around the base of her sundae glass. She liked what Ken was saying. She liked the idea of being Emily's best friend.

It occurred to her that this was the first time in as long as she could remember that anyone had said anything to her that had made her feel better rather than worse, something that made sense of her world, and she felt something hard and heavy lifting from her chest that she hadn't really noticed was there until that very moment. She felt a lightness come upon her, a sense that there was a center to everything after all. And as she sat there, in the steamy warmth of Morelli's Ice Cream Parlour, her dismantled world spinning around her head in a dozen separate pieces, she suddenly knew what that center was. It was Ken.

She wiped a tear from her cheek with the back of her hand and smiled at Ken. Then she took his hand in hers and squeezed it, really hard.

"Are you my friend?" she said.

"Of course I am," he said.

"Will you always be my friend?"

"I'll be your friend for as long as you'd like me to be."

"Well," said Melody, "that will be forever then."

Ken squeezed her hand back and smiled.

"Good," he said. "Good."

They got back to the house at nine o'clock. Melody had pictured her mum on the front step, pale with worry, pacing and panicking, wondering where her daughter was. But she wasn't on the front step. Neither was she in the kitchen or in the bathroom or in their room in the attic. Melody and Ken ran around the whole house twice, looking in all the rooms, and in strange places like airing cupboards and larders. Then Melody noticed that her handbag wasn't in the hallway. And Laura said she'd heard the front door slam at about five o'clock, so they all calmed down and assumed she'd gone out for dinner, or to see Auntie Susie.

Melody washed herself in the chilly bathroom that evening and tried to picture her mother sitting at her auntie Susie's table, laughing and giggling and forgetting the time. It didn't seem right at all, so she tried to imagine her mother sitting alone in a restaurant, at a table for two, her face in flickering candlelight, tucking into a steak and chips. That was completely wrong too.

As she slipped under her quilt and closed her eyes, the silence in her room overwhelmed her and she started to picture different things. Her mother squashed flat by the wheels of a huge truck. Her mother facedown and blue in the sea. Her mother sliced into segments by the metal wheels of an express train. She didn't know where these images had come from. She'd never thought about things like that before. But then she'd never not known where her mother was before.

She fell asleep after a long, long time and then, before she knew it, she was awake again, and it was still dark and her mother's bed was still empty. She decided that she felt scared and alone and that she needed to see a face, so she tiptoed quietly down the stairs and up the landing toward Ken and Grace's room.

A remarkable vignette greeted her upon pushing open the door. Ken and Laura lay on the big white bed, naked and wrapped around each other, while Grace, in a long blue nightdress, lay on a mattress on the floor with Seth by her side. The window had no curtains and a fat white moon bathed them all in an inky light. Although it was altogether wrong, there was something beautiful about the scene, something like the production of *A Midsummer Night's Dream* that Jacqui and her dad had taken them to see at Regent's Park Open Air Theatre that summer.

The only person to hear her come in was Laura, who gazed at her glassily through one open eye. She rubbed her eyebrows with her fingertips and rolled toward her. Her breasts were small and pointy, like little fairy cakes, and her rib cage was bony like a chicken's carcass. As she stared at her, Melody could see that she was still asleep. Her open eye fell shut, she rolled over onto her back, and Melody tiptoed quietly out of the room.

Matty's room was next door. She knocked gently and let herself in. Matty was on his side, one leg hanging off the edge of the bed, snoring very gently.

She watched him for a while and wondered what he was dreaming about. And then, deciding that he looked far too peaceful to disturb, lay down on his scruffy sheepskin rug, covered herself with his bath towel, and finally fell asleep.

Ken called the police the next morning. Two men in helmets arrived at the door and came in to ask questions, to which nobody seemed to have any answers. No, she hadn't told anyone where she was going; no, nobody had seen her leaving. They took down Melody's description of where Auntie Susie lived ("in a bungalow, with hedges round it, not near the sea, but not far from the sea, with a blue front door and floaty curtains") and then they looked at all her mum's stuff in the bedroom.

"Did she have any reason to disappear?" asked the younger of the two policemen.

Melody looked at Ken, who looked at her. "Well," he ventured, "she has been under some stress. Her husband is living with another woman, who has just given birth to his child. And, er, I think she's been suffering from, well . . ."—he glanced again at Melody—"some other issues. Of the emotional variety."

"So you're saying she's unstable?"

"Well, not exactly unstable, but . . ."

"Right, I think in that case we should give it twenty-four hours and then check the beaches. Particularly around Ramsgate."

"You mean, you think . . . ?"

This time the policeman and Ken both looked at Melody.

"I don't know, sir, but it is possible. We see a lot of it, you know, with women. Hormones can be powerful things. If there is no news about Mrs. Ribblesdale's whereabouts by this time tomorrow, we will start a search."

They took Melody's dad's phone number, which was the only phone number in the whole world that Melody knew off by heart, and then they left.

Matty wanted to know every last thing that the police had said when he came downstairs five minutes later. "I was trying to listen at the door, but it was too muffled!"

"They think she might be on the beach. Because of her hormones."

"What—dead?"

"No, I don't think so, just upset. But they're not going to look until tomorrow."

"Why not?"

Melody shrugged. "Don't know," she said.

"Well, that's rubbish," said Matty. "Anything could happen between now and tomorrow. It could be the difference between life and death. I say bollocks to waiting. I say, let's go now."

He disappeared for a few moments and returned clutching a cloth bag, which he hung across his chest.

"What are we going to do?" said Melody.

"We're going to find your mum."

They walked together through town to the damp, seaweed-strewn sands of Viking Bay. It was completely empty. They tramped up and down the quay, past the deserted café. Matty stopped every now and then to scan the horizon with a pair of battered army surplus binoculars that he'd stashed in his big bag.

"Any idea what she was wearing?" he said.

Melody shook her head. "She was still in her nightdress when Ken took me to London."

"Color?"

"What?"

"Her nightdress. What color was it?"

"Green. With a cream bit, here." She touched her chest.

"Right. And her hair is brown. And she's of medium build. Right?"

"Right," said Melody.

"OK. Nothing here, let's keep moving."

He let the binoculars drop and turned back toward town.

Melody followed him, silently, for what felt like a very long time. He stopped every now and then to examine small fragments of flotsam and oddments of litter.

"What kind of things does your mother like doing?" he asked, in due course.

"Erm, reading?"

"Hmm, we could try the bookshops, or the library, but I don't suppose she'd have been there all night. Anything else?"

Melody gave it some thought. "She likes cats."

"No, that's not going to help. Christ. This is tough. Think, Matty, think." He tapped his head with the palms of his hands. "A woman, thirty years old, feeling sad, what would she do? Where would she go? I know! I know! Come on, follow me."

It started raining as they approached the train station and Melody was tired and hungry. She hadn't had any breakfast and she hadn't had any lunch and it was now nearly two o'clock.

She was excited and glad to be spending time with Matty, but she also wanted to get back to the house, because the more she thought about it, the more convinced she was that her mother was probably there waiting for her. But she didn't want to annoy Matty so she followed him along the platform, down the sidings, over the bridge, and down into the undergrowth, and she waited patiently while he rooted around among empty beer cans and old carrier bags with a big stick.

Matty finally gave up his search at about four o'clock.

Melody's feet were rubbed raw inside her too-tight plimsolls and her stomach had given up growling and resigned itself to hunger.

They wandered slowly back into town, and up the High Street. Melody caught sight of their reflection in the window of Woolworths. They looked bedraggled and thin, like two little orphans. Melody gulped at the thought. This was as close as she'd ever been to having no parents and it felt terrifying.

They were almost home, two streets away from the house, when something caught Melody's eye. It was a fragment of fabric, just glimpsed through the steamed-up windows of the coffee shop. It belonged to a jacket that was very familiar to her. A blue jacket with black flowers on it. Her mother's.

"Matty! She's in there! Look!"

They cupped their hands to the glass and peered through. Jane sat with her back to the window, a red mug by her left hand, a bunch of dead flowers by her right. She sat alone and motionless, the angle of her head suggesting that she was watching someone, intently.

They stepped into the shop and as they got closer, Melody saw that she wasn't in fact watching someone, but that she was staring into nothingness, so deeply that at first she didn't notice the two small children by her side.

"Mum." Melody touched her arm.

Jane continued to stare into the distance.

Her jacket was grubby and her hair looked matted and tangled. There was mud under her fingernails and she smelled briny and damp.

"Mum." Melody tugged at her sleeve, a bit harder.

Jane finally broke her gaze and turned very slowly toward Melody.

"Yes?" she said.

"What are you doing?"

"What?" she replied vaguely.

"What are you doing? Where've you been?"

"Melody?"

"Yes. It's me."

"Why are you here?"

"We've been looking for you. You've been lost. We called the police! Where have you been?"

"Oh, here, mostly. I think."

"But all night, last night—where were you?"

Her mother paused, and rubbed her elbow. "Somewhere, I think. The beach . . . ?"

Melody paused and tried to make sense of the situation. Her mother was smelly and vague, and sitting in a café all on her own, having spent the night sleeping on the beach. In October.

She stared at her mother's muddy fingers and then at the dead flowers and then she said, "Mum, are you unstable?"

It was nice having her mum back in the bedroom with her that night, seeing the hump of her sleeping body across the room, hearing her rhythmic breathing and the rustle of her bedsheets as she moved around. But Melody couldn't sleep. Every time her eyelids got heavy, every time her thoughts grew unfocused, she snapped back to a state of awakeness. She didn't want to sleep, because if she slept, she might wake up and find her mother's bed empty. So she lay, just five years old, in her bunk bed, under the eaves, staring at her sleeping mother until the sun came up the next morning.

Chapter 25

Now

Melody sucked the last traces of English fudge ice cream off the back of the spoon and let it drop into the goblet. She'd forgotten breakfast this morning and hadn't realized how hungry she was until she'd stepped inside Morelli's Ice Cream Parlour five minutes ago.

Of all the places that Melody had been since the unlocking of her memory two weeks earlier, Morelli's held the greatest resonance. Her certainty of place here was stronger than anywhere else. She knew this place had been special—an oasis of happiness in what, she was becoming increasingly certain, had been a turbulent and uncertain childhood. She had sat in every booth in this parlour, she could picture herself at each and every one of them, her long spoon held in her small right hand, her lemonade on a paper coaster, candy sprinkles on her tongue, and Ken at her side.

Her resolve to unearth the secrets this town held strengthened by her visit to Morelli's, she turned and headed for the library. The local history section. It had been Ed's idea. "It's not just books in a library, you know, Mum. They have other stuff too. Papers and stuff. And lots of local history." She cut back through Chandos Square, through a couple of streets she hadn't ventured down before, and as she walked, Melody felt it again, a sense of pattern to the lefts and rights of the route, a cadence to the soft beat of her feet against the pavement and the way it changed when they crossed the tarmac road. This was a walk she'd done before, she decided, and not just once, but numerous times. She knew exactly where she was going.

Melody remembered everything, the moment she saw the squat yellow brick façade of Upton Junior School. She saw a gray duffel coat, a rip in a jacket pocket, a playground brought to silence by the poisoned taunts of a tall sad girl with her hair in plaits.

Chapter 26

1978

Penny Clarke was a big girl. She was a year behind, because she was what was then described as "educationally subnormal," but she would have been big anyway. She had coarse blond hair, which she wore in two fat plaits over her shoulders, and a very greasy forehead with a crease in it.

"For a child of seven to have a frown line is a very worrying sign indeed," said Melody's mother the first time she saw Penny outside the school gates.

Penny had befriended a girl called Dana, who was half her size and painfully thin and always had a stain down the front of her school sweater. The two of them stood in the corner of the playground at break times, looking cross and staring at people. Sometimes they chewed gum. They rarely spoke to each other.

One morning, shortly after the day she and Matty had found Melody's mum in the café, Penny and Dana approached her in the playground. Dana was wearing a gray duffel coat and her thin hair was in a ponytail. Penny was wearing a black Harrington jacket with a rip above the pocket.

"What's your name again?" said Penny.

Melody thought this was a strange question, as Penny had been in her class for nearly two months and was there every morning when Mrs. Knott read out the register. "Melody," she said.

"Oh, yeah, that's right. Knew it was something posh."

They shuffled around in front of her for a moment, and as they shuffled, Melody suddenly knew without a doubt that something bad was about to happen.

"Where you from then?"

"I don't know," said Melody.

The two girls exchanged a contemptuous look. "You don't know where you come from?" said Penny.

"No."

Penny laughed, a dreadful sound like a metal girder landing on a small dog. "But that doesn't make any sense," she said. "Everybody knows where they come from."

Melody gulped. She knew she had to say something sensible, and say it quickly. "My dad lives in London. I live here."

"Right then. So your mum and dad are divorced?"

She shook her head and stared at her feet.

"Then why don't they live in the same place?"

"Because they're cross with each other."

"Right." Penny sniffed and gave Melody a strange look. "You live in that hippy place in town, don't you?"

Melody wasn't entirely sure what a hippy place was, but suspected that she was referring to Ken's house.

"I live at Ken's house," she said.

"Yeah, that hippy bloke who hangs around town. I know the one. Looks like he could do with a good wash. Always trying to get people to give him money for his crappy leaflets. My mum says he's a pervert."

"What's a pervert?" said Dana.

Penny threw her a disdainful look. "You know," she said, "someone who does dirty things to people. Sex and stuff."

Melody shook her head. "No," she said. "You're wrong. Ken's really nice."

"Well, that's not what my mum says. She says he's got women in and out of his bed the whole time, sometimes two at a time. Mum says he brainwashes them and makes them his *disciples* and then uses them for dirty stuff. Mum says he's disgusting. And you live with him. And that makes *you* disgusting."

Melody gulped.

"And your mum too," added Dana.

"Yeah," said Penny. "And your mum too."

They stood there for a moment, staring at her expectantly.

Her head throbbed with words she wanted to say, with indignation, and with terror. She knew what they were saying wasn't true. She knew that Ken was a good, kind man. But she also knew that there were things that happened in her house that she couldn't explain, things that she knew were wrong, but that seemed, in the context of Ken and his house, perfectly all right.

"It's not like that," she said eventually. "It's just not like that."

"Oh, right, then what is it like?"

"Ken's really kind. He let us come and live with him when my mum was feeling sad and he takes me to London on his motorbike to see my dad and he's got a lovely wife who cooks for everyone and he's gentle and generous."

"Oh my God," said Penny, a cadaverous smile playing around her mouth, "you're in love with him, aren't you? Oh my God, do you do stuff with him too? You do, don't you? You and your mum and that hippy, all together. God, that's *disgusting*."

Melody had become aware that a kind of stillness had fallen upon the playground as other children interrupted their play to hear what Penny was saying.

Penny noticed her audience and addressed them. "She's *dirty*," she exclaimed, pointing at Melody. "Don't go anywhere near her. You'll get the clap."

The other children stared at her, blankly, while Penny's eyes flashed triumphantly.

The silence lingered for a long-drawn-out moment until it was shattered by the sound of the end-of-break bell being shaken.

Penny and Dana threw Melody one last dreadful look before turning away and Melody made her way slowly, and numbly, to her classroom.

Melody's mum moved out of their bedroom shortly after that. She was never very specific about where exactly she was going to sleep, but it didn't take long for Melody to work it out when Grace and Seth moved into her bedroom the following night.

Asking Grace questions about things was much easier than asking her mum questions about things, so she waited until she was on her own with her in the kitchen the next day and said: "Grace?"

Grace looked up from Seth's elbow, which was grazed and bleeding from a fall in the yard.

"Yes, sweetheart?"

"Why are you and Seth sleeping in my room and Mum's sleeping in Ken's room?"

"Ah, well." Grace paused for a moment and tore the paper wrapper off an Elastoplast. "Your mother's going through a bit of a bad patch." She stuck the plaster onto Seth's elbow. "She's feeling a bit confused and Ken wants to keep her close to hand. So that's why she's going to be sharing his bedroom. And I hope you don't mind me and Seth taking over your mother's bed. Just for a little while."

Melody nodded, though she was far from happy about this new development.

"Don't you mind, though?" she said. "Don't you mind that someone else is sleeping in your bed?"

"Well, beautiful girl, the thing is, we don't really think of things in this house as 'ours.' Or anyone else's. We don't believe in possessions. The bed that Ken and I sleep in belongs to *everybody*. And right now, your mum needs it more than I do."

Melody pondered this. As far as she could tell, the bed in their attic room was very comfortable. In fact, she remembered her mother commenting on more than one occasion on what a comfortable bed it was. So why did she need to sleep in another one?

"Is Ken's bed very comfortable?" she asked eventually.

Grace smiled, one of those strange smiles that adults used that were impossible to interpret and therefore very unsettling. "Yes," she said, "it is. It's very firm."

"And is that why my mum wants to sleep there?"

"Well, I'm sure that's one of the reasons."

Melody paused for a moment. If there were "other" reasons for her mother's being in Ken's bed she wanted to know what they were. "So why else?"

"I told you," Grace said, "she's feeling a bit confused. Ken wants to . . . comfort her."

Melody squirmed. That word, "comfort," seemed suddenly imbued with all sorts of shadowy submeanings and undercurrents.

"Why does Laura want to sleep with Ken too?" she asked. "Does she need comfort?"

Grace gave her that smile again, but this time it just made Melody feel angry. She may have been only six years old, but she really wasn't stupid.

"Yes," said Grace, "sometimes. Sometimes Laura feels lonely and then she comes into our room to sleep."

"Hmm." Melody picked up one of Seth's rattles from the kitchen table and squeezed it into the palm of her hand. There was something soothing about the feel of the baby's toy, something reassuring about the gentle chicka-chicka of the beads rolling around inside it. "What's the clap?" she asked.

"What?"

"A girl at school said it."

"A girl at school? What sort of girl?"

"Penny. She's a year older than us. She's nearly seven. Is it a disease?"

"The clap? Well, yes. It is. It's one that only adults can get, though."

Melody nodded and moved the rattle into her other hand. She wanted to tell Grace that Penny had said that people could catch it off her, but she had a strong feeling that this would lead to even more trouble. "What happens when you get the clap?"

"Well, there are lots of different types of . . . clap. But they're generally all around the fanny area."

"The fanny?"

"Yes. The vagina. And the penis. And women catch it off men and men catch it off women. But only grown-ups."

"Grown-ups who share a bed?"

"Yes, that's right. Grown-ups who share a bed."

"So could my mum catch it off Ken?"

Grace laughed and lifted Seth off her knee. "No," she said. "No. That's highly unlikely. I wouldn't worry about that. But really, I'm quite shocked that a six-year-old girl should be talking about things like that at school."

"Well, she's nearly seven. She's the oldest girl in the class."

"But still. Have you told a teacher?"

Melody shook her head and passed the rattle to Seth, who was standing at her feet, looking at it expectantly.

"Well, next time this girl comes talking to you about things like that, you just walk away. Just walk away immediately. And you tell me. Because that's not right. That's not right at all. There is nowhere else in the world where you could be safer or more loved than this house, and anyone who says differently is just talking out of their big fat derrière, OK?"

Melody smiled and nodded.

"Good things are happening here," Grace continued, "happy things. Everything is on the up. Now come over here and let me give you a big hug, you precious, precious thing."

Melody stepped into the long, tangled embrace of Grace's arms and allowed herself to be held, appreciating the gesture but wishing more than anything that instead of Grace's bony rib cage and pancake breasts, her face was being held warm and safe against the yielding and slightly pungent bosom of Jane Ribblesdale.

Chapter 27

Now

Broadstairs Library was an ugly red-brick building. Melody found the local history section and started to leaf, somewhat randomly, through obscure-looking books with titles like *Broadstairs and St. Peters During the Great War of 1914–1918*. It struck Melody as an entirely pointless activity. She wanted to know about a squat in the late eighties, not fishing in Viking Bay in the 1800s. She caught the eye of a middle-aged woman, small and neat in gray trousers and a polo-neck, her eyeglasses on a chain around her neck, leafing through a book about the local area.

"Excuse me," Melody said, "do you live in Broadstairs?"

"Yes," said the woman, "I do."

"Oh, good, I wonder if you could help me. I lived here for a short time when I was a child. I lived in Chandos Square, just behind here. Do you remember much about Chandos Square, thirty years ago?"

"Well, that depends . . ."

"The house I lived in—it's a guesthouse now—it's called the House on the Square. You know, it's very smart?"

"Oh, yes, I remember that house all right." The woman chuckled and closed the book she'd been looking at. "That house was the bane of everyone's life."

"That's right, it was a squat, wasn't it?"

The woman leaned forward conspiratorially. "That," she said, "was only the half of it."

Melody caught her breath, readying herself for the unknown.

"There was this man, like a hippy, he was kind of like the boss of the house, if you like . . ."

"What was his name?"

"Ken," she replied immediately, "Ken Stone."

Melody inhaled sharply. There it was again, another gleaming piece of the jigsaw, another flighty notion turned to fact.

The woman continued, "He was some kind of, what do they call it, like a political activist, always off on some march or other, always shouting off about stuff, but never actually changing anything, you know the type. And he believed in what they used to call 'free love.' All very 1970s. He wrote all these daft pamphlets about freeing the mind, about letting go of the shackles of conformity. All that rubbish. All talk and no action except when it came to the ladies . . . Here," said the woman, taking off her reading glasses and letting them fall to her lap, "this Ken fellow, was he anything to do with you?"

"Well, I lived there as a child, and he was my friend."

"But you're not related to him, then?"

"No, no, I'm pretty sure I'm not." Melody laughed brittlely as the realization that, heaven knew, she might be, suddenly dawned upon her.

"Well, anyway, he had this wife, at least she called herself his wife, though I can't imagine that they ever did anything as conventional as getting married, you know. And she was a strange creature, always looked to me like one of those Art Deco figurines, all sinewy, wrapped up in scarves and bangles. They had a little boy together . . ."

"When?"

"God, I don't know when. I suppose it must have been around the time our youngest was born, so about thirty years ago."

The baby on the floor, sucking the plastic spoon.

"Anyway, there were always people coming and going, odds and ends of people, and the talk around town was that they were all having a mass orgy, you know, like a love-in."

Melody thought about the woman called Laura she'd remembered this morning. Had she been part of this strange orgiastic commune? And then, of course, another thought struck her: Was it possible that something terrible had happened to her in this unsavory house? Was it possible that Ken Stone had violated her in some way, that she had been involved in something dark and unspeakable, and that was why her memory had ceased to function? Was it possible that she had been abused, not, as Ed had suggested, by her father, but by this stranger she barely remembered? Suddenly a dozen dreadful scenarios sprung to mind—she had been kidnapped from her safe Canterbury home by this woman called Jane and brought to this place to be used by adults in the most terrible way imaginable. And if that was the case, then maybe the same had been true of the house in Fitzrovia. Maybe she had been given to the man with the kind face by the woman called Jacqui. Maybe there were more houses, more stories, maybe she'd been passed from place to place, maybe—it was unthinkable, but they wrote about these things in the newspapers—maybe her parents had been behind it all. It would explain her abnormal ambivalence toward them, the gaps in their history. But even as soon as these notions appeared in her head, she quashed them. That wasn't right. It just wasn't. She couldn't remember much but she remembered that Ken was good, she remembered that the man in Fitzrovia was good, and she remembered, more than any of that, that however strained her relationship with her parents had been, they both cared about her deeply and truly. There was another story behind the doors of the houses on Chandos Square and Goodge Place and Melody was pretty sure that this neat little woman with her seaside accent and her Marks and Spencer slip-on pumps was about to turn the page to the next chapter.

Chapter 28

1979

A cold January morning, Melody's breath in icy clouds around her face. A revolving door, a pile of suitcases, a cabdriver in a gray sweatshirt and early morning stubble, smoking a cigarette and slamming the boot of his car.

Charlotte in a long brown fur coat and a purple bobble hat, complaining about how cold she was.

Her father looking sad and tired, pulling out his battered wallet and sliding out a ten-pound note.

Emily in a white, all-in-one zip-up suit, regal and upright in Jacqui's arms.

The sudden heat of the terminal as they walked through the revolving doors.

Her father's arm around her shoulders, the thunder of Tannoy announcements, the swirling bustle of a thousand people.

Melody's first ever time at an airport.

But she wasn't going anywhere.

Melody's dad went to live in Hollywood with Jacqui, Charlotte, and Emily when Melody was six and a bit.

Jacqui had signed a contract with a big film studio to work as a makeup artist on three back-to-back movies that would be filming over the next year. She would be earning more in a year than Melody's dad would earn in a decade, so there never seemed to be any question that they would take Charlotte out of school, request a sabbatical for her father, rent out the Fitzrovia house, and emigrate immediately.

"You'll come over at Easter. And we'll be back here in July for a fortnight. A year is not all that long, not really, not in the big scheme of things."

Melody nodded, mutely, wishing that that was true, but knowing instinctively that a year was a very, very long time indeed, especially for a baby.

A sign on a TV screen said that they had to go through customs immediately, and all of a sudden it was time to say goodbye, and Melody felt it was much, much too soon.

She kissed Jacqui on her perfumed cheek, then she hugged Charlotte, who squeezed her back hard enough to suggest that she might actually be a little bit sad. She threw her arms around her father's neck and let him swing her about for a while and then she turned to Emily.

Emily was four months old. She had a neat helmet of golden-brown hair and the beginnings of hazel eyes. She was a serious, quiet baby, who liked staring at people and looking at books. "I have no idea where this baby came from," Jacqui would say. "So still, so quiet. Nothing like me."

Melody didn't really understand why Jacqui expected her baby to be just like her. It was as if she'd forgotten that Melody's dad had had anything to do with her existence, as if she felt that her genes were so powerful and superior that they should be stamped, brandlike, all over everything she came into contact with. But it was clear to Melody where Emily had come from. She'd come from her. They were made of the same stuff, the same ingredients, like two identical cakes.

Melody did everything she could to imprint herself upon the baby. She rubbed her nose against her nose, she tickled her with her hair, she blew raspberries into her tummy and cuddled her almost constantly. Her dad thought it was cute. "Look," he'd say, "Emily's mini-mum."

But Jacqui didn't feel the same way.

"Too rough! Be gentle! Don't poke her! Don't stroke her! Leave her be! Leave her be!"

This had been the almost constant refrain for the first few months of Emily's life as Melody had attempted, in her own slightly overenthusiastic childlike way, to get to know her sister. She could see the fear in Jacqui's eyes, especially in the early days. Jacqui would look at her as if she were a drooling, befanged wolf, about to rip the meat from her baby's bones. She could almost smell the disgust that Jacqui felt for her, hear it in the terminology she used.

"Get your huge feet out of her cot."

"Keep your grubby hands away from her face."

"Melody, you're breathing garlic all over her. She doesn't like it."

Charlotte, on the other hand, appeared to have little interest in the baby aside from choosing outfits for her occasionally, showing her off when her friends came for tea after school, and complaining when she'd been crying in the night. When Melody was at Jacqui's house, she had Emily all to herself. And that was just the way she liked it. She didn't want to share her. She didn't even really like it when Jacqui touched her, though she never let Jacqui sense this in case it made her cross and stop her from coming to see her.

When her dad had told her that they were leaving the country, Melody's first thought had been: Emily, what about Emily? It had taken a second or two to digest the fact that she'd also be losing her father, and another long moment before it dawned upon her that now there was nowhere else to be but Broadstairs, and no one else to be with but her mother.

Melody lunged forward and buried her face into Emily's neck. "Bye-bye, Milly," she said, "I love you, my Milly."

Melody tried as hard as she could not to, but the smell of Emily's baby breath and the soft touch of her hands against her skin was too much to bear, and her shoulders started heaving and her jaw started wobbling, and right there, in front of a thousand strangers, Melody started to cry.

She cried as they turned and wheeled their towering trolley toward the customs queue, she cried as she headed back toward the taxi and the stubbly driver, and she cried the whole way back to Victoria Station in the back of his car, silently and heavily, with every fiber of her being.

Her mother met her at the station, but even the unexpected sight of a forced smile and a bag of chocolate peanuts wasn't enough to soothe her pain, because every time Melody closed her eyes she saw the back of Emily's head, her neat golden head nodding up and down, her little body zipped into its cozy white suit, absorbed into the core of her family and heading away from her. And every time she looked at her mother's sallow, haunted face, she felt more and more alone in her strange and unpredictable world.

Chapter 29

1979

Melody's mum was whistling.

Melody stopped what she was doing and stared across the kitchen at her.

She was sweeping the kitchen floor, and she was whistling.

She hadn't whistled for two years.

"Mum? Are you all right?"

Her mum looked up at her and smiled. "Yes," she said, "I'm fine."

"Then why were you whistling?"

"Was I?"

"Yes. You were whistling a hymn."

"Oh," she said airily. "I didn't realize."

Whistling wasn't the only strange thing her mother had done recently. On Tuesday she'd worn lipstick. And yesterday she'd made a cake. It was clear to Melody that her mother was feeling happier, and the only possible explanation that Melody could find for this was that her father, Jacqui, and baby Emily were no longer a part of their lives.

It had been twenty-one days since they'd left for America and twenty-one days since Melody had felt complete. The fact that something that made Melody feel so gnawingly sad could also make her mother want to whistle and bake struck her as somewhat unfair. But the vision of her mother bustling with a broom, the lightness of her actions, the flick of her hair, worn loose and a little longer, these things overrode any sense of injustice and made Melody want to turn a cartwheel of anticipation. Suddenly things that had seemed impossible for the past three years unfurled themselves from the darkest corners of her imagination:

Made-up stories at bedtime.

Swinging side by side in the playground, seeing who could reach the clouds first.

Bowls of cake mixture.

Cat's cradle.

Hugs.

Kisses.

Conversations.

"Can we go to the wool shop?" she asked, seizing the moment.

"Of course," replied her mother. "Let me just finish off in here. We can go for tea and a sticky bun at the cake shop after, if you like?"

Melody caught her breath and nodded. For a moment swapping her baby sister for her proper mother seemed like a fairly good deal.

In the wool shop she chose a length of pale blue angora that was on sale for 20p and a big ball of white wool for 48p. Grace had been teaching her how to knit. It was very difficult and she wasn't very good at it, but she wanted to try to knit a scarf for her Baby Blue Eyes (charitably passed down to her from Charlotte during one of her occasional and unsettling agreeable moods) and a hat for the rabbit she'd had since she was small. Her mother chatted to the shop assistant while she ferreted around in the big bins and Melody thought how long it had been since she'd heard her mother talk so warmly with a stranger and how different her mother's voice sounded when she was happy.

For so long the opening of her mother's purse for any reason whatsoever had been a painful event, accompanied by tuts and groans, and expressions of dreadful discomfort, so Melody could hardly believe it when her mother passed a pound note to the shop assistant without even glancing at it.

Melody hugged her paper bag of wool to her chest as they left the shop.

"Here," said her mum, "I'll take that." She gently took the bag from Melody's arms and smiled at her, before slipping it into her big shoulder bag. "Come on," she said, grabbing hold of Melody's shocked, unexpecting hand, "let's get that sticky bun."

Melody felt proud as she walked through the chilled, busy streets of Broadstairs that Saturday afternoon, holding her mother's hand, proud and hopeful.

In the tea shop they talked about school and Aunt Susie and hairstyles, and anything at all in fact that Melody could think of to talk about that wouldn't puncture her mother's newfound buoyancy.

"You know," said her mum, sliding a bit of snowy icing off her plate with the tip of her finger, "you're a very good girl. A very good girl indeed. You do know that, don't you?"

Melody shrugged.

"I know I don't say it very often and I know that a lot has happened these last few years and I haven't always been very . . . *present.* But however it may sometimes seem, I really do love you and I really do treasure you. I couldn't have got through any of this without you."

Melody allowed herself a smile. "I love you too," she said.

"Ah, but do you still think that I'm the best mummy in the world?" Her mum smiled tightly and Melody gulped. That was what she used to say, back in the past, back in London, back when her dad was there and they had parties and everyone seemed to like each other. "You're the best mummy in the world!" And Jane would smile and hug her and say, "And you're the best girl in the world!"

Melody glanced at her mum. She didn't look like the same mummy anymore. She was still fatter than she'd been before and her hair wasn't as nice, even though she'd started growing it out of the square shape, and she looked older and sadder and less likely to break into a huge spontaneous grin at the merest glimpse of her, but still, thought Melody, she was a nice mum. She didn't hit her or shout at her and she'd bought her exactly the Pippa doll she'd asked for for her birthday and she always said sorry if she pulled a knot in her hair when she was combing it. But "the best"? Was she the best? Melody thought of Jacqui, of her state of perpetual motion, the way she zoomed in and out of Charlotte's bedroom on a tidying blitz without stopping to say hello, zoomed in and out of the house without stopping to say goodbye, the way she only ever noticed if something had gone wrong, been spilled, been broken, but never when something had been done rather well, and she decided that yes, all things considered her mother probably was still the best mummy in the world.

But only just.

"Yes," she said. "Definitely. The best!"

Jane smiled and Melody saw her eyes fill up with tears. "Thank you," she said, "thank you."

They hugged across the table, Jane's sleeves hanging in the sugar bowl, Melody's face buried in her mother's soft shoulder, and Melody felt safe for the first time since she was three years old.

Chapter 30

1979

Jane's good mood lasted for eight weeks. During the fourth week of happiness, Jane and Melody got the train up to London, then sat on a tube for half an hour and ended up at Aunt Maggie's house in Ealing. This was the first time that Melody had been to Aunt Maggie's house since they'd left London and it gave her a strange sense of remove from herself to be in a place that hadn't changed at all, when everything else had.

Maggie met them at the ornate stained-glass door and held them both for what felt like ages. She smelled of cats and candle wax, and her hair was too long. Nicola and Claire had grown into leggy adolescents with ideas about clothes and pictures of boys on their bedroom walls. But the house was exactly the same, from the vase of silk orchids on the windowsill, to the Chinese paper balls that covered the ceiling lights and the green Trimphone on the hallway table.

"It's been far, far too long," Maggie said, ushering them through into the living room at the back of the house, which overlooked the apple trees and fig trees in her garden. "Two years. *Two years*, Janie!"

"Well," said Jane, draping her coat across the back of the sofa, "it doesn't feel that long."

"Doesn't it?"

"No, not really. Life's been a bit, you know, a bit of a blur."

"Well, not for me it hasn't. It's been a long old wait. And you, look at you!" She grabbed Melody's knee with her angular hands. "So big, so pretty, so grown-up. What happened to those fat cheeks of yours?"

Melody didn't know what had happened to her fat cheeks. She wasn't aware that she'd ever had them to begin with. "I don't know." She smiled, wanting to be polite, hoping, for some inexplicable reason, that Aunt Maggie would think that their life was all lovely and perfect, like a TV show, instead of all weird and echoey like a spooky dream. "Maybe they fell off!"

Aunt Maggie laughed loudly and looked delighted. "Maybe they did. Fell on the pavement. Got swept up by the road sweeper! Ha ha ha!"

Melody felt that Aunt Maggie was laughing a little bit too loud, and it struck her that maybe she was feeling nervous.

Claire and Nicola stared at her shyly from across the room. Claire was wearing eyeliner and Nicola had on a very short skirt. Melody had a feeling that neither of them was about to whisk her upstairs to their bedroom to play with dolls.

"Why don't you girls go out in the garden for a while?" said Maggie. "Me and Aunt Jane have lots of things we need to talk about."

Melody followed her cousins out into the garden, but stood near the side window so that she could hear the women talking.

"Have you told him?" she heard Maggie saying.

"Yes," said her mum. "I told him last night."

"And?"

"Well, he's delighted."

"And you?"

"Never felt happier."

"Well, I'm happy for you, if you're happy. But I just hope you know what you're doing."

"What do you mean?"

"I don't know. This Ken. Who is he? What's he like?"

"He's, well, he's not like anyone else. He's *special.* He's got a kind of power over people."

"Hmm," said Maggie, skeptically.

"Oh, no, in a good way," her mother said urgently. "He's not arrogant. He's not cruel. He's just . . . he makes life simple. No decisions. No options."

"You mean, he just tells you what to do and you do it?"

"No! The opposite. He expects nothing. He accepts me. Just as I am. Fat and a mess and full of all this shitty rage and sadness and . . . and . . . pain. He just takes it. Absorbs it. He is a great man. Honestly."

There was a brief silence. Melody held her breath.

"Well," said Maggie. "I'll take your word for it. I'll have to since I'm never going to meet him. And Melody? Have you told Melody?"

"No! No, absolutely not. Not yet."

"Does she get on with him?"

"She adores him. Idolizes him."

"Good," said Maggie. "That's good."

"And what about you? How are you coping?"

"Oh, you know, good days, bad days."

"And have you seen him yet? Have you seen Michael in prison?"

"No, no, no. Not yet. Not ready yet."

"So you think you will?"

"I really don't know. It's so dreadful. Like a nightmare. Sometimes I dream about him. I dream that it never happened, that everything's back to the way it was. But then, nothing ever really was the way it was, was it? It was all an illusion, Jane—my perfect life, my perfect husband, all a sick, beautiful illusion. And sometimes I have nightmares too. I see those girls, those lovely, lovely girls, and . . ."

From her vantage point at the window ledge, Melody could hear her aunt Maggie crying.

". . . And I feel so guilty, Janie, so horribly, horribly sick with guilt. I mean—I've got two daughters, and the idea of . . . of . . ."

Melody heard her mother sighing sympathetically. "Don't, Maggie," she said. "Don't do it to yourself. There's nothing you could have done."

"Oh, but there is, Janie, there is. I should have wondered more, I should have questioned things: his absences, his moods, his distance . . . but it's too late now, there's nothing I can do now. Those poor girls' lives are ruined forever and that's just something I'm going to have to live with for the rest of my life."

Melody tugged at her mother's skirt. "I need to do a wee," she whispered.

Her mum smiled at her. "Can you remember where the bathroom is?"

Melody shook her head.

"I'll take you," said Nicola, who'd followed her in.

Melody followed her cousin up the stairs. On the landing she saw the same painting of a hairy cow on a windswept dale, and in the bathroom the same pine-framed mirror over the same heavy Art Deco sink.

"Nicola," she asked, as she came out of the bathroom a moment later, "can I see something in your room?"

Nicola smiled sweetly. "I haven't got my babies anymore," she said. "We gave them to the hospital, for the ill children."

"I don't want to see babies," Melody replied, "I want to see something else."

It was there, just as she'd known it would be, hanging on the wall between posters of David Bowie and Queen: the Spanish girl with the blue eyes and the black hair and the red polka-dot dress. She stared at it in silence and felt something hot and cold slither down her spine.

"Are you OK?" said Nicola.

"Mm-hm." Melody nodded.

"Do you like David Bowie?" Nicola asked.

Melody didn't answer. She was mesmerized by the painting and puzzled by her reaction to it. "Have you always had that painting there?" she asked after a while.

"Yes," said Nicola. "Since I was a baby. Why?"

Melody sighed. "I don't know," she said. "It just . . . reminds me of something, that's all."

"Do you like it?"

She nodded. "Yes," she said, "I really do. I love it."

"Well, you can have it, if you like?"

"What, really?"

"Yes. I'm not that keen on it anymore."

"But won't your mum mind?"

"No," said Nicola. "She doesn't mind about things like that. Not anymore."

Melody sensed something sad in Nicola's voice and thought about what she'd just overheard Maggie and Mum talking about. Their dad had done something really bad and now he was in prison, but Melody decided not to ask Nicola about it.

Nicola got off the bed and stood on her tiptoes, reaching to pluck the painting from the wall. "Why do you live so far away now?" she asked.

Melody shrugged. “I don’t know,” she said. “I wish we didn’t. I wish we still lived in London.”

“Maybe you’ll come back now,” said Nicola, blowing a thick layer of dust off the top of the painting and smoothing the glass with the side of her hand. “Maybe your mum will change her mind.”

Melody nodded. “Yes,” she said, “maybe.”

Nicola passed her the painting and she held it in her hands. “Thank you,” she said. “I really, really love it. I’ll keep it forever and ever. And it will always remind me of you.”

Nicola smiled then and put her arms around Melody. “You’re so sweet,” she said, hugging her, “so, so sweet.”

Melody hugged her back, intoxicated by the smell of her big-girl hair and watermelon lip gloss, and amazed that there was this person, flesh and bone, solid and real, whom she hadn’t seen for two years, who was her *family*. Not a pretend family like Ken and Grace and Laura, not a patchwork family like Jacqui and Dad and Charlotte, but her real family, the one she’d had before everything had changed. She squeezed her back and hoped her tears wouldn’t leave a wet patch on the shoulder of her lovely blue Chelsea Girl sweater.

Chapter 31

1979

A lady called Janice accompanied Melody to Los Angeles that Easter. She told Melody that she had a daughter who was six and a half too and that her name was Rebecca.

"Where is she?" asked Melody.

"She's at home," said Janice, "with her dad."

Melody smiled and clutched her blanket to her, feeling that although she was neither home nor with her dad, and a hundred miles up in the air, she was exactly halfway between the two and that was as good a place to be as any.

"I'm going to be with my dad soon," she said.

"Yes, you are," said Janice. "Are you excited?"

Melody nodded and smiled. "Really, really, really, really, really excited! I haven't seen him since January."

"Wow. Three months. That's a long time not to see your daddy, isn't it?"

"And my sister," she replied. "My baby sister, Emily. She can sit up now. And play with toys."

"Wow," said Janice again. "I bet she'll be so excited to see you."

"I hope so," said Melody, "I really hope so."

Charlotte's bedroom had a bed with a gilded canopy, like one that Melody had seen in one of the state bedrooms at Sandringham last summer. Cascading from the gilded canopy was a circle of white chiffon that draped itself around the bed like a wedding dress. The carpet in her bedroom was soft cream shag pile and she had a dressing table with gold curly bits on it and a triptych mirror on top. A door to the left led to a small bathroom, with a shower cubicle, a bidet, and *two basins*, which was, apparently, only for Charlotte to use and was called an "on sweet."

"And look at this," Charlotte said, pulling Melody across the shag-pile carpet toward a pair of glazed doors at the rear of the room. "My very own sun terrace!"

The terrace was semicircular and furnished with a teak lounger and a giant orange parasol. It had a view directly over the small turquoise swimming pool in the back garden and a lantern that clicked on and off whenever anyone stood near it.

"No one's allowed on this terrace, except me. And you, when you're here. If I say it's all right. So—what do you think?"

Melody took another look around the grand suite and exhaled. She had never before encountered such opulence, such glamour and elegance. It wasn't a big house, not by the standards of the surrounding mansions and haciendas, but it was so modern and so thrilling. "I think it's the nicest bedroom in the whole wide world."

"Good." Charlotte smiled with satisfaction and flopped backward onto her big double bed. "You know, some of my friends at my new school have got *much nicer* bedrooms than this. You know, Christie's got *two* double beds, and her own pool. *And* a real diamond necklace. But then, her dad's a big producer—and she's an only child, so, you know, she gets more stuff."

Melody nodded, mutely. The idea of there being a bedroom somewhere close to here that was nicer than this one was impossible to conceive of. Melody herself would be sleeping in what Jacqui uncharitably, and perhaps insensitively, referred to as "the maid's room." It was a tiny whitewashed room near the utility room behind the kitchen with a small window overlooking the driveway. Someone (Melody hoped it was Jacqui, but thought it probably wasn't) had made an attempt to cheer it up a bit, with a Mexican blanket and a vase of orange blossom from the garden, but it was still an altogether gloomy box of a room.

"Where does Emily sleep?" she asked Charlotte.

"In the nursery," she replied.

"Can I see it?"

Charlotte looked at her in confusion, as if having seen the eighth wonder of the world that was her own bedroom she should have no reason ever to wish to see another bedroom as long as she lived. "If you want," she said, "it's next door."

Emily's nursery was big and airy, with arched shuttered windows that shared Charlotte's view across the pool. She had a large white cot with a mobile overhanging it and huge cartoon decals all over the walls. Melody breathed in deeply, relishing the scent of talcum and detergent, the piquant undercurrent of nappy and scalp.

There was a large framed portrait on the wall outside Emily's nursery, a studio photograph of Charlotte in a cream crocheted minidress and waist-length plaits tied with wool pompoms, holding Emily on her lap. Charlotte looked self-consciously beautiful and Emily looked slightly precarious in a matching cream dress with a pink Alice band holding back her curls.

Melody gulped. They looked so complete, the two sisters. Nobody looking at that photo would ever stop and wonder where the other sister was. No one would think that there was someone missing, a sister with Emily's hazel eyes and determined jaw, the same dreamy, faraway look in her eyes, the same spirit. They would just look at it and think: Look at those lovely sisters, so beautiful, what a pretty family.

"When did you have that photo taken?" she asked Charlotte.

Charlotte glanced up at it, as if she'd never seen it before. "Oh, that," she said. "A couple of weeks ago. It was your dad's birthday present to my mum. Do you like it?"

Melody nodded. "It's beautiful," she said.

"Yes," said Charlotte, "though I *hate* my teeth in it. Look at the way that one overlaps that one." She shuddered. "Horrible. So I'm going to an orthodontist next week. I'll probably have a retainer. They might even have to pull one or two, but it'll be worth it, worth it to have nice straight teeth . . ."

But Melody wasn't listening. She was staring at the photo of Emily and Charlotte, thinking: For the sake of a couple of weeks, why didn't they wait for me?

Jacqui cooked a chicken and avocado salad for supper that evening, which they ate at a long marble table on another terrace by the pool. Emily sat in a plastic high chair, slowly chewing on a hunk of French bread. Her dad sat at the head of the table, casual in an unbuttoned linen shirt and cut-off denim shorts. His hair was longer than he wore it at home, and his chin was shaded with stubble. He seemed restless and fidgety, and Melody wondered if it was because of what her mum had said, because he didn't have a job anymore and spent all day looking after Emily.

Jacqui sat next to him in a floaty chiffon top and flared white jeans. Cicadas chirruped from the flowerbeds and a sprinkler in the next-door garden made a shimmying noise as it sprayed water over orange trees and cactus plants. Charlotte, in a shirred muslin top and matching gypsy skirt, was kicking her feet against the table leg and pushing her salad around her plate with her fork.

Melody stared at them all in wonder. This Hollywood Hills family looked tanned and lean and foreign. They looked like a TV show.

"So, how's your mum?" asked Jacqui, pouring more wine into her father's glass.

"She's fine," said Melody.

"Good," Jacqui said. "All better then after . . . ?"

"Jacqui means after the time she went missing," said her dad, noticing Melody's confused expression.

"Yes." She nodded. "She's not unstable anymore."

Jacqui and her father exchanged one of those irritating smiles that made Melody want to throw her cutlery down and scream, "It's not funny!"

"Oh, that's good," said Jacqui. "I'm glad to hear that. And how's everything else? How's school?"

"It's OK," Melody replied. "Although there's this girl, called Penny, and she hates me."

"Oh, no, I'm sure she doesn't hate you . . ."

"Yes," said Melody, "she does. She says awful things to me, about Mum and about Ken."

"What sort of awful things?"

"Oh, you know, that they're disgusting and I'm going to get the clap."

The smile fell from Jacqui's lips. "What?"

"They say that me and Mum and Ken are doing dirty things to each other and I'm going to get the clap."

Charlotte snorted into her napkin and her mother threw her a look.

"Have you told Mummy about this?" asked her father.

"No! Of course not!"

"Why not?"

"Because she'd say something to the school and then Penny would hate me even more."

"Have you told anyone?"

"I've told Grace."

"And what did she say?"

"She said that was a wrong thing to say and that if she said it again that I should just walk away. And I tried that, but they just follow me around and say it even more."

"But why would they say such a thing?" said her dad. "I don't understand."

Melody shrugged. "I don't know," she said. "Just because they don't like me."

"Oh," scoffed her dad, "now that's just silly. Of course they like you, everyone likes you."

"No, that's not true. Only adults like me. All the kids hate me. They say I'm dirty and I smell and I live like a tramp."

Her father's face fell. "But, sweetheart—I mean, why would they . . . what sort of . . . is there anything wrong at home? Anything you're not happy about?"

She shrugged again. "I don't like it when Ken has his meetings."

"Meetings?" He looked concerned.

"Yes, when all the people come and talk about stuff and they all get loud and shout at each other. And I don't like it when Seth cries in the middle of the night—"

"Who's Seth?" Jacqui interrupted.

"He's Grace's little boy. He cries a lot. But apart from that I like everything."

Her father paused, licked his lips. "So, Mummy and Ken, are they still . . . friends?"

Melody nodded and chewed on a garlicky lettuce leaf. "Yes, and they share a bed now because Ken wants to keep her close at hand."

Jacqui and Dad threw each other a strange look.

"You mean," said Melody's dad, cautiously, "that they sleep together?"

"Yes. In Ken's room. Laura was sleeping in Ken's room but she's moved out now to live with a wizard, and Grace and Seth sleep with me in my room, in Mum's bed, and Matty's still got his own room because he said if anyone makes him move he's packing a bag and heading for the hills."

Melody stopped to catch her breath and glanced around the table. Jacqui, Charlotte, and her dad were all staring at her in amazement and she got the distinct impression that she'd said some things they weren't expecting to hear. They were, she suspected, strange things for a girl of six and a half to be talking about, but she'd had no one to talk to about things for so long and here she was, in paradise, bare skin warmed by humid, camellia-scented air, brand-new flip-flops licking the floor, a captive audience, a million miles from home. She wanted to make an impression on this glittering Hollywood Hills family, wanted to make them sit up and notice her. So she continued.

"And Matty said that Ken's no good, that all he wants is for women to make babies for him and clean him in the bath, but I know that that's not true because he's been so kind to us and Mum's never made a baby for him or cleaned him in the bath. I think Matty's just sad because Ken's not his dad and he's not allowed to see his dad because he drinks too much and he once put a man's head through a pub window. I think if Matty just gave Ken a chance he'd see that he's a good man. And if Penny ever came to my house she'd see that everyone is kind and good and no one is doing anything dirty at all. Except for when Matty goes hunting for rats with his harpoon that he made himself."

She stopped again and smiled. "Sometimes he comes back with bloody hands," she finished.

"Well," said her dad, "it sounds like you're living a very colorful life."

"Yes," she said.

"And this Penny character sounds like a nasty piece of work."

"She is. I hate her too."

"Well, actually, I think you should feel sorry for her. It's rather sad for a six-year-old girl—"

"She's seven."

"OK, a seven-year-old girl to have such thoughts, to think such things. She must come from a very unstable home."

Melody nodded thoughtfully. She wasn't sure what an unstable home might be like, but if her own brief experience of an unstable mother spending a night on the beach was any measure, it seemed to her it must be a thoroughly bad thing.

"We saw Aunt Maggie a few weeks ago," she said. "We went on the train and went to their house."

"Oh," said her father, "Maggie. How is she?"

"She seemed a bit sad. She said she's having nightmares."

"Oh dear," he said.

"But we had a really lovely time and Nicola gave me her painting and Mum seemed to be so happy when we got home. I think we're going to go back again soon. And Nicola says we might even move back to London."

"You'd like that, would you?"

Melody nodded. "Yes, then I'd be near them and near you and I'd be able to see Emily every day!"

She turned to smile at her sister, who was attempting to slice up her bread with a plastic spoon. She squeezed her hand and nuzzled it against her lips. "Tomorrow," she said, feeling brave, "can we go to the place where you took Charlotte and Emily to have their picture taken and have one taken with me in it?"

Her father threw a look at Jacqui. "Oh, yes, well," he said, "I'm not sure about that. It was very expensive and you have to make a booking."

"But"—Melody felt tears pricking her eyes—"it's not fair that Charlotte has a lovely picture with Emily and I don't have one. I'm her sister too."

Her father smiled and put his hand on her shoulder. "Absolutely," he agreed. "You are absolutely right. Wait right there. I'll be back in a tick."

He came back two minutes later holding a large camera.

"This," he said, "is a magic camera. Now, you go and stand next to Emily, that's right. OK, now smile!"

Melody opened her mouth and pushed her teeth together and smiled as hard as she could. There was a pop and a flash and then a strange whirring noise and something emerged from the front of her father's camera. He pulled it out and waved it back and forth.

"There you go," he said a moment later, "it's coming."

She stared at the piece of shiny white paper in his hand and, as she watched, a ghostly image appeared, the luminescent outline of a small girl and a baby. Details surfaced one by one, the buttons on her shirt, the clip in Emily's hair.

"It's us," she breathed.

"That's right," said her dad. "It's called a Polaroid."

She took it gently from his hand and watched the colors intensify. And there they were, Emily and Melody, almost identical with matching shy smiles and dark eyes. "Look," she said, showing the photo to Emily, "look. It's us. You and I. Look."

Emily glanced at the photo inquisitively and squeaked.

"Can I keep it?" said Melody.

"Of course you can," said her dad. "It's yours. To keep forever."

Melody smiled and propped it up against her tumbler on the table. It was, she decided, a truly magic photograph, in every way, and a hundred times better than the stupid portrait outside Emily's nursery.

Melody couldn't sleep in her little room at the back end of the house. Cars kept zipping past on the road that ran past the driveway and there was an extra-loud cicada right outside her window. After about half an hour she took her pillow and her Mexican blanket and climbed silently up the open-tread stairs to the first floor. She tiptoed down the parquet-floored landing until she got to the nursery and then she pushed open the door.

Emily was asleep in her cot, with her arms above her head, snoring gently. Melody stared at her for a moment or two, resisting the temptation to stroke her lovely cheek, before laying herself down on the floor by her cot and nestling under her blanket.

From here, all Melody could hear was the gentle lap of the swimming pool, the scratch of distant cicadas, and the murmur of Jacqui and her father still chatting on the terrace. She was drifting peacefully off toward sleep when she was startled by the sound of her own name.

"Melody's only a child," she heard her father say. "She's six years old. She doesn't understand about sex, or manipulation."

"Oh, of course she does. I mean, she may not know exactly what sex is, but she knows when something's right or wrong."

"How can you say that?" snapped her father. "If that was the case then there'd be no sex abuse. All it takes is a smooth talker—"

"Are you saying that you think she's being sexually abused?"

"No," he said impatiently, "I'm saying that she's living in a house with sexually promiscuous people and a mother who hasn't cared for her properly since she was four years old. I'm saying she's *vulnerable*."

"Hmm . . ." Jacqui acquiesced.

"Imagine if it was Charlotte," he said. "Or Emily. Imagine if one of them was living miles away from you, with a depressive parent, in a house full of hippies and political activists, God knows who coming in and out of the house."

"Of course I'd be concerned," Jacqui said gently. "But, John, you made this decision, you committed to us, to this family. You have to live with the consequences of that."

"No, Jacqui, I don't. She can come here. Come and live with us."

"How, John, how? Do you honestly think Jane would let her go? And where would she sleep? She can't sleep in the maid's room forever. I would actually like to put a maid in there at some point."

"She could share with Charlotte."

"*With Charlotte!* Are you kidding! Can you imagine what Charlotte would have to say about that?"

"Well, then, with Emily?"

"Hmm, maybe." Her tone softened again. "But what about school? I can just about stretch to Charlotte's school fees. And I'm sorry, John, I'm incredibly fond of Melody, I really am, but she's not my child. I will not have my own children going without to pay for your daughter's education."

"So you can afford to pay for a maid, but not for my daughter's school fees?" said John in a raised voice.

"Yes," snapped Jacqui, "a maid to clean my house and cook meals for my children and my boyfriend. A maid so that I don't have to clean the whole house when I get back from fifteen hours on set. It's not a luxury, you know, it's a necessity."

There was a brief silence then and Melody heard her father strike a match and breathe in on a cigarette. "Well," he said softly, "I'm up shit creek without a paddle then. Because I want my daughter to come and live with me but I haven't got any means to support her. And if I go back to England to look after her I won't be with you and Emily."

Jacqui sighed. "That's the long and short of it, yes."

"Fuck. What a fucking mess."

"Yup," said Jacqui. "That's life for you."

"Poor Melody," he said. "My poor little Melody." And then he started to cry.

Melody sat up. She'd never heard her father cry before. It was a strange noise, a little like a dog snuffling and worrying at a bone.

"She's had such a rough ride these past few years and she's such a little trooper, so sweet and so uncomplaining, and none of what's happened to her is her fault. It's all so unfair, so unfair. On everyone . . ."

"Oh, John," Melody heard her stepmother say soothingly. "It'll be all right," she said. "We'll be home in eight months. Only another eight months and then we can take care of Melody. She'll be fine, you know, just fine."

Melody lay back down on Emily's floor and closed her eyes.

Eight months, she thought, *only another eight months*. And then she could go and live with her dad.

Melody eked out every last moment of pleasure from her two weeks in America. She ate ice cream every day and taught Emily how to hold a crayon. She went to a baseball match and accompanied Charlotte to her appointment at the orthodontist and played football on the beach at Santa Monica with her dad. But mostly she just spent time with Emily, helping her play with her toys and trying to teach her things.

"My little babysitter," Jacqui would say whenever she came upon the two of them absorbed in some activity or another, "what will I do without you?"

Jacqui and her dad let her continue to sleep on the floor in the nursery and even put some cushions down for her to use as a bed.

By the end of the fortnight, Melody had a tan, a fat belly, and a beautiful gypsy sundress like Charlotte's, that Jacqui bought for her as a leaving present.

She didn't feel so sad saying goodbye at the airport as she'd felt when they'd left London three months earlier. She didn't feel so sad because she knew they'd all be home for a fortnight in the summer and that by this time next year she'd be living with them in London.

Janice was her escort again on the trip home.

"I asked for this trip specially when I saw it was you," she said, smiling. "We had such a lovely time on the way out. You've put on weight!"

"I know," said Melody, tapping her tummy. "I ate too much ice cream!"

"So, you had a good time, did you?"

"It was brilliant. I played with Emily every day. And look"—she pulled the precious Polaroid out of her travel bag—"Daddy took this picture of us with his magic camera."

"Oh, aren't you both lovely," said Janice. "Your sister looks just like you."

"Yes, I know. We are the same. We look the same and we like doing the same things, even though she's only six months and I'm six years. And Daddy wants me to come and live with them in America but Jacqui can't afford to pay for my school, so I'll go and live with them next year when they come to London."

"Oh, that sounds like good news. And what about your mother? Won't she mind?"

"No." Melody shook her head. "She hasn't cared for me properly since I was four years old. I think she'll be glad."

"Oh, now, I'm sure that can't be true."

"Oh, but it is. She really loves me and everything. But I don't think she particularly likes looking after me. No"—Melody nodded her head decisively—"she'll be glad."

Janice nodded slowly with a tight smile on her mouth and then turned to look out of the window.

She didn't say anything else to Melody for another ten minutes and when she did, there was a mascara streak below her eyes, as if she might have been crying.

Chapter 32

1979

It seemed as if a huge game of musical chairs had been going on while Melody was in America. When she got back to the house at Broadstairs, her mother was in Matty's bedroom, Matty was in hers, Grace and Seth were back in Ken's room, and a couple called Kate and Michael were in the spare room.

The first Melody knew of any of this was when she ran upstairs to her bedroom, threw open the door, and found Matty cross-legged on the floor dissecting a frog with a scalpel and a pair of surgical tweezers.

"Well, if it isn't Melody Ribblesdale, back from her sojourn across the Atlantic Ocean."

"What are you doing in here?" she asked, dropping her travel bag on the floor at her feet.

"Your mum gave me five pounds for my room."

"What?"

"She didn't want to sleep with shit-breath anymore and then those moon-faced idiots moved into the spare room and she bribed me with a fiver to give me her room. I got all this stuff with it"—he pointed at the full set of gleaming surgical equipment in front of him—"so it was well worth it."

"But—why didn't she want to stay in here with me?"

Matty shrugged. "I didn't ask too many questions. Just took the money and ran. You'll have to ask her yourself."

Melody ran down two flights of stairs to the living room, where her mother was chatting to the new woman, Kate. "Mum! Why did you give our room to Matty? And where did you get five pounds from?"

Her mother sighed and gave the woman a long-suffering look. "I didn't 'give' our room to Matty, Melody, I asked him to swap. Just for a while."

"But why?"

"Because," she sighed again, "because I am thirty-one years old and I haven't slept alone for two years. Because I needed some space. Because I wanted to be . . . *alone*. It's nothing personal, darling. It's nothing to do with you. Besides, I thought it might be more fun for you to share with Matty. You could have fun together after lights out."

"Yes, but I don't like the same sort of fun as Matty likes."

"Well, then, don't have fun, but please, darling, let me have this space. Is it really too much to ask? Just for a little while. Just for a few months?"

Melody grimaced. It was too much to ask. It wasn't fair. She didn't want to sleep in a room with Matty and his scalpels and dismembered animals. But then she remembered that in a few months' time her dad and Jacqui would be coming back and she'd be going to live with them, and then her mother could have the big attic room all to herself, and she thought how happy that would make her, so she didn't complain.

Instead she smiled and said, "OK. That's fine," and went to look for Ken.

Ken was the only person she'd missed in America.

Ken was the only person in the whole world, apart from Emily, who made her feel like she was important and exciting. Whenever anyone else looked at her—when Jacqui looked at her, when her mother looked at her, when Charlotte or Matty or Penny or even her dad looked at her—she felt like they were looking at a beach of dull pebbles, an endless uninspiring expanse of grayness with nothing to catch the eye. When Ken looked at her it was as if he'd just come upon something sparkling and thrilling, something that he hadn't expected to see. There didn't seem to be one activity that Ken found more engrossing than talking to Melody, or one vision more compelling than the sight of her standing at his study door.

She found him sitting on his balcony in the spring sunshine in a huge hat and a coat that looked like a soldier's coat, big and scratchy with shiny buttons. He turned at the sound of her footsteps and beamed at her. "Oh my God, you're back! Thank God! I missed you so much! I've had no one to eat ice cream with, no one to go for bike rides with, no one to have interesting conversations with!" He put down his book, took off his huge hat, and spun her round his study until she felt like her head might snap off and fly out of the window.

"I like your coat," she said, feeling the rough wool of the sleeve. "Is it new?"

"Yes, indeed it is. I bought it from a jumble sale for twenty-five pee. What a bargain! Feel the quality of that!"

Melody fingered the wool and smiled at him shyly.

"So," he said, "are you happy to be back?"

She nodded, a small, uncertain nod.

"Did you miss us?"

She nodded again. "Well," she said, "I missed you the most."

"I bet you did." He smiled. "Come on," he said. "It's a beautiful day, I've got nothing going on. And the best cure for jet lag is fresh air. Let's take the bike out for a spin!"

All thoughts of sliced-up frogs and distant sisters and mothers who didn't want to sleep with her fled Melody's thoughts as she sat in her little rocket capsule next to Ken, racing along the coastal roads. It was amazing to think that just a few hours ago she'd been asleep on a plane in the sky and now she was wide awake and zooming around the seaside on a motorbike.

After an hour or so Ken brought the bike back round to Broadstairs and pulled up in front of Morelli's. An old couple sitting in the window stared curiously at Ken as he pulled off his helmet and then at Melody as she pulled off hers. Melody thought their faces looked strange and sour, like a pair of large fish who'd eaten something unpleasant. They carried on staring at Ken as they walked toward the counter and then the woman said something to the man and tutted and they both turned to look at them again.

"Why are those people staring at us?" asked Melody.

"What people?"

"Those old people, over there."

"Oh. Never mind them. They've just got empty heads and empty souls."

"Why?"

"I don't know. Some people are just born that way. Voids. Vacuums. Put on this earth to touch no one, to change nothing, to exist and then to die."

Melody didn't know what voids or vacuums were but thought it sounded awful anyway. She glanced back at the old couple, at their pinched, gray faces, their thin clothes in shades of black and navy, their dusty air of superiority, and she smiled at them.

The woman glanced away but the old man gave her a sly wink. Melody smiled to herself and addressed the altogether less depressing issue of ice cream.

"So," said Ken, as they slipped into a booth a moment later. "Did you have a good time in America?"

Melody nodded. "It was brilliant," she said. "Everything about it was brilliant."

"Do you wish you were still there?"

Melody thought about the question. She would like to be swimming in the small turquoise pool and she would like to be in Emily's nursery doing jigsaws and she would like to be sitting on her dad's lap playing with the hair on his tanned forearms. But she didn't wish she was still there, not really. It wasn't her home. She'd just been a guest. "No," she said, "I'm glad to be home. Though I'm not pleased about Matty being in my room."

"No," said Ken, "I didn't think you would be. But it's not for long. Kate and Mike are only staying for a few weeks."

"Who are Kate and Mike?"

"They're my friends."

"And why aren't they living in their own house?"

"Because they haven't got their own house."

"So where do they live the rest of the time?"

"Well, all over the world, really. They're just back from India for a couple of months because Kate's mum died, and then they're off to Pakistan."

"But why do they live over there when they're not Indian?"

"Because some people are born with it inside them, like a little pea, a little grain of sand, that rubs and rubs, and even though it's only tiny it's really uncomfortable and when it rubs enough you just want to get away, to see something new, to smell something different. Some people like to travel. It feeds their souls. And then some people, like those two over there"—he glanced at the old couple in the window—"some people just want to sit and fester and make assumptions about things, because they're too lazy and too small-minded to get off their backsides and find out for themselves."

Melody thought about this for a moment. "I like to travel," she said. "I liked going to America and I like going on trains and seeing the backs of people's houses. And I like going in your bike and seeing things moving really fast."

"Well, that doesn't surprise me to hear you say that, Melody. You are a very interesting little girl and I expect great things of you when you're a grown-up. I do not expect to walk past Morelli's Ice Cream Parlour in the year . . . 2034 and find you sitting in the window looking miserable and pulling bitter faces at lovely little girls."

"What do you expect then?"

"Oh, Melody, I'll be dead when you're as old as them, but I'd hope that you would be a lovely, serene old lady, surrounded by happy grandchildren, with a face filled with experience and joy. And no regrets. Regrets are worse than any mistake you could ever make. Far, far worse . . ."

Melody nodded sagely, and relished the image that Ken had just painted of her future. "Will I still be here," she asked, "in Broadstairs?"

"Oh, I doubt that very much," said Ken. "Nobody should stay in Broadstairs forever."

"But what about you? You'll be here forever, won't you?"

Ken paused. "Maybe," he said, "maybe not. While there's work for me here. While people need me. But if I ever find myself alone and unnecessary, I'll move on too."

"And what about my mum? What do you think will happen to my mum?"

"Well," said Ken, "she's been on a bad journey, but the end's in sight now. I think that you and your mum are about to enter a bright new phase. I really do."

Melody smiled at this heartening assertion and attacked her knickerbocker glory with renewed gusto.

The pieces of her jigsawed life seemed finally to be fitting together.

Chapter 33

1979

Another memory:

Jane, sitting on her bed in Matty's old room, cross-legged and fat, her hair in a plait and her feet in clogs.

The window open onto the street, letting in wafts of chip-fat smell and the banter of Cockney holidaymakers.

A fat ball of aquamarine wool at her feet.

The dog running up the stairs, clickclickclick against the wooden steps.

The morning sun landing in stripes across the far wall.

A radio being tuned in someone else's room.

Her mother, smiling, glancing down at her fat belly and saying the words: "Mummy's going to have a baby."

Melody wondering, How can Mummy be having another baby when Daddy's living in America? And then realizing, without anyone grown-up having to tell her, that Daddy wasn't the father of Mummy's baby. Ken was.

Jane's baby was due in November. She got fat very quickly. All day long she ate bread and cheese and bananas, and she was sick, loudly, voluminously, and frequently. The summer came and went, and by the time Melody went back to school in September her mother was the size of a house and had chopped off all her hair again into the square helmet shape.

Penny's face did the strangest thing when she saw Melody's mum for the first time that Wednesday morning. She blinked and then she blinked again, then her jaw slowly lowered and her eyebrows slowly lifted and her nostrils flared open until she looked like her whole face was trying to escape from her head.

"Your mum's having that hippy's baby!" she declared with glee in the corridor outside their classroom a moment later. "She's having his fucking baby. That makes me want to be *sick*."

Melody turned away toward the classroom door.

"Don't ignore me," hissed Penny. "I'm *talking to you*."

"Yes, well, I don't want to talk to you."

"No," said Penny, looming over Melody like a vulture, "I don't suppose you do. I wouldn't want to talk to anyone if my mum was up the duff by some dirty old hippy."

"He's *not dirty*," said Melody. "Why do you keep saying he's dirty?"

"Because he is. They all are, hippies. My mum said so."

"Yes, well, your mum doesn't know anything about hippies. And anyway, Ken's not a hippy. He's a polickital ativist."

"Same thing," said Penny, "same thing. All dirty. All perverts. All fucking disgusting. Just think." Her face broke into a terrible smile. "You're going to have a little brother or sister who's a hippy too. A dirty little hippy! Heh heh heh . . ." Penny trailed off with a contented smile and pushed past her into the classroom.

Melody followed quietly behind, staring at Penny's thick yellow plait and wishing more than anything that she could grab hold of it and pull it so hard that Penny's ugly head rolled off her shoulders, out the door, down the corridor, and straight onto the busy street outside.

"What are you going to call your baby?" Melody swung back and forth in the bamboo chair that hung from the ceiling in the front room.

Her mum looked up from a crossword and smiled at her, distractedly. "Oh," she said, "I haven't really thought."

"How about Jonathan?"

"That's a nice name."

"Yes, or if it's a girl, Rowena?"

"Hmm . . ."

"Or Bettina? Or Matilda?"

"Wow," said her mum, "you have been thinking about it."

"Yes. I've thought of lots more girls' names than boys' names, though. They're much easier to think of."

"Yes," said her mum, "that is true."

"Why did you call me Melody?"

"Ah." Her mother's face softened for a moment. "We called you Melody because we thought that Ribblesdale was a bit rough around the edges and it needed something to soften it. We almost called you Emerald, for the same reason."

"Emerald?"

"Yes, like the green stone."

Melody paused for a moment, trying to imagine the other version of herself, the one that never existed, the one called Emerald. Emerald was exotic and exciting and had jet-black hair and a haughty demeanor. Emerald wouldn't be picked on at school by a pig like Penny. Emerald would have Charlotte quaking in her boots. Emerald was *remarkable*.

"Can we call her Emerald then," she said, "if she's a girl?"

"Oh, I don't know. We'll have to have a look at her and see what we think, won't we? Only a certain sort of little girl could carry off a name like Emerald . . ."

Melody mulled this over. She stared at her mother's burgeoning belly and decided that whoever was in there deserved a name like Emerald and that even if she didn't look at first as if she'd be able to "carry it off," the very fact of having such a name bestowed upon her would be enough to see her through anything.

"What will the baby's last name be?" she asked.

Her mother paused and stared for a moment into the distance. "Hmm," she said, "good question. I suppose, since Ken and I aren't married, the baby should have my name. My maiden name. Newsome."

"What's Ken's surname?"

"Stone."

Emerald Stone. It was perfect.

"So, where will we all sleep when the baby comes? Will you and the baby sleep with Ken? And Grace and Seth too?"

"Oh, Melody, you and your questions, questions, questions. Do they never stop? I don't know what's going to happen, all right? I don't even know what's happening tomorrow, let alone next month."

"But, there's no room for a cot in Matty's room, so you'll have to sleep somewhere else and—"

"*Melody!* For God's sake! Please!"

"But—"

"Argh!" Her mother threw down her newspaper and pen. "Melody—there is not an answer for every question! I do not know what is going to happen! I do not know anything! I barely know what my own name is half the bloody time! Now please, be quiet and leave me alone."

Melody closed her mouth, really hard, so that no more questions came tumbling out of it, and let the bamboo chair spin her, very slowly, away from her mother.

Late in October when Melody was almost seven and her mother was fit to pop, Ken took her out for ice cream.

It was a strangely balmy day, a soft breeze being blown across the drear and deserted town from somewhere far away with white beaches and palm trees. Ken's bike was broken and a man called Pablo was fixing it for him, so they walked the short distance together in a companionable silence. That was one of the best things about Ken—unlike most other adults, he didn't think it was necessary to keep talking all the time. He waited until he had something interesting to say or to ask, and then he said it. Or mostly, he just let Melody do all the talking.

But today his silence seemed more pointed, like he was being quiet on purpose. He didn't say anything until they were sitting down in their usual booth at Morelli's, and then it seemed to take him a long time to say it.

"So," he began, "your mum's nearly ready to have the baby then?"

Melody nodded and nibbled on a biscuit wafer.

"The baby in there is very big now, you know. If she had the baby now it would be big enough to cuddle."

Melody nodded again.

"It's funny, isn't it, when mums' tummies get all big and fat like that? Looks quite strange, like a huge balloon!"

Melody giggled.

"So, have you felt the baby moving yet?"

Melody looked at Ken to see if he was joking, but he wasn't. "How could I do that?" she said.

"Like this," he said, cupping his hand to his own stomach. "When babies get as big as your mum's baby, you can feel them moving around inside."

"No"—Melody shook her head—"I don't think that's true."

"Oh, but it is. I used to feel Seth when he was in Grace's tummy all the time. He used to kick me," he said, "and once I even saw the outline of a little foot through Grace's skin."

"No!" Melody looked at Ken in wonder.

"Yes. Honestly. So, your mummy hasn't let you feel the baby move then?"

Melody shook her head.

"Well, babies move around the most when their mummies are sitting still, so tonight, when she's relaxed and everything's quiet, ask her if you can feel it."

"OK," said Melody, "but I don't think she'll let me."

"Why not?"

She shrugged. "Don't know. Just don't think she will. Maybe she thinks I'll hurt it."

Ken laughed. "You can't hurt a baby by feeling it moving."

She shrugged again. "Well, you know that and I know that but Mum, well, she's just a worrier, isn't she?"

Ken smiled and patted her hair.

"She is that," he said. "She certainly is that."

Melody's mum didn't let her feel her bump that night.

"No," she said, "the baby's sleeping. I don't want you to wake it up."

She didn't let her feel it the next night either.

"No," she said, "the baby's sleeping again. There's nothing to feel."

Thinking that this baby seemed to like a nap in the evenings, Melody asked again the following morning.

This time her mother smiled. "Why the sudden need to feel the baby?" she asked.

Melody shrugged. "I don't know," she said. "I just want to."

"Well, I tell you what, this baby isn't much of a wriggler, not like you were. You wriggled and kicked nearly twenty-four hours a day! But this one"—

she patted her big belly gently—"this one just seems to like lying around, contemplating its navel. But when I feel it kick, I'll let you know. OK?"

Melody smiled and kissed her mum's tummy. "OK," she said. "And you," she said, addressing the bump, "wake up!"

Her mum laughed then and the two of them walked to school slowly and contentedly.

Chapter 34

1979

The baby arrived the next day. No one was expecting it as the baby wasn't due for another three weeks, but there she was, pink and fat and surprisingly alert for a newborn.

Ken had come to get Melody from school, in the middle of the day. She'd been pulled out of science; twenty-eight curious pairs of eyes followed her as she left the classroom.

"She's here!" Ken had said, hopping around the corridor, grinning from ear to ear. "The baby's here!"

They'd run home, the whole way, breathless and panting by the time they reached the house, but still taking the stairs up to Jane's room two at a time.

Jane was sitting up in bed, wearing a voluminous nightgown and drinking a cup of tea. The baby, dressed in a pink babygro and knitted hat, was lying at the foot of the bed, staring at the ceiling and kicking its fat legs in the air.

"Well," said Jane, smiling groggily, "what do you think?"

Melody stared at the corpulent creature on the bed and thought how different she looked from Emily when she'd first seen her. Emily had looked diaphanous, otherworldly, like a mystical creature from fairyland. This baby looked solid and fully formed. The baby caught Melody's gaze and stared at her. Then the baby smiled and Melody knew then that something wasn't right. But she didn't say anything. Instead she smiled and stroked the baby's soft brown hair and said, "I think she's beautiful."

"Your mother," said Ken, perching on the side of the bed and stroking the baby's foot, "is a *goddess*. Do you know why?"

Melody shook her head.

"Well, just after she dropped you at school this morning, her waters broke and she *walked* all the way to the hospital, on her own, which is mad, but also quite spectacular. Then she pushed out this magnificent baby—all eleven pounds of her—had a cup of tea, and came home! I have never known anything like it!"

Melody stared at the baby and then at her mother. She couldn't remember the last time anyone had said anything so complimentary about her mother, the last time her mother had looked so proud and so happy. She liked the idea of her mother's being a goddess, a creature worthy of worship and respect. She liked the atmosphere in this room, the joy on Ken's face, the enervating scent of new life, the way that new babies seemed to come along and temporarily clean the stains out of everything. So she smiled and she lay down on the bed next to her new sister and she kissed her cheek and tried to put the strange things she was feeling to the furthest corners of her mind.

"Are we going to call her Emerald?" she asked, even though she wasn't sure that it actually suited the big doughy-faced baby on the bed.

Her mother smiled and shook her head. "No," she said, "not Emerald. But close. It's a precious stone. Can you guess what it is?"

"Er, Diamond?"

"No. Try again."

"Ruby? Sapphire?"

"No—we're going to call her Amber. Amber Rose Newsome. Do you like it?"

Melody glanced once more at her baby sister and considered it. It wasn't quite as thrilling as Emerald Stone but it suited her better she thought. She nodded and kissed the baby's cheek again and said, "Yes, I like it. I like it a lot."

The baby turned at the sound of her voice and put one small fat hand out toward Melody's cheek and for a moment the two sisters stared deeply and thoughtfully into each other's eyes. Melody offered her sister a finger and the baby took it in her small fist, grasped it tightly. Melody stared at the fleshy tangle that their hands had made and felt a deep, dark yearning, for continuity, for meaning, for something everlasting. *Stay with me*, she willed the tiny girl, *stay with me. Please.*

But then Amber started to cry and Jane whisked her away from Melody and Ken was sent down to the kitchen to make up a bottle and Grace came in to coo at the baby and the spell was broken. But for one moment in time Melody had made a connection with this little person, a connection that would stay with her for far longer than Amber would.

Chapter 35

1979

The first Melody heard of the baby who'd been stolen from outside the newsagent's on Nelson Place was two days after Amber was born. There were news posters all over Broadstairs emblazoned with the headline "10-Week-Old Baby Snatched While Mum Shopped."

The baby in question was called Edward James Mason and he'd been taken while his mum was in the newsagent's buying a paper and a packet of envelopes. The mother's haunted face peered out at Melody from the front cover of every newspaper that day. She was young—only nineteen years old—and she clutched a blurred photograph of her lost baby to her chest. Her husband was a sallow-faced eighteen-year-old with a pudding-bowl haircut and wire-rimmed glasses. "I only popped in for a minute," she said at a press conference in London. "Broadstairs is such a safe place. I never thought that something like this could happen."

The baby was described as being dressed in white trousers, a blue jacket, and blue bootees and was wearing a "very distinctive" cream woolen hat, knitted by his maternal grandmother. He had brown hair and blue eyes and weighed approximately fourteen pounds. The baby-thief had taken just the baby and left behind a large Silver Cross perambulator, a quantity of baby bedding, and a wooden rattle.

"Somebody must have seen something," said a Detective Inspector Philip Henderson. "This occurred on a busy shopping street at ten o'clock in the morning. The baby was taken out of its perambulator so the sight of a person, possibly in a state of high excitement, carrying a small baby through the streets of Broadstairs could have struck somebody as peculiar in some way. If anybody remembers seeing such a sight on the morning of Wednesday the twenty-fourth of October, please do get in touch with Scotland Yard."

There was a small black-and-white photograph of baby Edward beneath the article, a bit creased and a bit blurred. It showed a newborn baby in a knitted hat looking blankly into the middle distance.

"And he was fast asleep too," said Kate, passing the newspaper to Grace across the breakfast table. "I mean, what sort of person would lift a sleeping baby out of its pram?"

Grace eyed the photo of the missing baby and sighed. "Poor wee thing," she said. "Imagine that. One moment you're fast asleep, the next you're staring at some stranger's face. Horrific, quite horrific."

Melody's mum sat at the head of the table, baby Amber asleep on her shoulder, nodding her agreement.

"I mean, to think, you can't even leave your baby outside a shop for a moment. I don't know what the world is coming to." The three women all sighed and shook their heads and Melody stared from one to the other and asked herself the question: *Don't you know? Doesn't one of you women know what's going on here?*

Because Melody knew. She knew exactly what was happening. Baby Amber wasn't baby Amber at all. She was baby Edward. And this she didn't just suspect, but she knew, because last night when her mum wasn't looking she'd unpopped the poppers on the baby's babygro, and she'd hooked one finger inside the damp terry toweling of its nappy and she'd seen, with her own eyes, a small pair of leathery red testicles and a tiny penis.

She'd then, spurred on by the details coming to light in the news reports, searched her mum's room when she was in the bathroom and found, in her wastepaper basket, underneath yesterday's newspaper and a ball of old hair, a small knitted woolen hat and a pair of blue bootees.

She hadn't shared this knowledge yet with anybody. It was living in her head, like a ball of fire, burning and gnawing and eating away at her consciousness. She had never before in her life been privy to such an extraordinary secret. It felt bigger than everything that had happened to her in her whole life added together and timesed by a hundred. She didn't know what to do with it. It felt so big that it might just burst out of her head and spill all over the floor, flooding the streets of Broadstairs with pure undiluted sensation. She wanted to tell Ken, but Ken would be so disappointed that the baby wasn't really Amber. And she wanted to tell her dad, but he was in America, and today, for a split second in PE, she'd even wanted to tell Penny, just to see her face do that weird thing where it looked like her features were trying to run away, just to know that she'd said the most shocking thing to Penny that anyone had ever said to her in her life.

Melody knew she shouldn't be excited about her discovery. Every time she thought about that poor mother in the newspapers she felt bad because she knew that all that stood between her heartbreak and her ecstasy was Melody and her secret. But she didn't want to let go of it. And she didn't want to let go of the baby and the excitement that his/her arrival had brought into this strange house.

But what seemed strangest of all to Melody was that nobody else seemed to have noticed that something was so very, extraordinarily wrong. Nobody had noticed that the baby could smile and that the baby could hold things in its hands and that the baby could see things across the room. Nobody noticed the way that Jane turned down every offer to change the baby's nappy or to help her bathe it at night. And nobody wondered why Jane had had her baby all alone at the hospital on *the very same day* that baby Edward was stolen from the shops.

It seemed she would be carrying her shocking secret around with her in overwhelming solitude until late that night, when she awoke to find Matty hissing in her ear.

"What?" she said.

"Wake up," he said.

"I am awake. What do you want?"

"It's the baby," he hissed. "I know something about the baby."

Melody sat up in bed and switched on her bedside lamp.

Matty looked scarecrow-haired and wide-eyed. "Your mum's baby! It's him! The one that was stolen!"

Melody sighed. Those were her words, that was her secret, her remarkable declaration of fact. "I know," she said. "I've known for ages."

Matty looked deflated. "How?" he said.

She shrugged. "I just had a feeling. So I looked inside his nappy, and he had a, you know, a . . . *boy's thing*."

Matty's eyes boggled.

"And I found the blue bootees and the hat in my mum's bin. How did you know?"

"Because I heard my mum saying something."

"Saying what?"

"She was talking to Kate in the kitchen after your mum went to bed and I was in the toilet and they didn't know and I heard my mum saying: 'Something's not right about that baby. Are you thinking what I'm thinking?' and then I accidentally banged the chain against the wall and they heard it and shushed each other, and that was all they said, but it got me thinking because it doesn't seem right, does it? I mean, for a kickoff, that baby is way too big to be new, so just now I snuck into your mum's room and I took Seth's piggywig because I remember that piggywig was exactly the same size as Seth when he was born and I put piggywig next to the baby in the cot and the baby was just *massive* compared to it. And now it's clear, isn't it? Cut-and-dried case? Your mum stole that baby from the shops, Melody Ribblesdale, and we're the only people who know about it."

Melody gulped and nodded.

"You know that the grown-ups are about to work it out though, don't you? And once they've worked it out they'll go to the police and the police will take the baby away and put your mum in prison, and Ken too, for being a willing accomplice? It's all about to come crashing down, the whole thing, and you need to decide what you're going to do about it."

"Do about it?" Melody felt her breath catch.

"Yes. Are you going to run and hide, or stay and face the music?"

"I don't know," she whispered breathlessly. "What would you do?"

"Run," he said, "run for the hills."

"But what about the baby?"

Matty shrugged. "Leave the baby here," he said matter-of-factly. "The police will sort it all out. But you and your mum should pack a bag and just go. Now. Tonight. As far away as you can get. I won't tell a soul." He zipped his lips with his fingertips and stared at her solemnly.

Melody's heart was racing. Her big secret no longer felt like a showy gift but like moldering poison. She hadn't thought about her mum's going to prison. She'd only thought about her being sad that the baby was gone. If her mum went to prison and Ken went to prison, then who'd look after her? She'd have to go to America and share a room with the maid and not go to school and wear ragged clothes, like Cinderella. Or she could go and live with sad Auntie Maggie in London, which wouldn't be so bad, although they didn't have a bedroom for her either, so she might end up sleeping on the floor, and their house wasn't all clean and luxurious like the house in Hollywood. There was Auntie Susie, of course, who had plenty of room for her, but didn't know anything about children, or she could stay here with Grace and Seth and Matty, but that might not be allowed on account of their not being related to her.

She sighed heavily and stared back at Matty. "You're right," she said. "I'll go and wake her up."

Her mother was nestled right next to the baby in the little single bed and if you didn't know better you'd have said that they were the perfect mother and child, slumbering peacefully, sharing each other's breath. Jane stirred as the door opened and then awoke with a start.

"Shhh," she said, "don't wake the baby!"

"Mum," said Melody, "we've got to go. We've got to go now. We know about the baby. Everyone knows about the baby. And if we don't go now, they'll call the police and you and Ken will be sent to prison!"

"Melody, what are you talking about?"

"We know the baby is Edward Mason. I know. Matty knows. And I know Grace and Kate are thinking it too. Leave the baby and let's go!"

"I really have no idea what you're talking about."

"*They're going to call the police! They'll put you in jail!*" she cried, tugging at her mother's arm. "Don't you understand? Mum! Don't you understand?"

Jane tutted and pulled her arm from Melody's grip. "Honestly, Melody. Please will you be quiet? You'll wake Amber."

Melody stopped then and looked at her mother, really looked at her. She was mad. It was suddenly horribly and utterly clear to her. Not unstable. Not imbalanced, but actually properly mad like the old lady on the seafront with the stuffed ferret and the crinoline. She was quiet for a moment while she considered her next move. She realized that even if she were to stand here for the next hour and a half repeating over and over the words, "That baby is

Edward Mason," it would make no impact at all in her mother's current delusional state of insanity. So instead she sighed and stroked her mother's cheek and said, "It's OK. Why don't you go back to sleep?"

Her mother stared back at her, breathing heavily, a look of panic starting to fade from her features. "Yes," she said, "yes. I will. I'll see you in the morning, darling. Get some rest."

Melody backed out of the room, watching as her mother laid her head back on the pillow and pulled the blanket closer around the baby's shoulders.

She tiptoed slowly back to her bedroom.

Matty sat bolt upright in his bed as she walked in. "Well," he said, "what happened? Are you going?"

Melody shook her head. "No," she said sadly. "She didn't want to go. I'll try again tomorrow."

Matty tutted impatiently. "There won't be a tomorrow, don't you realize that? Tomorrow is officially canceled, on account of your mum being arrested and carted off in a bloody great Black Maria!"

"Yes, I know that," she said defiantly, "but she won't go and there's nothing I can do to make her. We'll just have to let it happen."

Matty tutted again and shook his head. "Your lookout, Melody Ribblesdale," he said, "your life. But you'll regret this when you're in a children's home sleeping on a thin mattress and eating slops. You really will."

He turned over then and Melody contemplated the curve of his back for a while and thought about what he'd said. The idea of a children's home chilled her to the bone. But then the idea of disappearing into the cold, dark night with her unhinged mother, with just a change of clothing and not a penny between them, chilled her even more. She closed her eyes and let sleep carry her away.

Chapter 36

1979

The next morning, it was tempting for a while for Melody to believe that everything that had happened last night had been a dream. Her mother sat at the kitchen table with the baby asleep on her shoulder, while she ate a slice of wholemeal toast and read the papers. Grace poured tea from a giant pot into mugs for the adults. Seth sat on his shaggy dog and wheeled himself up and down the terra-cotta floor. Kate sat on Michael's lap while they both read dog-eared paperbacks. And Ken polished his big old army boots with a yellow cloth and a tin of Cherry Blossom.

In some ways it was just like a normal morning. But there was a humming undercurrent of tension, of expectation. Nobody smiled. Nobody moved. It was as if they were all waiting for a taxi.

At ten o'clock the doorbell rang. The adults all glanced at each other nervously and Ken went to answer it. A moment later three policemen walked through the kitchen door and Ken pointed at Melody's mum and they walked up to her and one of them said, "Are you Jane Victoria Ribblesdale?" and she nodded and then he said, "I am arresting you under suspicion of the abduction and imprisonment of Edward James Mason. You do not have to say anything, but anything you do say will be taken down and may be used in evidence in a court of law. Do you understand?"

Her mother nodded mutely and a lady officer came forward clutching a white blanket. "Now, Mrs. Ribblesdale," she said, "I need you to give me the baby. Can you do that?"

Jane's face started to crumple then and she pulled the sleeping baby closer to her. "She's sleeping," she said. "Can't you wait until she's awake?"

"I'm sorry, Mrs. Ribblesdale, but we'll have to take him now. The mother is waiting anxiously. Please, let me take him."

A tear rolled down Jane's cheek then, and she held the sleeping baby out in front of her to look at him. His head flopped pathetically and he grimaced as he struggled to hold on to sleep. "It's time to go now, my beautiful angel," she said, her voice catching on every word. "I've had a lovely time looking after you, I really have, but it's time to go now." She glanced up at the WPC. "She'll need a coat," she said. "It's cold out."

"That's OK," the policewoman said kindly. "I've got a blanket. He'll be fine."

Jane nodded mutely and kissed the baby once, on the cheek, before passing him to the WPC. "Bye-bye, Amber Rose," she said, as the WPC and the baby left the room. "Bye-bye, my beautiful baby."

The two remaining police officers looked down at Jane. "We'll need you to come with us now for questioning. Is there anything you need to do before we go?"

Jane looked blankly around the room, at the worried faces of her friends and her daughter, and she shook her head. "No," she said, "there's nothing. Shall we just go?"

She got to her feet and smiled at everyone. "It's OK," she said, "I don't mind. I really don't mind."

Grace passed her her coat and smiled back at her. They all followed her up the stairs and to the front door, and it wasn't until she was about to get into the police car parked outside that the younger of the two officers said to Jane: "What about your daughter?"

And Jane looked up, slightly surprised, stared right at Melody, and said, "Oh, she'll be fine here, won't you, darling?" before smiling wanly, and allowing herself to be lowered into the car.

Melody stood at the front door and watched as the car pulled away and waited for her mother to turn round, just once, turn round and wave. But she didn't. She stared straight ahead, smiling benignly, unconcerned about her parentless child, looking not scared, not upset, but really very relieved.

Chapter 37

Now

The cuttings in a carrier bag made a swishing sound against her denim jeans as Melody walked up the Mall, toward Charing Cross. It felt remarkable to her that the people she passed by, heading for home, for drinks, for trains, had no idea of what lay within that innocuous plastic bag. It was similar to the way she'd felt when she was first pregnant, before she'd started to show, like she was carrying around an incredible secret, something so big that it could turn the world on its axis if it got out. In this bag was proof, solid, black and white, irrefutable, that her real name was Melody Ribblesdale, that her mother had been called Jane, that she'd lived in a squat with a man called Ken, and that her clinically depressed mother had stolen a baby from outside a newsagent's. There was proof also that her father had been called John, that he lived in LA with a woman called Jacqui Sonningfeld and his other daughter, Emily. It was all in here, every detail of her life, of her existence, in the year 1979, two years before a house fire in Canterbury had taken away her memory and saved her from the terrible truth. But there was more, she knew there was more, she'd seen something that had hinted at it and had stopped reading because she'd absorbed enough already, enough for now, and any more could wait.

Ed was out when she got home half an hour later. She breathed a sigh of relief. She didn't want to see him. She didn't want to have to explain to him that he came from a family of lunatics and criminals. She didn't want to have to explain anything to him.

She unscrewed the cap from a bottle of something white that had been in her fridge for weeks, something that Stacey had left there after a girls' night in, and she poured it into a large glass. She dipped her shaking hand into her handbag and pulled out her Marlboro Lights, indifferent to the fact that she didn't really want one, needing to do something physical to give her the resolve she needed to make it through the next few moments. She didn't taste the cigarette, just welcomed the instant softness the nicotine brought to her head, the blurring of too much reality.

She spread the cuttings out onto the kitchen table and she arranged them into date order. She wanted to start from the beginning, and she wanted to end at the end. She wanted to read her story properly.

Chapter 38

1979

The day after the police came to arrest Jane, a social worker called Beverly, a police officer called Cheryl, and Melody's auntie Susie all came to the house for a meeting, to discuss Melody's future. Ken sat in on the meeting too.

Melody wore her best dress, the gypsy dress that Jacqui had bought for her in America, because her mother didn't like her wearing it, and now that her mother wasn't here she could wear whatever she wanted. She put it over a brown ribbed polo-neck and wore it with brown tights and lace-up shoes. She also had on her mum's wooden-beaded necklace and a slick of Green Apple lip gloss that Charlotte had given her. She wanted to look grown-up and elegant, the sort of sensible little girl who could fend for herself quite nicely, thank you very much.

Auntie Susie looked shocked to find herself sitting in a house that wasn't hers. She was wearing a lime-green kaftan and jade-green sandals, and her bleached blond hair was piled on top of her head like the whipped cream on top of a fruit salad. "Awful," she kept sniffing into her lace-edged handkerchief. "Just awful."

The social worker called Beverly was also overweight, but dressed more soberly than Susie, in a brown sack dress and thick ribbed tights. She wore horn-rimmed glasses and had square hair the color of toffee apples. She didn't smile much and kept giving Melody suspicious glances as if she thought she might be about to commit a terrible crime right under her nose.

The social worker wanted to have the meeting without Melody's being there, but Ken insisted. "She's a very wise girl," he said, "old for her years. She needs to know exactly what's happening."

Beverly pursed her lips and said nothing, but she didn't tell Melody to go, so she stayed where she was, perched on a piano stool.

"Well," she began, "we have made contact with the father, in Los Angeles. He will be flying back to the UK at his earliest possible convenience. Possibly today. Hopefully tomorrow, at the latest. In the meantime Mrs. Ribblesdale has asked that Melody be put in the care of her sister Miss Susan Newsome."

"No!"

The adults all turned to look at Melody and she gulped. "Sorry," she said.

Her aunt patted her hand. "I know," she said, "I know how awful all this must be for you. But you mustn't be worried. I'll take very good care of you."

Melody felt guilty for not wanting to go and live with her aunt, but really, the thought of all those rich meals and dull evenings and talk of Jesus Christ Our Lord was more than she could bear.

"You know," she said, in her most organized voice, "I'm a bit worried about something. If I'm living with Aunt Susie, who's going to walk me to school in the mornings?"

The grown-ups all looked at each other and then at Susie.

"Well," began the social worker, "your aunt, I would imagine . . ."

"No, but you see, Aunt Susie can't really walk, on account of her hips, you see."

Aunt Susie threw the social worker an apologetic look. "It's true," she said. "I'm far from mobile."

"I could walk her," said Ken. "In fact, I could take her in to school every day and pick her up too. I have a motorbike," he added.

Aunt Susie threw him a look. "I'm not sure the back of a motorbike is a very suitable place for a six-year-old girl."

"I'm seven next week," Melody interjected.

"Or a seven-year-old girl," Susie continued.

"And it's not the back. It's the sidecar."

"Well," she said, breathing in heavily and conclusively, as if a sidecar were somehow intrinsically evil.

"I tend to agree, Miss Newsome," said the social worker. "Is there any other option?"

"Well, I could just walk there and back. Though from where Miss Newsome lives, it would take over half an hour."

"And, Mr. Stone, who are you, exactly, in relation to the minor?"

"I'm her, well, I'm her—"

"He's my friend," Melody interrupted. "My best friend."

"I'm her guardian," he said. "I've been caring for her during her mother's illness."

"And you, Melody, where would you like to stay until your father arrives?"

"Here," she said, relieved that someone was finally asking her a direct question. "I want to stay here with Ken and Grace and Matty and Seth."

The social worker stopped and wrote something in her notepad. "The thing is, Melody," she said a moment later, "it's very important for your mother, and for us as the people responsible for your welfare, that you are staying with someone as closely related to you as is possible. I appreciate that you are comfortable here, that this is the place that you call home, but an environment of this type, an illegally tenanted house, it's not the best place for you to be without the care of your mother. And given that your aunt is both local and has the space to accommodate you, I feel it is in the best interests of everyone involved that you stay with her until your father gets back to England. Now, if you could just go upstairs and pack a little bag, we'll get you to your aunt's as soon as possible."

"But what about getting to school?" Melody said.

"Mr. Stone will be responsible for collecting you and dropping you off. It's only for a day or two. Just until your father gets back. After that we'll have to review the situation. OK?" She smiled, acknowledging that this wasn't a question but a statement of fact.

Melody felt a blackness begin to engulf her then, a sense of everything familiar being stripped away from her. But then she thought of her father, sitting on a plane, possibly even now, on his way to England, on his way to get her. She smiled.

"OK," she said brightly.

"Would you like someone to help you pack your things?" Beverly asked.

"No." Melody shook her head. "I'd rather do it myself."

Matty looked at her with curiosity when she walked into their bedroom a moment later.

"So," he said, "are they sending you to a children's home?"

"No," she said, taking her mother's big canvas shoulder bag out of a drawer and beginning to fill it with things she thought she might need. "I'm going to my aunt Susie's."

"What, that big, fat lady who can't breathe properly?"

"Yes."

"Well, I guess that's better than the home."

"I told them I wanted to stay here, but they weren't really listening."

"I told you they wouldn't. There's no way they'd let you stay here. Not with a bunch of old hippies and unmarried mothers and God knows what. It was never going to happen." He shook his head sagely.

"Well, my dad's coming back really soon, so I'll probably end up going to America to live with him, so it's only for a little while. I don't mind, just for a little while." She smiled bravely, but there were tears prickling at the backs of her eyeballs and a lump like a grapefruit in her throat.

Matty got to his feet and took the bag from her. "Here," he said, "let me hold that for you."

"Thank you," she said.

She placed underpants, socks, vests, and tights in the bag. Then she chose two dresses, her school uniform, some books, a hair clip, and, on a last-minute whim, a scarf of her mother's that smelled like her.

"What about a sweater?" said Matty, helpfully. "It's winter, after all."

Melody smiled gratefully and put two sweaters in the bag. She put out her hand to take the bag from Matty, but he slung it over his shoulder. "It's all right," he said, "I've got it."

The two children walked slowly together down the stairs and as they walked Melody suddenly remembered the first time she'd walked up these stairs, two years ago, her mother by her side, wondering what sort of place it was and what on earth they were both doing there. And now she was leaving this strange house, without her mother and with no idea whether or not she'd ever see it again.

Everyone kissed and hugged her at the door. Grace made sure her coat was buttoned up and Ken gave her a five-pound note and the phone number for the house on a small piece of paper. She got into a car with the social worker and the police officer and Auntie Susie, who had to be wedged in because it wasn't a very big car, and all her friends stood on the curb, smiling but looking sad.

"I'll be at yours first thing tomorrow morning for school," said Ken, his eyes looking damp with tears even though he was trying to sound stern.

Matty put his mouth to the car window and blew his cheeks right out. "*Arrivederci*, Melody Ribblesdale!" he shouted through the glass, and Melody laughed, but inside she was wishing that he hadn't done it because it reminded her too much of what a funny boy he was and how much she was going to miss him.

She craned her neck as the car headed away from the house and watched the small group of waving people recede from view. And then she turned her head to face the front. To face her new future.

Chapter 39

Now

"What are you up to?"

It was Ed, back from a day in the park with his mates. His face was pink from too much sunshine and too much beer. The sunshine worried Melody more than the beer.

She quickly shuffled the photocopies into a pile and put her wineglass down on them. "Nothing much," she said, stretching out her tense neck muscles, "just some bills and stuff. You look happy."

"Yeah, I am. Tiffany Baxter just stroked my hair."

Melody smiled. "Did she?"

"She did. Like this . . ." He put the palm of his hand against Melody's head and shook it.

"More of a ruffle, really," said Melody.

"Yeah, I guess it was a ruffle. But it was a meaningful ruffle."

"So things are moving on, are they?"

Ed smiled and pulled a can of Coke from the fridge. "Kind of," he said. "I've invited her to my birthday party. She says she'll come. And that other bloke, the one with the car, he's going to stay with his dad up north for a month, which means *no competition*."

"Yay!" said Melody, pulling an old copy of *Exchange & Mart* over the pile of papers and moving the whole thing to the other side of the table.

"So," he said, pulling up a chair and sitting down next to her, "how was Broadstairs? Did you find the Matthew bloke?"

"Nope," she said. "Looked everywhere. Not a trace. I asked about him and apparently he often disappears, goes home somewhere to dry out."

"Oh," said Ed, looking slightly deflated. "Anything else?"

She shook her head, hating the feeling of lying to her son. He was so keen to get involved. He thought it was some great adventure, like a story line in *Hollyoaks*, and she wanted to share this with him, but she needed to know how it was all going to end first. She needed the full picture. The truth would have to wait. "No," she said, smiling regretfully, "nothing else."

"Did you try the library?"

"Uh-huh. Nothing there. Just loads of old shipping news and stuff."

"Well, then," he said simply, getting to his feet. "Looks like you'll just have to call your parents. Either that or spend the rest of your life in blissful ignorance."

When he had gone Melody glanced down at the table and let her gaze wander across the edges of a headline, the headline of a story she hadn't read yet, but that suggested a truth so awful that maybe blissful ignorance would be the better state to choose.

Chapter 40

1979

Another memory:

Basil Brush on the TV.

Boom boom.

A half-peeled satsuma in her hand.

The late afternoon sun shimmering through Aunt Susie's net curtains, alighting on motes of dust and filling the air with sparkles.

A hole in her tights, her only pair of tights.

The fearsome smell of supper being prepared, a smell that would turn out to be sole meunière and honey-glazed carrots.

The phone ringing in the hallway.

Aunt Susie's labored footsteps.

"Good afternoon, Susan Newsome speaking. Who is calling?"

Then, a silence.

"I see. I see. Yes, I see. How did this happen? Oh, I see."

Her aunt Susie standing in the doorway, in a rose-print apron, clutching a blue and white striped tea towel and uttering the words, "Sweetheart, I have some bad news for you. Some very bad news."

Boom boom.

Jane's court case was heard three months later, at Canterbury Crown Court. Except nobody called her Jane anymore. She was now known as the Broadstairs Baby Snatcher. Or Evil Jane. Similarly, nobody really referred to Melody as simply Melody anymore. She was poor Melody. Or tragic Melody. Or poor, tragic daughter of Evil Jane, Broadstairs Baby Snatcher.

Her whole world had been assigned new adjectives. She was now part of a "Cursed Family" to whom "Tragic and Terrible" things happened. Including three days after her mother's arrest, and on the eve of Melody's long-anticipated seventh birthday, the arrival by telephone of the news that her father had been killed in a multiple pileup on the freeway out of Hollywood and toward Los Angeles International Airport.

And it was for this fact, more than for the years of indifferent mothering, more than for not loving her the way a lovely little girl deserves to be loved, more than for being so horrible to her father that he'd left her and gone to live in America with Jacqui, and more than for stealing somebody else's baby and letting her believe that she finally had a sister she could keep, that Melody now despised her mother. Because if her mother hadn't got herself arrested, then her father wouldn't have been on his way to the airport to fly home to look after her, and he would still be alive, and everything else in her life might, eventually, have rearranged itself into something vaguely resembling normality. As it was, normality, even of the living-in-a-squat-with-strangers-and-strange-sexual-practices type, seemed a nebulous and unlikely state of affairs.

Parents, Melody realized, were the linchpin of normality, even when they were far from normal themselves. Parents, even distracted, slightly ambivalent parents, acted as a kind of strainer through which life got poured. They were there, in essence, to catch the lumpy bits. Without a parent, life felt oblique and directionless. Without a parent, the world was too close for comfort.

Melody had a dozen people looking out for her. She had Aunt Susie, Aunt Maggie, Ken, Grace, Kate, and Michael. The teachers at school were extra nice to her and even Penny seemed to think it beyond the pale to torment a girl who'd lost both parents within a week of each other. Beverly the social worker visited regularly and her grandmother on her father's side had even come to spend a week with her at Susie's house, the first time she'd set foot outside of Ireland since her husband had died twenty-two years previously.

Everyone cared about her. And Susie was, in some ways, a better carer than her mother ever was, especially since Beverly had explained to her that duck and grape fricassee wasn't really a suitable supper for a seven-year-old, and that she'd probably be happier with sausages and mash. Susie didn't seem to realize that children should be encouraged to look after themselves and did everything for Melody, including doing up the buckles on her shoes and brushing her teeth. Sometimes Melody felt like she should tell Susie that it was OK, that she could do those things for herself, but she didn't because deep down inside, she liked being treated like a three-year-old.

But in spite of all the fuss and attention, and in spite of all the grown-ups who cared about her and worried about her, Melody still didn't feel safe. She still felt like she was tiptoeing blindfolded around the perimeter of a very large, very deep hole. She still wanted her mummy.

But sadly, access to her mummy was somewhat restricted.

Jane's conditional bail had been overturned after she'd told the police that if they let her go, she'd go straight to Ramsgate and throw herself off the cliffs, and she'd been held in a secure unit in Rochester pending trial ever since.

Of course, Melody didn't actually know that her mother had threatened suicide. She also didn't know that her mother barely thought about her between visits and mainly sat in her bedroom thinking about her lost babies (she included Melody in this category, having read somewhere that a child leaves the opaque and semi-formed world of infanthood and enters the clearer, more unyielding world of adulthood around their seventh birthday). There were, as ever, a million things that Melody didn't know about her life, cogs and wheels turning in dark corners that would affect her entire existence forevermore. But for now all she knew was this: It was Wednesday. It was January. It was cold. She'd had kedgeree for breakfast. And today instead of PE and science, she was going to visit her mother in prison.

Once upon a time there was a little girl called Melody. She had long wavy hair the color of conkers and eyes the color of burnished gold and she lived by the seaside in a big house with a smiling face with her mummy, Jane, and a man called Ken. Melody had a daddy too. He was a printer and he lived in London with a makeup artist called Jacqui, Jacqui's daughter Charlotte, and a lovely little baby called Emily Elizabeth, who was Melody's only sister. Melody sometimes stayed with her other family in the house in London and always felt sad when she had to come back to the seaside, because, you see, Melody's mum wasn't very happy and didn't give Melody many cuddles or kisses. But Melody was happy by the sea because of Ken, who was kind and good, and took her for ice cream every week on a motorbike with a sidecar.

Then one day, a very sad thing happened. John and Jacqui went away to a far distant land and they took Melody's little sister with them. Melody was very sad, and cried and cried for days. But then something happened to make her feel happy again. Her mummy made her a new baby sister. Everyone loved the new baby sister, especially Ken, but Melody knew that there was something wrong. The new baby didn't look like it was brand-new. And then the newspapers said that a baby had been stolen from outside a shop and Melody knew that that was what had happened.

The next day the police came and took the baby away and then they took Melody's mum away. They said she was very unwell and that she couldn't come home, because if she did she might hurt herself. Melody's daddy wanted to come to the seaside then, to take Melody away with him to the far distant land, but a terrible thing happened and he died on the motorway trying to get to her. So now Melody had nobody at all, except for her strange auntie Susie.

After three months Melody's mum went to a court and the judge told her that she was to be sent to prison for two years.

Melody never saw her again.

The next thing she knew, she was lying on her back outside a burning house with some other people called Mum and Dad.

And they all lived happily ever after . . .

Chapter 41

Now

The following day was Cleo's eighteenth-birthday party. Melody opened up a carrier bag and put inside it two wrapped gifts: a set of lingerie from Ted Baker and a crystal-encrusted silver cross from H. Samuel. Then she opened a card on the kitchen table and let her pen hover above it for a moment while she tried to find the right words. She didn't know where to start. That person, the one called Melody Browne, who'd stood at the side of Stacey's hospital bed all those years ago, fifteen years old, nine months pregnant, scared and elated, holding this new life in her arms, this tiny little scrap of stuff that was destined to become a woman called Cleo—that person didn't exist anymore. She'd been erased, taken out with a click of Julius Sardo's fingers and the swoosh of a photocopying machine in Broadstairs Library.

There was no such person as Melody Browne, so who was this, writing a birthday card to the firstborn child of her oldest and dearest friend? She tried to imagine what she'd have written two weeks ago, before her life had been whipped up into a sensational maelstrom, but couldn't put herself there. She wanted it to be poignant, meaningful, loving. She had watched Cleo grow from a scrappy, tufty-haired infant, into a skinny, knock-kneed child, and then blossom from a gangly adolescent into a stunning five-foot-ten flame-haired beauty with a double-D chest. She had loved her as her own. And that was when it came to her, an echo of something that Ed had said to her before everything had changed. She put the pen to the card and she wrote: "To Beautiful Cleo, the daughter I never had and could only have dreamed of. I am so proud of you. Happy Birthday, from your loving auntie Mel xxx."

As always, Pete and Stacey had found the money from somewhere to hire a function room above the smartest Italian restaurant in Hackney and fill it with helium balloons, banners, and Easter lilies (Cleo's middle name was Lily). Tall sash windows opened out onto the noise of Mare Street and paper-covered trestle tables bowed under the weight of bowls of pasta, platters of cold meat, and piles of whole ciabatta. Melody and Ed were the first to arrive, a full half an hour before the designated start time of seven thirty.

Cleo's remarkable eighteen-year-old body was wrapped up in a tight purple satin dress from TK Maxx and her red hair had clearly been arranged by a professional hairdresser into intricate snakes that twisted around themselves and left the nape of her neck naked, except for the clasp of a stunning Swarovski necklace. Her eyes were heavily kohled, and she looked to Melody like a creature directly off the pages of one of the daft celebrity magazines that Stacey always had lying around at her house.

She hugged her to her and breathed in her perfume, looking for that smell of smallness and newness that she'd exuded for so long, which was, of course, long gone now, and anyway indistinguishable beneath the overwhelming aroma of Agent Provocateur, her signature scent.

"Happy birthday," Melody said, stroking the bare skin of her back, the same back she'd rubbed all those years earlier from time to time, trying to dislodge a bubble of gas. "You look absolutely beautiful, Clee, seriously, like a film star!"

"Oh, thanks, Mel!" Cleo hugged her back.

Stacey was scurrying around in a tight red rip-off of the Roland Mouret Galaxy dress from ASOS, her hair also professionally preened and a cigarette hanging from her painted lips. She kissed Melody distractedly and directed her to a table on the other side of the room where gifts were to be deposited. Ed was talking to Cleo. Melody watched them fondly. Her boy and her best friend's girl. Of course she and Stacey had fantasized over the years that they would become teenage sweethearts, get married, and make them both beautiful grandchildren to share, but inevitably a lifetime of living in each other's pockets, of bickering, rowing, and stubborn ignoring, had put paid to that, and now they rarely saw each other. Besides, Cleo had a boyfriend now, a man of twenty, tall and sinewy with a fine-boned face and very thick hair, called Jade, with whom she was deeply in love.

"You all right?" Stacey narrowed her eyes at her.

"Yes, I'm fine."

"You sure? You seem a bit . . ."

"What?"

"I don't know. A bit *off*."

"Honestly," said Melody. "I'm fine." She wanted to tell Stacey about everything, now that she knew that she wasn't mad, now that she had hard evidence that her mind was sound, but she couldn't, not tonight, not here.

"Oh, Mel," said Stacey, pulling her toward her for a hug, "my baby! Look at her! She's not a baby anymore." She smelled of nicotine and beer and felt tiny inside Melody's embrace.

"Oh!" Melody had remembered something, something so important that she could barely believe she hadn't already asked. "The test! Did you do it?"

Stacey let go of her and put her finger to her lips. "No," she said softly, "not yet. I want to get this week out of the way first. I'll do it on Monday. Another few days isn't going to hurt."

Melody nodded distractedly. She didn't agree. This baby, if it was a baby, was yet another gift in Stacey's overflowing basket of life. She should treasure it, nurture it, respect it, if for no other reason than to show gratitude for her myriad blessings.

Stacey looked at her pursed-up mouth and smiled. "Don't you go all moral majority on me, Melody Browne! You know as well as I do that there's nothing there yet, just a bunch of bubbles. I can't get my head round the idea of a baby right at this very moment. And tonight is my *first* baby's big night and I am not going to miss out on that when for all I know I might not even be pregnant. So, unpurse those lips and go and get yourself a beer!"

Melody felt detached from the celebrations that night. The whole affair came to her like a painting in a gallery, like a scene from a stage play. She saw the guests as characters, whom she stood and observed from somewhere in the cheap seats. She saw Cleo, the beautiful princess; her mother, Queen Stacey; and her father, King Pete, in his Burton suit and the Paul Smith shirt that Stacey had bought for him in the sale last summer. She watched as Princess Cleo moved to her father's side and pulled herself into him, she saw King Pete lean down and kiss her head, not his daughter in any biological way, but his daughter nonetheless. She saw the new princess, Clover, in a mauve velvet dress from Monsoon that she had helped Stacey pick out last Saturday, her hair held back with a velvet rose, dancing with her cousins, her tiny face alive with excitement. She saw Stacey's mum, Pat, the Queen Mother, looking ragged and confused, leaning into her walking frame on a chair in the corner, and she saw Stacey's brother, Paul, looking chipper, cheery, and whippet thin in jeans and a Nike sweatshirt, underdressed as ever. His pregnant wife stood next to him, clutching a glass of Coke with both hands and watching her children dance with Clover, her eyes filled with pride.

Melody absorbed the scene, and then began, subconsciously, to paste strange, new faces over the familiar faces in front of her. She put the gentle, equine face of a man called John Ribblesdale over the face of Pete and the startled, bloated, but distinctively pretty face of a woman called Jane Ribblesdale over the face of Stacey. The children she transposed with the faces of a baby called Edward Thomas, bald and creased and freshly hatched, and a lovely little girl called Emily Elizabeth, whose face she had to invent because there'd been no pictures of her. She saw the sad, faded faces of her parents, the other ones, the ones who'd saved her from the fire, and she saw a man called Ken, beautiful and kind, just as she'd pictured him, with a face like Jesus Christ. Her family. Her real family. Not this borrowed family that she'd lived vicariously through for the past eighteen years, and not the tiny family she'd made for herself, the one that consisted of just her and Ed, but another family, a big one, one that belonged exclusively to her, a family with roots and feet and legs and arms, a family that had crumbled into pieces and been blown across the world by a cruel breeze.

This could have been her life, she thought, this rich, dizzying whirl of humanity with all its faults and foibles and oddness. But something sad and irreversible had happened when she was too young and unformed to understand or even to remember, and now she was left here, in limbo, between a place she thought she knew and a place she might have known. She looked again at Pete, big and strong, kind and shy, and she thought of the man who'd died on an American freeway twenty-seven years ago on his way to get her, and she wanted, more than anything in the world, for him to walk through the door, in his best suit and shoes, smile at her, and say, *Hello, Melody, where've you been?*

The party went on until past midnight, until the tightly coiled snakes of Cleo's hair had unfurled into shaggy tendrils and the kohl around her eyes had smudged into grayness. Melody got into a minicab and let out a sigh of relief. Ed had stayed behind, invited back to Stacey's house to carry on the party, and Melody was glad to be alone. Feeling softened with the warmth of celebration, Melody pulled her mobile phone out of her handbag and opened up the last text message from Ben, the one she'd read on the train on the way to Broadstairs yesterday. She pictured Ben as she read it—his name suited him so well—Gentle Ben, a gentle man. She smiled. And then she imagined him waiting for her in her flat, cross-legged on her sofa, reading a book (he seemed the type of man who would read). She imagined him glancing up at the sound of her footsteps in the hallway, putting down his book, smiling: *How are you? How was your night?* And then she imagined herself kicking off these stupid heels, curling up next to him, resting her tired heavy head against his strong shoulder, and saying: *Lovely, really lovely. I wish you'd been there, though.* And she felt it, for the first time in her adult life: a hole, a space—room for someone in her life. And soon, when she knew exactly who she was, she'd press "reply" and let fate dictate the rest.

She switched off her phone, and let it rest in her lap while she turned to face the moving scenery.

Out there, she mused, as the neon lights of an East End Saturday night flashed and flickered at her through the window of the cab, out there was a girl called Emily, a girl who was her sister. And out there was a man called Edward, who'd been stolen from his mother by her own mother. Out there, right now, maybe there, in that Turkish restaurant, there was a woman called Jacqui who'd lived with her father for two years. And out there, maybe, was another woman called Jane who'd given birth to her.

She'd read her story again and again over the past few days, gone through the copied cuttings until they were worn through by her inquisitive fingertips, and now she knew nearly everything. She knew what had happened to her from the ages of four till seven. But she still didn't know what had happened before. And she still didn't know what happened next. What twisted knot of fate had brought her to a Broadstairs squat, and how had she ended up living in a Canterbury cul-de-sac with a pair of strangers called Mum and Dad?

Chapter 42

1980

Ken took her to see her mum in prison, in his sidecar.

Ken had put in a few hours over the past months, sweet-talking Auntie Susie, who was now no longer of the opinion that he was "an unsuitable companion for a young child," and now thought of him as a "fine young man," and even "a sweetheart." She allowed Ken to take Melody to school every morning and bring her home every afternoon (particularly after an attempt to walk there had been marred by people stopping and staring at Melody and saying things in stage whispers, like, "That's her, the baby-snatcher's kid!") and twice a week to take her out for ice cream at Morelli's, or back to the house in town for tea with Matty and Seth.

Her mum was sitting in a big patterned chair with plastic sleeves on the arms when they were let into the visiting room at the prison. Melody and Ken sat on stools without backs and drank water out of plastic cups.

"How are you, darling?" asked her mother.

"I'm fine," Melody said, trying not to be put off by her mother's strange demeanor. Ken had said that they'd had to give her special medicine to stop her feeling so sad and that she might not seem quite herself, but she hadn't expected her to look quite so swollen and gray. Her face was all shiny and tight, and her eyes were all sunken and beady, like raisins stuck in dough. Her hair was scraped back into a greasy ponytail and she was wearing gray prison clothes that made her look like a street cleaner. But what was worse was that she was wearing lipstick, just a touch, peachy pink and poorly applied. Melody's mum hardly ever wore lipstick and Melody knew she'd put it on, a) because she was mad, and b) because she thought it would make her look nice. Which it didn't. It just made her look like a fat, mad, greasy woman in lipstick.

"And how is school?"

"School's fine," Melody replied.

"Is everyone being kind to you?"

"Yes," she said, "even Penny."

"Penny?" said her mother vaguely. "Do I know Penny?"

"I shouldn't think so," Melody said. "I didn't tell you about her because I thought you might make a scene. She was picking on me for ages, about living in the squat with you and Ken and everything. But since you stole the baby, she's been all right to me."

"Good." Her mother nodded distractedly and looked mildly pleased with herself for having relieved Melody of Penny's attentions. "And how are you getting on with Auntie Susie?"

"Fine," said Melody, staring at a swirl on the worn-out Axminster carpet and thinking that it looked a bit like a running dog. "She makes me proper food now sometimes. And she bought me some clothes for Christmas. Nice clothes."

"Oh," said Jane, "that's nice. I'm glad it's working out. And did she give you the gift from me?"

"Yes." Melody nodded, thinking of the far-too-babyish cuddly chimpanzee that had arrived in the post three days after Christmas in a slightly battered, poorly wrapped parcel with a note that said, "With love from Mum (& Father Christmas)," when everyone knew that there was no such thing as Father Christmas. "Thank you."

"Sorry it was a bit late, but it's hard to get organized in this place. You know. So many rules and regulations." She laughed and put her hand to her hair, and Melody squirmed and thought that she wanted to go now. The woman sitting in front of her was not her mother. She was not the mother she'd lived with in London, who'd had a job and a throaty laugh and a penchant for rum punch, and neither was she the mother she'd lived with in Broadstairs, who was pensive and sad and prone to doing absentminded things like forgetting to cook her tea. This woman was like someone in a rubber suit doing a poor impersonation of her mother. No, in fact this woman was just like a rubber suit without a body in it at all. This woman was *empty*.

"And how are you, Ken?" Jane turned and fixed her unsettling smile upon him.

"Good," he said. "Well. Fine."

"And how's everyone else? Grace? Matty?"

"Fine," he said again, "everyone's fine."

It fell silent for a moment and Melody looked around the room. She wasn't the only kid here. All the people in this prison were women, so quite a few had their children here to see them. There was a girl, just by the window, about the same age as Melody, with a much younger brother of about two. Their mother didn't have the same strange, glassy look that Jane had. Their mother was crying, and trying to look brave all at the same time. Their mother had a scrunched-up tissue in her hand and kept squeezing both her children's hands. Their mother looked horrified to find herself talking to her children in a prison lounge.

Melody stared at her mother's hands for a while. They were very pale and she had a little bruise on the top of one of her veins and a little scab. "What's that?" she asked, pointing at the mark.

Her mother glanced down, vaguely. "That? Oh, I don't know, some kind of injection. They're always injecting you with something or other in this place. If it's not going down your gullet it's being pumped down your veins." She laughed inappropriately.

Melody paused then and waited, to see whether if she was quiet for a moment her mother might say something about her father, but she didn't. Instead she smiled at Ken and said: "So, how's everyone?" for the second time, as if she'd forgotten that she'd already asked him.

"Did you know?" Melody interrupted impatiently. "Did you know about Dad?"

"Yes," said Jane. "It's very, very sad. And you . . ."—she looked at Melody quizzically, as if something had just occurred to her—"you must be feeling very sad, I suppose. Are you?"

Melody nodded sulkily.

"But you know, he should never have been there in the first place, should never have followed her over there, given up his job, his livelihood, his daughter, just to idle by a pool all day long."

"And you," shouted Melody, "you should never have stolen a baby and made him come back for me!"

"Well," said her mother, softly and in a considered tone, "perhaps not. But now we're all paying the price for our mistakes, aren't we?" She said this with an air of great wisdom, as if there were some kind of divine justice at work in all of their lives rather than just chaos, madness, and tragedy.

Melody didn't want to hug her mother when they left ten minutes later. She didn't even want to kiss her on the cheek. She just wanted to get into Ken's sidecar and feel the icy wind against her hot skin. She wanted to feel clean and she wanted to feel free. A lot had happened to Melody over the past few years, but she barely thought about the three-year-old girl in the yellow bedroom in Lambeth these days. She had a vague recollection of a funeral and a man with funny hair and another slight feeling of having been present when her mother was in labor, but, like most children, Melody lived mostly in the present and in the future, with the occasional foray into last year, and she was old enough now to know that she would never again live a normal life with her mother and her father, and that what lay ahead of her was unconventional and slightly scary. There was no point in wallowing around in thoughts of what might have been. Clearly what might have been wasn't going to be, and so for now her main concerns revolved around whether or not the woman from the social services would let her live with Ken and Grace and save her from a life of Jesus and too much central heating with Auntie Susie. Melody didn't want perfection, she just wanted second best.

But even that option was going to be cruelly snatched from her that afternoon, for as Ken's bike rounded the twists and turns of the country lanes, heading back toward the coast, something terrible was happening at Auntie Susie's house, something that would rip gentle destiny from Melody's hands one more time and scatter it to the winds.

"Oh God, get her away, Ken, get her away *now*!" Aunt Susie was standing outside the house, ashen, in a summer dress and sandals, and wrapped up in a blanket. "For God's sake, don't let her see!"

But it was too late. Melody had already seen.

The front of Aunt Susie's immaculate cream bungalow had been daubed from top to toe in red and white paint with words like "Rapist's spawn!" and

"Accursed child!" and "Blood is thicker than water!!" But worse than that was the fact that the front porch had been ripped apart by some kind of explosion.

"It was a petrol bomb!" sobbed Auntie Susie, sipping sweet tea given to her by a kindly neighbor. "Imagine that! Someone made a bomb and put it through my letterbox! Here, in my house, with me inside, and thank God Melody wasn't here!"

The wall around where Susie's front door had been was jet black, and there was still smoke coming out of the exploded side windows. "Look!" she said, pointing at the gaping holes. "My stained glass! Gone! That was original you know, you can't replace stuff like that. I mean, what sort of person, what sort of person . . . ?"

A few neighbors milled around on the cold pavement, the fire brigade had been and gone, and the police were coming back later to take a statement. But for now, Susie was left here, cold and alone, outside her violated, insecure home.

"OK," said Ken, "let's get some timber, get that door boarded up. Here"—he turned to face the appalled neighbors—"have any of you got some old timber?"

Ken was taken to a neighbor's shed, while Susie and Melody were soothed and comforted in the teak-lined front room of an elderly lady called Evelyn.

"Dreadful thing," she tutted quietly, "a dreadful, dreadful thing," in a tone of voice that suggested that she was always half expecting dreadful things to happen, so when they did she was only half surprised.

But Melody was concerned not so much with the dreadfulness of the situation as with the detail of it. Why had someone called her a rapist's spawn? She knew what a rapist was. Grace had told her one day when she'd heard them say it on the radio. A rapist was a man who had sex with someone who didn't want to have sex. A rapist was a bad, bad man. And it was as she was wondering about this strange detail and thinking that she might ask, but feeling that it wasn't very nice to talk about things like that in front of an old lady, that she saw a copy of the *Kentish Gazette* on Evelyn's armchair and saw a headline that nearly took her breath away.

BABY SNATCHER IS AU PAIR RAPIST'S SISTER-IN-LAW!

Melody discreetly perched herself on the armchair and turned to read the text beneath the headline:

> It emerged today that Jane Ribblesdale, the Broadstairs Baby Snatcher, is in fact the sister-in-law of Michael Radlett, the infamous Au Pair Rapist. Radlett, 41, is married to Mrs. Ribblesdale's older sister, Margaret Radlett, 37. Last year Radlett was convicted in the Crown Court of six counts of rape committed against young women. He has been dubbed the Au Pair Rapist due to the occupation of five of his victims. He was sentenced to life imprisonment and is currently carrying out his term at Pentonville Prison in North London. Mrs. Radlett refused to comment on this story from her home in Ealing, West London.

Melody couldn't read everything but she absorbed enough to understand why there was paint on Aunt Susie's house. She put her hands in her lap and sighed. She thought of her cousins Nicola and Claire, and wished she could see them again. She thought of poor, sad Auntie Maggie, and of the last time she'd seen her. She thought about all the adults she knew and how difficult they all made it seem, just the ordinary business of getting on with life. And then she thought of Ken, the only person she knew who made being a grown-up look like something she might one day want to do, and hoped that this terrible unfolding of events might just have a silver lining, that it might make someone at the social services think she'd be much better off being taken away from her aunt and sent back to the house by the sea.

Melody *was* taken away from her aunt, a few days later, after someone posted a packet of human excrement through the letterbox of the newly refitted front door, but she wasn't sent to Ken's house by the sea, she was sent somewhere altogether different. She was sent to Canterbury to live with a couple called Clive and Gloria Browne.

Chapter 43

Now

Melody had never been into an internet café before. She'd never even been on the internet before. Stacey, who worked in an office and did most of her shopping online, always teased her about it: "You're a sodding troglodyte, Melody Browne!"

So she felt slightly nervous as she set her handbag down on the worn blue carpets of the easyInternet Café at Trafalgar Square on Sunday afternoon. The café was half full: European teenagers in generic jeans and T-shirts, their hair and skin dulled by insufficient showering facilities in scruffy hostels; tourists in shorts and sandals; immigrants applying for jobs and instant-messaging their friends and families.

She looked at the computer screen. She'd paid in advance for an hour. An hour should be enough, she assumed, though having never really used a computer before she had no idea how long this was going to take. She really didn't know where to start and the clock in the corner of the screen was ticking down the minutes.

"Excuse me," she said to an overweight Chinese teenager sitting to her left. "How do I look things up on the internet?"

The girl eased herself away from her computer and silently pressed a few buttons on Melody's keyboard.

"There"—she pointed at a box in the middle of the screen—"put in what you want to find there. Put these"—she made quotes with her fingertips—"around the words to make it more accurate. OK?"

Melody nodded gratefully. "Thank you," she said. "You saved my life."

"No probs," said the girl, returning to her seat and to a website that appeared to be selling dancewear.

Melody opened her pad, the one she'd written in on the fire escape this morning while fending off her hangover with full-fat Coke and four slices of toast:

PEOPLE TO FIND

Emily Elizabeth Ribblesdale/Sonningfeld?

Charlotte (Sonningfeld?)

Jacqui Sonningfeld

Ken Stone

Grace (Stone?)

Seth (Stone?)

Matty ??

JANE RIBBLESDALE (NEWSOME?)

Susie/Susan Newsome

Mum and Dad (?)

She started to type. Nothing came up for Emily Elizabeth, nor for Charlotte (though without her surname, she hadn't expected it to). Jacqui Sonningfeld, on the other hand, brought up a few pages.

As she read through the results, Melody learned that Jacqui was born in Leicester in 1950, that she'd been nominated for an Oscar in 1994 for her makeup effects in a film called *Beatlemania*, and that she lived in Beverly Hills with her husband, a film editor called Tony Parry, and their two teenage children. There was no mention, that Melody could see, of any former husbands or older children, but the picture that accompanied one of the articles showed a dyed-blond woman in designer glasses with a slightly leathery mouth and very thickly applied mascara who was, Melody was absolutely certain, the woman with whom she'd stayed in the thin house in Fitzrovia.

She made a note of Jacqui Sonningfeld's agent's phone number and address and then began to look for Ken Stone. This was harder, as where there was only one Jacqui Sonningfeld, there seemed to be dozens of Ken Stones. There was no way Melody would be able to uncover precisely the Ken Stone she needed from among the hundreds of results that came up, so she tried Grace Stone instead. This brought up an interesting selection of results—including barbecues and duvet covers—but one in particular caught Melody's eye: a yoga instructor in Folkestone. The location was right, as was the occupation. She made a note of the accompanying mobile phone number and then took a breath. She was about to search for her mother.

As she'd suspected, there was only one Jane Ribblesdale in the world, and that Jane Ribblesdale had done only one thing of any note—she'd stolen another woman's baby. She found a couple of references to her, but nothing to suggest what might have become of her since her sentencing over twenty years earlier, so instead, Melody looked up the name of the prison where she'd been kept on remand and took a note of the phone number.

She found no mention of a Susie or Susan Newsome, and was about to slide her notepad back into her handbag and leave when she realized that there was one person on her list she hadn't looked for. She typed in the name "Seth Stone" and to her amazement, Google came back with more than thirty thousand results. Seth Stone was famous! Seth Stone was the lead singer of a band called the Mercury. Melody had heard of the Mercury. She'd even, now that the context had changed, heard of Seth Stone. She quickly checked a biography on a fan site, just to be sure, and there it was: Seth Stone was born in 1977, in Broadstairs, Kent.

She scrambled through the results, looking for a contact number, looking for an address. She found the details of his record company and his management company and then, just as she was about to see if she could find any more biographical details, the screen went blank. Her hour was up.

Ed was out when Melody got home half an hour later. It was a dirty gray summer's afternoon, with gathering rain clouds on the horizon and a dank breeze stirring the litter on the ground, but it was warm enough to sit outside, so Melody pulled a kitchen chair out onto the fire escape and opened a can of Sprite. She rested her notepad against her knees and took the lid off her pen with her teeth. She wanted to write a letter to Seth Stone. Seth Stone was, she'd decided, by far the best person to begin this search with. He would definitely know where his father was, his mother, his brother, and once Melody had found Ken, the rest would fall into place.

"Dear Seth," she began. "I'm sure you don't remember me, you were only a baby the last time I saw you, but . . ." She stopped, and tutted, unable to decide what to say next. It seemed such a simple thing to ask: What happened to my family? What happened to my friends? What happened to me? But she couldn't find the right words, and the longer she stared at the sheet of paper, the fewer ways she could think of to continue.

She put down her notepad and stared at the comings and goings of the estate beneath her feet. Two small Somalian boys played with a football; an old lady called Violet sat on a candy-striped deck chair, resting her arms on a stick; a man called Peewee with a learning disability polished his boots in a patch of sunshine; and a Cambodian baby in a pram sucked on a large pink dummy and stared into the middle distance while her mother chatted at high speed to a friend in the doorway. There was nobody to wave at, no one to call out a cheery hello to.

Melody had been here for almost half her life, yet had formed no allegiances and barely a handful of acquaintances. People came and people went. And the people who stuck around were somehow just beyond her reach; single men she'd avoided, in case they got the wrong idea; couples she'd avoided because she thought they might look down upon her; elderly people she'd avoided, in case they took advantage of her; and foreigners she hadn't made an effort to get to know because she couldn't speak their language. She'd kept herself very much to herself over the years and it was only now, as she unpeeled the layers of her own personal history, that she began to wonder why she'd allowed herself to become so cloistered. And then she realized—she kept her distance because the closer people got to you the more questions they asked, and the more questions they asked, the more inadequate she felt, and now, although they were still unformed and only half-baked, she finally had some answers. Now, she thought, now she was almost someone.

She turned back to the letter and she started writing.

The following day, Melody did two more remarkable things: first, she left a message with a PA at the LA agency that represented Jacqui Sonningfeld. "My name is Melody Ribblesdale," she'd said. "I'm sure she'll remember me. She used to be my stepmother." And then, half an hour later, she slid the letter to Seth Stone into a letterbox on Endell Street, her fingers crossed tight for luck. She sat for a moment on the fire escape after that and breathed in deeply, savoring the calm before the storm. She'd set the ball rolling, put the cat among the pigeons. Nothing would ever be the same again.

Chapter 44

Now

Every waking moment of Melody's life was now taken up with questions. Her head was constantly bubbling over with things she'd like to ask, mentally composing letters to Jane Ribblesdale, to her parents, to Jacqui Sonningfeld, and to her sister. There was a whole cast of characters out there, all lined up and waiting to meet her, but that's all they were, characters.

Until 9:17 a.m. on Tuesday morning.

Melody was in the living room, watching breakfast TV and trying to decide what to do with the rest of her day, when her mobile phone rang. It was an unknown number.

"Hello?"

"Hi, is that Melody?" It was a strident female voice, slightly salty, and underlain with a transatlantic twang.

"Yes, speaking."

"Oh my God, this is unbelievable! It's Jacqui here, Jacqui Sonningfeld! I just got your message!"

"Oh God, Jacqui, I . . ." Melody jumped to her feet and pulled her fingers through her hair.

"I haven't got you up too early, have I?"

"No, no!" she exclaimed. "It's fine! I've been up for—"

"My God! How are you?"

"I'm fine, I'm good. *I'm excited!* How are you?"

"Yeah, I'm fantastic. Couldn't believe it when I got your message. Just such a shock. I've been wondering about you for years, always wanted to know what had become of you. Listen, Emily's in London! She moved over about two years ago, working for the BBC. You must track her down. You're like a mythological figure in our house! She talked about you her whole childhood! Here, take her number down, call her, she'll be totally amazed!"

"Oh, right, yes . . ." She scrabbled around in the drawer of the coffee table to locate a pen and take down the number. "And Charlotte?" she said. "How is Charlotte?"

"Oh, Charlotte is Charlotte, you know. Just filing for divorce from husband number two, still hasn't given me any grandchildren, still waiting for her big break, still a pain in the arse. And you? Tell me what happened to you?"

"Oh, nothing much to tell. I had a son, very young, I work in a school, I'm single."

"And what happened to you, after, you know . . ."

"What, after my dad died?"

"Yeah, after your dad died."

"Well, I don't know, I'm not really very sure. My childhood's all a bit of a blur. I mean, I only just remembered you, and Emily. I walked past a house, in Goodge Street . . ."

"Oh, wow, the old place in London! How did it look?"

"It looked fine, it looked great. I went in and they told me that Charlotte had sold them the house . . ."

"They're still there, then, the American family?"

"Uh-huh. But it's taken me a while to put the pieces together."

"I should say. You had a very disjointed childhood. But what happened to you after, you know, your mother . . . ? You were with your aunt, right?"

"Yeah, I think so, but then I ended up living with a couple called Clive and Gloria Browne."

"You mean you were adopted?"

"I don't know. I think so . . ."

"Wow . . ." Jacqui's voice trailed off. "Jeez, I'm really sorry, I didn't realize, I . . ." She paused, and Melody could hear her inhaling on a cigarette. "Well, look, it's late here and I've got to be on set in four hours. I have to go get some zeds. But listen, call Emily, call her now. She'll be the happiest girl in the world! And stay in touch. Please. I mean, in a strange way, it's almost like you're family . . ."

Melody switched off her phone and let it fall on the sofa. Lorraine Kelly was still gabbling excitedly about a fake tan product, just as she had been before Melody's phone had rung. Melody switched off the television. And then she squeaked with excitement.

"Oh my God!" she whispered to herself. "Oh my God! I've found my sister! I've found my sister! Oh my God!" She ran around the flat a few times, unable to settle or rest in one spot before screaming again and running to the next place. Eventually she sat breathlessly on the edge of the sofa and stared at her phone in amazement. She could pick it up right now, press eleven buttons, and one minute later she'd be talking to her sister, her actual sister. And then, as she stared at it, it suddenly began to ring, loudly, aggressively. She jumped and picked it up. She didn't recognize the number. Could it be her? Could it be Emily? She pressed "answer." "Hello?"

"Hi, is that Melody?" It wasn't Emily. It was a man, with an accent that suggested the London suburbs.

"Yes."

"Hi! This is Seth. Seth Stone."

"Oh God, Seth, I didn't think you'd get my letter . . ."

"Yeah, our PA opened it this morning, got all excited, phoned me straightaway. How are you?"

"I'm fine. I'm . . . having quite a morning. I mean, do you even remember me? I don't suppose you do."

"No, I don't remember you, seen you in photos, though."

"You have?"

"Yeah, my mum had a few from the days of the squat. There's this great one of you that my dad took, down on the beach at Viking Bay. You're wearing red sunglasses and pink jelly shoes. It was always up on the pin board in our house . . ."

"What, seriously?"

"Yeah, my mum loved that picture. She used to touch it when she passed by. I think she felt bad, you know, that you got taken away, that she lost touch."

"So your mum, is she, still . . . ?"

"Alive? Oh God, yeah, well and truly. She's coming up for seventy now, but she's still teaching yoga."

"In Folkestone?"

"Yeah, in Folkestone. How did you know that?"

"I found her on the internet, on a website about yoga teachers."

"Oh, right, well, yeah, she's still teaching, she can still do the splits, still full of zest, you know. God, you'll have to call her. She'll be so amazed to hear from you. She'll be so happy, I swear . . ."

Melody took a deep breath before asking the next question, her heart fearing the worst. "And what about your dad? What happened to Ken? Does he still live in Broadstairs?"

"Ah, no, not quite, dear old dad lives in Spain now, moved there when I was about three, after the squat got repossessed. Had it with the UK. Gave up trying to make a difference, and then he and his mates Kate and Michael bought an old farmhouse for about ten quid and turned it into an eco-lodge, and this was like decades before it was fashionable. Growing their own food, killing their own meat, living off the land, no chemicals, all that business. He's married to a Spanish woman now, they've got about six kids, plus there's always loads of people moving in and out. I think there might have been another couple of Ken sprogs along the way."

"So, do you still see him?"

"Yeah, of course, I'm there every other Christmas. I always stop by for a few days when I need to wind down, after a tour or whatever. You should go over and see him—he'd be over the moon, seriously."

"Does he remember me then?"

"God, yeah, of course. I think he always half expected you to just walk into the room at any moment. He always said you and he had this bond, that you'd find each other again. And looks like he was right . . ."

Melody smiled victoriously. Of course. Of course! The sense of significance that she'd had about her relationship with this man called Ken, from the very first moment he'd reentered her consciousness two weeks ago, the feeling of a deeply shared love, of kindredness, it was all real!

"And what about Matty? What happened to Matty?"

"Oh, yeah, Matty. He's, well, things didn't turn out so great for Matty. He kind of lost his way a bit."

"Oh, why, what happened?"

"Oh, lots of things. His dad died, his marriage didn't work out, he started drinking."

"Like his dad?"

"Yeah, just like his dad. He lives with Mum now, mostly, except when he's on a bender."

"Then what?"

"Well, then he just goes AWOL, missing, no one sees him for a few weeks, living rough, I expect, down in Broadstairs."

"Oh!" said Melody, suddenly putting two separate pieces of her jigsaw together. "Matthew!"

"Yeah, he's Matthew now, been Matthew for years."

"But I know him! I mean, I met him, in Broadstairs. He's the man with the curly hair, the man who talked to me."

"And how was he? How did he seem?"

"Well, drunk, mainly."

"Yup, that's Matthew."

"God, I can't believe I didn't recognize him."

"Yeah, well, he's a long way from that little kid with the bag full of scalpels and rabbits' feet."

Melody thought about the scraps of memories she had of the boy in the squat, the serious, olive-skinned boy, always looking for the drama in life, always searching for a narrative. Now it appeared he'd abandoned his search and allowed his life to unravel completely.

"That's so sad."

"Yeah, it is. It's a bit of an unhappy ending, really. I don't know what happens to him after Mum goes, you know. I fear for that day, because then there'll be nowhere safe for him to be, no one to look out for him . . ." He paused. "Look, I've got to go now—we're at the studio, the guys are waiting for me—but give my mum a ring. She'll be made up, totally."

"And your dad, how can I get in touch with him?"

"Well, that's a bit trickier—no phones—but drop him a line or, better still, book a flight. Turn up on his doorstep. Make his dream come true."

Melody hung up a moment later and stared at the notepad by her hand. She had collected, within the space of half an hour, a phone number for her sister, a phone number for Grace, and an address in Andalusia for Ken Stone. She had spoken to her former stepmother and a boy she'd lived with in the squat in Broadstairs, and discovered that she'd already met Matty without even realizing it. But in all the excitement and fluster of new discovery she'd failed to do the most important thing of all. She hadn't asked anyone what had happened to her mother.

That night in bed, filled with a sense of encroaching completeness, Melody picked up her mobile phone and opened the last text message from Ben. She pressed reply and wrote: "Hi. Sorry been out of touch. Too much to deal with right now. How about dinner here one night next week?"

She had just put the phone back on her bedside table when it lit up.

"No worries about going AWOL. Totally understand. Would really like to have dinner at yours. Monday night too soon?"

"Monday good. Ed will be here too. Hope that's OK."

"That's cool. Are you too tired for a chat?"

Melody stared at the message for a while. This was fine, this texting business. This was within her control. She texted back: "Yeah, a bit. Need to sleep. Let's chat on Monday."

"Sure," came Ben's reply. "Sleep tight. Etc. etc."

"Zzzzzzzzzz"

"Xxxxxxxxx"

Melody smiled, switched off her phone, and turned off the bedside lamp.

Chapter 45

1980

Melody stood in front of the small neat house in Spinners Way and appraised it. It was very new, very modern, the ground floor built from red bricks, white plastic cladding on the first floor, and a chimney built out of bricks that were lots of different colors. It sat in a neat circle of similar houses in a road shaped like a horseshoe. It had a small driveway, leading to a garage with a blue up-and-over door, and a monkey puzzle tree in the front garden. It was a nice house, it looked clean and fresh and happy.

At Melody's feet were her possessions: a small suitcase filled with all the pretty clothes that Aunt Susie had bought for her; her painting of the Spanish girl, tied up with string; and a small rucksack filled with schoolbooks and mementoes, including a dried mouse that Matty had given her.

Aunt Susie put a clammy hand on her shoulder and said, "Shall we ring the doorbell?"

The door was opened by a lady with soft blond hair teased into the shape of a tulip, wearing a fawn cardigan, a fawn skirt, fawn tights, and fawn loafers, with a string of creamy pearls around her neck. She ushered the visitors through the porch and into the house, kissing Aunt Susie twice, once on each cheek, and then leaning down to address Melody.

"Hello, Melody." Her voice was tiny, like a small girl's. "I'm Gloria. It's very nice to meet you."

Melody smiled, not sure what to say.

"How was the drive?" Gloria addressed Aunt Susie.

"Oh, fine, fine. Lovely day, isn't it?"

It was a fine day, warm and springlike with a softness in the air that felt like summer. It was the sort of day that made Melody want to put on a pair of sandals and run down to the beach with a bucket and a spade, and tuck her skirt into her knickers for a paddle. But there would be no paddling and sandcastles today, because today she'd said goodbye to Broadstairs. Canterbury was only a few miles away but as far as Melody was concerned, she may as well have been in Timbuktu.

"Thank you so much, Gloria," Susie said to the lady in fawn, "such short notice. I really do appreciate it. But it's not safe for her, not anymore."

"Of course not, no, I totally understand." Gloria looked down at Melody and smiled fondly. "You'll be much safer here. We'll make sure of that."

She ushered her into a neat living room furnished with two floral sofas and a blue Dralon wing chair. On the table in the middle of the room were three plates. One bore eight triangular egg and cress sandwiches with the crusts cut off, one a quintet of coconut macaroons, and the third, a small coffee and walnut cake with a silver cake slice resting next to it. A tall thin man with ash-colored hair, thin and lovingly swept across the top of his otherwise hairless skull, emerged from the kitchen as they entered the room, holding a tray upon which was balanced a teapot in a quilted cozy decorated with illustrations of small English birds, four cups and saucers, a bowl of sugar lumps, a small jug of milk, and a pile of incredibly shiny teaspoons.

"Hello there!" said the man, setting down the tray and smiling warmly at Melody. "You must be Melody."

Melody nodded.

"I'm Clive." He offered her a large dry hand to shake. "Very nice to meet you. I hear you've been having a rum old time of it."

Melody shrugged and slipped her hands underneath her legs.

"Well," he said, "it's nice and quiet here, nothing untoward likely to happen round here. Now, can I pour anyone a cup of tea?"

Melody gazed around the room. It was a bit like Auntie Susie's house inasmuch as it was quiet enough to hear a clock ticking, but nicer than her house because they had pretty paintings on the walls, and things that looked like antiques, and their curtains were thick and snug looking and you could tell that they had lots of visitors, unlike Auntie Susie, who never had any and didn't even own a teapot.

"So, Melody," said Gloria, smoothing out her fawn skirt, "I've phoned the local school this morning and as chance would have it they've got a space free for you, so this afternoon we'll head into town and get you a uniform. You can start tomorrow morning. That's good, isn't it?"

Melody nodded stiffly and smiled. It was only for a few weeks, and the prospect of attending a school that didn't have Penny in it was almost worth being taken away from Broadstairs for.

"And your aunt Susan tells us that you like crafts, so I've registered you for some arts and crafts lessons in the local church hall, and, if you thought you might enjoy it, we could even arrange for you to join the Brownies. I'm a Brown Owl for the local Girl Guides, so I'm a bit of an expert." She paused and smiled again. She seemed somewhat out of breath, as if she'd had to do everything in a terrible hurry. "Would you like to see your bedroom?" She nodded and shook her head simultaneously, then giggled nervously. It was almost as if she had something wrong with her and couldn't stop talking. "Maybe later," she replied to her own question, almost immediately. "Anyway, I think it's all going to work out very well." She turned to her husband and gripped his hand, quite tightly. "Don't you, Clive?"

Clive nodded and slipped his arm around Gloria's shoulders, a gesture that Melody found immediately reassuring. "I do indeed. Just what this house needs, a child. Will do us all no end of good. Oh, and the house next door—two girls, ten and eleven. Someone for you to play with."

All three adults turned and smiled at Melody, and she knew she was expected to say something, preferably while sounding grateful, but it was hard, because she wasn't really grateful because she didn't mind about people posting poo through the letterbox or painting rude words on her house—well, not nearly as much as she minded being here in a strange house miles away from Ken, from all that was left in her world that was familiar.

"Thank you," she said eventually, "thank you for having me."

All three adults smiled at her, their faces softening with relief, obviously thinking that despite her reticence, she was happy to be here.

"It's a pleasure to have you," said Clive expansively, "a real pleasure. And don't worry—we'll make sure nothing bad happens to you, nothing at all."

Melody smiled tightly and pressed her fingers into her thighs, thinking that really, it was a bit late for that.

Aunt Susie stayed at Clive and Gloria's house for about three days and then headed back to her house in Broadstairs, slightly tearfully.

"You be a good girl," she said, ruffling Melody's hair with her big doughy hand. "I know you will be, because you always are. And I'll send for you when I think it's safe again. When those terrible people have found something more interesting to worry about than an innocent seven-year-old girl. It's only for a little while, just a few weeks." She pulled a grubby handkerchief from the sleeve of her voluminous dress and blew her nose into it, slightly too noisily. "You're a lovely, lovely girl, Melody Ribblesdale. I shall miss you."

Melody took her arms from around Susie's squashy waist and let her kiss her awkwardly on the cheek, a tiny hint of sharpness around her lips suggesting whiskery stubble. "I'll see you really soon," said Melody, "really, really, really soon."

Susie nodded and wiped a tear away with her old handkerchief. "You most certainly will," she said. "Now in you go; let me say goodbye to Clive and Gloria."

Melody stood by the front door, listening as the grown-ups chatted in low serious tones on the front path.

"I'm sure it'll be fine," she heard Susie saying. "The doctor says it's very common, particularly in people of a larger frame, and all the drama, all the stress, it doesn't help. A few days' peace and quiet and I'll be fit as a fiddle."

"You know, you can stay as long as you like. There's no need for you to rush off, we've plenty of room."

"No, I need to be at home. I need my creature comforts. You know what it's like. But thank you, thank you so much, for everything. I'm sure Melody will be no trouble at all. She's a very good girl, really she is."

Melody lifted the heavy curtain in the front room when she heard the engine of Aunt Susie's car starting up a moment later. She watched Aunt Susie struggling to look over her shoulder, the girth of her neck offering little in the way of flexibility to her movements. And then she watched as Aunt Susie reversed her car out of the driveway, found first gear with some difficulty, and then drove slowly and circumspectly out of the cul-de-sac and back toward the sea.

Melody liked it at Clive and Gloria's house. Gloria made sure she was busy all the time, ferrying her in her fragrant Fiat Panda across the pretty city of Canterbury, with its spires and ancient fat-bricked walls, between school and dance classes and Brownies and friends' houses for tea. In many ways it felt to Melody as though Gloria had been waiting all her life to have a little girl living with her. She seemed to be so good at it. And Clive was so much fun. He was always doing silly things to make her laugh, and offering to go out in the garden with her to throw a ball around or play Swingball. He was springy and scampery, like a playful retriever, always wanting fresh air and activity. It amazed Melody that Gloria and Clive had no children of their own.

"Why don't you have any kids?" she asked one afternoon while she and Gloria were in the kitchen, painting hard-boiled eggs for Easter.

"Ah," said Gloria, in her little-girl voice. She was wearing an apron with sprigs of cherry blossom printed on it and frills around the edges. "Not everyone can have children, unfortunately."

"Why not?" Melody asked, painting in the petals of a tiny daisy.

"Well, it's to do with biology." Gloria stopped and dried her hands absentmindedly on the crisp cotton of her fancy apron. "Do you know about biology?"

"I know about things that grow in Petri dishes, and bacteria and things."

"Well, this is more like *human* biology. To do with our insides, our bodies, and how they work, and the thing is that I have something wrong with my biology, I don't make the right . . . *things*, the things that ladies need to make babies . . ."

"You mean, like, eggs?"

Gloria looked at her in surprise. "Yes," she said, "like eggs. My body stopped making eggs a bit early and by the time I met Clive, they'd all gone. So that's that, no babies for us."

"Are you sad about that?"

Gloria smiled, but only with her mouth. "Yes," she said, "I'm very sad about that. Now," she continued briskly, pulling a second pan of hard-boiled eggs from the kitchen sink, where they'd been cooling, "what shall we paint on these ones? I think happy faces, don't you? Yes, lots and lots of lovely happy faces."

Melody stared at Gloria, at her tiny waist and wispy hair, and thought about the inside of her body, her *biology*, and the poor empty spaces inside her that should have had eggs in them, the poor empty spaces in her house that should have been filled with children, and then she thought about her dead baby sister, Romany, she thought about the baby her mother had stolen to satisfy her own strange emptiness, and she thought about the sister in America she might never see again, and thought that really, when it came down to it, babies were nothing but trouble.

When she had been at Clive and Gloria's house for just over two weeks, Ken came to see her. He arrived on his motorbike, wearing his big scratchy coat and a scarf that looked like a tea towel. When he took his crash helmet off, Melody could see that he'd grown a beard, not a normal one that covered his whole chin but a pointy sort of one that sat just on the very tip.

She hugged him to her, as tight as she could, and breathed in the smell of him, the slightly damp, slightly musty, slightly herbal smell of home.

"This is Ken," she said, introducing her friend to Clive and Gloria.

"Nice to meet you, Ken," replied Clive, while Gloria smiled primly, her small hands folded neatly in her lap.

Ken looked strange sitting in this house, in his old clothes with his straggly hair and his faded tattoos. The flowers on the Brownes' sofas seemed almost to be recoiling in horror. Ken had suggested taking Melody for a ride into town and a glass of lemonade, but Gloria had vetoed that, on the grounds that it was "a bit chilly" and that Melody already had "a bit of a sniffle," so they sat in the pretty front room, sharing a plate of digestive biscuits and a pot of tea, shuffling around the edges of a hundred awkward conversations.

"So, Ken, what do you do?"

Ken put his tiny teacup down with a rattle. "Well, this and that, really. I suppose you might call me an agent for change."

Clive raised his eyebrows and leaned forward. "An agent for change? Sorry, you'll have to enlighten me."

"Well, in my younger days I was an activist, a crusader, you know, trying to change the way the world is run, trying to make it a better place for my kids, you know, so it was all marching around with flipping great placards and hassling politicians, but these days, well, I've mellowed, you could say. These days I'm more . . . *subtle*. A well-placed letter in a newspaper, a few intelligent, well-worded pamphlets *slipped*"—he mimed posting a letter—"through the right front doors. I'm too old for charging around the place screaming at people." He smiled and picked up his teacup again. "Drip drip effect," he said, and winked.

"And you live in a squat, is that right?"

"Well, yes, you could call it a squat, or you could call it an empty house lovingly occupied by decent, respectful humans." He said this much as he said everything, in such a charming tone of voice that no one, not even the slightly uptight Gloria, could possibly take offense. "But not for much longer . . ." He turned and picked up Melody's hand. "Bad news about the house," he said, his gray eyes looking sad and watery. "The owner's copped it and it's been left to some distant great-nephew who wants to sell it. He's got a court order on us, we've got to be out by the weekend."

Melody went stiff. "What," she said, "you mean all of you? You mean Grace and Matty and Seth and Kate and Michael and—" She was going to say "Mum and me," but stopped herself just in time.

"Yes, sad to say, but yes. It's all over."

Melody dug her fingernails into her kneecaps, really hard. She wanted to scream. She wanted to break something. She wanted to scratch her own eyes out. It was all over. *It was all over.* No Ken, no Grace, no Matty, no Seth. She pushed her fingernails into her flesh until the pain turned numb and then she looked up. "But where will you go?" she managed to utter, in a voice so small that she wasn't sure if she'd actually said it or not.

Ken shrugged and scratched his cheekbone with grimy fingernails. "Gracie's taking the boys to Folkestone, her mum's old place, just for a while. And me and Kate and Michael are heading off to Spain for a few weeks, just to get some space, you know."

Melody nodded but she didn't really know. Why was Grace staying here and not going to Spain with Ken? What sort of space was he talking about?

"But what about Mum?" she said, beginning to panic. "What's going to happen to Mum, when she gets out of prison?"

Ken took her hand again and squeezed it extra hard. "Oh, well, I can't really say about that. It's tough, because, well, I mean, nobody's really sure what's going to happen to your mum."

Melody continued to stare at him, willing him to do what he always did and to make everything better. Nothing he was saying made any sense. How could nobody be sure about her mum? She'd been sent to prison for two years. She'd been in prison for six weeks. By Melody's calculations that meant that she'd be leaving prison in one year and ten and a half months. Melody had always assumed that on that day she and her mother would return to the house on Chandos Square, hand in hand, to reclaim their shadowy room in the eaves. But now she was being told that there would be no house on Chandos Square to return to and that her mother might never get to leave prison anyway.

"Did you see her?" she asked, in the biggest voice she could muster.

"Yes, I visited last week. She's not very well, Melody. It could be a long time before they think she's well enough to send her home again."

Melody gulped. "What do you mean by a long time?"

"I don't really know, but they're doing everything they can to make her well again. All I'm saying is, not to expect anything. All I'm saying is that anything could happen."

Ken's words made Melody feel cold and scared, as if she were all alone in a big, echoey room, with cobwebs everywhere and a creaking noise and no handle on the door. But she felt too sad to cry and too scared to ask for help, so instead she picked up a digestive biscuit and offered it to Ken, who took it from her outstretched hand, silently and with a very sad smile.

Ken left half an hour later. He was off to the passport office, needed to get there before they closed, but before he went he stood for a while in the garden, with Melody, smoking a lumpy roll-up and staring thoughtfully up through the overhanging trees. After a moment he cleared his throat and turned to her.

"They seem like nice folk, those two." He gestured awkwardly at the back door.

"Yes, they are nice. They wanted a baby and couldn't have one so they're extra nice to me."

"You could do a lot worse," he said.

She nodded, not really grasping his full meaning. They both turned again to gaze into the shimmying leaves of the overhanging branches. Melody licked her lips. "Can I come with you?" she whispered into his arm, quietly so that Clive and Gloria wouldn't hear and be upset. "Can I come to Spain, with you and Kate and Michael?"

Ken turned to look at her. His face was wistful. He crouched down and took her hand. "Melody," he said gently, "there is *nothing* I would like to be able to do more right now than to take you to Spain with me—heck, to take you to

Broadstairs with me. I'd like to take you everywhere with me, forever and ever. But the people in charge of this big old ugly grown-up world we live in say that can't happen. For some reason, which I really cannot fathom, I am not allowed to be responsible for you. I cannot put you on my passport. I cannot live with you. This"—he gestured around the immaculate flowerbeds of Clive and Gloria's garden—"is what they want for you. This, no matter what you or I may feel, is what 'they' think is best. For now, at least. So, you need to carry on being the brave, special girl you've always been, and be nice to these good people and work hard at school and one day they might all change their minds."

"They?"

"Yeah. *Them.* The trained monkeys and lab rats who tell us how to live our lives. But you know me, the eternal fighter, I haven't given up yet. There's always a way to beat the system, there's always a way to make it do what you want it to do, so just hold tight, little one, hold tight and stay strong. For me." He kissed the top of her hand with his velvet lips, and then he kissed the top of her head, quite hard, like he was trying to suck something out of her soul, and then he got to his feet.

"Oh," he said, putting his roll-up between his lips and suddenly feeling the pockets of his coat. "I brought you things, some stuff, hold on, they're here somewhere." He finally pulled out a book, a matchbox, and a red hair clip. The book was *Anne of Green Gables*. "Grace bought it for you, she thought it was up your street." The matchbox contained a small dead frog, painstakingly coated in gold leaf. "Matty made it for you, he found the frog down by the sidings." And the red hair clip was one of hers that had been found down the side of her old bed in the attic.

"Was there . . . did Mum have anything for me?" she asked, sliding the matchbox closed.

"No, nothing from your mum, I'm afraid. She's not really capable of that kind of thing, right now."

"But did she ask about me?"

Ken glanced at her from the sides of his eyes. "Oh, yes, of course. She wanted to know if you were OK."

"And what did you tell her? Did you tell her that I was here? Does she know where I am?"

"Yes, she knows, she knows you're here."

"What did she say? Did she mind? Was she cross?"

"I don't think," said Ken, gently grinding the burned-out tip of his roll-up into the soil beneath the Brownes' neat lawn and putting the butt into his inside pocket, "that your mother is really well enough to feel cross about anything. Come on"—he held out his hand for hers—"I'd better go. Come and wave me off."

Melody had to use all her strength not to cry when she saw Ken putting on his old crash helmet and straddling his bike a moment later. She stared longingly at the empty sidecar and pictured herself squashed into it, wearing the furry coat that Aunt Susie had bought her from Fenwick's last month, and her new Fair Isle mittens, taking off on an adventure, one that would inevitably involve lemonade and ice cream, and then going back to the house in Broadstairs with pink cheeks and a belly full of sugar.

She smiled bravely as Ken revved up the engine and she waved at him as hard as she could. When she couldn't see him anymore she turned and ran inside, straight up to her bedroom, where she landed cross-legged on her bedroom floor and began to wail. She stared round the room through tear-soaked eyes, and her gaze alighted upon the Spanish girl. She stared back at Melody, reassuringly, her wide eyes still the same improbable, iridescent shade of blue as the wings of an Emperor butterfly, her hair still as dark and glossy as a saucepan of melting chocolate, her dress still as vibrantly scarlet as raspberry sauce.

"It's not fair," Melody sniffed between gulps, "it's not fair. None of it. None of it. None of it." The Spanish girl smiled at her sympathetically. "I want to go home," sobbed Melody, "I want to go home. I want my mummy and I want my daddy and I *want to go home*!!!"

Melody closed her eyes, and let the tears run down her face. When she opened them again, she saw Gloria, her face set with sadness, closing her own bedroom door very slowly behind her and heading away across the landing and toward the stairs.

Chapter 46

Now

Melody blow-dried her hair on Saturday morning, not her usual hasty, heavy-handed flurry with her fingers, but a proper blow-dry, with a cylindrical brush that had come free with the hair dryer. She teased it and rolled it until it fell to her shoulders in shiny layers. Then she pulled out her old makeup bag and applied some eyeliner, some cover stick to her under-eyes, and a coat of brown mascara. It was a fresh morning again, with no evidence of summer in the air, so she put on some jeans, a white camisole top, and a heavy ribbed cardigan in baby blue. On her feet she wore her brand-new Geox trainers, and in her ears, a pair of large silver hoops. She appraised herself in the mirror, wondering what sort of impression she would make. She didn't look like a dinner lady, nor did she look like a single mum who lived on a council estate, but she didn't look like a girl from LA called Emily who worked for the BBC and whose mother was an Oscar-nominated makeup artist, either. She sighed and pushed her shiny hair behind her ears. Her clock radio told her that it was 11:58. She was late.

She met Emily on a bench outside a café in Ladbroke Grove.

"Hello," she said, approaching her softly. "Emily?"

Emily turned and smiled, and Melody's heart turned over. Chestnut hair, hazel eyes, soft, round face, light eyebrows, and a smile that turned her from haughty to sweet. It was like looking in a mirror: a rather flattering mirror.

"Melody! Oh, oh, omigod!" Emily got to her feet and Melody discovered that they were exactly the same height. Emily stood for a moment and stared at her, her eyes taking in the details of Melody's face, her mouth agape. "This. Is. Un. Real."

Melody nodded, absorbing her sister, taking in her shiny white teeth, her double-pierced ears, her pointy green pumps and skinny gray jeans. "Wow. This is amazing," she agreed.

"You look exactly like I expected. You look just like Dad, just like . . ."

"You?"

Emily laughed. "Yeah," she said, "just like me."

"So, how old are you now?"

"I'm nearly twenty-eight. Getting old!"

"Oh, no, twenty-eight—you're still a baby."

"Well, it doesn't really feel like it. Though my lifestyle might suggest someone *considerably* younger. Hey, look, I thought we might go for a coffee?"

They headed into a café around the corner, full of Saturday families and Portobello shoppers. Melody ordered a cappuccino and Emily ordered an herbal tea.

"That was the most amazing phone call of my life," said Emily, taking off her denim jacket and revealing a plum cotton vest top and a pinstripe waistcoat. "Seriously. I was with my roommates and they were all like, omigod, I can't believe that just happened, and I was like, yeah, I know, my actual sister, and we were all screaming, because, wow, you're like a legend, you know?"

Melody smiled and pushed up the sleeves of her cardigan. "Well," she said, "I'm not sure that's exactly how I'd describe myself."

"No, seriously, when I was growing up, there was this picture of you, in my sister's room—"

"What—Charlotte?"

"Yeah, in Charlotte's room, in her, like, her dressing mirror thing, and you're wearing this like gypsy dress and you have a camellia in your hair and you're smiling at the camera and you look like *the most interesting* girl, you know, like someone who you'd want to know, want to talk to. And I just . . . oh, shit, this is really embarrassing . . . I made you into my imaginary friend. Seriously. I would talk to you all the time, in my bedroom, I would tell you what I was doing with my dolls and I swear you talked back to me. My mother sent me to a therapist, because she thought I was nuts. And I guess I was kind of a weird kid . . . I didn't have any real friends, just you . . ." She smiled at Melody, almost apologetically. "So, you can imagine how freaky this is for me. My imaginary friend—come to life. Wow."

Melody looked at her in amazement. "This photo," she said, "where did it come from?"

"God, I don't know. My dad—well, shit, I mean *our* dad—took it, when you came to stay?"

"I came to stay? You mean in Goodge Place?"

"No, in LA."

"I came to stay in LA?"

"Yeah! You came on your own, on a plane. I always thought that made you the bravest, coolest girl ever, to get on a plane on your own."

"I went on a plane, to LA?"

"Yeah! You don't remember?"

Melody shook her head, and picked up her coffee cup. "No," she said, "I really don't remember anything about it at all." She paused and stared at the tabletop for a moment, feeling for the first time the dreadful reality of her broken memory. Forgetting another mother, another father, another house, another life, that was one thing, but to forget a trip to LA struck her as strangely appalling in every way.

"Wow. That's bizarre. I mean, you stayed for, like, two weeks. You slept on the floor in my nursery."

"I did?"

"Uh-huh. Mom always talks about it. She said you were 'the little babysitter,' that you sat with me, like, all the time, didn't leave my side."

And then it hit her: a white room, Tweetie Pie stuck to the wall, a mobile swaying gently in the breeze, an open window, the lazy symphony of cicadas, ruffled palms, the bubble of a swimming pool filter and murmur of just-heard adult conversation. She felt the stone floor, hard beneath her body, and felt the presence of something precious, a small life, beneath the cut-out animals of the wooden mobile. Her sister.

"I remember!" she said, slamming down her coffee cup, dizzy with the joy of remembering. "I remember! You had Tweetie Pie on your bedroom wall. And there was a swimming pool and the air . . . it smelled like . . ." She sniffed the air. "It smelled like . . ."

"Jasmine?" said Emily.

"No, not jasmine—*chlorine*! I do remember."

"Wow, I can't believe you remember the Tweetie Pie decal! There was Minnie Mouse too, on the other wall. Remember that? They were there until I was, like, nearly ten! Then I scraped them off myself with a palette knife and painted the whole room *aubergine*. Mom was *not impressed*. So, do you . . ." Emily cast her eyes down toward the floor. "Do you remember much about Dad?"

Melody smiled wistfully. "Not really," she said, "and anything I do remember is pretty new to me, but I remember he had a kind face, that he was tall, that he really loved us both, a lot."

Emily smiled and fiddled with a tube of sugar. "Yeah," she said, "that's what Mom's told me. I mean, I was, like, *one* when he died. I don't remember him at all, you know, not even a little bit. Just what I've seen in photos. And he looks like the nicest, kindest man. I wish I'd known him."

"Yes," said Melody, "so do I."

"Well, you got, you know, six years?"

Melody shook her head sadly. "Not really," she said. "I don't remember anything about the first nine years of my life."

"What, like nothing at all?"

"No." She shook her head and smiled wryly. "Up until a week ago I thought my name was Melody Browne and that my parents were called Clive and Gloria and that I'd spent my whole life in a house in Canterbury."

Emily threw her a confused look. "What, seriously?"

"Uh-huh. I had some kind of amnesia and it seems like while this was happening, my mother got sent to prison, my dad died in a pileup, and I got adopted by a pair of strangers who lied to me my whole life."

"You're kidding, right?"

"No," said Melody, "no. I'm not. But I really wish I was."

They spent another hour in the café, ordered more tea, more coffee, and talked ferociously and almost manically about absolutely everything. Emily lived in a flatshare off Golborne Road with three other girls, she worked for the BBC in their marketing department, and she was writing a novel in her spare time, about a girl trying to find her long-lost sister.

"You know," she said, "I came to live in London to be near you. I wanted to breathe the same air as you. I wanted to give serendipity a head start . . ."

She really liked her mother's new partner, and her two younger half brothers, but she couldn't get on with Charlotte, however much she tried. "She's just, like, a *diva*. And she's so smart but she plays it dumb all the time. I can't connect to her, you know?"

She liked cooking and socializing and she had a boyfriend of fourteen months whom she was thinking about splitting up with because "he's nearly thirty-one and he's ready for, like, having a family and settling down, and I'm like twenty-seven going on seventeen and that's just not what I'm about right now."

She was amazed to hear about Melody's son. "You're a *mother*? Omigod! That means I'm, like, an *aunt*! And you were fifteen? Jeez, you know, I just knew that you would be different and amazing, and you are, you just totally are!"

By the time they left the café Melody felt like all the strange and dreadful fragments of her forgotten childhood, all the sad revelations and bleakly gothic truths that had emerged from the shadows of her mind and shown their awful selves to the light, had somehow come together and formed a new bright, glossy picture, embodied in this girl, this bouncy, beautiful, sweet, silly, and unblemished girl. It was as if it had all been distilled down to one small shiny pearl of goodness: her sister. And in this new person she saw not only a person she might have been close to had fate sent her down a less potholed road, but another person too—the person she might have been if her father had not died on the freeway coming to bring her home, if he'd made it to London, helped her pack a bag, and brought her back to Los Angeles.

"Do you have to rush off?" said Emily, grabbing hold of Melody's hand.

"No," she replied. "Not at all."

"Good," said Emily, "there's something I really, really want to show you."

By the time they reached Tooting, it was raining heavily and they huddled together beneath a small Hello Kitty umbrella pulled out from the bowels of Emily's roomy shoulder bag. Emily wouldn't tell Melody where they were going, but she seemed quieter as they approached the cream stone walls of Lambeth Cemetery.

"Here we are," she said.

Melody threw her a questioning look.

"We're going to see Dad," said Emily. "Are you OK with that?"

Melody gulped. She'd planned on spending a day at the Family Records Centre in Clerkenwell, thought about finding her father's death certificate, discovering where he'd been buried, but she hadn't found the impetus. Now she was here, a moment away from his final resting place. She took a deep breath and nodded.

"Good," said Emily, "that's good.

"I come here once a month," said Emily as they meandered through the pretty cemetery, dodging puddles. "At least once a month. This was another reason I came to London. So that I could see him whenever I wanted. And I always half-hoped that maybe one day I'd come along and find you here, you know, just paying your respects . . . But I guess, now I know a bit more about you, that that wasn't ever going to happen."

As they walked, Melody felt shivery waves of familiarity. She saw a stone angel and a chipped crucifix, ivy-draped walls and pointy conifers, and she knew she'd seen them before. And then she felt a wall of sadness, a bleak certainty—this was a place of personal tragedy and of desperation.

"Here," said Emily, pausing between two rows of small stone plaques embedded into the earth. "Here he is. Dad."

Melody stopped and gazed at the ground. His plaque was dark gray and the words were hammered out in cream:

JOHN BAXTER RIBBLESDALE

1944–1979

Beloved father, stepfather, and husband

Taken from us much too soon

Will remain forever loved

She put her hand to the damp stone and stroked it gently. And as she touched the stone she felt the world start to wrap itself around her head, darkly and softly, and she closed her eyes and saw a hole in the ground, and a tiny white coffin and a woman in an old gray dress trying to climb into the hole. She opened her eyes and the image was gone, but there were tears in her eyes.

"I've been here before," she said.

"Yes, of course you have," said Emily, "you must have been here for the funeral."

"Yes, I suppose I must have." She looked around and saw a familiar tree.

"But it feels like it was something else. A different funeral . . . maybe a . . ." And then she stopped and gasped, because she had just seen the inscription on the plaque to the left of her father's—a small cream plaque, streaked green in places:

ROMANY ROSEBUD RIBBLESDALE

4 January–6 January 1977

The sweetest rose

Plucked before her time

Our hearts forever darkened

It took a moment for Melody to absorb the full meaning of the inscription. At first she thought perhaps it was the grave of an ancient ancestor, a tragic child born and perished in some other century, unconnected to her life, but then she absorbed the numbers properly and realized that this was a baby born when she was four years old and that probably, given the nature of her recent flashback, the woman she'd pictured trying to climb into the hole in the ground must have been her mother, Jane Ribblesdale, the Broadstairs Baby Snatcher, and that she therefore must also have been the baby's mother and suddenly everything made a kind of blinding, awful sense.

Emily saw her staring at the baby's headstone and touched her arm. "Poor little baby, huh?" she said softly.

"Did you know?" Melody asked. "Did you know she was my sister?"

"Our sister. Yes, uh-huh. I knew before I came to London. My mom always said that was the start of everything. You know."

Melody shook her head. "No," she said, "I don't know. Start of what?"

"Well, you know, your mom and dad splitting up, your mom going nuts, taking you to live in that dive by the sea, stealing that baby, killing herself . . ."

Melody gasped, her body rocked. Her mother was dead. She'd suspected it, but not known it, and knowing it hurt more than she'd imagined.

"Oh God." Emily paused and stared at her. "I thought you knew."

"No, no, I didn't."

"Oh, shit, Melody, I'm so sorry. I just assumed because you knew all about what happened with snatching the baby and everything . . ."

"I knew she took the baby and I knew she went to prison but I thought maybe . . . I don't know what I thought."

“There,” said Emily, pointing to the other side of their father’s grave. “Look.”
Melody followed her arm to a small gray plaque, framed in soft green moss.

JANE VICTORIA NEWSOME

1948–1981

A Mother above all else

Loved and missed

She fell to her haunches then, and let her head drop in her chest. The rain was falling heavier now, running down her crown and over her face. She looked up and glanced from left to right at the three small rectangles of stone, marking three small boxes of dust and ash. Her mother, her father, her sister. Her family. Shadowy, unknown strangers, faces seen only in smudgy black-and-white photocopies, a baby she’d never known, dead at two days, leaving her parents with “hearts forever darkened,” a tiny world pinched out by the fingers of fate in less than five years.

“What happened to the baby?” she asked.

“Um, I’m not sure. Heart defect, I think. I’d have to check with Mom. But that sounds right to me.”

“And what happened to Jane? What happened to my mum?”

Emily shrugged and grimaced. “She hanged herself,” she said apologetically, “I think.”

Melody inhaled, suddenly, as though she had been kicked in the chest. An image flashed through her mind, a featureless woman in a big gray dress hanging from the ceiling in a prison cell. Had she been there? No, of course she hadn’t. It was just an offering from her imagination. But she must have been told. Who would have told her? How did she feel? Had her mother left her a note? Had she made any provision at all for her only daughter?

“And what . . . what happened to me?”

Emily shrugged again. “That’s the biggest mystery of all. One minute we knew where you were, the next we didn’t. It was like you just disappeared. It was like,” she said, staring through the stirring trees into the brightening sky, “it was like we’d just dreamed you.”

Chapter 47

1981

The news about Melody's mother came via a phone call from Auntie Susie, one breezy Sunday afternoon, while Melody was playing ludo on the coffee table with Clive and awaiting the removal of a fragrant Victoria sandwich from the oven in the kitchen.

"Oh, darling, darling thing," said Susie, her breath labored and thick. "I can't believe I have to say these words to you, not after everything you've already been through, but a terrible, terrible thing has happened and I need you to be terribly, terribly brave."

She was calling from the recovery ward of the Queen Elizabeth Hospital, having suffered a minor heart attack upon hearing the news. Her words were punctuated with beeps and tears and gulps and other unsettling noises that made her sound less like an auntie and more like a creature from *Doctor Who*. The words made no sense at first. She used terms like "gone" and "passed away," and Melody thought maybe she was trying to tell her that her mother had escaped from jail. But once the truth of her garbled words hit her, Melody felt gravity being sucked from the room, her legs soft as jellies, her head filled with mist, everything leaving her, drop by drop, until all that was left was a small heap on the floor, not crying, but slowly seeping away.

Melody had a good mind; she'd always managed to make sense out of most things. And she was a flexible girl: she went with the flow, she tried not to get in the way of other people's plans. If a man in a courthouse had decided that what her mother had done when she took the baby from the newsagent's was bad enough to warrant two years in jail, then Melody would just have to wait two years for her mother to be released. If her mother was too sick to see her, or even to write her letters or funny little postcards, then Melody would have to stop fantasizing about letters and funny little postcards and accept that there wouldn't be any, and if her auntie Susie had decided that her home was not a safe enough place for her to be and that she would be better living with her "dear old friends" here in Canterbury, then that was fair enough. Melody could even justify the fact that her mother had stolen the baby in the first place, reasoning that she'd only done it to make herself feel happier and that if she'd felt happier maybe she would have been a better mother to Melody. Melody could accept most of the unpleasant things that had happened to her over the past few years, as she knew that fundamentally, everyone was just doing what they thought was best. But it didn't matter how hard she thought about it, or how much she tried to understand it, nothing about the fact that her mother had decided that she didn't want to be alive anymore made the slightest bit of sense. How could being dead possibly help anyone, or make anything in life better or easier? How could leaving Melody all alone with strangers be the right thing to do, for her or for anyone?

Melody's mind lost all clarity as it fought to make sense of this development, and for a while as she lay there on the muted Axminster carpet, her cheek pressed down into its scratchy fibers, her fingertips tracing the silky fringed trim of the floral sofa, she lost her connection with the world. She knew it was there, she was aware on some level that Gloria was stroking her hair, that Clive was trying to persuade her to stand up, that there was a half-played game of ludo on the table behind her, that Gloria's Victoria sandwich would probably burn if she didn't take it out of the oven now, but couldn't think where these facts bore any relevance to her. Underneath the sofa, she could see a small ball with a bell attached. She assumed that it must have belonged to the fat marmalade cat called Puss, who'd played the role of Gloria's surrogate child until his demise last year under the wheels of a National Express coach full of tourists. She stretched out her arm and reached for the ball, and pulled it toward her, held it close to her cheek, rolled the cool metal of the bell across her hot skin and tried to imagine what would happen if she were ever to stand up again. It didn't seem possible to her that she could do such a thing. The idea of her legs' supporting her head, this heavy, numb lump on her shoulders, seemed unthinkable. No, she decided, she would just lie down here, lie here and wait to see what happened next.

What happened next was that Gloria shrilled, "The cake!" and ran from the room, and that Clive helped Melody gently from the floor and folded her onto the sofa. She sat on the sofa in the very same form that Clive had placed her onto it, as if she were a pliable rubberized dummy. In her hand she clasped the cat toy and her gaze fixed onto a counter on the ludo board, blue, shiny, brittle. She leaned forward stiffly and picked it up. She could almost see her reflection in it, a tiny blue haze of features, not recognizably her own, specter-like. It occurred to her that she had not thought about her mother's being dead for quite a few moments and as she thought this she felt a pinch of pain in her stomach, like someone giving a hot burn to her insides. She dropped the ludo counter to the floor and allowed some external noises into her head.

"Melody," she heard Clive saying, "Melody, love, please, talk to me."

But she couldn't. Talking seemed so very far away from anything that she would want to do. To talk would mean to resume her connection with the world, and she really didn't want to, not when the world could do such mean things to her.

A column of smoke curled across the room and she could hear Gloria cursing gently in the kitchen.

"Get her a glass of water, Gloria!" Clive called out.

Gloria came back into the room and passed the water glass to Melody. Melody pushed it away. She didn't want water. She wanted her mum.

"I'm so sorry, love," said Gloria, pushing Melody's hair away from her eyes. "So so sorry."

"Rum luck," sighed Clive. "More rum bloody luck."

"But don't you worry about anything. We'll sort everything out, we'll make sure you get everything you need. We're here for you, Clive and I, completely." Gloria pulled Melody's numb body toward her own and kissed her on the shoulder. It was the first time she'd ever kissed her. Melody had been secretly hoping for a kiss from Gloria since her first night here, had been willing her to squeeze her tight at bedtime and kiss her hard on the cheek like Auntie Susie used to, like Ken used to, like Mum had sometimes done in her rare phases of contentment. But the kiss on her shoulder felt strangely unpleasant and Melody arched her body away from her.

"Yes, we'll sort everything out," agreed Clive.

"Is there anything we can do for you now? Anyone you want to phone? Anyone you want to speak to?"

Melody rolled the cat toy around between the palms of her hands and stared through the window opposite. A high wind was blowing around the tops of the trees, a piece of litter flew by, someone in the house opposite was doing the housework. She looked at the toy and she thought about Puss, the cat she'd never met, she thought about him squashed under the fearsome tires of the National Express coach, then she imagined the horrified faces of the passengers on board the coach, all on their way for a nice day out in Canterbury, as they watched his fat orange body being crunched to a pulp. And then she thought about a freeway in LA, the sound of screeching brakes, the scream of twisting metal, her father's face flattened against the shattered windscreen, and then she felt that soreness in her stomach, the hot burn, and a small space opened up in her mind, a space she didn't even know she had, like a little safety deposit box, and she thought it seemed like a good place to put the horrible picture of her dad on the freeway. So she slipped the thought into the box and pushed the box back into the hole in her head and the moment she did so, she felt the soreness in her stomach fade away.

"Melody," she heard Gloria asking, softly, "Melody, please, say something."

But Melody didn't want to say anything. The thought of saying something made Melody feel like she was about to push her hand into an electric socket or a live flame. So she kept her mouth closed. It felt good. It felt smooth and gentle and strong. Words were messy. Thoughts, she now realized, were far superior. Thoughts could be arranged into boxes, filed away. Words were too public, too immediate. Words were for idiots.

She got to her feet and left the room, then climbed the stairs slowly and heavily to her bedroom.

She stayed up there for the rest of the day, finding new places in her head to put the things she didn't want to think about anymore, and she didn't come down until it was dark, until her tummy was rumbling so hard that the burned Victoria sandwich sitting on the kitchen counter looked good enough to eat.

Chapter 48

Now

"You just got about a hundred text messages!" Ed called out to her from the living room, where he was restudding his football boots. Melody, who'd just had a shower, tucked her towel around herself and padded toward the kitchen, where her phone was recharging. She had four new texts. The first was from Ben. She opened it, presuming that he was canceling their date, but he wasn't.

"Did you say it was your son's birthday next week? Let me know, I have a plan . . . B x"

Melody grimaced, then smiled. How on earth had he remembered that? She smiled again and texted back: "Good remembering skills. I'm impressed. He's 18 on Wednesday. But what's this 'plan'? You're making me nervous . . ."

She pressed "send" and then looked at the next three messages. They were all MMSes from the same number, one that she didn't recognize. She took her phone into her bedroom and stepped quickly into her underwear while she waited for the attachments to download. Then she perched herself on the edge of her bed and opened them one by one. They were from Emily, each one annotated with the words "Proof that you were here!"

They were photographs, small and grainy, depicting a small girl and a baby sitting on a parquet floor, the bright pieces of a giant jigsaw puzzle on the floor between them, both staring upward into the lens with dark, serious eyes.

Melody called Emily immediately.

"Oh my God," she said breathlessly, "it's us!"

"Yes, I know!" cried Emily. "Mom emailed them to me last night. Aren't they the cutest?"

"I love them!" said Melody. "I really do. I used to have—" She stopped, suddenly unsure of the provenance of what she was about to say, the substance of it, but then seeing it clearly, in her head, a faded Polaroid, its edges worn thin with tender handling. "I used to have a photo of us," she continued, sure now that she had. "You were in a high chair, I was standing next to you, orange blossom behind us. I'd forgotten it, and now I remember. It was one of my most precious things. And I suppose"—she felt the sour tang of resentment rising in her throat—"I suppose it must have gone in the fire, gone with everything else."

What else, she wondered, what else had been taken by that cruel and life-altering fire? What else had been lost? Which clues to her childhood, to herself?

A text from Ben arrived a few seconds after she hung up the phone to her sister. "Don't be nervous," it read. "Also, shall I email you a photo, in advance of Monday, to remind you of what I look like?"

Melody smiled, then typed: "No need. Short, fat, bald, and ugly, right?"

He texted back a moment later, a wink and a kiss.

Melody sat on her bed for a while in her underwear, the phone held close to her cheek, her heart aglow with some unknown joy.

The following day, Melody left the gloom of yet another disappointing summer's day behind and caught a train to Folkestone, where the sun was shining happily upon the Kentish seaside resort.

Grace lived in a third-floor apartment in a slightly shabby 1950s block, two roads back from the seafront. Its architect had decided that a lack of sea view was no obstacle to adorning the front of the building with ungainly balconies and huge picture windows, which looked hopefully out toward the unpretty back end of a terrace of Georgian houses.

In a cool, faintly grease-scented corridor lined with green-marbled stone and threadbare carpets, Melody rang on a doorbell. She inhaled and prepared herself for an Art Deco vision of sinewy arms and opulent headdress, but what greeted her instead was a vaguely disheveled-looking man in a dark-green polo shirt and baggy shorts with a half-smoked cigarette in one hand and a can of Diet Coke in the other.

"Fuck," he said. "Melody fucking Ribblesdale!"

It took a moment for Melody to make sense of this man who knew her name. His cropped hair and clean-shaven face had thrown her slightly. But it was Matthew. Matty. The boy from the squat. The drunk from Broadstairs. Grace's son.

"Matthew!" she said.

"Wow. Fuck. You remember me?"

"Yes, well, we met quite recently."

"We did?"

"Yeah, in Broadstairs, about two weeks ago."

"No!" He looked simultaneously aghast and unsurprised. "Christ, what did I say to you?"

"Oh, nothing much, just asked me if I needed any help. I must have looked a bit lost."

"I hope I wasn't obnoxious. I can be, you know, when I'm drinking like that."

She shook her head and smiled. "You were fine," she reassured him, "really."

"Thank fuck for that!" he said. "Christ, anyway, come in, come in, welcome."

He led her barefoot down a narrow hallway, toward a bright room at the end. The flat was small and eclectically furnished, with objects from all the major continents: African masks and Indian wall hangings and Chinese lanterns. The living room ended with a full plate-glass window and doors onto a balcony upon which sat a majestic lady with a cup of tea and a newspaper.

"Melody!" she exclaimed, unfurling herself from her deck chair and padding barefoot into the living room. "Oh, Melody!"

She was very slim and dressed in gray leggings and a purple blouse bunched in at the waist with a silk scarf. Her hair was pure white and cut short, in a pageboy style, and she wore heavy gold earrings that looked Indian in design.

She grasped Melody's forearms with long, strong fingers and stared into her eyes urgently, as if she'd lost something inside them. "Beautiful!" she exclaimed after a moment. "Beautiful. I always knew you would be." She released Melody's arms from her firm grip and sighed, almost with relief. "Come and sit down. What can I get you to drink?"

"Oh, a Diet Coke would be nice," she said, gesturing toward the can in Matthew's hand.

"Matty—get Melody a Coke, will you, sweetheart? Here"—Grace patted a scruffy sofa, dressed in a length of green sari silk—"sit. Let me look at you."

Melody sat down and let Grace stare at her for a while. "Just exactly the same, but also so different. You look . . ."—she paused—"*mature*. You've lived a life, yes?"

Melody gazed at the woman, trying to find something familiar about her, trying to find a place in her head where a memory of this exotic woman might still be residing, but nothing came to her. "Well, that depends on what your definition of living a life is." She smiled. "I've lived a big life, in a small way."

"Children?"

"Yes, one, Edward . . ."

"Edward? Edward like the baby . . . ?" Grace paused, uncertainly.

"Like the baby my mother stole, yes. Completely unconnected, pure coincidence, though . . ."

". . . possibly subconscious in some way?"

"Yes. Possibly."

"Interesting." Grace pulled one lithe leg up beneath herself. "And how old is he, your Edward?"

"Seventeen," Melody replied, "eighteen on Wednesday."

"Huh! A man! You had him young."

"Fifteen, yes."

"Well, good for you. I always partly regretted not having my children earlier. Too busy 'finding myself.' Thing is, I was too young to know what I was looking for. Should have had the kids first, when I was young and stupid, then found myself afterward, but, there you are, *c'est la vie*. And what have you been doing together, you and your Edward?"

"Oh, just drifting along really. In a rut. But a nice rut." Melody laughed nervously. There was something unsettlingly penetrating about this woman's gaze, like she was trying to find some meaning behind Melody's eyes.

"Working?"

"Yes. I work at Ed's school. In the kitchen."

"You're a dinner lady?" asked Matthew with a smirk as he walked back into the room with Melody's Coke.

"Yes!" she answered playfully. "And?"

"God, of all the things I thought Melody Ribblesdale would become, a dinner lady was not on my list."

"What's wrong with being a dinner lady?" she countered, resisting the temptation to say that of all the things she'd thought Matthew would become, a pathetic drunk was not on *her* list.

"Nothing," he said, putting his hands in front of his chest defensively and smiling. "God love 'em, where would we be without them? But I just always thought . . ."

"What?"

"I dunno, there was always something special about you. I always thought you might end up being famous, you know, that I'd switch on the telly one day, and there you'd be."

"Instead it's your little brother!"

"Yes, indeed, I am Brother of the More Famous Seth."

Melody didn't really know what to make of that so she said nothing and thought instead about the little girl called Melody Ribblesdale, who'd been of so much interest to everybody, the little girl for whom everybody appeared to have such high hopes, and wondered what on earth had happened to her.

"So," interrupted Grace, "you work in a school kitchen and you live in . . . ?"

"Covent Garden."

"Oh, how glamorous." She smiled. "I always dreamed about living in the middle of town, slap-bang in the middle of the chaos. Is it thrilling?"

"It's OK," Melody said. "It's just a council flat."

"And those people, your parents, Roger and Gloria, was it . . . ?"

"Clive," said Melody, "Clive and Gloria."

"That's right. What happened to them? How are they?"

Melody shrugged and took a sip of her Coke. "I haven't seen them for quite a long time."

"Oh, why is that?"

"Oh, all sorts of reasons. I haven't seen them since before Ed was born. It was all very messy. But how did you know about them? I thought I went to live with them long after I lived with you."

"Well, yes. First of all you were with your auntie Susie, that's right, poor old Auntie Susie . . . and then she sent you to live with that couple. I never met them, sounded quite pleasant. I believe the woman, Gloria, was Susie's second cousin."

"You mean, we were related?"

"I believe so, yes. And then, of course, after your poor mother lost her battle with her demons and left you all alone, well, there was a bit of a fight."

"A fight?"

"Yes, between Ken and me, and the couple. We found out that they were registering themselves as private fosterers, so that they could adopt you, and we thought, well, that's not right, who are these people, utter strangers, keeping our lovely Melody all to themselves—they wouldn't let us see you, you know—so we started adoption proceedings too. Ken even had his hair cut short. We played the happy suburban couple, here, in this flat, visit after visit, questions, *interrogations*, like the fucking Gestapo. Ken got a job—believe that? Yes, as a road sweeper. I wore a skirt and my mother's fucking pearl necklace. We made these people cup after cup of tea, had them in and out of here for months. We knew we didn't stand a chance, not really. I mean, those people, they were related to you, you were already there, they were *normal*. It didn't matter how much Ken and I pretended to be normal, we weren't going to fool anyone. The stress on our marriage was appalling. And then, when we found out that our application had been rejected, it all sort of imploded. Ken ran off back to Spain and bought his flea pit there and I . . . well, my mother was elderly, she needed me here, so I just sort of *stopped*." She paused and looked around her flat, describing it with her eyes as a kind of well-furnished prison. "Anyway," she continued, "we went back to see you, you know, a few months later. We got sick of our phone calls being ignored and our letters being returned and, you know, there was no house! It had been razed to the ground! A neighbor told us there had been a terrible fire, but that you and that couple had escaped. But nobody knew more than that. Nobody knew where you were. You disappeared, Melody, simply disappeared!"

Melody stared at Grace, mutely. This stranger, of whom she had no recollection whatsoever, had attempted to be her mother. This unconventional creature, this nonconformist with a rock star and a drunk for children, had worn pearls and humiliated herself in order to appear as an acceptable parent for her. The stress of trying to adopt Melody had broken her marriage, changed the direction her life would take forever. All this struck Melody as both exhilarating and appalling.

"But here you are now." Grace smiled, revealing perfect white teeth and Audrey Hepburn cheekbones. "Beautiful and alive and happy. Are you happy?"

Melody nodded. "Yes," she said, "I think so."

"Good," said Grace. "And are you in love?"

Melody smiled, questioningly. "Urm, no."

"No one in your life?"

"No, not really. Well, there is someone, but it's kind of on hold at the moment, until I can get to grips with all the stuff that's been going on."

"Ah, you mean the strange unlocking of your mind?"

"Yes, exactly."

"Remarkable," Grace continued. "The mind is a remarkable, remarkable thing. Never fails to amaze me. So, this man, this hypnotist, he just clicked his fingers and suddenly it all came flooding back?"

"Well, no, not suddenly, just in dribs and drabs really. Every now and then something triggers a memory."

"And me—do you have any memory of me?"

Melody shook her head. "I remember Ken had a wife and I remember Seth being a fat baby, sitting on the kitchen floor, and I remember sitting in the garden with Matty and talking about Ken, but I don't remember you."

"Ah, how sad to be so forgettable." She feigned sorrow and then looked up and smiled. "I remember you, my darling. I remember you so well. Every last thing about you. Do you remember, I taught you to do finger knitting?"

Melody shook her head.

"Ah, well. And do you remember telling me about that girl in your school, that dreadful creature. Penny?"

At the mention of the name Penny, Melody saw an image in her head. A thick-skinned girl, heavy featured, with a deep crease in her forehead. *Penny.* That was her name, the girl she'd remembered outside her old school last week. Penny.

"Yes," she said, "I remember a girl called Penny. She was horrible."

"She made your life miserable. I wanted to go to the school and punch her for you, but you wouldn't let me. You always wanted to deal with your own battles. You were always so *self-possessed.* I admired you greatly, the way you dealt with everything. Particularly your mother. You were wonderful with your mother."

"Was I?"

"Oh, yes, endlessly patient and understanding. You gave her so much leeway, allowed her to be so . . ."

Melody searched Grace's eyes for a clue to what she might be about to say next.

"So *absent.* Not her fault, obviously, poor Jane. Depression. The Black Dog.

A terrible affliction. And then to lose another baby like that, at twelve weeks, well, that would tip most people over the edge, but your mother was weak, you know. I'm sorry if that sounds like a heartless thing to say, but she was. I would never have allowed any unhappiness I was experiencing to stop me from being a proper mother. But there you go, everyone is made from different stuff. And your mother, I'm afraid, was made from very brittle stuff indeed . . ."

Melody wasn't surprised by Grace's words. It was clear to her from her few memories, from the newspaper reports, from the fact of the powdered remains of her thirty-three-year-old body in a hole in the ground in Lambeth Cemetery that her mother had been made of brittle stuff, but Melody had secretly hoped for more. She had hoped for words of admiration, for a suggestion that there'd been more to Jane Ribblesdale than dead babies, insanity, and suicide, that she'd been a good mother and that she really hadn't wanted to leave behind her lovely little Melody.

Matthew was watching the conversation from a stool at a breakfast bar that formed an opening into an open-plan kitchen. His knee was jigging up and down frantically, and he seemed to be waiting for an opportunity to ask a question.

"So, who's the father?" he asked Melody, as his mother paused for breath.

"I'm sorry?"

"Your son. Who's the father?"

"Oh, Matthew, so rude," admonished Grace.

"It's OK," said Melody. "The father was a boy called Tiff, an Irish boy. He was two years older than me . . ."

"And he didn't want to know, right?"

"Right."

"So you've brought this boy up all by yourself?"

She nodded.

Matthew shook his head appreciatively. "That's pretty bloody impressive, Melody Ribblesdale."

"You think?"

"God, yeah. I couldn't even be trusted to look after a hamster, let alone raise a child on my own. And he's all right, is he, this boy of yours? Not out happy-slapping and knifing teenagers on the streets?"

Melody smiled. "No," she said, "he's a good boy. A good man. I made a good man."

"Good on you," he said, appraising her with respect. "Good on you, Melody Ribblesdale."

Melody glanced down at her feet, feeling strangely touched by his comments.

"So," he continued, "what does he make of all this weird shit, all these strange people coming back from the dead?"

She cleared her throat and replied, "I haven't told him yet."

"You haven't told him? Why the fuck not?"

Melody paused. "I don't know. I think I just don't want to get halfway down the path with all this, and then find out it was all—I don't know—all a mistake, that I'm mad, that none of it ever happened. I want to be able to give it to him like a whole new world, like a . . ."

"Like a gift." Grace smiled and nodded.

"Yes," said Melody, relieved that her reasoning made sense to someone other than herself. "Like a gift. For his birthday"—she smiled—"for his coming of age . . ."

They fell silent for a moment, until Matty suddenly jumped to his feet.

"Remember that day?" He planted himself on the sofa next to her. "Remember that day your mum went missing and you and me went searching all over town for her? Do you remember?"

Melody shrugged. "Doesn't ring a bell," she said.

"Yes, remember, after your dad had another baby, she lost the plot, went off and slept on the beach, you and I trawled the town, top to toe, found her in a café."

She shook her head. "I don't remember that exactly, but I did feel things when I was in Broadstairs, things that felt familiar."

"You found the old house, then?" asked Grace.

"Yes, just before I bumped into Matty. It's a guesthouse."

"Yes, poncy bloody shithole," said Matthew. "That woman thinks she's royalty. I knocked on the door once, just after she'd done the place up, asked if I could have a look. Should have seen the look she gave me. Well, granted I was probably a bit the worse for wear, but it wasn't as if I wanted to make off with her heirlooms, you know, just wanted a quick look at the old place."

"I went inside," said Melody.

"Did you?"

"Yes, pretended I wanted a room. It's very nice. She's done a very nice job of it."

"So you remember it the way it was?" said Grace.

"I remember the outside, I remember seeing Ken on the balcony in an old coat, I remember our bedroom, and the kitchen and the strange paintings on the garden wall. They were happy times, weren't they?"

"Yes," said Grace, "on the whole. Obviously the time with your mother was an emotional time. It took us all a long time to get over the incident with poor baby Edward. And then of course we all missed you horribly after you went away. I kept a picture of you, look." She got to her feet and wafted into the kitchen, where she unpinned something from a cork board. "Here"—she passed the photo to Melody—"look at you. Look at that wonderful little girl."

Melody held the photo between her thumb and finger and stared at it. It was her, smaller than she'd ever seen herself before, her back against a shingled, graffiti-daubed wall, sitting on a pebble beach. She was wearing pink-framed sunglasses and red jelly shoes and a denim skirt with red patch pockets. Her hair was redder than it was now, and hung from a middle parting in twisted ropes. "Who took this?" she asked.

"Ken. On one of your jaunts."

And there, on the beach, just by her feet, Melody could see it—her crash helmet, the one she'd remembered right at the start of all this. And then, looking closer, she saw something else remarkable—a reflection in the lens of her sunglasses of a man, holding a camera, a man with long hair and a beautiful face, a man who looked like Jesus. Ken.

"It's a lovely photo, isn't it?" said Grace.

"It's . . . *amazing*. I mean, I've never seen a picture of myself so young before. I had no idea what I looked like at . . . ?" She looked questioningly at Grace.

"Five," she said, "you were five."

"Wow," said Melody, continuing to stare at the little girl in the sunglasses and jelly shoes she had no recollection of ever owning. "Can I take this?" she asked. “Get it copied? I’d love to show it to my son. He’s never seen a picture of me as a child. I never thought to take any with me when I left home.”

“Of course!” said Grace. “Please, take it. I just wish I had some more. But Ken will have more. He was always snapping away. Are you going to see him?”

“In Spain?”

Grace nodded.

“God, I don’t know. I can’t really afford it . . .”

“EasyJet!” she exclaimed. “Last time I went I got a flight for fifteen pounds. And once you’re there, it’s all free. It’s not exactly nights on the strip in Puerto Banús when you’re staying with Ken! You should go!” she exclaimed. “Ken would love to see you. He would just . . . well, he’s had a hole inside his soul ever since we lost you to those people. If he saw you, it would heal him. He’d be whole again . . .”

Melody said goodbye to Grace an hour later. It was early afternoon and Grace was due at a local Weight Watchers group to give a yoga class. She clasped Melody to her in the hallway, and breathed into her hair. “Strong as you ever were,” she muttered, “strong as I knew you would be. So much to take in. So much to accept. Such a good, good girl.” She let her go and kissed her hard on each cheek. “Now off you go and move on. There’s nothing holding you back now. Nothing to stop you. Knock ’em dead!”

And as she said this Melody noticed a mole on the side of her face out of which grew a solitary black hair. It rather marred the perfect symmetry and fine lines of her features and she thought it showed a remarkable lack of vanity that she hadn’t attacked it with a pair of tweezers, and at that very moment she remembered. She remembered a tall woman in the kitchen at Ken’s house, a woman in a turban and clattering bronze bangles. She remembered Grace.

She smiled to herself and hugged her one last time.

There was one more place to go before Melody caught the train back to London, and Matthew took her there in a battered old Vauxhall Astra.

She watched his hands as they manipulated the gear stick. They were weather-beaten hands, tinged a strange shade of yellow in the places where he clutched his cigarettes. His nails were ripped and torn and his legs were scuffed and scarred. He was a man of the street. There was something quite unsettling about being driven on a busy A road by a man she'd last seen careering drunkenly around the streets of Broadstairs, drinking 69p cider from a can. But there was also something real about him, something that made her feel strangely reassured about everything that had happened to her and everything that was still to come.

"So," she said, "what's the deal with you and Broadstairs? Your other 'life'?"

He turned and smiled at her, glad, she could tell, of her candor. "Ah yes, dear old Vagrant Matty, my alter ego. Well, it's the same old story really. Young man has alcoholic father, young man loses alcoholic father, young man feels searing disappointment with the world, young man finds oblivion in the bottom of a bottle. And then every now and then he can't take it anymore and wants to go home and have a bath and not feel like a piece of shit for a while. Until the searing disappointment with the world hits him again and then the bottle starts calling and his mum kicks him out and it's back to square one."

"You mean Grace won't let you stay when you're drinking?"

"No. I'm out the door the minute she gets a whiff of it. I don't even bother waiting now. When I get the calling to the bar, I just pack my duffel bag and head straight for Broadstairs, straight for the wine shop."

"So, why Broadstairs?"

He shrugged. "Not sure really. Just didn't want to shit on my mum's doorstep, you know, have all the neighbors going, ooh, look, Gracie's boy's fallen off the wagon again, look at him, vomit all over his shoes, his knob hanging out of his flies. That wouldn't be fair on Mum. Because, as you can probably tell, my mother is a very refined lady." He smiled and chucked a cigarette butt through the open window of the car. "And Broadstairs, well, it's my spiritual home, it's where I had my first drink, my first fag, my first shag. It's where I came of age. So that's my life, a shitty tale of two cities. Spineless mummy's boy in Folkestone, pathetic drunk in Broadstairs. Can't say I'm proud of either of my rather tragic personas."

Melody stared ahead, not sure what to say next. "And you can't find a way to break the cycle?" she asked.

"No." He smiled sadly. "I've tried rehab, I've tried true love, I've even tried the Church of fucking England. None of it worked. This is me. This is it. And you know what?"

She glanced at him.

"It's not so bad. I've got a good mother. My brother looks out for me when he can. I've got people who love me. You know, there are people out there who've got no one. People out there like islands, floating around, nothing to anchor themselves to. I've got it good, compared to some. The choices I make are *my choices*, not ones that have been landed on me from a great height by the powers that be. And you know something else? I like being drunk. I do. As fucked-up as that might sound, I love being so blitzed that the world turns inside out. I love the randomness of it, the madness of it. I like that I've taken myself out of the equation, you know, that I don't count, that I don't matter. And I like fucking people off, always have done." He turned and winked at her and she smiled. There was something unfalteringly, blisteringly honest about this man. He was utterly transparent and completely without guile. He was, she suddenly realized, a child, a big, gruff, scuffed, pickled, hyperactive, and self-obsessed child, who cared only what his mother thought about him.

She smiled at him again and resisted the urge to squeeze his grazed knee.

He signaled left and pulled the car down a small turning off the road. A large wooden sign at the top of the turning said "Elm Trees Residential Care."

At the top of the driveway was a large pebble-dashed house with mullioned windows and barley-twist chimney stacks.

Once inside, Matthew smiled at a woman in a nurse's uniform and said, "Hi, we've come to see Susie Newsome."

"OK." The nurse smiled. "I'll just locate her for you."

"How long has she been here?" asked Melody while they waited.

Matthew shrugged. "Years," he said. "Pretty much since you were adopted. Since the heart attack."

"Heart attack?"

"Yes. She had a weak heart. There was all the stress with the court case, then she had a minor attack after your mum's suicide, and then a massive heart attack when she heard about the fire at your place, when you went missing. She was clinically dead for four minutes, came out of it with brain damage, affected her sight, her bowel control. Now she can't see, and she poos in a bag, and she's been in here ever since. Mum's been really good about keeping in touch with her. She visits quite a lot, I think."

"Miss Newsome's in the residents' lounge," said the nurse.

Melody followed Matthew down a corridor and into a large, heavily plastered room overlooking a manicured garden. A television was on in the corner, showing *Deal or No Deal*, and a dozen or so elderly people sat staring at it from oversized chairs. In a chair under a window sat an extraordinary-looking woman, fat as a walrus, fluffy white hair backcombed into points. Wearing a lime-green tracksuit and dark glasses, she looked more Hollywood Hills than suburban Kent.

"Well, hello, Miss Susie Newsome. It's me, Matty."

Susie looked up toward him, unseeingly, large wattles of crêpey flesh flapping from side to side as she did so. "Matty. That's nice. Who are you with?"

"You'll never guess."

"No," she agreed, "I don't suppose I will."

"Someone you haven't seen for a very long time. Someone you've thought about for thirty years. Someone really special."

"Let me feel," said Susie, holding out two plump white hands. Melody moved toward her and let her touch her face. It was an odd sensation but not altogether unpleasant. "No"—Susie smiled, running her hands down Melody's hair—"no idea, you'll have to tell me. Who are you?"

"I'm Melody."

Susie stopped then, her face frozen in surprise. "Melody?" she gasped. "*My* Melody?"

Melody nodded. "Yes."

Tears sprang to the old lady's eyes. "Oh, my! But where did *you* come from?"

"We came from Grace's flat. We've just—"

"No no no!" she cried. "I mean—*where have you been*?"

Melody explained everything, from the Julius Sardo show to the trips to Broadstairs and her visit to her mother and father's graves the day before with her sister.

"And this is all new to you? All this, this other world?"

Melody nodded, then remembered to speak. "Yes. I thought it was just me and my son. I thought I was alone, but, well"—she paused, emotion stopping the words halfway up her throat—"I'm not." She started to cry then, tears of hope and tears of gladness, because it was true. She wasn't alone, not anymore.

Susie took her hand between hers and squeezed it.

"So what happened to you?" she asked. "All those years ago, after the Brownes took you in, what happened?"

"I don't know," Melody replied, "I'm a bit of a mystery."

"I'd say," said Susie. "Those bloody people, promised me they'd stay in touch, but all I got every year was a cheap Christmas card, no return address, no news about you, but always signed, Clive, Gloria, and Melody. And then even they stopped." Her voice cracked. "You know, I'd never have left you with them, never have supported the adoption if I'd known they would steal you away like that, away from me, away from Grace and Ken, your poor little sister in America, everyone who cared about you! It was the saddest thing that ever happened to me, and believe me, *a lot* of sad things have happened to me." She forced a smile with trembling lips. "But this," she continued, "this is happy! This is my Melody, back from the dead! This is like a *miracle*."

She took Melody up to her room, the weight of her terrible, bloated body being supported by a metal walking frame as she shuffled slowly toward a small passenger lift. "Here," she said, pushing open her bedroom door and heading for a chest of drawers, "here. I've kept this all these years, hoping that one day I'd have the chance to give them to you, and in all honesty, I'd just about given up on that day ever coming. But now you're here, and I can finally pass it on. Here . . ." She pulled a cardboard box from one of the drawers and laid it on the bed. "Come. Come and see."

Melody stared at the box. "What is it?" she asked, perching herself on the edge of Susie's bed.

"It's your mother's things, what they gave me when she passed on. And a letter, for you."

"From . . . ?"

"Yes, from your mother. Still sealed."

Melody paused for a moment. She wasn't sure if she could do this. The past twenty-four hours were starting to make themselves felt around the edges of her mind. Her thoughts were becoming dense and unfathomable. Her heart felt like a clockwork toy that had been overwound. She needed space from this experience. This elderly, overweight woman with the candy-floss hair seemed like a very nice person, but Melody had no recollection of the weeks that she'd spent living in her home, she couldn't remember the bedtime stories or sitting on her soft lap to watch the television, or her gentle hands plaiting her hair in the mornings. She felt moved that she was related to this woman, and a sense of fascination about being with someone who shared her DNA, but beyond that, there was nothing. She didn't want to share this moment with this woman, she didn't want to share this moment with anyone. She wanted to take her box home and open it sitting on her own bed, far away from this parallel world of strangers and revelations.

"You don't have to open it now," said Susie, reading her hesitation. "Take it home. Open it when you're ready. But will you do one thing for me? Will you tell me what the letter said? I'd love to know, just as a kind of final goodbye, you know. Because I never really spoke to her, not after she was taken away; she was never really there, not the real Jane. And this"—she touched the box—"this was written by the real Jane, I know it was . . ."

Aunt Susie touched Melody's hair as she held her to say goodbye a few moments later. "Mmm," she said, rubbing it between her fingers. "Such good hair, you always had such good hair. And tell me, does it still have that lovely auburn shimmer, in the sunlight, your hair?"

"No"—Melody smiled—"not anymore. The red faded a long time ago."

"Ah, well, yes," said Susie, letting the hair drop, "red does tend to do that. Red does tend to fade."

Melody stroked her aunt's hand, just once, and then kissed her on the cheek. "Thank you," she said, "thank you for everything you've done for me, even if I can't remember it."

"Oh," said Susie, "I don't think I was awfully good at it, but I did the best I could. I'm just so sorry I let you go. If I'd been healthier I would have found a way to track you down, but after the attack, well . . ."

"You did the best by me," said Melody, "that's all that matters."

Susie smiled sadly. "I hope that's true," she sighed, "I really do hope that's true, otherwise I shall go to my grave with a pain in my heart and a stain on my soul. I love you, Melody. I always did. And I always will. Now stay in touch. I've lost you once, I'm not about to lose you again."

Melody and Matty left the home at four o'clock and drove toward the train station.

"Weird, huh?" said Matthew.

"Mm," agreed Melody. "Very weird indeed."

"Your mum's sister and you don't even remember her."

"Do you remember her?" she asked.

"God, yeah, you don't forget someone that fat in a hurry. She was the fattest person I'd ever seen! And she invited me over for tea once, when you were living there, and do you know what she made us to eat, bearing in mind that I was, what, twelve and you were seven? She made us a smoked salmon and quails' eggs salad, seriously, with, like tinned anchovies and watercress and stuff. You and I just sat there making vomit faces at each other behind her back and trying to stick quails' eggs up our noses. It was really fucking funny. But hey"—he turned to her and smiled—"I guess you had to be there."

A short distance from the train station, Matty pulled the car up to the curb and peered over Melody's shoulder at a small shop. "Look at that," he said. She glanced out of the window. It was a photography shop, with a small bay window filled with slightly startling photographs of unpretty children and stiff businessmen in suits.

"What?" she said.

"Ring any bells?" he asked, pointing at the shop front.

She peered at it, but could see nothing at all familiar. "Nope," she said. "What am I supposed to be looking at?"

"That. The name of the shop." He pointed at the sign.

It said "E. J. Mason Photographic Services."

It still meant nothing to her.

"E. J. Mason," said Matthew. "Edward. James. Mason. Otherwise known as baby Amber Rose."

"Oh my God," said Melody, "you mean that's his shop? The baby?"

"Yes. That's his shop. Fine upstanding member of the community, our

Eddie. He is a Rotarian. And a keen golfer. And I'm pretty sure he's married with two point four kids . . ."

"How do you know all this stuff?"

"Mum. Mum knows everything about everything. If Mum doesn't know about it, it hasn't happened. And oh, look, there he is! The man himself . . ."

They both turned and watched as a tall, casually dressed man walked out of the shop, clutching an aluminum box and with two cameras hanging from his neck in nylon cases. He had fine hair, and thin-rimmed glasses, and walked with a sense of purpose.

"God," said Melody, watching him climb into a silver Honda Civic, "you'd never guess it to look at him . . ."

"What, that for three days he was called Amber Rose Newsome and lived in a squat in Broadstairs? No, you really wouldn't. But I tell you what, I don't suppose it's done him any harm. In fact, it's probably made him feel special. Look, you can tell just by looking at him that he thinks he's a bit special, a legend in his own gray little seaside town. A bit like me, I suppose, you know, not famous, but *infamous* . . . the Legendarily Pissed and Appalling Matthew Hogan. And you too, I suppose, Melody Ribblesdale, the Girl Who Came Back from the Past." He put the car back into gear and started to pull away from the curb. "And I wonder," he said, turning and smiling at her, "I wonder if maybe, just maybe, you've come back for a reason . . ."

Melody didn't open the box from her mother when she got home that evening. There were some things she wasn't ready to know.

Chapter 49

Now

Despite spending her working days in a kitchen, Melody had no interest in cooking. Her son had been raised on a diet of fish fingers, toasted sandwiches, microwave meals, and the occasional takeaway from the fish-and-chip shop up the road. She'd once attempted a homemade Bolognese, inspired by one that Stacey had cooked for the kids' tea when they were all about five years old, and it had been disastrous. She didn't have any of the right knives and had resorted to slicing an onion with a dinner knife, and because she'd left its preparation until the last minute she'd only cooked it for a quarter of an hour. Ed had eaten one forkful and spat it out. "I don't like it!" he'd cried. "You liked it at Stacey's house last week," she'd responded. "Yes," he'd said, "that was different. *That* was nice."

She'd never cooked for him again. In fact, she'd never cooked for *anyone* again. So it was with some surprise that she found herself in Marks and Spencer on Monday morning bypassing the ready meals department and heading toward the fresh produce. She'd seen a recipe in one of her magazines for seared tuna and spicy noodles and had thought it sounded both delicious and easy to cook, and decided, on a whim, that she would attempt to reproduce it for Ed and Ben tonight. She wasn't sure where this sudden, unexpected culinary inspiration had come from, but she embraced it nonetheless, as she now embraced every new and uncharted sensation. The old Melody, the one who didn't look in the mirror before she left the house, who wore her son's football shirts, who smoked and stayed in and kept the world at arm's length, was beginning to fade away, and in her place was the beginning of a new Melody, not yet formed, but feeling her way cautiously along the pathway. She felt like she'd been subtly upgraded, in her sleep, and was just starting to try out her new features, one by one. And so here she was, handling a bunch of fresh spring onions and wearing a skirt. Not a big deal by most calculations, but big enough to give her a slightly fluttery sensation in the pit of her belly.

She took her carrier bags home and as she walked she did something else she hadn't done before—she made eye contact with the people she passed. It amazed her how few people even noticed her attention, and that those who did weren't appalled by it. She felt like a creature born to reside on the bottom of the ocean floor, dark and flat and half-blind, slowly rising through the icy water to the glittering light above.

She appraised her flat when she got home, this home that she had allowed to accumulate so many layers and piles. She saw it for the first time through the eyes of someone who didn't really know her and wondered what it said, and she realized with a shock that it didn't speak only of a loving mother and a small but happy family, but also of an obsession with the past, a fear of letting go, and a lack of pride and imagination. The clear-out that she'd always feared would strip her home of all its "memory" would, in fact, breathe new life into this pretty set of rooms. What would happen if she threw away Ed's trainers, the ones she'd kept for two years because he'd been wearing them the day he got his GCSE results, and therefore she associated them with the proudest moment of her life? Would she forget all about her pride? Would she forget the feeling of warm satisfaction that had suffused her body, the smell of sixteen-year-old scalp in her nostrils as she held him to her, the relief that the ordeal was over and done with, and they could move on to the next stage? No, of course she wouldn't. Those things would stay with her forever. Her memory was not as puny and unreliable as she'd thought. It was all there, in color and detail. It had just needed a kick-start.

She went to the kitchen and pulled out a large bin bag. She flapped it open and then she filled it. She filled it with old trainers and clothes she hadn't worn in five years and dinner plates that always stayed on the bottom of the pile and calendars from 1998 and blankets that she would never get round to cleaning and saucepans without handles and paperbacks she wouldn't read, and, finally, the aged, overgrown spider plant, sad and resentful, done with life and ready to go. She tied a knot in the bin bag and she hauled it downstairs to the putrid concrete room where the communal bins were stored, and she heaved it over the top and listened to it land at the bottom with a satisfying metallic boom. Then she went back to her flat, washed her hands, and started on the dinner, feeling in some way as though she had exhaled her way another few feet higher, toward the warm golden sun at the top of the ocean.

Melody took off the high heels. That looked better she thought, appraising her reflection in the mirror, not like she was trying too hard, not like she wanted to be wanted. And besides, she had pretty feet, why not show them off? She was wearing an ankle-length tiered skirt in brown cheesecloth and a turquoise vest top, and she looked very nice. Not amazing, not spectacular, just nice. She jumped at the sound of the intercom buzzing and glanced at the time: 8:01 p.m. One minute late. A man who remembered birthdays. A man who kept good time. *Too good to be true*.

Melody shook the negativity from her head. She was done with all that. She took a deep breath and went to meet him at the door. He looked better than she remembered. He hadn't shaved and she thought he suited a slightly rougher look. He wore a gray jersey hooded top and jeans that were just the right side of trendy. He'd brought Ed a gold envelope with his name on it.

"What's this?" she asked. "The Plan?"

"Yes"—he smiled—"this is the plan."

"Oh, Ben, God, you didn't have to get Ed a present."

"Why not?" he said easily.

Melody couldn't answer that question so she just smiled and watched as Ed opened it. It was a pair of tickets to see Prince at the O2 later in the month. "I don't know if you're a fan or not, you're probably a bit young, but if you don't want them you could get a good price for them on eBay. They'll be good seats: my brother works for a ticket agency."

Ed smiled at the tickets. "Cheers," he said.

"I don't know," said Ben, addressing both of them, "do eighteen-year-olds like Prince?"

Ed shrugged. "I don't really know his stuff, but I reckon I'll go—could be a bit like missing Elvis otherwise."

Ben laughed and Melody felt her stomach softening. The worst bit was over, and it seemed to have gone all right. In the kitchen she put the dressing onto a salad and lit the flame underneath a frying pan lined with olive oil. She took two bottles of beer from the fridge and brought them through to Ben and Ed.

"What a brilliant place to live!" said Ben. "I mean, God, you've just got everything on your doorstep. It must be amazing."

People had been telling Melody that living in Covent Garden must be amazing for as long as she could remember, but she'd never really seen it that way. Melody didn't live in Covent Garden, she lived in this flat. Her life was about these four walls and what happened within them. Her location was wasted on her. She may as well, she mused, have stayed in Canterbury, her life would have been every bit as mundane. "I can't say I really make the most of it," she said. "I could be anywhere."

"What a shame," said Ben, and Melody realized that that was the second time he'd used those words about her since their first date.

"What about you?" He addressed Ed. "What's it been like for you, growing up around here?"

Ed shrugged. "Don't know any different," he said. "It just feels normal to me. I've got my school up the road, my friends round the corner, I've got the gym and the pool, football in Lincoln's Inn."

"So, do you reckon you'll stay around here, once you've left home?"

"Ed's not leaving home, are you, Ed?" Melody smiled and winked at her son. He smiled back.

"No. Why would I leave home? I've got the best mum in the world." He leaned over and kissed her on the cheek and Melody felt slightly embarrassed, unused to the intimate machinations of her relationship with her son being played out in front of anyone except Stacey and her family.

"I can see that," said Ben, "and if I were you and I lived here with your mum, I wouldn't leave home till I was forty."

"At least," said Ed, and they both laughed and clanked their beer bottles together.

Melody watched them and felt a small shiver of what she at first took to be apprehension, but then realized was actually *anticipation*. Something seemed to be happening here tonight, something that she had decided long ago would never happen. They were moving on, she and her son, slowly, inch by inch, and it looked as if this man, this tall, fit man with his golden glow and perfect teeth, might, against all her early instincts, be about to play a part in it.

In the kitchen, Melody poured herself a glass of wine and stared at the frying pan to ensure that it was issuing forth the required levels of smoke, to ensure a properly seared tuna steak. It was, so she threw the steaks into the pan and recoiled as they snapped and sizzled with alarming ferocity.

"You don't want to overcook those," Ben said, appearing behind her.

"I know," said Melody, "three minutes each side."

"Hmm," he said, "they're quite thin, I'd just give them a minute."

"Really?"

"Yeah."

"You can cook, then?"

"I'm reasonable," he said. "I can do the basics."

"What, you think searing tuna steaks is *basic*?"

"Well"—he shrugged and smiled—"yeah. Kind of. Ed tells me that you're not exactly a natural in the kitchen?"

"No, not my natural habitat."

"Which is strange, considering your occupation."

"Or maybe it's exactly why." She smiled. "No," she said, "I don't like cooking. But it's something I want to work on. I always used to say I didn't have time to cook, but now I've got all the time in the world. I'm running out of excuses. In fact, you know, I'm running out of excuses for everything."

"You are?" he asked meaningfully.

"Yes." She paused. "Shall I turn them now?"

Ben peered into the pan. "Yeah, and then, literally, thirty seconds on the other side. What sort of things?" he continued.

She flipped the steaks over with a fork and sighed. "God, I don't know. My whole life I felt like something was missing, and then Ed came along and filled in all the gaps for me. So that was me, you know, *Ed's mum*, sorted. I haven't really looked outside of that. And now, well . . . shall I take them out?"

He nodded, and she slipped them onto three waiting dinner plates. "Now, with everything that's happened, and Ed turning eighteen, it's forced me to reevaluate and I've realized that there's potentially much, much more to me than being Ed's mum. You know, I discovered I've got a sister?" She lowered her voice.

"Wow! You did?"

"Yes, I met her on Saturday and she's just like this little ball of energy, full of plans and ideas, and she's only five years younger than me but she just seems so much younger, and I thought, that could have been me. If all this *stuff* hadn't happened to me, if the truth hadn't been kept from me, I could have been like that, a girl about town, on the career ladder. But I don't feel resentful, I feel great, like this couldn't have happened at a better time. I met this woman called Grace, she said to me how lucky I was to have had my family so young, because now I can find myself, and she was right. I'm only thirty-three, I've got this flat, I've got a fairly decent brain, I can be whatever I want to be."

"Well, hallelujah!" said Ben.

"What?"

"Well, you're just waking up to the woman I saw on a number fourteen bus three weeks ago."

"Ha! I thought you just saw a pair of shoulders."

"Yes, I saw a pair of shoulders, and then I saw a woman who looked not only incredibly gorgeous but also incredibly interesting."

Melody turned and smiled at him. "That's what my sister said, about a photo of me she had as a child. She said I looked like a really interesting little girl."

"And I bet you were. And thank God for Julius Sardo for doing whatever it was he did to your head to help you remember who you really are. To Melody Browne, a very interesting little girl." He raised his beer bottle toward her.

"Yes," she said, "and to Ben whatever your surname is, for not giving up on me."

"Ben Diamond," he said, "my name is Ben Diamond."

Ben Diamond. She should have guessed. She smiled and turned to light the gas beneath the noodles.

• • •

Ben stayed that night. He didn't take his underwear off, just lay down next to Melody and embraced her with one smooth, heavy arm. "Dinner was excellent," he whispered into the silence.

"It was, wasn't it? Thanks to you. Would have been a bit of shoe leather and some rank old noodles without you."

"Stop putting yourself down. You *allowed* me to take over. If I hadn't been there you'd have made a fine job of it."

"You reckon?"

"Definitely."

Melody laid her hand against his forearm and stroked the soft fur. They had already agreed that there would be no sex, so she felt safe that her small display of affection wouldn't be misconstrued as an overture of some kind.

"Your son is great," he said, curling his arm through hers so that their arms were now tightly entwined. "Really great."

"He is, isn't he? I've spent all these years worried I was doing it all wrong, and now here I am, two days away from his eighteenth birthday, and I can suddenly see that I did everything right."

"And so, that's it, you can pretty much write the whole story now, the story of you?"

"Well, not quite."

"One more chapter to go?" said Ben.

"Mm," said Melody. "One more chapter to go." And then she reached for the switch of her bedside lamp and brought the room to a reassuring darkness. "Night-night, Ben Diamond," she whispered.

"Night-night, Melody Browne." He leaned over and kissed her cheek in the darkness.

The moon outside was bright and full, and cast a purplish hue across the dark room and the undulating outline of Ben's body. Melody could see the white stain of it showing through the thin cotton of her curtains and its perfect circle took her back to another night, twenty-five years ago, when she'd woken up from some strange, unknown slumber and found herself a hollow, insubstantial girl called Melody Browne with parents she didn't belong to and a life she didn't possess.

There was only one way to find out how she had ended up on the grass that night, staring at the moon. Only two people who could finish her story for her and they were the two people she had vowed never to see again. Her parents.

She closed her eyes against the thought and tried to pull herself toward sleep, but with her head full of her parents and her bed full of a strange man, sleep eluded her until well into the next day.

Chapter 50

Now

The weather forecasts on the radio the next day for Ed's birthday were for a fine, bright day, with a high temperature of twenty-four degrees. Melody breathed a sigh of relief. Ed had turned down her offers of meals out, bowling alleys, and go-kart racing and said that all he wanted was a picnic in Lincoln's Inn Fields with some beer, some sandwiches, some mates, and a Frisbee.

She walked to the tube with Ben that morning at nine o'clock, where they exchanged a small, but significant kiss, and then she walked slowly down to Tesco on Bedford Street to shop for the picnic. She glanced at the time. It was 9:09 a.m. This time eighteen years ago, she recalled, she'd been in her tenth hour of labor. This time eighteen years ago she and Stacey had been in her new flat, unfurnished except for the secondhand sofa and the table and chairs, Stacey sitting cross-legged on the floor, desperately trying to get the screaming week-old Cleo to latch on to her breast, Melody doubled over in silent agony on the other side of the room (the moment would have made quite a picture, two motherless children, trying to control new life, all alone). This time eighteen years ago, Melody was about to observe that her contractions were coming less than five minutes apart and Stacey was about to say, "Get in a cab and go, there's a fiver in my jacket pocket." And this time eighteen years ago, Melody was fourteen hours away from pushing out an eight-pound baby boy in a small white room, with no one at her side but a midwife called June.

Those hours between leaving her flat and delivering Ed had been the loneliest of her life. She'd pined then, not just for *her* mother and father, but for *any* mother and father, until the midwife had put her baby into her arms and she'd known then, she'd known immediately, that she didn't need anyone at all, least of all Clive and Gloria Browne. But now, here she was, eighteen years on from that moment, and she needed them once more. The thought filled her with horror and dread.

She filled her basket aimlessly with pre-sliced cheeses, and processed hams, packets of cocktail sausages and large bags of Doritos. She knew where her parents' phone number was. It was in an old diary from 1989 that she'd come upon the day before when she'd been clearing things out. She could go home now and phone them, her mum and dad. She could do it today, this morning. She had no idea what was awaiting her on the other side of the phone call. A disconnected number? A stranger's voice? The news that her parents were dead? Or a conversation with her mother or her father that might finally explain how she'd been allowed to live her life as half a person?

Ed was eating his breakfast when she got back to the flat half an hour later.

"You were up early," he said, tipping the cereal bowl to his lips to drink the sweetened milk.

"Walked Ben up to the tube and then went to Tesco's for your picnic stuff."

"Did you hear the weather forecast?" He gestured toward the radio on the table.

"I know." She smiled. "It's great, isn't it?"

"Are you inviting him, tomorrow?"

"What, Ben?"

"Yeah."

"Do you want me to?"

Ed shrugged and got to his feet. "Yeah," he said, "yeah. I liked him."

Melody glanced at her son. He was slightly pink, almost embarrassed. Melody took this to mean that Ed liked Ben more than he felt comfortable admitting and this thought left a soft feeling in the pit of her stomach. "Cool," she said circumspectly. "I will then. Though he might not be able to take the time off work."

"That's cool," said Ed, disappearing into the kitchen with his empty bowl. "Whatever."

Melody unpacked her shopping bags in the kitchen and noticed that it was spotless. "Did you clear the kitchen up?" she asked suspiciously.

"Yeah." Ed smiled. "Me and Ben did it this morning, when you were in the bathroom."

"Blimey," she said drily, "and whose idea was that?"

"Mine, of course." Ed winked at her.

"Yeah, right." She smiled at him disbelievingly, and moved him out of the way of the fridge. "What are you up to today then, the last day of your childhood?"

"Thought I'd go to the playground, go on the swings, then ride my scooter home and have a tantrum."

"Ha ha!" Melody nudged him in the ribs.

"I don't know," he said, "I suppose I should do something, though maybe I'd be safer staying at home. Imagine if I got run over by a bus the day before my eighteenth—how tragic would that be?"

"Oh, stop it!" shrilled Melody. "Not even as a joke!"

Ed was about to leave the room when he turned back and opened his mouth. "Mum?" he said.

"Yes?"

"Who's Emily?"

She spun round from the open fridge. "What?"

"Emily. American-sounding. Called on your mobile, while you were out?"

Melody caught sight of her phone, plugged into the charger on the kitchen counter.

"Oh, Emily, she's just a friend."

"Oh, right, because she said a really weird thing. She said she was my aunt."

"She said *what*?"

"Yeah, she said, you must be Ed, and I said, yeah, and she said, guess who I am, and I said, no idea, and she said, I'm your long-lost aunt, and I just sort of laughed and said, oh, right, 'cause I didn't know what else to say, and she kind of laughed and that was that."

Melody breathed in deeply. "What else did she say?"

"Nothing really, just for you to call her back. What's the deal with her, then, is she OK?"

"Yeah, she is, she's fine. She's just . . ." Melody was about to tell her son that the woman he'd spoken to on the phone was just a little weird, just a bit daft, but then she looked up at him, this man who was three inches taller than her, this man who'd cleaned up her kitchen while she wasn't looking, who wanted the best for her, for his mum, and she suddenly wondered what exactly she was trying to protect him from. From the fact that the grandparents he'd never met and didn't care about weren't his real grandparents? From the fact that his mother had had a sad and terrible childhood that she'd only just remembered but that she actually felt *better* for knowing the truth, not worse? "She's my sister," she said, exhaling with relief.

"But you haven't got a sister."

"No. I didn't have a sister before, but I've got one now. Turns out my mum and dad weren't my real mum and dad. Turns out you were right, I was adopted. Listen"—she leaned across and took his hands from where they hung between his knees—"this is a really long story. And I don't know the end of it yet. I need to make a phone call, and then I need to go and see somebody. Let me go and do that, and then I'll take you out for a Nando's and tell you everything—how about that?"

"OK." Ed shook his head and smiled bemusedly. "Shit," he said, "brain fuck."

"Yeah," agreed Melody. "Just a bit."

Melody took her phone into her bedroom and arranged herself on her bed. She pulled open the musty little diary that started with the day she left her parents' home for the last time and ended with a health visitor's appointment when Ed was ten days old. The inscription on the inside cover said: "THIS DIARY BELONGS TO: Melody Browne, 4 Trojan Close, Canterbury, KENT, CT1 9JL." Written underneath was a phone number, seven familiar digits, written in red pen in her still immature handwriting. Melody took a deep breath and tapped the numbers into her phone.

She waited for three, four rings, until a click, a breath, a small girlish voice: "Hello?" Her mother. Melody gasped and hung up.

No, she thought suddenly, she couldn't start this on the phone; she needed them to see her face. And she needed to see theirs.

• • •

Melody stood outside 4 Trojan Close and looked up at the house. It was startlingly familiar, as if she'd only just left it. The cul-de-sac was silent, all the driveways empty except for this one, a small red car to Melody's right. Her mother's car. Not the car she'd had when Melody was growing up, but still, unmistakably, a car that belonged to Gloria Browne. Melody rang the doorbell, feeling strangely confident. It was opened almost immediately by a small old woman in a blond wig. Melody didn't recognize her at first. The wig was slightly askew, as though she had thrown it on in a hurry, and her features were pale and ill defined. And she was smaller, much smaller than Melody remembered.

They stared at each other for a short moment. Gloria's face started to smile, before suddenly falling. "Melody," she whispered.

Melody nodded.

"You phoned earlier?"

She nodded again.

"I knew it was you. I felt it. Come in. Please, please, come in." This was said not as an invitation, but as a plea.

Melody stepped inside the house. Gloria let her pass, her eyes never leaving her. "Sit down, sit down," she entreated as they entered the living room. Melody sat and looked around the room. It was all there, every last porcelain animal, cut-crystal decanter, and gilt-framed reproduction. And there, on the mahogany sideboard, Melody Browne, astride a chestnut pony, legs in beige jodhpurs, a rosette pinned to her chest, eleven years old and every inch the privileged young Canterbury princess. It shocked her, the contrast, what she'd been, what she could have been, what she'd turned out to be. So many twists and turns, so many permutations. And now it had all boiled down to this: a ticking clock, a silent house, a small woman, the final pages of the book.

"Are you OK?" Gloria Browne's pale eyes searched Melody's face for clues to her sudden reappearance. "Is everything all right?"

"Everything's fine," Melody said, her voice flat. "How are you?"

"Oh, me, I'm fine. You know. Fine as I can be, really. And it's Edward's birthday tomorrow?" She smiled.

"Yes." Melody felt a rush of surprise. "Yes, how did you know?"

"How would I not know? He's my grandson. I think of him all the time, especially on the second of August. And he'll be eighteen?"

"Yes, that's right."

"And how is he? How is Edward?"

"Ed's great. Just waiting for his A level results, then working out what to do next."

"Oh." Her mother seemed relieved to hear this. "Oh, I'm so glad. And it's so nice to see you, Melody. It's wonderful. And you look very pretty . . ."

"Well, I wouldn't say that . . ."

"No, you do, you're a woman now. A beautiful woman. I'm very proud of you."

Melody felt a burst of anger at these words. Gloria Browne had no right to be proud of her, no right at all.

"Where's Dad?" She changed the subject.

"Oh, dear, he passed away, last June, yes, last June."

"Oh." Melody waited a beat for a feeling, any kind of feeling, but none came. "What happened?"

"Alzheimer's. On top of the strokes. Yes, it was a relief. It really was. The last few years had been very difficult. Very difficult indeed. But still, life seems sort of . . . *barren*. Without him. Lonely, you know?"

Melody nodded. She felt sorry for this woman, she really did. But she'd brought it all on herself. She'd lived a lie, the full extent of which was as yet unknown, but it was undoubtedly a lie. It was clear that Clive and Gloria Browne hadn't deliberately wiped her memory clean of her life before she'd met them, but they certainly hadn't done anything to help her unlock it.

"What happened to your hair," she asked gruffly, almost spitefully.

"Oh, yes"—Gloria touched the hairpiece regretfully—"my hair, well, it was always so poor and then"—she drew in her breath—"after your father passed away, well, it just sort of gave up altogether, a bit like me, really." She smiled, a watery smile. "It's not nice being bald, you know, when you're a lady, not nice at all . . ." She pulled herself out of her sad reverie and smiled again. "And you, Melody? How have things turned out for you? Did you have any more children?"

"No, I didn't have any more children. Ed was enough for me, and apart from that I never met anyone I'd want to have children with."

"Oh, that's a shame, so Ed's father . . . ?"

"Tiff was never Ed's father. He didn't even come to see him after he was born and the last I heard he was back in Cork, working on a pig farm."

"So, it's just been the two of you, has it? All these years . . . ?"

"Yes, just the two of us."

"And you've been happy?"

"Well, yes, as happy as a person can be when their life is just a . . . a . . . *mirage*."

"A mirage?" Gloria repeated dreamily.

Melody looked at Gloria Browne, blinking at her in confusion, as though she hadn't the slightest idea what she was talking about, and snapped at her, "Oh, come on! You know exactly what I mean!"

"Well, no, I'm not sure I do."

"Look, I didn't come here today to make small talk, I came to get some answers. I know what happened. I know you're not my real parents and I just want the truth now. I want you to tell me what happened after my mum died, what happened between Aunt Susie taking me to your house and the day I woke up on the grass outside our burning house."

The small room fell silent again. The clock ticked on, oblivious. Her mother sighed. And then, finally, she began to talk.

Chapter 51

1981

The man with the black hair and the steel-rimmed glasses looked a bit like Mr. Spock from *Star Trek*. His ears had a strange shape to them, almost floral. He smiled kindly at her and sighed.

"So, Melody. My name is Dr. Radivski, and I am a doctor who looks after children's heads, do you see?"

She stared at him, wondering what would happen if she opened her mouth and issued forth a particularly large burp. The thought made her smile, which he seemed to find very interesting. "Yes," he said, "I know that sounds strange, and, of course, I am not talking about this bit of your head"—he knocked his knuckles against his own skull—"but this bit." He pointed at it. "Inside your head. Your mind. Your thoughts. What makes you tick. Do you know why you are here?"

She continued to stare at him. He had a very shiny nose and his eyelashes looked extra thick through the magnifying bits of his bifocals.

"You are here because your foster parents are very concerned about you. You are here because you have not spoken for nearly three weeks. I understand you had some upsetting news and I understand that sometimes when we hear things we don't like, it seems somehow easier and safer just to go . . ."—he rolled his hands toward him—". . . inside. Is that what you have done, Melody? Have you gone inside?"

Inside, thought Melody. She liked that word. Inside meant warm. Inside meant safe. Inside meant sofas and telly and nice things to eat. She liked being inside this room. It was very nicely decorated and lined with books. It felt, in fact, a little like the inside of her own head, the little cubbyholes all filled neatly and snugly with interesting things.

There were some toys in the corner. She stood up and walked across the room, suddenly curious to know what they were.

"Ah," said the doctor, "you've seen my little toy shop. Come"—he got to his feet—"let's look together." He was very tall when he stood up and it struck Melody that some children might actually be a bit scared of this tall man with his odd ears and his thick glasses and weird accent, and wondered why he'd decided to become the sort of doctor who looks after children's heads. The toys were neatly laid out: wooden dolls, paper, pens, a small wooden house, a bed, a car, a bear.

"I'll just watch you playing for a moment, if I may?"

She glanced at him curiously, wondering why a grown man would want to watch an eight-year-old girl playing with dolls, and then picked up a small wooden doll with blond hair and a red cotton dress. She picked up the car with the other hand and slid the blond doll into the passenger seat. Then, not because it was something she really wanted to do for fun, but just because she knew it would make this doctor think all sorts of interesting things about the inside of her head, she pushed the car, with the doll in it, really, really hard and it zoomed across the varnished wooden floor and crashed into the skirting board on the other side of the room.

She turned to look at the doctor.

He smiled.

"Melody," said Gloria, knocking gently against her bedroom door, "Melody, can I come in?"

She pushed the door open and stood with her back against it. Melody put down the book she was reading and glanced curiously at her.

"We've had some news. Some good news. Would you like to come downstairs and we can tell you all about it before supper?"

Melody knew what she was going to say. She was going to say that their application to adopt her had been accepted. She picked up her book and carried on reading.

"Melody, love, please, this is important."

She put down her book again and folded her arms. If it was important, she thought, then she could tell her here.

Gloria sighed and perched herself on the edge of Melody's bed. "We've had a call from the social services," she said. "We've been accepted. That means that you can be our little girl. Properly. Isn't that wonderful?"

Melody turned her head to gaze out of the window. The news was neither wonderful, nor bad. She was bright enough to realize that the alternative to being adopted by the Brownes was to be put into foster care or into a children's home and she knew that not many people wanted to adopt eight-year-old girls, especially ones with elective mutism (which is what the doctor with the funny ears had told them she was suffering from). She knew that Ken and Grace had had their application turned down weeks ago, that her auntie Susie was far too ill to be able to look after her, and that her aunt Maggie had given her go-ahead to the Brownes' application and so obviously had no intention of stepping into the breach and taking her into her own broken little family. She knew all this. She was a bright girl. The Brownes were her only option. The Brownes were all she had.

She picked up her book and carried on reading.

Melody blew out the candles on the homemade chocolate cake. There were nine of them. It was November 1981 and she had been called Melody Browne for nearly six weeks. In the room were seven other people: Gloria (or "Mum," as she was now known); Clive (otherwise known as "Dad"); Clive's brother, Peter; his wife, Cheryl; and their two hyperactive children, Samantha and Daniel, who were currently kicking an empty cardboard box around the living room. Gloria's elderly mother, Petunia (she liked to call herself "Granny"), sat on the wing chair, watching the children in bemusement. Melody herself sat at the head of the table, surrounded by extravagantly wrapped gifts, and tried not to think about what she'd been doing this time last year, when she was still at Auntie Susie's and the news had just arrived about her father. The memory of that day was still there, tucked away in its little compartment, but it was blurred, like a vivid dream, fading away as consciousness ascended. She couldn't remember what was said, how she'd felt, the order in which things had happened. It was almost, but not quite, as if none of it had ever happened.

Gloria divided the thick chocolate cake into eight large slices and put them onto pink paper plates. Melody stared at her slice for a moment, relishing its dense brownness, the oily sheen on the butter icing, the dry crumbs of a broken Flake bar sprinkled on top. Gloria made lovely cakes. Gloria also made lovely stews and lovely roast chickens, and made perfect replicas of Chelsea Girl pedal pushers on her Singer sewing machine. Gloria was a lovely, lovely mum, better than her real mother had ever been, when it came to things like cakes and hobbies and looking after her.

She stuck her fork into the cake and broke a chunk off. She slid it into her mouth and as the flavors hit her taste buds, a sound slipped from the depths of her lungs, a loud and quite surprising *Mmmm*. Everyone in the room turned to stare at her. She put the fork back into the cake and launched a second load toward her mouth. Again she let loose a guttural moan of pleasure as the cake slid down her throat. Sensing the sudden shift of focus in the room, the unexpected tension, she did the same again. She did it a total of twelve times until the slice of cake was gone from her plate and entirely inside her stomach. And then she dropped her fork onto her empty plate and smiled. Gloria and Clive stared at each other, in amazement, and then, slowly, and rather oddly, they gave her a round of applause.

Three days after Melody's ninth birthday, Gloria and Clive were invited to a dinner party at the home of the new neighbors across the street. The new neighbors were young, and vaguely glamorous, and were called Sean and Janine. Gloria seemed to be in what she might call "a bit of a flap" about the event, and had taken Melody on three separate shopping expeditions to find exactly the right dress. Now that Melody was able to utter sounds, she had been of at least a little help, making approving and disapproving noises every time Gloria emerged from behind the fitting-room curtain. Melody had begun to think about the possibility of speaking again; she'd been practicing when she was alone in her bedroom, talking to the Spanish girl. And there was a girl in her class called Melissa, who was really pretty, but really kind, and she'd whispered some words into her ear at break time, but made her promise not to tell anybody.

As the hour of the much-anticipated dinner party arrived, Gloria became slightly distracted, and kept running up and down the stairs, having forgotten something vital on her last journey. She appeared, eventually, at three minutes to eight, dressed in a pale blue dress with a high neck and leg-o'-mutton sleeves, with a band of blue rhinestones around the collar. Her hair had been teased, with the aid of a pair of newly purchased BaByliss curling tongs, into a veritable riot of blond sausages, and her lips were tinted a hot salmon pink.

"Well, my goodness, don't you look special?" said Clive, who himself was attired rather smartly in a brown suit with a wide velvet collar and a navy-blue ribbed wool polo-neck.

Melody looked at them both and smiled. They looked nice. They weren't her real parents, but they looked nice. She felt something tiptoeing across her consciousness that felt a bit like pride, and when they came to her to say good night, instead of just allowing them to hold her in their arms, she held them back, both of them. They smelled good, of Avon perfume and Brut aftershave.

A teenage girl from two doors down, called Rachel, was being paid the princely sum of five pounds to sit with Melody for the evening and the two of them saw Clive, Gloria, and a tissue-wrapped bottle of Blue Nun to the door at three minutes past eight, whereupon they returned indoors and, instead of going upstairs and allowing herself to be put to bed, Melody joined Rachel on the sofa and together they worked their way through a packet of After Eights and watched a particularly scary episode of *Within These Walls*.

Melody was fast asleep by the time Clive and Gloria returned from their dinner party at close to midnight, pink cheeked and a little wobbly on their feet. She didn't hear them make themselves a pot of coffee in the kitchen and she had no idea that they danced together a little, in the dark of the living room, Gloria giggling, her face lit up by the pearlescent glow of the fat, full moon. Thankfully, she was unaware that they'd tiptoed upstairs, holding hands, and fallen clumsily into their king-size double bed, where they'd begun breathing heavily and fumbling frantically with the fastenings on each other's clothing. She had no idea that just as Clive had managed to wriggle his way out of his brown trousers and was halfway to relieving his wife of her brand-new royal blue silky camiknickers, Gloria sat bolt upright and said, "What's that smell?" And she was blissfully unaware of the ensuing panic as it was ascertained that the spare bedroom was, in fact, on fire. Because her bedroom was next door to the spare room and because she slept with her door open, her room was filled immediately with thick, plasticky smoke and within a moment or two Melody was entirely unconscious.

Between her state of sleep, her state of unconsciousness, and her state of consciousness as she lay beneath the moon, on the lawn, in front of her burning house twenty minutes later, something very peculiar happened inside Melody's head, a sort of housekeeping. By the time she awoke from a deep sleep in her uncle's spare room twenty-four hours later, Melody could remember nothing about the tangled mess of her previous life. She couldn't remember Ken, or Broadstairs, or her mother, or her father. She couldn't remember LA, or Charlotte, or her baby sister called Emily. All she could remember was that her mum and dad had saved her from a burning house, that she was nine years old, and that her name was Melody Browne.

Chapter 52

Now

It was the BaByliss tongs that had caused the fire, carelessly left switched on in the spare bedroom, next to a used tissue, on the nylon quilted bed, by her socially anxious mother.

The only question that now remained was why they had left her with a broken memory. The answer was unsurprising.

"We thought it was for the best," said Gloria.

"I knew you'd say that!" Melody growled.

"Well, it wasn't an easy decision to make. You'd been so unhappy before. You wouldn't talk, your behavior was very worrying—I felt you'd already compartmentalized the whole terrible saga even before the fire. So when you came round and you smiled and you called us Mum and Dad, well, it would have been heartbreaking to have taken a step backward from that. You came out of that fire as a different child. And we waited and we waited for you to say something about the past, you know, about your mum or Ken, and you just didn't. It took months for us to realize that you *just didn't remember*. And, you know, it just seemed a perfect opportunity to make a fresh start, what with the house gone, and you happy at last."

"But my family!" Melody cried. "My aunts! My sister! Ken!"

"I know," sighed Gloria, "I know. As I say, it wasn't an easy decision to make. It was the hardest decision I've ever had to make, in fact. Apart from the decision to let you go . . ."

"What do you mean, let me go?"

"Well, eighteen years ago. If you love someone, set them free, if they love you, they'll come back." Her voice began to crack. She paused and smiled sadly, then pulled in her breath to continue. "And you never did. So I had to resign myself to the fact that you'd never loved me. And I had to ask myself if I was to blame, for the decisions I made—*we* made—all those years ago."

"Well, I think you probably know the answer to that question. How could you possibly have thought it was OK for me to go around my whole life not knowing who I was?"

"We didn't," Gloria replied matter-of-factly. "We didn't think it was 'OK.' We just thought of the two possible options, both of which were nigh on unpalatable, it was the best."

"For you, you mean?"

"No, not for us, for *all of us*. So that we could be a happy family."

Melody stared at Gloria Browne, aghast. Is that really what she believed, this silly, kind, nervous little woman, that their tiny suburban unit was the happier option?

"A happy family?" she shouted. "What the fuck is a happy family? A family without a history? A family without roots? A family stuck in a cul-de-sac in Canterbury, too scared to let anyone in in case they spoiled the mirage? We weren't a happy family, we were just three people going through the motions. And you know what's so sad? If you'd let me know, *allowed* me the privilege of keeping my identity, I might have been happy to be with you, because I would have known what you'd done for me. And I wouldn't have felt trapped with you. I'd have had people, other people, to care about me too. I've met them now, the people you stole from me, and they all remember me and they all care about me, and I already feel a million times more special than I ever did before because of them, and if I'd felt that way my whole childhood I might have ended up being more than a teenage mum and fucking dinner lady, and you and I might still have been, you know, *a mother and daughter*."

There was a short silence, and Gloria issued a small sob. "I know," she said. "I knew from the moment you left our house that night, I knew we'd done the wrong thing. And I've lived with that ever since. It's the greatest regret of my life. And now, well, I don't expect us to be able to salvage anything from this terrible mess but it would really help me if I thought you might be able to, well, not to forgive us, but to maybe just try to *understand* why we did what we did."

Melody paused. Her head of steam was subsiding. She thought of this woman, small and broken, all alone in her cul-de-sac, surrounded by photos of her long-lost family, her beloved husband and her truant daughter, and she felt something inside her soften. She thought of the electric-blue harem trousers and white cotton pirate shirt that Gloria had made for her for her first school disco when she was thirteen years old, the outfit that had been the envy of every girl at the school; she thought of the private exhilaration of their trip to Boots, the following summer, to buy her a packet of jumbo-sized sanitary towels when her first period had arrived. She thought of her fourteenth birthday party, how she'd managed to persuade Clive and Gloria to let her host it alone and how proud Gloria had been to return home at ten o'clock to an empty house, clean and tidy, a small smudge of Um Bongo on the living room floor and a smudge of blue eyeliner on the tablecloth the only evidence of the festivities that had preceded. "It's so nice to know that we can trust you, Melody," she'd said, surveying her tidy home, "it means so much to us." And then she thought of her face less than a year later when she first saw Tiff turn up in the cul-de-sac on his buzzing scooter, full of attitude, face hard as wood. "He's not what I'd have hoped for you," she'd said gently. "You could do so much better."

She thought of a dozen different moments where Gloria had been patient, proud, attentive, and loving and she realized that even though this woman wasn't her mother, and even though her feelings toward her had never been those of a daughter toward a mother, this woman had, in actual fact, been a very good mother indeed. And with that thought she took a deep breath and said, "OK, I'll try. But I can't promise anything."

Before Melody left, Gloria gave her an envelope. "For you," she said.

"What is it?" Melody asked.

"Open it."

Melody opened the envelope and pulled out a sheet of cream parchment.

"It's your birth certificate," Gloria said. "I've kept it all these years, always thought you'd come back for it, that you'd need it. For a passport application or for a job. Thought that would be the moment, that would be when I'd tell you everything."

Melody had never been abroad. She'd never needed a passport. If only she had, she thought, staring at the details penned in thirty-three-year-old ink, of her real parents, the name of the hospital in South London where she'd really been born, an address in London, SW8, where she'd really spent the first few years of her life.

She could have known all this time. All she'd needed to do was ask for this piece of paper and she'd have known everything. But she never had. She folded the certificate back into a rectangle and put it in the envelope. "Thank you," she said, "I'll be needing this. Thank you." And then she kissed the little lady in the wig, just once, on a powder-soft cheek, and left her there on her Canterbury doorstep, alone once more, but no longer wondering.

Melody sat for a while, after she got home that afternoon, and tried to decide how she was feeling. The sun flooded her bedroom with light and sparkled off her mirror. Hanging from the corner of her mirror was the necklace, the one she'd stolen from Gloria's jewelry box all those years ago, the one she'd taken to a pawnshop when Ed was two months old to get some cash to pay her bills and had been told was worth about five pounds. She'd almost taken the five pounds but something had stopped her, something had made her snatch the necklace back off the counter and stuff it into her handbag. She'd never really thought about that moment before now, but now she knew what it was. It was about her *mother*, the very essence of who she was and what she represented. She needed to keep something, one small thing, something that had touched her skin, that still, remarkably, smelled of her. The necklace was a talisman. It was there, in the absence of an actual mother, in some strange, unknowable way, to protect her.

And with that thought, Melody got up from her bed, opened her wardrobe door, and kneeled down to pick something up from the bottom. The box, the one her auntie Susie had given her. The box that contained, she imagined, the essence of her other mother, her *real* mother. She brought the box back to her bed and, very slowly, with her heart gently racing, she sliced open the tape that secured it. The flaps popped open and Melody peered inside. She removed the contents, slowly, one by one. First a large pair of jeans, pale blue, scuffed at the knees and hems, a label in the back that said they were Lee jeans and in a size 36. Then a loose tunic top, navy polyester with a pale blue print, slightly stained under the arms, with a graying satin label in the back that said "Dorothy Perkins."

After the dress came a coat. It was blue denim with a black splodgy print and a matching belt. Melody recognized it immediately. The thought flashed through her mind in a nanosecond. *It's Mum's coat.*

She put her hands into the pockets and brought out a creased tissue, a tube of Lipsyl, and a Polo mint. She held these objects in her open hand for a moment and stared at them. Where had her mother been when she'd bought the mints? When had she last wiped her nose on this tissue, rubbed this balm on her lips?

Beneath the clothes (which included, also, a full set of underwear, from Marks and Spencer, and a pair of oatmeal socks with holes in both heels) was a floral wash bag containing a jar of deodorant, a tube of Crest toothpaste, a rather battered turquoise toothbrush, a damp terra-cotta emery board, and a wooden hairbrush, filled with wiry brown hairs. Finally, at the bottom of the box, Melody found a large manila envelope. She unpeeled it and let the contents fall onto the bed.

There were three small envelopes, one with the name Romany written on it, one with the name Amber, and the other with her name, Melody, in a neat handwriting very similar to her own. Melody shivered slightly with the kind of excited anticipation that had once accompanied the unwrapping of childhood gifts. What would she find—locks of hair, fallen teeth, letters filled with words of tender mother love?

She couldn't decide which envelope to open first. Amber's, she thought. She wasn't real. She peeled apart the ancient tacky seal and pulled out the contents with shaking hands: a photograph of Edward James Mason, taken from a newspaper; a pink bootee; and a lock of brown hair, taped to a piece of card.

Next she opened the envelope with her own name on it. She could feel through the manila the outline of an A5 envelope, the lines of a letter, and she'd waited long enough, long enough to hear what Jane Ribblesdale had to say about everything. Sweat crackled on the palms of her hands as she pulled apart the flap. Inside was a lock of soft auburn hair, a tiny white mitten, a plastic hospital bracelet with the words "FI of Jane Ribblesdale 3 November 1972, 5:09 a.m." written on it. There was also a smaller envelope, her name written on it again, in a less confident script. Melody took a deep breath and opened it. It was written on lined paper, but the words didn't follow the lines. They ran around the page erratically, almost as if they were drunk. Melody had to concentrate to decipher the scrawl.

My dearest, most darling Melody,

How are you? I have been meaning to write for a long time now but the days here are so complicated somehow and as soon as I've started it's time to go somewhere or sleep or eat or take some more infernal pills it's all I ever do. But how are you? I think of you often my lovely girl and wonder about you with your new family. Are they kind to you? I'm sure they must be, I think they are my cousins so they are as good as family and one day soon maybe they'll let me out of this place and you and I could be together again. Would you like that? they are trying to make me better but I'm not so sure about it. I wish I could explain to you how it's been for me these last few years but I'm not sure I can. It's been a blur, baby girl, a big long blur and you've been so good. It's something to do with babies, you see, something to do with all the time and effort it takes to make them, all the waiting and the hoping and the way they feel when they're inside you and all the dreaming and wondering and the anticipation and then fate comes along and takes them away from you, takes away everything good, leaves you with nothing, an empty hole, empty arms, an empty heart you know maybe some people could find things to fill themselves up with again but I never could not even you, you were always so good at finding other people to take care of you, such an appealing little girl you are.

I do miss you all I miss Ken, I miss the house, but its better for me here. I want to get better but I'm not so sure it will happen, so many black holes in my head baby girl, so many bad things. Thank god you're not like me, you are daddys girl, you always were if only he hadn't gone and left you, should never have gone away in the first place with that woman at least she managed to make you a sister though, not like me, poor Romany, and then poor little baby Amber, gone at twelve weeks, all over the bathroom floor, how could I tell Ken that I'd lost his baby, poor little baby Amber and then my terrible sin, to take that girls baby, what a terrible person I have become, no good for you, no good for anyone. I think this pen is running out of ink. Sorry. I do love you Melody, you are my baby girl. Be good.

Mummy xxx

Melody sat for a moment, entirely motionless, the letter held in her open hands, and tried to piece together a person from the jumble of words, the bundle of unpretty clothes, and the photos she'd seen in the newspapers. There was something childlike about her haphazard style of dressing, her explanation of the cycle of unhappiness that had brought her to incarceration in a mental facility and her eventual suicide, and even her floral wash bag. It was clear to Melody that this woman would have been incapable of looking after her properly. There would have been no Brownies, no cakes, no visits to professional hair salons and perfectly executed birthday parties. But more than that, Melody felt overwhelmed by a sense of empathy. She thought back to the first few months of Ed's life, the constant fear of losing him that had accompanied every simple afternoon nap or trip to the supermarket. This woman, Jane Ribblesdale, had experienced the worst thing that could possibly happen, she had held her baby in her arms and then watched that baby die. There could be nothing worse, Melody thought, nothing worse in all the world.

She put the letter to one side and then she brought the third envelope onto her lap: Romany's envelope. This, as Emily had told her, was where it had all begun. She peeled it open and then gasped at what she saw: another white plastic ankle band; a red rosebud, dried to the color of sediment; and a photograph. She hadn't been expecting a photograph. And there she was, her baby sister, tiny and pale, skin the color of distemper, head bald and blotchy, hands held in tiny fists, staring directly into the camera with enormous dark eyes. On the back were the words: "Romany Rosebud, 4 January 1977." The picture had been taken when she had just been born, perhaps before they knew that there was something wrong with her, when her parents were still happy and life had been set on a different course altogether.

Melody brought the photo closer to her and stared deeply into her sister's eyes. "Hello," she whispered, "hello, Romany. I'm your big sister. It's lovely to meet you, you're very lovely, very lovely indeed . . ."

She sat like that, for a while, her dead mother's clothes bunched up in her lap, emitting a strange, damp aroma, her sister's photo in her hands, and she let herself cry for a while.

She glanced up at the portrait of the Spanish girl beside the window and she smiled at her. "You knew," she chastised gently, "you knew everything, and you never told me."

Then, she put the objects back in the box; slid the photo of her dead sister into the glass of her dressing-table mirror, next to her mother's necklace; and went to find her son, to take him out for lunch, to tell him the whole story.

Chapter 53

Now

True to the forecast, the next day dawned bright and warm. Melody let Ed sleep until midday and then she awoke him with eggs and bacon on toast, a mug of tea, and a pile of gifts. He smiled when he saw her sitting on the end of his bed. "Morning," he said.

"Morning," she replied. "How does it feel to be a man?"

He smiled again. "Kind of cool," he said. "How does it feel to be the mother of a man?"

She laughed. "Bloody weird," she said. "Not sure how we got here so quickly."

"Doesn't feel quick to me," said Ed. "I feel like I've been a kid all my life!"

He took the mug of tea from her and balanced the tray on his lap. "Everything feels different today," he said, "not just because of my birthday, but because of all that stuff you told me yesterday. I just feel all kind of . . . *excited*."

"You do?"

"Yeah! I mean, my whole life's been full of all this missing stuff—you know, my dad, my grandparents—and I was all right with all that because of you, and now it's like, suddenly, all these new people, all this . . . history. Makes me feel like life is just starting, you know what I mean?"

Melody stroked the top of his hand and nodded. "Yes," she said, "I know exactly what you mean."

"Did you ask her?" he said.

"What, Emily?"

"Yes."

"Yes. And she's coming. She said she's going to pull a sickie. She can't wait to meet you. And Ben's coming too. He's got a hospital appointment about his wrist anyway, so he'll just come straight on from there."

"Cool," said Ed, picking up his cutlery.

"You not going to open your presents?" she asked.

"Do you want me to?" he asked.

"Yeah." She smiled. "Go on."

He unwrapped the iMac first. "Excellent!" he said. "Thanks, Mum."

He pulled her to him and kissed her on the cheek. And then he opened his other gift. Melody held her breath. It was a small photo album that she'd filled the night before, with precious, irreplaceable pictures. There was a picture of Ed in her arms, the night he was born; the photo of Melody on the beach at Broadstairs that Grace had given her; a photo of her father that Emily had posted the day after their meeting; a photo of Ed with Cleo and Charlie when they were all tiny; pictures of Jane Ribblesdale, Ed's real grandmother, taken from the news cuttings; a printout of a picture of Melody and Emily she'd taken on her phone; and there, on the last page, was Romany Rosebud, his perfectly formed little auntie.

"I want you to keep this forever," Melody said, "and fill it with photos that really mean something to you, not just nights out with your mates, but the important things, your first love, your first baby, treasured things."

Melody looked at him. She knew it wasn't as exciting to him as the iMac and that he was probably wondering why she'd given it to him, but one day, when he was older, when he had a history of his own, she knew he'd appreciate it, he'd show these pictures to his own children and tell them about the aunt he never had a chance to know, the grandmother who let tragedy pull her under, and the grandfather who never had a chance to make things right.

"Thanks, Mum," he said, leafing through the pages. "Next page . . ."—he pointed at the blank page—"*Tiffany Baxter!*"

"If she's got any sense at all," Melody agreed. She put her arms out toward her son, she pulled him to her and hugged him as hard as she knew he'd let her.

Stacey, Pete, and the kids were already there when they got to Lincoln's Inn two hours later. They had installed their Swingball, laid out blankets, and already opened a bottle of champagne. One of Stacey's many extravagances, for which she always seemed to have just enough cash, was champagne. There was little in the way of celebration that she would consider unworthy of the uncorking of a bottle of champagne.

"Gorgeous day!" she trilled, heading toward Melody with a full glass and outstretched arms. They hugged and Melody noticed that her breath was minty fresh. She took the glass of champagne from Stacey's hand and looked at her quizzically. "Any news for me?" she said.

"Well, yes." She smiled. "I am officially pregnant. Six weeks today. And feeling like shit. Yay!"

"Yay!" agreed Melody, and squeezed her best friend. "That's fantastic! Are you happy?"

Stacey shrugged. "Yeah," she said, "I am. I'm not looking forward to getting fat again and all I can think about is booze and fags, but another baby, yeah—I can't wait!"

And neither, thought Melody, could she. There hadn't been a new baby since Clover, three years earlier, and now, with her heart full of little holes where babies should have been, Stacey's news couldn't have come at a better time. "That's brilliant!" she said, squeezing her again. "I'm so happy for you, I really am. Am I allowed to tell people?"

"Yeah, of course you can. Everyone'll guess the minute they see me without a fag in my hand anyway, so you may as well. And what about you?" She gestured at Melody's hand. "Are you still off the fags?"

"Yes," said Melody, "I had one a few days ago, just made me even more sure that I really don't like it anymore."

"Weird," said Stacey, "really weird."

"I know," said Melody. "The whole thing's been weird, really weird indeed." And she was about to start trying to explain what had been happening to her for the past fortnight, when someone tapped her on her shoulder and she turned round and it was Emily.

"Hi!" She smiled. "Sorry I'm early!"

Stacey looked from Melody to Emily, and then back again, her eyes wide with incredulity. "Oh my God," she said, before Melody could squeeze in an introduction. "You two look like twins!"

Melody and Emily smiled at each other and then at Stacey.

"Emily," said Melody, "this is Stacey. My best friend. That over there is Pete, her husband, and her kids, Cleo, Charlie, and Clover. And in there"—she pointed at Stacey's stomach—"is another little one on the way."

"Oh," said Emily, "congratulations!"

"Thank you," said Stacey, throwing Melody a curious look.

"Stacey," she said, "this is Emily. Emily is my baby sister."

Stacey looked at both of them again, her face a picture of confusion. "Well," she said, "I think I could have guessed that. And the reason I've known you for eighteen years and you've never told me about a baby sister before, is . . . ?"

Melody smiled and took her friend's hand. "I've had quite a couple of weeks," she said. "Help me get this food unpacked and I'll tell you all about it."

The afternoon unfolded before Melody's eyes like something out of a dream. The sun shone without a pause, the champagne and beer flowed, and for once Melody wasn't using Stacey and her family as a kind of prop. She had her own people here today. Ben, tall and handsome in his business suit, pared down in the hot afternoon sun to a pale blue shirt, unbuttoned, sleeves rolled up, smart suit trousers, and bare feet; Emily, giggly with champagne and the excitement of being somewhere she'd always dreamed of being; and Melody's own, beautiful son, stripped to the waist and leaping high into the sky to reach for a Frisbee, his young body taut and unfurled, ready to take on the world.

She saw Pete gently cup his wife's tiny stomach while Cleo and her boyfriend sat entwined beneath a tree, sharing a bowl of strawberries. Clover was being spun in circles by her big brother, Charlie, and Ed's friends from school, kids she'd been serving beans and chips to every day since they were eleven, hung around in little groups, tucking into the buffet that Melody had provided, drinking beer from bottle necks, and flirting with each other.

Behind a tree, hidden from view, Melody and Stacey lit the candles on a huge chocolate cake, made by Stacey and Cleo, and brought it out to a chorus of "Happy Birthday to You."

Melody stared in awe at her son's face as he blew out the eighteen candles. She thought of that face over the years—three years old, five years old, ten years old—those same cheeks filled with air, that same look of concentration, that same beautiful profile that had once made her think only of his estranged father and now made her think of a man called John Ribblesdale and a woman called Jane Newsome, and she felt even prouder than she had before.

The cake was divided into large blocks and passed around on paper plates. Ben sat down next to Melody and draped his arm across her shoulder. She liked it there, and gently pushed her body closer to his. Across the blanket, she could see Ed talking to Tiffany Baxter, the object of his affections. How much more he had to offer her now, she thought—not just a mother, but a mother with roots, a mother on the brink of something new and wonderful, a real family.

Emily sat down next to her and Ben, and crossed her legs. It amazed Melody to think that for Emily it was completely normal that Melody should be sitting here with a man, that to Emily, Melody's having a man in her life was unremarkable and entirely to be expected.

"Wow," Emily said, looking around her, "I really *love* your world!"

And that was it, thought Melody, that was exactly it, succinctly and completely. Melody had always loved her son, always loved her friends and her flat, but until this exact moment, she had never loved her world. And more important, until the doors to her memory had been unlocked two weeks ago by an over-tanned prat in a mohair suit, she had never really loved herself.

Melody brought her other arm around her sister and sat there for a while, safe, and happy, full of champagne, chocolate cake, and hope for the future.

Melody Browne is dead! she thought to herself. *Long live Melody Ribblesdale!*

Epilogue

Late August

The taxi driver refused to take his car up the potholed dirt path that led to the farmhouse, and dumped Melody and her rucksack on the side of the road. She gave him a tip anyway, primed as she was to give everyone she met at every juncture of her first trip abroad a tip, just to be on the safe side.

She eyed the road ahead warily. It didn't seem possible that there could be a house up there, with people living in it, but this was definitely the right place, unless there was another dirt track next to a wind farm with a sign outside saying "El Dorado."

She slung her rucksack over her shoulder and started to walk, the afternoon sun burning overhead like a ball of fire, sweat trickling down her spine and dampening the underarms of her T-shirt.

The rucksack was Ben's. It was scuffed and weathered and festooned with old airline tags. Ben's rucksack was more widely traveled than Melody. He'd seen her off at the airport at 5:40 this morning, bleary eyed and full of sleep, but insistent. "I want to see you go," he'd said. "I want to watch you so I know what it looked like when you finally found your wings."

She walked for over five minutes, until she was thoroughly convinced that she was in completely the wrong place and that she would die out here, of heat exhaustion and dehydration, her body ultimately stripped of its flesh by the vultures that circled overhead, her bones left to bleach in the harsh Spanish sun. But just as she was starting to panic, a vista appeared on the horizon, a set of rustic, low-rise buildings; a cluster of fig trees; a vine-draped footpath; a line of washing; three small white goats, clustered around a metal tin; a white camper van, a moped, and there, to the left of it, an aged, rusted motorbike with a sidecar. Her heart leaped in her chest. This was definitely the right place.

A woman smiled at her as she saw her approaching. She was about Melody's age, dark haired and very thin, wearing loose jeans and a floral camisole top. "*Hola*," she called.

"*Hola!*" said Melody. "Hello! Do you speak English?"

"Yes." The woman smiled. "I speak *perfect* English. My name is Beatriz. Can I help you?"

"Yes, I'm, um, I'm looking for Ken? Ken Stone. Is he here?"

"Ken, yes, he is here. Who are you?" She asked this in a friendly tone of voice.

"Oh, I'm Melody, I'm an old friend, I'm kind of a . . . *surprise*."

A small girl with dark hair and wide blue eyes appeared from behind Beatriz's legs and eyed Melody curiously. "Hello!" said Melody. "I mean—*hola*!"

The little girl blinked at her and then ran back into the house. "That's Daria. She's a bit shy. Come in. Follow me."

Melody followed Beatriz into the house. She'd been expecting it to be basic, from what Grace and Seth had told her, but was still surprised by the lack of modern living on display inside the home. The kitchen consisted of three walls of open shelving, an old gas hob, and a butler's sink. The floor was bare concrete covered over in places with threadbare rush matting. Two more small children sat at an old table in the middle of the kitchen, eating oranges and reading a comic. But it was cool in here, and smelled good, of roasting meat and orange zest.

Beatriz led Melody through the house and out the other side, down a footpath lined with orange trees and sun-bleached old garden furniture. At the other end of the path was a smaller building and outside this house, sitting astride a stool and combing the thick hair of the biggest dog that Melody had ever seen in her life, was a tall, slim man with long hair and a kind, beaten-up face. He looked up at the sound of their footsteps and squinted.

"*Hola!*" he called.

"Hello," said Melody, smiling.

He got off his stool and walked a few paces toward them, his face still scrunched up in concentration, as he tried to place her face. "I know you," he said.

"Yes," said Melody, "you do."

"Oh my God," he said, his blue eyes starting to shine with tears. "It is, isn't it? It's you."

"That depends," said Melody, "on who you think I am."

"Melody! It's Melody. Oh my God!" He ran toward her and held her before him by the arms, his eyes taking in the details of her face. "I knew it!" he said. "I knew you'd come. I dreamed about you last week. I dreamed that you and I met on a boat, by chance, that you had twelve children and that you'd dyed your hair blond! You don't, do you," he said, "have twelve children?"

She laughed. "No. Just one. And I've never dyed my hair blond."

"This is just—wow—like something out of a novel. This is the most perfect moment. Beatriz!" He pulled the dark-haired woman toward them. "This is Melody. Remember, I told you about her, the little girl who used to live with me when I lived by the sea, the little girl I tried to adopt. This is her! This is her! She came!"

Melody smiled at Beatriz, and then at Ken, and as she looked at him she felt something warm wrapping itself around her heart. She'd been worried that the real Ken wouldn't live up to the Ken of her memory, that he'd be just a sad old man, a man whose life had been a failure, the man that Matthew had warned her about. But he wasn't, she knew that already. He was everything that she remembered and everything she'd hoped. She put out her arms and he entered them.

Her story was complete.

Acknowledgments

Thank you to Judith Murdoch and Louise Moore. My debt to you both is huge and I miss you both enormously.

Thank you to Jenny C for being my buddy, generally, but in particular during the stormy weather of April 2008, which I don't think I could have got through without you.

Thank you, for similar reasons, to Jascha. You are always at your best in a crisis and this was no exception.

Thank you to Jonny Geller and Kate Elton for steering me so patiently and gently through the choppy waters. You made it as painless as could reasonably be expected and I look forward to many years of smooth sailing with you both.

Thank you to my lovely girls, Amelie and Evie, the smallest of whom was a mere pillow up my top when I first started writing this book and is now a little girl with burnished gold curls, slate blue eyes, and a fondness for the word "mine."

I am a lucky mother.

Thank you to everyone at Century and Arrow Books who has worked so hard to transform my typed sheets of A4 paper into a thing of great beauty, get it into bookshops and under everybody's noses. And thank you to everyone who sells a copy and everyone who buys a copy. It's all a bit pointless without you.

Lastly, but never leastly, thank you to my friends on the Board. You know who you are and you know the score.

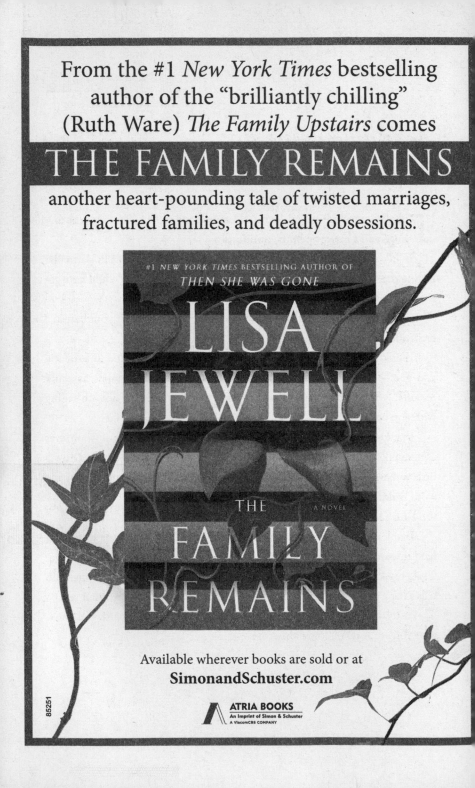